TURN TO STONE

TURN TO STONE

An Ellie Stone Mystery

JAMES W. ZISKIN

SEVENTH
STREET
BOOKS®

Published 2020 by Seventh Street Books®

Cover image: Alamy
Cover design: Jennifer Do
Cover design © Start Science Fiction

Inquiries should be addressed to
Start Science Fiction
221 River Street, 9th Floor
Hoboken, NJ 07030
Phone: 212-431-5455
www.seventhstreetbooks.com

10 9 8 7 6 5 4 3 2 1

978-1- 63388-552-3 (paperback) | 978-1-63388-553-0

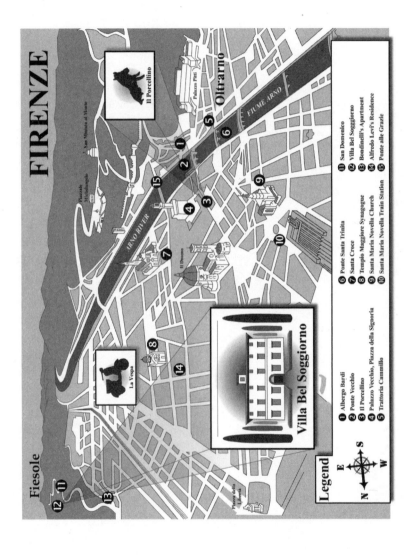

FIRENZE

Fiesole

Oltrarno

ARNO RIVER

FIUME ARNO

Piazzale
Michelangelo

San Miniato al Monte

Palazzo Pitti

Piazza della
Libertà

Il Duomo

Il Porcellino

La Vespa

Villa Bel Soggiorno

Legend

N
W — E
S

❶ Albergo Bardi	❻ Ponte Santa Trinita	⓫ San Domenico
❷ Ponte Vecchio	❼ Santa Croce	⓬ Villa Bel Soggiorno
❸ Il Porcellino	❽ Tempio Maggiore Synagogue	⓭ Bondinelli's Apartment
❹ Palazzo Vecchio, Piazza della Signoria	❾ Santa Maria Novella Church	⓮ Alfredo Levi's Residence
❺ Trattoria Cammillo	❿ Santa Maria Novella Train Station	⓯ Ponte alle Grazie

In the summer of 1963, Paul Anka and Neil Sedaka scored hits on the Italian pop charts. Andy Williams and Petula Clark, too. That fact, in and of itself, might have provoked nothing more dramatic than a shrug if not for the oddity that the songs were actually sung in Italian. All in Italian. It's a jarring sensation to hear a voice you recognize singing in a foreign tongue on the radio. Language is an emotional, intensely personal faculty. Men have conquered nations to impose its dominance, written poems to document its beauty, and defined it at its most elemental as "maternal." From our earliest days, we absorb language. It nourishes and sustains us, and we never manage to wean ourselves from its diet. It remains fundamental to our identity. No intellectual acquisition is more essential to our human distinctiveness. Nothing. Except perhaps a name. We are tagged with names and become what we are called. But, using language as a tool, names can deceive. They can hide secrets as discreetly—and discretely—as a mask. As faithlessly as a lie.

CHAPTER ONE

MONDAY, SEPTEMBER 23, 1963

The young lady in the blue pillbox hat tore the outbound coupon from my ticket, handed the booklet back to me, and wished me a pleasant flight. Moments later, I boarded a gleaming Pan Am 707, destination Rome, and found my seat next to a ruddy-faced business-man in a tight-fitting seersucker suit. He introduced himself—Harvey Turner of Portland, Maine—and, squeezing my hand in his death grip, nearly crushed four of my favorite fingers and three perfectly fine knuck-les. With growing dread, I soon realized that my chatty neighbor intend-ed to chew my ear off for the next nine hours whether I liked it or not.

Once we were airborne, he puffed away on a cigarette, going on about himself and chuckling at his own wit. My attention strayed. I won-dered where middle-aged men got their wealth of confidence with young women. Surely not from the mirror. Still, I had to be polite, listen to his golf jokes, and endure his accolades of my beauty, which—apparently— grew more bewitching with each cocktail he consumed. At length, the Old Fashioneds worked their magic and, head back and mouth open wide, he commenced to snore louder than the four jet engines roaring outside the window.

TUESDAY, SEPTEMBER 24, 1963

Upon arrival in Rome, I cleared customs at the spanking-new airport, where the immigration officer welcomed me to Italy with a wink, fol-lowed by a smart tap of his stamp in my passport. I'd been inoculated against pertussis, tetanus, and diphtheria, but not the charms of hand-some Italians in uniform. I resisted my reckless impulses, inspired by the very first man I'd clapped eyes on in the *paese del sole*, and, without further temptation, found my way to the Pan Am transport bus for Rome. An hour later at the Termini station, I boarded the train for Florence and claimed my seat in a gray second-class compartment. I was impervious to Italian sex appeal with the second man in uniform I met, a pudgy, middle-aged train conductor. He appeared above me with indifferent, sleepy eyes, and said simply, "*Biglietti.*" He punched my ticket and moved on without further comment.

I'd been warned about thieves and, of course, never to sleep on trains. So from time to time I dug into my camera bag to make sure everything was in order. My precious Leica was there, along with three dozen rolls of Kodachrome, Ektachrome, Kodacolor, and Tri-X film. A secondhand—brand-new-to-me—135mm Elmar lens I hoped to put to good use while in Italy was tucked safely in its case. There hadn't been enough room in my luggage to pack flashbulbs, so I was resigned to buying them on site at a premium if necessary. The experts had also told me that such items were prohibitively expensive in Europe.

Confident my photographic supplies were present and accounted for, I opened my purse. Passport still there, as was the packet of American Express Travelers Cheques as thick as two decks of cards. Then, sitting back to watch the Lazio countryside blur into Umbria, I fell asleep, only to wake as we pulled into the Santa Maria Novella station in Florence with all my possessions intact. What is it they say? God protects fools, children, and drunkards.

Settling into my room at the Albergo Bardi, I unpacked my bags and scrubbed my face. The light streaming through the window shone a glorious goldenrod, tinged with approaching orange. It was nearing five o'clock, and I figured I had a couple of minutes still before the sun set over the Arno.

Camera in hand and purse slung over my shoulder, I skipped down the stairs to the lobby and into the street. Barely ten minutes later, I'd already cranked nearly two full rolls of Kodacolor through my Leica. Only one frame remained in the camera, and I decided to save it in case the perfect subject presented itself.

Having crossed the Ponte Vecchio to the north side of the river, I strolled through the narrow streets and landed in the tiny Piazza del Limbo. There, I treated myself to a Campari and soda in an outdoor café. The waiter leaned against the railing of the terrace, eyeing me whenever he wasn't picking at his fingernails. I was the only patron in the place, prompting me to wonder if he was ogling me or merely doing his job.

No matter. I paid the bill, left him a little something extra as a tip, and made my way back to the Ponte Vecchio. Pausing at the center of the bridge to soak in the warm rays of the sinking sun to the west, I couldn't help noticing a young couple—newlyweds—holding hands and gazing into each other's eyes next to the bronze bust of Benvenuto Cellini. Then, just so I wouldn't feel left out of the romantic moment, a strange man sidled up to me, pinched my behind, and offered me a proposition of sorts.

I scurried off toward the south bank of the Arno, nearly losing my hat as I fled. Once on the Oltrarno side, I chanced a look back over my shoulder. The creep, a slim, wormlike sort in dark glasses, had slithered to the end of the bridge in pursuit of me but gave up the chase there. I raised my camera, aimed it at him, and snapped a picture, which I intended to show to the police. He must have figured I was a lost cause and there were plenty of other foreign girls upon whom he might ooze his charm. Throwing one last glance over my shoulder, I saw him gazing after me longingly, ruefully, as I—his prey—loped away to safety. He'd hunt again. I was sure of that.

Back at the hotel two minutes later, I glanced at my watch: 5:35. It had taken barely thirty minutes for me to run into my first pincher.

FLORENCE, ITALY
WEDNESDAY, SEPTEMBER 25, 1963

Squatting in the small bathtub and holding a hand shower over my head, I succeeded in spraying most of the water onto the floor. Mission accomplished on my first morning, if the mission had been to flood the place. But at least I was clean and temporarily safe from the dive-bombing mosquitoes.

Zanzare. Mosquitoes. No one had prepared me for such misery, the scourge of sultry Florentine nights that frustrated all attempts to sleep with their maddening buzzing. The same know-it-alls who'd told me not to drink the water or to sleep on trains, had said nothing about mosquitoes. Desperate for relief, and willing to try anything to repel their attacks, I'd steeped myself in perfume, left the lights on, and hunted down the elusive little beasties with a rolled-up newspaper. But the onslaught resumed as soon as I'd let my guard down. Eventually, despite my discomfort and determined vigilance, fatigue triumphed and I drifted off to sleep. In the wash of the morning's sunlight, evidence of the mosquitoes' transit became all too plain in the form of welts, stippled and swollen, on my arms, ankles, and neck. Larger bites than I was used to back home, and they itched like all get-out.

But I was determined not to let a few insects ruin my first trip to Italy since 1946, when my late father had dragged me along on what, at the time, felt like a never-ending tour of dusty academic institutions and stuffy colloquia. Now I was in charge of my own itinerary, at least once I'd paid the piper, who in this case was a man named Professor Alberto Bondinelli, founder and Secretary General of the Società Filomatica Dantesca. He'd heard my father lecture in Milan in the late thirties, shortly after he—Bondinelli—had finished his *laurea* degree, and set out on a distinguished if dry career in medieval Italian studies. Bondinelli had invited me to represent my father at a symposium in Florence and accept a posthumous award on his behalf. The academic portion of the proceedings promised to be as dull as ditchwater, but the agenda also included a relaxing weekend in a country house in Fiesole after the close of the seminar. In his letters to me, Bondinelli had assured me that there would be food and wine aplenty and no talk of medieval literature.

I headed down to the *sala colazione* for breakfast where I was to meet Bondinelli before setting out to do some sightseeing on my free day before the symposium. The waiter, a middle-aged man with a baldpate and a pencil mustache, showed me to a table in the center of the room. Once I was seated, he unfolded my napkin with great ceremony, laid it across my lap, and noticed the red bites on my arms. Maurizio, as I later learned his name was, fetched me a *caffellatte*, a pot of yogurt, some cold ham, and a brioche. Then he disappeared behind a door only to re-emerge a few moments later with an aerosol can of something called Super Faust.

"*Insetticida*," he said, enunciating the word with great care. Then he aped a back-and-forth spraying motion. "*Per le zanzare.*"

I thanked him warmly and made a mental note to leave a good tip after breakfast. Then, waiting for my host to arrive, I retrieved the envelope—a welcome packet—that Bondinelli had left for me at reception. Inside I found the symposium schedule, meal vouchers for local restaurants, a map, as well as information on some of the local attractions. For my reading enjoyment, he'd also included a list of the scholars, students, and professors who'd be presenting papers and sitting on panels, some of whom were staying in the hotel. I was happy to see Bernie Sanger on the list. He had been my father's last and perhaps favorite doctoral student.

After my breakfast meeting with Bondinelli, I intended to set out and explore the city I'd last seen in 1946. I didn't remember much about Florence. Our visits to nearby San Gimignano, with its forest of medieval towers, and Siena, where we'd watched the Palio from a balcony overlooking Piazza del Campo, had left deeper impressions on my ten-year-old mind. Then there was the Coliseum in Rome. My father's stories of gladiators and slaves and wild beasts dying for the entertainment of thousands of citizens had both horrified and fascinated me. That evening so many years before, for my edification and enjoyment, he'd even sketched a ferocious lion rending a poor Christian slave to shreds. Once he and I had returned stateside in September of that year, my mother scolded him for scaring and scarring me so with his stories. I still have the drawing, along with hundreds of others he made.

A voice from over my shoulder interrupted my memory. "*Scusi, è lei la Signorina Stone?*"

I turned to see a squat, barrel-chested man with a mop of salt-and-pepper hair atop his tanned face. He wore a pair of thick, black, horn-rimmed eyeglasses on his broad nose.

"Professor Bondinelli?" I asked, extending a hand to him from my seated position. Somewhere somehow I'd come to think of him as a taller, younger man. But perhaps I'd been mistaken. Then I noticed the two uniformed policemen behind him.

"I am Inspector Peruzzi," he said. "*Polizia di Stato.* You were expecting Professor Alberto Bondinelli?"

"Yes, he's my host. That is he arranged for my visit here in Florence."

He considered me for a long moment, the way men do when they're not sure how much respect is owed the woman they're confronted with. Was I someone important or merely the professor's bit of fun on the side? He produced a small notebook and fountain pen from his breast pocket. I could see that his right forefinger and thumb were stained black, as if he'd sliced them open and bled ink. He propped his glasses up onto his forehead and aimed his naked right eye at the notebook as he scratched something onto the open page. He asked when I'd last seen Bondinelli.

"I've never seen him."

That surprised him. "*Mai?*"

"*Mai.* We corresponded by mail, but I've never met him in person. Can you tell me what this is about, Inspector?"

He closed the notebook, slipped it and the leaky pen back into his breast pocket, and stared me down, again leading with his right eye.

"*Il professore è morto,*" he said. "Drowned in the Arno."

CHAPTER TWO

Having helped himself to a seat at my table, Peruzzi retrieved his notebook again and flipped through the pages. We embarked on a conversation in Italian. He really didn't speak any English beyond the most basic greetings and common words. While I'd never met Bondinelli, he was my only contact in Florence—at least until Bernie Sanger arrived—and his death came as a bigger shock to me than I might have expected. I asked the inspector when it had happened.

"Yesterday evening," he mumbled, looking at his book. Then he explained that it wasn't known exactly how Bondinelli had ended up in the river, only that he'd been spotted in the water under the Ponte Santa Trinita, one bridge to the west of the Ponte Vecchio. A young couple, necking on one of the bridge's piers as the sun was about to set, noticed a dark shadow in the water drifting under the central arch of the span, directly below the gaze of the fierce Capricorn escutcheon. Squinting into the murky river, with the fading glow of the sun's last rays as the only light, the pair distinguished what they thought was the shape of a man. The girl screamed, according to the cop. And her lover ran to summon the police, who, rushing to the scene in a powerboat a few minutes later, caught up with the submerged body and, using high-powered flashlights and a mooring hook, fished the corpse from the water just beyond the Ponte alla Carraia, the next bridge downstream.

"How awful," I said. "That must have been shortly after I'd returned to my hotel. I was taking photographs on the Ponte Vecchio."

"Yes, I've heard tourists do that kind of thing."

I ignored his comment and asked if dead bodies floated.

Peruzzi twisted in his seat and made eye contact with one of the uniformed policemen standing by a few feet away. The officer signaled to the waiter, and Maurizio arrived at a trot.

"*Un caffè*," said the inspector barely moving his lips. Then, turning back to me, he explained that bodies didn't float until they'd started to decompose.

"So that means he wasn't in the water long."

"It appears not."

I gulped. "Does he have any family?"

"A daughter. Fourteen years old. She's away at school in England. His wife died six or seven years ago."

"My God, that poor girl is an orphan. Does she have any other relatives?"

"An uncle here in Florence. We've contacted him. And there's a *donna di servizio*, a cleaning lady, who lives in the Bondinelli household."

"This is such terrible news," I said. "How tragic for that girl."

He nodded. "*Già. Poverina.* We've spoken to the headmistress of her school. She's making travel arrangements for the girl to return to Florence."

Across the room, a man entered from the corridor, surveyed the tables, then approached ours.

"Excuse me," he said. "Are you Signorina Stone? Eleonora Stone?"

Peruzzi considered the gentleman, and I did the same. A well-built man of about forty, the new arrival offered his hand, which I took, and he introduced himself with an exaggerated bow, "*Professor Franco Sannino.*"

"*Piacere*," I said in my best Italian.

He raised my hand to his lips but didn't quite make contact.

Peruzzi interrupted the niceties and said, "Signorina, if you must, save your flirting for your own time."

I must have looked mortified, as Sannino came to the defense of my honor. "This is a proper signorina from a fine family."

The inspector offered a dismissive wave of his hand as reparation. If he realized that he'd misjudged me, it didn't show. Of course he couldn't possibly have known, but my interaction with the males of the species was hardly above reproach. I was what people called a "modern girl," and I apologized to no one for the way I lived my life. Still, I appreciated the effort to defend my good name.

Eager to get on with his business, Peruzzi wanted to be done with the presentations, but Sannino had other ideas. Resisting all attempts by the inspector to break in, he prattled on and explained in heavily accented English that he'd read every word my father ever wrote.

"I am the *assistente* of Professor Bondinelli," he said. "That's the same as assistant professor in America. I am helping to organize the *simposio*. I study the poetry of the *Medioevo*. The Middle Ages. Like your father."

Franco Sannino wasn't quite charming. Nor was he self-conscious, despite speaking English—as the French would say—like a Spanish cow. Switching to Italian, he described his field of study, which seemed so utterly arcane and tedious that I wanted to stick a knife in my ear, just to see if bleeding would make the droning stop.

"That sounds fascinating," I said.

I found him almost handsome. But his brow jutted a fraction of an inch too far over his hungry eyes, and his chin looked to have been fashioned with a chisel tap or two too few. The result went beyond virile, crossing the line into coarse. A touch too hulking to approach the suavity of, say, a Marcello Mastroianni. I kind of had a thing for him, by the way.

Peruzzi had heard enough. He finally managed to interrupt.

"What did you say your name was?" he asked.

"Sannino," said the man. "Professor Franco Sannino. I'm a colleague of Alberto Bondinelli's at the university."

"*Dottor Sannino*. Yes, you're on my list. Please sit down."

"And who are you?" asked Sannino, still standing and, by all appearances, miffed at having been called "*dottore*."

The inspector indicated the uniformed policemen with a subtle nod. Franco got the message.

"*Ispettore Peruzzi*," said the cop almost as an afterthought.

"What's this about? Where's Alberto? I was supposed to meet him here this morning with Signorina Stone."

The inspector repeated the story of poor Bondinelli's last swim in the Arno. Sannino's smile vanished, and his jaw dangled on its hinges like the sprung trapdoor of a gallows. He stammered a barely comprehensible question asking what had happened, and once Peruzzi had given the abbreviated version, he took the seat he'd been offered.

"*Morto?* I can't believe it," he said, staring blankly at the policeman, clearly unwilling to accept the reality of the news. "I spoke to him just Monday afternoon on the telephone."

"Did he seem normal to you? Under any stress?"

"Of course not. He was the same as always. Busy, excited about the symposium. He was working on his opening remarks. Everything was normal."

Maurizio returned with Peruzzi's coffee, set it down on the table gingerly, and withdrew as though certain he'd be arrested if he lingered.

"I can't believe it," Sannino said again, then he fell silent.

I placed a hand on his shoulder to comfort him. "Can I get you some water?"

He muttered to himself, shaking his head, still reeling from the news. At length he found his wits and said, "*Grazie, no.*" Then he fumbled for a cigarette, slipped it absently between his lips, and lit up.

"Are you sure there's nothing I can get you?"

He took a deep drag and blew out the smoke. Then he asked if I'd be kind enough to fetch him some orange juice.

"Of course."

"And one of those prune brioches I saw at the buffet. *Grazie.*"

Having tended to Franco Sannino and his breakfast, I turned my attention back to the inspector. Notwithstanding his insistence that the police weren't sure how Bondinelli had ended up in the river, I pressed him again for an opinion. Did he think it had been an accident? Something more nefarious? A robbery gone wrong on one of Florence's bridges? Suicide?

"Suicide? Never," interrupted Sannino, chewing his brioche. "Alberto is a devout Catholic. He would never consider such an act, I assure you. Never."

Peruzzi frowned and said that, if there were no objections from the good *dottore*, the police would consider all possible theories just the same.

"But he has a young daughter," continued Sannino, reasoning with the inspector. "How could he kill himself and leave her an orphan? No," he concluded, shaking his head. "Suicide is impossible. And, please, if you don't mind, call me *professore.*"

Italians were quite particular about their titles. And while Sannino might not have held officially the position of "professor," I knew it was customary for academics in his situation to insist on being addressed as such.

Peruzzi drained his coffee in one go, leaned back in his chair, then addressed me. "We haven't ruled out anything. And that includes suicide, no matter what the illustrious *professore* says."

The police inspector excused himself to speak with the clerk at the reception desk, leaving me alone with Sannino. With the shock of the news tempered by a hearty breakfast, he reluctantly turned to more practical matters, namely, the symposium scheduled for the following day. I asked him if it would be canceled under the circumstances.

"This was Alberto's project, of course," he said. "But so many people are involved. So many participants have traveled to be here."

"Still, it seems wrong to go on without him."

Sannino lit another cigarette and inhaled deeply. Then, mugging a fatalistic moue, he said the symposium was Bondinelli's last labor. "We must see it to its end. He would have wanted that."

"What about the weekend in the country? Surely that will be canceled."

Franco's eyes narrowed. "Alberto was eager to give his students and you a pleasant finale to the symposium. Everything is planned. We should honor his wishes."

"It was very generous of him to welcome us into his home."

"Oh, no. It's not his place. It belongs to a friend of his. A man named Locanda."

It was noon by the time Inspector Peruzzi had finished making his inquiries. I'd spent most of the morning in the hotel lobby chatting with Sannino, who I learned was one of Bondinelli's protégés, in line for an associate professor position in modern philology at the university. As he droned on about the promotion process and other inner workings of the Italian university system, a young woman approached us. She stared at me as an owl might scrutinize an unsuspecting field mouse on her nocturnal perambulations.

Sannino introduced her as another symposium participant. *Introduced* might be overstating the case. He recognized her as a student of Bondinelli's all right, but he couldn't produce her name for love or money when the appropriate moment arrived. She provided the information. Veronica Leonetti.

The young woman looked to be in her early twenties. Her thick brunette hair, held in place by a pink plastic band, framed a pasty face and heavy eyebrows. Lips turned down in a half-frown, she watched the action unfold around her as she raked her chewed-down fingernails across a red patch on her neck. More an observer than a voyeur, she appeared to derive no pleasure at all from the exercise. Envy, perhaps. Or a repressed desire to participate. To be invited to participate.

"Did you know Professor Bondinelli well?" I asked her.

She blew her nose, rubbed raw to match her pink eyes, into a handkerchief in her left hand while her right fiddled with the cross hanging from her neck. "He was my mentor," she said in Italian. "A good man."

I told her I was sorry, sure that my words were inadequate under the circumstances. Should I have offered condolences instead? Or perhaps a hug?

"Did he appear upset or troubled the last time you saw him?"

She frowned. "No, why?"

I was thinking of suicide, but I didn't share my suspicions with her. She caught on anyway.

"The professor was not upset at all. In fact, he was excited and looking forward to the symposium. So, please, don't suggest that a good Christian like him would have committed the cardinal sin of taking his own life."

"I'm truly sorry," I said as she glared at me. "I never met him, you see. I was speculating." Hoping to defuse the tension, I asked her if she'd known him long.

"Two years. He rented me a room in his home in Via Bolognese. That is he gave me room and board in exchange for help around the house. I'm from Prato. Not far from here. He was very kind."

That was news. "You were living with him? I mean in the same house?"

I wondered why she hadn't mentioned it straight off. She averted her gaze and nodded.

"Then you must know his daughter."

She nodded. "She's in London but spends her school holidays here. I take her to church when she's in Florence. I can't say we're close." She cracked a sad, apologetic smile. "You know how young girls are. Interested in frivolous things. Popular music."

"Did you see him yesterday? The day he died?"

"Yes, of course," she said, wiping away some fresh tears. "I spoke to him at breakfast. He said he had some errands to run in preparation for the symposium. Then he planned to meet some people at his church to solicit donations for the *mensa dei poveri*, the soup kitchen."

"Is the church anywhere near the river?"

"No. Near the Fortezza da Basso," she said. "Chiesa della Madonna della Tosse. It's his parish church."

"The Madonna of . . . the *cough*?" I asked, wondering if my Italian was betraying me.

"Yes, that's right," she said in English as if there was nothing odd about the name.

CHAPTER THREE

I was, understandably, loath to traipse around Florence in light of the fact that Professor Bondinelli had just been fished out of the Arno the night before. Even though I'd never met him, I felt conflicted. Was it proper to enjoy such pleasant diversions while the man who'd gone to all the trouble of organizing a conference to honor my father lay so fresh on a slab in the morgue? While his fourteen-year-old daughter was packing her bags to return home an orphan? No, it wasn't right. But at the same time, I couldn't say it was entirely wrong either.

So with mixed feelings, I slipped into some flats, pulled a wide-brimmed sun hat onto my head, and hid myself behind a pair of Ray-Ban Meteor sunglasses. And, unlike my first visit years before, I set out to tour Florence, ready to appreciate the city for all its romance, art, and history.

Florence in September. There were still plenty of tourists, outfitted in breathable leisurewear, comfortable shoes, and embarrassing hats, aiming then clicking their cameras, all the while babbling in their foreign tongues. They bought trinkets and souvenirs, and even posed for caricatures in front of the Uffizi. They waited on line at the post office to buy stamps for their letters. Or to place phone calls back home, perhaps to ask for money. The foreigners, including me, were often surprised to be charged for full-letter postage if they scribbled anything more than "*ciao*" or "*saluti da Firenze*" on their postcards.

Commonplace items and local customs charmed or vexed the visitor, depending on his mood. The stubborn refusal of shopkeepers to place change in your proffered hand took some getting used to. They dropped it instead into a small dish on the counter; it was your job to retrieve it from there. And Americans weren't in the habit of drinking water from a bottle, never mind having to pay for it. My native New York City boasted the best-tasting water available anywhere—perfect for making bagels, too—

and it ran from the tap free of charge. Nor did we appreciate the scarcity of ice cubes, which could be had for the price of a "please" at home. And what American visiting Europe didn't feel claustrophobic in the Matchbox cars? Barely a third as long as an average Chrysler sedan. Even the homely, imported Volkswagens back in the U.S. dwarfed the tiny Fiats, which the Italians parked in a random, jumbled fashion on the streets—and sidewalks—of Florence, wherever they might fit. These differences and countless others leapt out at the tourist. I giggled at some, cursed others, but soaked them all in with a joyous curiosity.

First on my itinerary was a second crossing of the Ponte Vecchio. It was only steps from my hotel, and reasonably free of tourists at lunch hour on a Wednesday in late September. Nose pressed against the bridge's shop windows, I coveted the gold treasures on display. Rings, some filigreed with latticework, others brightly enameled, more still sparkling with diamonds, beckoned to me as if crooking a finger. Too rich for my budget, I thought, even as I calculated in my head how much I might afford. No, I told myself, pushing away from the showcase. The price of one bauble in particular dwarfed the sum of the Travelers Cheques in my purse by a factor of ten. I strolled up the slow incline toward the center of the bridge.

"Signorina," called a man from the doorway of the shop. "Come back. I show you beautiful jewels. I make you good price."

I flashed him a sad smile and shook my head. He shrugged and disappeared back inside.

"*Excusi mi*," said a middle-aged lady standing in front of me in a bright sundress. American. A sunburned, Baby Huey of a man stood behind her, smile at the ready. "*Tu fare foto noi per piacere?*"

"Of course," I said. "I'd be glad to take a picture of you."

She seemed thrilled that I spoke English, introduced herself as Millie Stueben and her husband, Big Bob, from Lebanon, Kansas. Under cross-examination, I gave my name and city of origin.

"We saw you this morning in the breakfast room at the hotel," she explained. "Are you staying at Albergo Bardi too? We're in room twenty-five. How about you?"

"Forty-one," I said.

Big Bob stepped forward, grabbed my hand with both mitts, and commenced to pumping vigorously. He pronounced himself happy to meet another American, even if I was from New York. Ha ha. I took the

AGFA Optima 1 camera from Millie, corrected the disastrous F-stop settings she'd dialed in, and focused on the couple. Not much that I could do beyond that; it wasn't a magic camera. Millie and Bob were satisfied all the same, and invited me and my husband—surely I was married—to visit them in Kansas if ever we were in the neighborhood.

"Or stop by our room anytime if you're missing some American company. Number twenty-five."

The Stuebens left me at the crest of the bridge, exactly where I'd been propositioned and pinched by the creepy man the previous evening. I watched them go, then loitered at the Cellini bust to admire the view. I retrieved my camera from my bag and snapped a roll of Kodachrome, half in each direction. To the east a couple of sculls were rowing on the river alongside the quays below the Uffizi Gallery. On the other side, to the west, the Lungarno stretched along the river with the Ponte Santa Trinita directly before me. That reminded me of poor Bondinelli. It was, of course, there that his body had been spotted the night before. I screwed my new Elmar lens onto the camera and focused on the bridge to the west. What exactly I hoped to see, I couldn't say.

Lowering my camera, I paused to pay a small silent token of respect to my late host. He'd been a religious man, I was told. Still, a prayer would only have confirmed I was a hypocrite. I wondered what the appropriate gesture should be, given that I didn't believe he'd been borne away to heaven on angel wings. Should I say "rest in peace"? Perhaps just "farewell." That suited me. And since I was standing in the middle of the Ponte Vecchio, I said it softly, under my breath, in Italian.

"*Addio.*"

Blinking away a couple of unexpected tears, I unfolded the map from my guidebook and puzzled over it. I have a strong memory, and something about the Santa Trinita bridge bothered me. I was sure it hadn't been there when I'd visited Florence in 1946. Maybe there'd been a wooden bridge? Or wood and steel? I couldn't quite remember. Considering the span in the distance, I had to admit that it indeed looked to be hundreds of years old. I shrugged and decided that perhaps my powers of recall weren't as sharp as I'd thought after all.

The sun was bright in the clear blue sky, which contrasted and complemented the greenish brown river, making for what I hoped would be some delightful souvenir photos. Again, the Arno conjured images in my mind of *povero Bondinelli* and his watery end. Pushing those thoughts aside, I fiddled with the camera's aperture settings and focused on the Vasari Corridor above the shops on the eastern side of the bridge. My father had taken me on a tour of the passage after the war. He explained it had been built as a secure conduit for Cosimo de' Medici to avoid the dangers and inconveniences of marching through the streets shoulder to shoulder with the hoi polloi. Now, standing there snapping photographs, I felt like a cliché of a tourist, but so what? That was what I was, after all. At least this day there was no greasy handprint on my bottom to ruin the moment.

I crossed the bridge and, a short distance farther along, found myself in the Mercato Nuovo, face to face with a bronze statue of a boar sejant. Forgetting for a moment Bondinelli and even the creepy man who'd propositioned me the night before, I nearly squealed with delight. Or, I suppose, like a stuck pig. This was the very spot where George Hamilton had bought flowers for Yvette Mimieux in *The Light in the Piazza*. I'd seen the movie a year and a half earlier with a date who paled in comparison to the bronzed, handsome Hamilton. I wouldn't say I measured up to Yvette Mimieux's standard of beauty either. But we're not talking about my date's disappointment with me, just mine with him. While perfectly nice-looking when the evening had begun, my escort paid the price for not being George Hamilton once the lights came up at the end of the last reel. I didn't invite him up for a nightcap after the show.

Now, having waited my turn, I reached out and rubbed the *Porcellino's* snout for good luck as all visitors to Florence do. In fact, for my photo souvenirs, I snapped a couple of frames of other tourists doing exactly that. In fairness to my forgettable date, none of them measured up to George Hamilton's beauty either.

From the *mercato*, I made my way to the nearby Piazza della Signoria, where the Palazzo Vecchio soared impossibly high into the blue Tuscan sky. A couple of memories of my first Florentine sojourn surfaced unexpectedly. As I shamelessly captured the David with my camera in all his Kodachrome glory, a murmur of Portuguese nuns loitered in front of the statue, averting their eyes from his . . . *pisello*. That was the word my father had used to describe the appendage, adding that the Florentines sometimes said *pimpero* instead. *Pisello* or *pimpero*, the sisters found the little thing objectionable. Or perhaps fascinating.

Next I stumbled across the slab marking the spot where Savonarola and two other monks had been hanged then burned as heretics in 1498. I distinctly recalled my father describing in rich detail the incineration of the three revolutionary priests. The story gave me nightmares until we left Florence a week later.

By one thirty, the blazing sun had driven me to seek a cool drink on the terrace of the Caffè Rivoire. Lingering over a bottle of mineral water for a half hour, I watched the tourists flood the piazza, dodging the cars and scooters as they did. I loaded a roll of Tri-X and again screwed the 135mm lens onto my Leica. I shot some of the more interesting-looking people passing by. There was a fresh-faced blonde girl, no more than twenty or twenty-one, crossing the piazza on the arm of a man in his sixties. She didn't seem to mind his age or, I could only assume, the aberrant behaviors he surely required of her in the boudoir. I considered myself broad-minded in such matters, especially where my own conduct was concerned, so I wasn't judging the pair for their choice of pastime. But I wondered if she shouldn't keep the hospital's telephone number handy on the bedside table in case the strength of his heart proved inadequate for the vigor of their exertions.

A group of Japanese tourists, outfitted almost entirely in white, marched past on my right, entering the piazza from Via Vacchereccia. Led by a prim man barking orders as he held a parasol high in the air, the group paused briefly in front of the Loggia dei Lanzi to admire Cellini's Perseus with the Head of Medusa. Then they steered around the Portuguese nuns, who were now transfixed by Giambologna's Rape of the Sabine Women, and veered off toward the Uffizi Gallery. A few minutes later, the sisters were gathering before the David again, as if one helping of his nudity had not been enough. When the crowds and traffic thinned, I got some fun snaps of their facial expressions. The long lens was remarkable. Large eyes and covered mouths. One novice in particular looked less shocked than enthralled.

As I was rewinding another roll of "exposed" film, a stately lady of a certain age plopped herself down at the table next to mine. Dressed in a silken flower-print dress, she adjusted her hat, a kind of blossoming-rose number, and huffed for breath. She waved a foldable souvenir fan in her face before reaching with a white-gloved hand to grab the bottle of San Benedetto mineral water from my table. She dashed some into her handkerchief, which she then pressed to her forehead, and uttered a distressed so-sorry but thank-you-all-the-same to me.

"It's just so hot, my dear," she said. "Haven't the Italians ever heard of air conditioning?"

A harried waiter materialized out of thin air. He was bearing a Chinese pug, holding it as far from his black vest as his skinny arms would extend. My neighbor glanced up at him, motioned to a spot on the terrace beside her. The waiter dropped the dog at her feet, a tad brusquely I thought, and shook his hands as if ridding them of mucus.

"Leon, my pet," said the lady to the dog. Then to the waiter, "Did he do his business?"

"*Prego, signora?*"

"His business," she repeated, vexed by the thickness of his skull. "Did little Leon do his business? Pay attention, man."

The waiter looked confused and explained in heavily accented English that the dog had done no business. "*Solo pipì.*"

She snorted her dissatisfaction then demanded a tuna salad sandwich and waved him away.

"*Signora?*"

She repeated her order and, when the waiter stubbornly refused to understand, she explained what it was. Finally the penny dropped. He pointed to the salade niçoise on the menu and kissed his fingers to indicate how delicious the dish was. With a theatrical sigh, the lady acquiesced and sent him packing.

"No tip for him," she said to me once he'd shuffled off. "Such poor service. But what can you expect from an Italian?"

Cracking an uncomfortable smile, I asked if I might have my bottle of mineral water back. She nodded.

"Little Leon needs to keep his regular schedule, you know, or he's cranky. Where are you from, dear?"

I explained, leaving out the details of my job as a newspaper reporter for a small upstate New York daily. She wasn't listening anyway. In fact her attention was on the pug. She cooed and patted Leon on the head, speaking loudly in a singsong baby talk that affronted both her own dignity and the dog's. Satisfied that her adoration would hold him for a while, she produced a compact from her gigantic purse and set about powdering her perspired nose. She said she was from Philadelphia.

"The Main Line, to be exact. I'm touring the Continent. What day is this? Wednesday, yes. Tomorrow I'm off to Rome. Then it's Venice and on to Vienna. Heavens, I can't wait for this wretched trip to be over."

After that, she lost interest in me, planting her nose in a *Fodor's Guide to Italy* instead. The book was out of date, 1958; I saw the year on the cover. Hardly heartbroken over my new friend's snub, I reached down to pet the dog as consolation, but he wasn't interested in me either. He licked something off the floor then waddled to the far side of the table and plopped down to pant for breath against a leg of his mistress's bentwood chair. I opened my own guidebook—*Baedeker's*—to plan the rest of my day, but a shadow from over my shoulder distracted me. I turned to see who was blocking the sun and discovered a tall, thin man hovering over me. But before I could tell him where to get off, he smiled.

"Ellie, I knew it was you."

"Bernie!" I jumped to my feet, prompting little Leon to utter a yelp and tumble backward in a most lumpish and inelegant manner. He righted himself and took up a sheltered position under his mistress's chair. I threw my arms around Bernie's neck. "I was wondering when you'd show up."

Bernie Sanger was the last doctoral candidate to work with my father before his passing. I'd met him three and a half years earlier in New York under the difficult circumstances surrounding my father's death. We'd butted heads at times during our brief acquaintance, but, somehow, tragedy endured together binds people, even through years, distance, and silence. He'd written to me months earlier to say he was planning to attend the symposium, and I'd been looking forward to seeing him in Florence under happier circumstances. His friendly presence, I was sure, would make the event bearable.

After a short stroll to Piazza della Repubblica, Bernie and I sat down to a late lunch on the terrace of the Giubbe Rosse. It was too hot and steamy for anything more than one course, so I settled on the *spaghetti alla chitarra* with fresh tomato and olive oil. Bernie got the same, and we ordered a carafe of Chianti and a bottle of sparkling mineral water—*acqua gassata*—to wash it all down.

"You look so handsome," I said once the waiter had vanished with our order safely stored in his memory.

Bernie blushed and aw-shucked for a few seconds before offering a reciprocal compliment that I was prettier than ever. But then his good humor evaporated, and he leaned in closer.

"This news of Bondinelli is tragic," he said in a near whisper. "Just like that, he drowns in the Arno. What do you think happened?"

I shrugged. "No idea. The police say they're not ruling out anything. Accident, suicide, or even something worse."

Bernie shook his head in woe then asked me what I thought of Bondinelli.

"I never even got the chance to meet him. He was supposed to join me for breakfast this morning at the hotel."

"I met him once a few years ago. Nice enough man. A little tight. Not at all your typical Italian."

"Not a caricature, you mean. What are we Jews like, Bernie?"

He smiled. "We're delightful."

"What about my father? What did he think of Bondinelli?"

"He didn't know him all that well. I remember he told me once that Bondinelli was a middling scholar but a good man."

Coming from my father, that amounted to a ringing endorsement. One could never be sure that his estimation of a colleague's scholarship wasn't unduly harsh and, therefore, not to be taken at face value. But when he passed judgment on character, it was money in the bank.

Bernie turned serious again. "I've been worried about you, Ellie. How have you been coping?"

Uh-oh. Here it comes. "Coping? What do you mean?"

"I haven't seen you since you disappeared after the memorial service three years ago. I never got to say goodbye."

I fiddled with the fork before me. This was a topic I'd rather avoid.

"You mean my father? We hardly spoke when he was alive. How should my life be any different since he died?"

Bernie didn't have an answer for that. He just squinted into the sun and dropped the subject. I took pity on him and offered a lukewarm smile.

"I've made peace with my dad."

That prompted a nod and the lighting of a cigarette.

"What was it he always said when he wanted to change the subject?" Bernie asked. "*Cangiamo discorso.*"

A sad smile crossed my lips. "He had his odd phrases."

"It was funny that he liked to use that antiquated form of the verb. And he mined the entire peninsula's linguistic riches, from Naples to Venice," added Bernie.

"Beyond Italy, too. Whenever he wanted my opinion, it was '*Was sagst du?*' or '*Qu'est-ce que tu en penses?*' It was maddening."

"I envy you a father like that."

"Let's change the subject, please, Bernie," I said, purposely avoiding the old Italian phrase my father had used, and lit a cigarette of my own.

A short time later, the waiter returned with a small basket of Tuscan bread—the kind made with no salt—and our water and wine. We stubbed out our cigarettes and picked at the bread instead.

"Is it true the Florentines don't put salt in their bread because of some ancient blockade by the Pisans?" I asked.

"More likely because the Florentines were poor and didn't want to pay the tax on salt. Whatever the reason, this stuff is an acquired taste."

"I rather like it."

"Sure. You've just buried it in salt and drowned it in olive oil."

And with the word "drowned," my thoughts returned to Bondinelli. I reviewed in my head the sparse details Peruzzi had provided. The professor had been spotted shortly before sunset the day before—Tuesday—drifting in the Arno under the Ponte Santa Trinita. Since bodies don't float for days after drowning, it was clear he hadn't been dead for long. Furthermore, Veronica Leonetti had seen him at breakfast that same morning, meaning the time of death was somewhere between ten a.m. and early evening. I wondered how long the professor had been in the water. And where had he gone in? Surely not from the Ponte Vecchio. Too many people. Someone would have seen. This was Florence in summer, after all. Early autumn to be precise, but still chock-full of tourists with cameras snapping pictures of every inch of the city.

So had he entered the river farther upstream? At the Ponte alle Grazie, the next bridge to the east? Or Ponte San Niccolò? And how long before twilight had he fallen in? What time had the sun set anyway? I decided to find out.

"Ellie?" It was Bernie calling me back to the present. "Anybody home?"

"Sorry. I was just thinking of Bondinelli."

"It's very sad."

"I'm curious to know when he died," I said. "Obviously yesterday. But when? Late afternoon? Early evening?"

"What difference does it make?"

"The difference between an accident and murder. So I'd like to know how he ended up in the river without anyone seeing? Sunset along the Arno is prime sightseeing time, don't you think?"

"Maybe he killed himself and did it quietly. Waded into the river east of here. No tourists in that part of Florence."

I shook my head. "Apparently he was a devout Catholic. People who knew him say suicide is impossible."

"I'm sure the police will figure it out," said Bernie, and we moved on to other topics.

"Have you met any of the other symposium people at the hotel?" I asked.

"Just a couple of the students who are helping with the organization. A girl named Giuliana—quite beautiful—and a young man named Tato."

"I haven't met them yet. Just Franco Sannino and Veronica Leonetti."

The waiter arrived to interrupt our discussion, placing two plates of steaming spaghetti before us and topping off our wine glasses. Taking notice of the nearly empty carafe, he asked if we'd like another. Bernie shook his head, but I overruled him. The waiter set off to fulfill the errand.

"Wine puts me to sleep," said Bernie, twirling his fork in his noodles. "Especially on a hot day."

"I don't need the temperance lecture, chum."

Bernie spooned some grated Parmigiano from a small metal dish onto his spaghetti. "This cheese is delicious. How can they call that stuff in the green can back home the same thing?"

"I know what you mean. When they first started making it, my father wouldn't allow it into the house. He called it *segatura*."

"Sawdust? Really?" he asked with a chuckle.

"Yes. And, of course, Elijah and I loved it, much to his annoyance."

I felt a twinge, prompted by my own mention of my late brother. Better to push those thoughts to one side. If Bondinelli's death had upset me,

I was sure to crumble if I allowed myself to think of Elijah. "Now that I've tasted the real thing," I continued, steering the conversation back to the cheese, "I can't imagine eating that *segatura* ever again."

We ate in silence for a long moment. Bernie knew all too well about my brother's death in a motorcycle crash, and he was giving me a moment to myself.

"What do you think of the weekend in the country?" I asked finally. "In light of Bondinelli's death, I mean."

"What weekend in the country?"

Me and my big mouth. "Bondinelli organized a retreat in Fiesole this weekend. A thank-you to the students who helped with the symposium, I believe."

Bernie frowned. "I wasn't invited."

"No great loss. I've decided to beg off. Under the circumstances, it doesn't seem right. And if you're not going, I won't either."

"Don't stay away on my account. I'll be fine."

"Not another word. I'll stay here with you and we'll have a grand time."

"How does a professor like Bondinelli afford a country house in Fiesole anyway?" asked Bernie.

"It belongs to a friend of his," I said, stabbing at a bit of cooling *chitarra* strings with my fork. I popped some spaghetti into my mouth, chewed, then swallowed. "A man named Locanda. I don't know anything about him. I suppose he must be rich if owns a place like that."

Bernie shrugged and turned his attention to his food. After a short while he asked if I was seeing anyone.

"You mean *going steady?* No. I'm playing the field."

Misjudging my answer for a willingness to discuss my love life, Bernie took that moment to remind me of my own dalliance three and a half years earlier with a torturously handsome Italian man named Gigi Lucchesi. I'd indulged in a white-hot romance with him in the days leading up to my father's death. The memory was not a welcome one for me, and again I tried to dictate a new topic. I asked Bernie to tell me about his new job teaching at Williams. That saw us safely through the meal and to dessert: *macedonia di frutta*.

Over coffee, Bernie tried to engage me again in talk of my father, but I can be as slippery as a Maremma eel. I told him instead that I'd been approached by an editor at UPI about a possible job as a feature reporter-cum-photographer.

"That's big news," he said, lighting another cigarette and inhaling deeply. "How did that happen?"

"Apparently he's some kind of horseman. He was in Saratoga last summer and saw some stories and photos I did for my paper. A rather sexy double murder."

"So what are you going to do? Leave Amsterdam?"

"New Holland," I corrected. "I'm not sure what to do. It's awfully exciting. A wire service. My stories would be published all over the country. The world. And there would be travel."

"Like where?"

"He mentioned Vietnam, for one. East Pakistan for another."

Bernie wondered if the offer was on the up-and-up. I asked what he meant.

"Nothing. Just that it sounds too good to be true. Maybe he's just trying to get somewhere with you."

I bristled.

"Putting to one side just how insulting that is to my judgment, what makes you think I'm not up to doing a job like that?"

Bernie retreated to a defensive position, issuing a full-throated apology. He hadn't meant it that way. Of course I'd make a wonderful reporter for UPI.

I let him twist in the wind for a moment like a sad, deflated tetherball on a line, then informed him that I was a fair hand with a camera and had caught a few murderers in the past three years, thank you kindly. In fact, I'd done exactly that the last time I'd seen him in New York. Finally, I explained that I had long experience dealing with men making passes at me, unwelcome or otherwise, and I didn't need him to tell me what that looked like.

"I'm sorry, El," he said once I'd paused to draw a breath. "It was stupid of me to say that. Please forgive me."

Bernie surely didn't realize it, but he'd uttered the magic word. An open sesame for my forgiveness. "El" was the name that my brother, Elijah, had called me, and hearing it still pricked something raw and tortured deep inside me. It always provoked surprise then sorrow. But just as soon, an overwhelming sensation of warmth would wrap itself around me like a bath. I missed Elijah fiercely, but his memory comforted me. As children, we'd walk to school together and he'd protect me. He shared my passions for radio shows and mail-order prizes. I remembered the Cheerios pocket-sized Disney comic books, for instance. We'd clipped coupons and hoarded box tops to win those treasures. In truth, some of the box tops had come into our possession without the requisite purchase, torn instead off cereal cartons at the market when no one was looking.

And more intimate memories of Elijah came to mind as well. He'd often declared himself in awe of my rather useless talent for naming classical music pieces at the drop of a phonograph needle. And he'd been my hero, comforting me—long past the time when I could use childhood as an excuse for the tears caused by my father's harsh disappointment in me. Elijah knew well how deeply my father's words cut me. And he realized, too, that I absorbed much of the attention that might have been aimed at him had I not been the failure I was. Elijah had his secrets as well. Secrets my parents never knew.

Yes, Elijah called me El. Likewise, back in New Holland, my dearest friend in the world, Fadge, also used that name for me. And now if Bernie was going to lay claim to it as well, he was surely going to benefit from my forgiveness, especially over something as insignificant as an ill-considered remark about my career prospects with UPI. I liked Bernie. He was a good egg. I could be direct with him without fear of causing hard or hurt feelings. And vice versa. But he was a devotee of my father's, and his loyalty and affection would always lie with him. I couldn't begrudge him that. My strained relations with my dad had nothing to do with Bernie. That mess had been spilled long before he'd come onto the scene.

CHAPTER FOUR

I wanted to do some more sightseeing before punching out for the day, while Bernie had some research to do in the Biblioteca Nazionale beyond Santa Croce. As Santa Croce was on my list, we made our way together, window-shopping on Via dei Calzaiuoli, then passing by the American Express office in Piazza dei Cimatori, where I cashed some Travelers Cheques. I spotted a yellow Kodak sign hanging outside a *cartoleria* across the tiny piazza and dropped off the film I'd shot that morning and the night before. The nice man in the shop told me the prints and slides would be ready Monday.

Bernie and I weaved aimlessly through the narrow *vie* for half an hour before finally emerging into a large rectangular piazza. At the far end loomed a great white basilica, Santa Croce. We parted company there, in front of the bell tower, with promises to meet at the hotel at seven for drinks then dinner.

I gazed up at the church, conflicting emotions roiling in my chest. I'd made my peace with my father's death and our limping relationship, but that didn't mean I welcomed reminders of its troubles. And Santa Croce, I recalled, was fraught with memories of him.

There was much in- and outside of the basilica that awakened gentle and some not-so-gentle remembrances of the man whom I'd loved and hated, who may have loved me but certainly didn't like me. The Pazzi Chapel just to the south of the church was my first stop. This was where my father had told me the story of the Pazzi Conspiracy, a failed coup against the Medicis in 1478. Dad had insisted the term "patsy" derived from the famous Florentine family name, though I do not recall his reasoning. Surely one of his many folk etymologies, whimsical imaginings about the origins of words and phrases.

Inside the basilica, frescoes by Giotto, a relief by Donatello, and

Cimabue's thirteenth-century crucifix bore witness to the rich history and culture and religion of Florence. Then there were the tombs. Michelangelo, Galileo, Rossini, and Machiavelli were all interred on the right-hand side of the nave. Most significant to me personally was Dante's cenotaph. My father's life's work was the study of the great poet, whose empty tomb stood steps from Michelango's. I contemplated the marble sculpture, concentrating on Dante's severe features. He sat frozen in stone, right hand raised to the side of his face as if answering a telephone, and stared down—seemingly—at whosoever was gazing up at him. In that very spot, seventeen years before, my father had held my hand and translated the inscription, "*Onorate l'altissimo poeta.*" "Honor the exalted poet." He went on to explain that it was a quote from Dante's greatest work, the *Divine Comedy*.

"Dante was a poet?" I asked. "But he looks like a wrestler."

My father ushered me away, granting as we went that the statue was an idealized physical representation. "He wasn't nearly so muscular in real life," he said.

I don't know how long I lingered inside, but my blouse, soaked from the hot, muggy Florentine air when I'd entered, was dry, and I felt a chill as I stood in the darkened basilica. Though not a Catholic, or a believer of any stripe for that matter, I nevertheless purchased three votive candles, lit them in memory of my brother, my mother, and my father, and placed them on the bye-altar among a forest of offerings from other supplicants. The candles, some crooked and others burnt-out puddles of solid wax, stood at varying heights, depending on how long they'd been there. My three slender flames, which provided little in the way of comfort to me or—I'm sure—to my departed loved ones, instead stoked intense regret and sorrow at the losses. I fought the tugging in my throat and resisted the welling of tears in my eyes, determined not to weep for my family. Not there. I did my grieving in private, usually with a whisky chaser. And I'd become quite adept at standing stoic, impassive, and dry-eyed when mourning my losses. So, there, among the tourists inside Santa Croce, I stared at my three pathetic candles, lonely but sure of the fact that I loved my family dearly. Even my imperious father. Even when I hated him. And he me.

My late father had been a professor of Italian and comparative literature. He spoke a few languages beautifully, Italian best of all. And I'd acquired a great deal of it by osmosis, listening to him converse with colleagues and friends, but also through opera, which he listened to every Saturday in his study. In preparation for my trip, I'd knuckled down and, determined to improve my rusty skills, embarked on a ten-month-long course of private Italian lessons with the elderly aunt of my landlady, Mrs. Giannetti.

Sister Michael, née Severina Scognamiglio, had arrived in the United States from Naples in 1913 at the age of twenty-four and landed as a nurse at Saint Joseph's Hospital on the West End of New Holland, New York, my adopted hometown. A few months later her younger brother, Nunzio, emigrated to be near her and began a long career as a weaver in the carpet mills on the Mohawk River. His third daughter, Concettina, grew up to be my snooping, judgmental landlady. Living below me in the duplex, she'd found a new zest for life after her husband's passing by monitoring my consumption of whisky, based on the empty bottles in my trash. She also took a particular scandalized pleasure in tracking my male visitors in some kind of ledger of sin. Each time I entertained a gentleman in my apartment, I pictured her sliding a billiards scoring bead across a wire with a cue stick to mark another stain on my character. Or perhaps she used an abacus.

"My aunt's Italian is excellent, dear," Mrs. Giannetti had told me. "She used to teach it at Saint Joseph's Academy. You'll learn all sorts of useful phrases. Like how to say no to men. Well, in Italian at least."

Seventy-five-year-old Sister Michael turned out to be a firecracker. A marvel. Not at all like her small-minded niece. She was cultured, energetic, sharp as a tack, and interested in learning about my Jewish background. And though she was disappointed to learn that I was not raised in the faith, thereby making me a less-than-ideal guide when it came to the finer points of Talmudic instruction, she proved to be a better teacher than my father had ever been. Though she'd been born in Naples and had lived fifty years in America, she'd learned standard Italian well and retained the grammar and "proper" pronunciation through the years. And she never did teach me how to say no to Italian men. The subject never came up.

I pushed through the Bardi lobby door at five thirty. Though it had been barely a half-day of sightseeing, I was flagging. A *caffè* had revived me after my lunch with Bernie. At this hour, however, I was looking forward to something stronger. And that was when I spotted Professor Sannino chatting with the clerk at the reception desk.

"Signorina Eleonora," he called to me, gesturing toward himself with his right hand in a quick raking motion. Italians beckon that way, with the fingers pointing down, not up as Americans do. "*Venga. Venga.*"

I was headed that way in any case; I needed to retrieve my room key. Still, he seemed pleased that I'd agreed to join him.

"Did you see the city today?" he asked. "Quite hot out there."

"Not inside the churches," I said.

"Will you join us for dinner this evening? I want to introduce you to some of the scholars from the symposium. The students who helped us organize everything."

I explained that I already had a date with Bernie.

"Professor Sanger?" he asked. "Invite him too. I want to meet him."

"Are you sure it's appropriate? After Professor Bondinelli's death, I mean."

Franco assumed a suitably doleful expression but insisted that one had to eat. "Life goes on," he said with a sigh.

Bernie and I got roped into joining Franco Sannino and four others for dinner, but not before I'd had a chance to freshen up and put on a new face. And down a quick couple of fingers of the Scotch I'd been provident enough to pack in my suitcase. With a healthy belt under my belt, I did my best to tame my unruly curls and dressed for dinner.

At eight thirty, seven of us were seated around a long table at Trattoria Cammillo on Borgo San Jacopo. A lively eatery with a long history on the Oltrarno, Cammillo was well known to locals and tourists alike. And for good reason. The friendly staff and traditional Tuscan menu kept the place busy, even on a Wednesday evening in late September.

While not actually setting out physical place cards, Sannino nevertheless dictated our seating arrangements. He blocked me into the chair on his right with the gentle encouragement of an all-American pulling guard. A curly-haired student of about thirty, Lucio Bevilacqua, was assigned the seat on my other side, while Bernie, looking tired and suffering from the time difference, landed at the opposite end of the table next to a very pretty young thing named Giuliana. A cold, aloof beauty. Her eyes met mine for a moment, then she turned away, looking bored and aggrieved. Rounding out our group were Veronica Leonetti, the shy girl from Prato who was living in Bondinelli's house, two places beyond Sannino; and a bright-faced young man of about twenty-five, Tato, in between. He had one of those smiles that, like the song "Take Me Out to the Ballgame," rendered ill humor an impossibility. Open and sincere, Tato Lombardi welcomed you. But there was a naiveté, as well, and I sensed that he was subject to hectoring, or at least ribbing, from more aggressive males. Perhaps even from women.

Once introductions had been made, we made do with small talk for a few minutes until the waiter had poured a glass of wine for everyone. Well, not quite everyone. Veronica begged off and declared herself content to drink *acqua minerale*. And flat, not even bubbly. Sannino cleared his throat and shushed us all.

"*Cari amici*," he began, "we have suffered a terrible loss. Our dear friend and mentor, Alberto, left us yesterday. A tragic accident that saddens everyone who ever knew him. The symposium he's organized will go ahead as planned. I know I can count on all of you to ensure a successful conference tomorrow." He reached for his glass of wine and raised it in a toast to his defunct colleague. "*Ad Alberto*," he said and took a sip. "*Che riposi in pace.*"

There was a general consensus of regret among those present, though Giuliana seemed less downcast than the others. Some offered dry anecdotes about the man, none rising to the level of an affectionate roast. Nor did I detect much fondness. Rather the reminiscences struck me as polite and respectful. If the tributes were to be believed, Bondinelli suffered no vices. No one joked that he chased women, was known to tell a ribald story, or liked his wine. In fact, just the opposite. Lucio, the curly-haired student next to me, explained in broken English that Franco's toast might never have happened had Bondinelli been present, as he was wont to stare down his long nose in disapproval at drinking.

"You know, I've never seen a photograph of him," I said. "Is it true that he was tall?"

"*Centonovantasette*," said Lucio.

I did a quick calculation in my head. A meter ninety-seven. Nearly six feet five inches. "Did he play basketball?" I asked in an ill-timed attempt at humor. Lucio didn't know the word in English, and I didn't know it in Italian.

"*Pallacanestro*," offered Bernie from the far end of the table.

Then Sannino butted into our conversation. "I have a picture of him. Here," he said, producing a small black-and-white ID photo from his briefcase under the table.

"You carry his photograph?" I asked, taking it from him.

"Just for the symposium tomorrow. Part of the documentation."

I turned my attention to Bondinelli's picture. A Leninine beard grew from his chin. He'd dyed it black. You can always tell when a man colors his hair. It's not so much the dye job itself—though there's that, too—as the mismatch with the skin tone and general age of the face. Human eyes are quite skilled at detecting deviations from the norm, anomalies, and incongruities. Even idiosyncrasies such as gait and gestures.

But back to Bondinelli. He was staring at the camera, eyebrows arched high on his forehead as if startled, though I believed he'd been aiming for intensely intellectual. His skin appeared pasty white, like Death's, and I wondered where he'd found parking for his pale horse in Florence's crowded streets. His upper lip, thick and partially obscured by a mustache, bulged ever so slightly, hinting that a set of honking-big choppers lurked inside the large mouth. His long nose called to mind Dante's. Perhaps the great poet was on my mind after my visit to Santa Croce, but the comparison was not an unfair one.

I looked up from my study of poor Bondinelli. Sannino had turned to his left and was deep in conversation with the young Tato. I found myself in one of those awkward social moments where everyone present has paired off with a partner, and you're left alone. To tell the truth, Veronica had also been orphaned by the others, but she was so far from me that we would have had to stand and holler at each other to be heard. I didn't mind the respite and took a moment to assess my fellow diners.

Unlike their waxen mentor, Bondinelli, the young people at the table glowed with the healthy blush of a fresh tan. I was sure they'd all recently returned from their August beach holidays, again with the exception of Veronica, whose complexion, much like Bondinelli's, called to mind chalk. They all seemed to be coping with their recent loss, which—it hadn't escaped my notice—Franco Sannino had pronounced an accident. I wondered if he'd spoken to Inspector Peruzzi or was he in possession of a crystal ball?

Lucio tapped my forearm. "Eleonora, how are you?" he asked, showing off his English. But he somehow managed to amputate the -h- from the word *how* and transplant it onto the -a- of *are*. The result was "Ow har you?"

Despite his awful English, he was adorable. I told him I was fine, thank you, and he explained that he was a student of medieval and Renaissance poetry, specializing in Petrarch.

"I love the poetry," he announced as if apologizing for his academic specialty. "And the song. I like sing and play the *chitarra*."

I corrected him as politely as I knew how that we said "guitar" in English, and, angry with himself, he loosed a stream of Italian profanities as if from a fire hose. The invective was aimed at—I can only assume— the English language and its maddening vagaries. As dry as Petrarch seemed—and despite the liberal dosage of salt in his language—Lucio positively sparkled with personality. He was not what one would call handsome in any traditional way, but his eyes and smile compensated almost poetically for nature's capricious allocation of beauty.

"*Scusami per le parolacce*," he said, apologizing for his language. "But I love the bad words. They are beautiful, no?"

To my left, Franco Sannino had rotated 180 degrees to fix me with a persistent stare from beneath his overhanging brow. With a glass of wine in the bank, he seemed to have loosened up and was grinning an unnerving smile in my direction. I swear he was flashing what he assumed were bedroom eyes at me. I'd have to stay on my toes or he'd have a hand under my blouse in no time. I inched closer to Lucio, seated to my right.

The conversation jumped naturally between Italian and English. Everyone at the table managed in both languages, with the exception of Franco and Lucio. They seemed to follow the English well enough but couldn't untie their tongues to pronounce a word that any of us could decipher without having to ask once or twice for them to repeat themselves. As for my Italian, I felt more comfortable with each glass of wine consumed, and probably caught eighty percent of what was being said. Sannino complimented me on my pronunciation, though he noted it bore faint traces of a Neapolitan accent.

He downed another glass of wine and was morphing before my eyes. More aggressive and displaying confidence in spades, he was at turns jocular then petulant, aggrieved that his audience was not suitably deferential. He was, after all, the heir to Bondinelli's position of power, at least in this group of students. What began as an amicable debate with Lucio over who was the greater Italian cyclist, Gino Bartali or Franco Coppi, soon devolved into an argument with raised voices. In fairness, raised *voice* would be a more accurate description, given that all the volume came from Sannino's side. Lucio was in mid-sentence, counting the titles and records of Bartali's illustrious career on his fingers when Sannino declared the discussion closed. I could sense an ugly scene brewing, so I took action.

"Franco, you're so funny," I said, opting for his first name. "Isn't he funny?" I asked the others. "*Che buffo!*"

Then I hazarded a friendly shove and faked my best phony laugh. I even sacrificed a measure of my dignity, hoping to diffuse the situation, and placed my hand on his forearm as platonically as I could manage. The last thing I wanted to do was give him ideas. There was a moment's hesitation before the boor to my left got on board. But then he produced a caricature of a smile that blazed two times brighter than the occasion or my humor called for.

"*Dai, Lucio, ridi,*" he said, mocking him good-naturedly and urging him to laugh. "I was kidding."

I doubted anyone believed him.

"*Domani mattina . . .*" Franco said, changing course. He paused to spear a bit of melon with his fork and used his knife to wrap a ribbon of prosciutto around it before gobbling up the neat package. He chewed thoroughly for several seconds and swallowed. Everyone waited for him to finish his thought.

"Tomorrow morning?" I prompted, happy that the subject had moved on from cycling.

"Tomorrow," resumed Franco, "we begin at nine in the Sala dei Cinquecento in the Palazzo Vecchio with the tribute to your father, Eleonora. Then we will reconvene at the university at eleven, and the panelists will begin presenting their papers."

He went on to outline the entire schedule for the day. When he'd finally finished, he took another sip of wine and leaned in close to me.

"How is it you're not married, *carissima Eleonora?*" he asked in a low voice, all but whispering in my left ear.

Not sure I wanted to answer, I told him, instead, that I preferred to go by Ellie. When that didn't deter him from his question, I asked him how old he was instead. That shut him up for a spell. He turned back to Tato and discussed some not-so-urgent errands he wanted him to run before the symposium in the morning.

By the time we'd polished off the antipasto of prosciutto and melon, it became clear to me that Franco and Lucio were both trying to lower my defenses with drink. Several toasts to my father's memory, to me, to themselves, and to the *Newark* Yankees were obvious ploys to get me to drain my glass. And I obliged them. But of course they'd only just met me and knew nothing about my tolerance for alcohol. Over the years, many unscrupulous-but-hopeful men had made the same mistake, only to end up under the table instead of my sheets.

Before our host, Franco, had noticed, we'd finished three bottles of wine collectively, and the first course hadn't even been served. He said something curt to the boys about the early start in the morning, and they assured him they'd take it easy.

"Eleonora—Ellie—is our guest," he said. "No more wine, please, until the second course is served. Let's maintain some dignity and sobriety, *perbacco.*"

By Bacchus, indeed. In order to survive this torture of a dinner, I was going to enjoy my wine whether the host approved or not.

His miserly hypocrisy was typical of selfish men. There was Franco, sopping it up like a thirsty sponge, but he begrudged the rest of us our share. Errol Flynn had once described this brand of hospitality best when he noted, wickedly, that the wine at Hearst's castle in San Simeon, "flowed like glue." Perhaps that was an exaggeration in our case—we'd squeezed the life out of three bottles after all—but the meanness felt the same. And, by the way, I kind of had a thing for Errol Flynn. Debonair, intemperate, and libidinous all at the same time. A shame he wasn't at our table that night. A shame he was dead.

For my first course, I enjoyed a delicious plateful of *paccheri* in a *tartufo bianco* sauce, while Franco and Lucio ordered a *puttanesca* and a light tomato-and-basil dish respectively. Veronica had a simple *pastina in brodo*, while Giuliana's *pappa al pomodoro* sat uneaten, as she spent fifteen minutes in the telephone cabin speaking in animated tones to someone on the other end of the line.

Franco and Lucio urged me to taste their dishes, and though I normally don't like to share food, I couldn't resist a bite of each. Once Veronica had finished her meager repast, she dabbed her lips and said she was heading back to her room at Bondinelli's place.

"Must you go?" asked Franco, though one could tell his heart wasn't in it.

"I'm feeling tired," she said, and scratched the red patch on her neck.

"Well, see you in the morning."

"Veronica, wait," I said, rising from my seat. "Don't go by yourself. I'll take you home in a taxi."

Franco grabbed my arm and held tight. "No, don't go. Your friend Bernard can accompany her."

He called to Bernie at the end of the table and indicated Veronica with a toss of his head. Bernie—reluctantly—dropped his fork and dragged his napkin across his mouth.

"You're coming right back, aren't you?" I asked.

He yawned and said he'd probably just turn in for the night, if I didn't mind. I envied him. He stood, and the two of them slipped out of the restaurant into the street.

"That girl is an idiot," said Lucio as he watched them disappear into the night. "Doesn't understand irony or humor."

"That's not a nice thing to say," I told him.

"No, not nice, but true," said Franco. "I don't know why Alberto let her continue her studies. She's not bright. He was just too kind."

"She's simple. Naïve," added Lucio.

Not two minutes after Bernie and Veronica had decamped, Giuliana returned from the phone booth and announced that she, too, was leaving. Tato sprang to his feet and volunteered to escort her home. She insisted it wasn't necessary, that she had her *motorino* and could find her way on her own. But Tato's ardor won out. I thought she looked annoyed, but she was a brooding sort in general. They wished us all *buonanotte*, and stepped outside onto Borgo San Jacopo. Through the window, I saw her climb aboard a little motorbike, kick-start the thing, and invite Tato to hurry up. He straddled the seat behind her, wrapped his arms around her waist, and held on as the bike lurched from its standstill off the curb. The engine whined high-pitched and shrill as Giuliana sped off.

Now, with just the three of us left at the table—Franco, Lucio, and me—our host loosened up in earnest. The battle for the female of the species was on. But while the flirting from Lucio was fun and entertaining, Franco remained serious and severe, as if seducing me were a dour enterprise requiring heavy lifting and perspiration. As we waited for our second courses to be served, the wrestling match nearly turned violent. In a manner of speaking. No blows were traded or threatened, but they jousted for my attentions all the same, first—literally—with *grissini*, then—figuratively—with their wits and attempts at humor. The breadstick fight did not win them any points with me. They looked more like zeroes than Zorros, but they seemed pleased with themselves.

In fact, despite the childish behavior, my escorts were growing on me. At least Lucio was. His open smile did lots to compensate for his lack of any conventional beauty. In his late twenties, of average height and weight, with a bushy head of curly black hair, he was delightfully flirtatious and funny in both Italian and in his thickly accented English. He gazed into my eyes with a purposely goofy charm as he told me I was the girl of his heart. "*La ragazza del mio cuore sei.*" I giggled. Franco, stewing over Lucio's little victory, informed me that Lucio was only quoting a popular song from the radio. I didn't mind. He was adorable.

I'd ordered the delicate *tagliata di manzo* with arugula. Throughout the main course, the spectacle continued until the wine began to hit its mark, and its first casualty was Lucio. He grew quiet, then he started to yawn and cross his eyes. Like a big-hearted palooka on the ropes, he rallied gamely once or twice, but in the end, it was a technical knockout. He threw in the towel and said he was going home. He advised Franco and me to do the same.

In fairness, he probably sensed that he was not going to bag his trophy that night anyway. He bowed to kiss my hand and clicked his heels in theatrical fashion. Then he slurred a *buonanotte* in my general direction, turned to the door, and weaved his way out of the trattoria.

And so I was left alone with Franco, a hungry-looking man of forty or so, who, once inebriated, had no shame when it came to suffering repeated rejections. Proper and well-behaved enough when sober, now he had one thing on his mind, viz. how to separate me from my virtue or, more precisely, from my skirt and blouse.

With no warning, and apropos of nothing, he covered my hand with his, as if to prevent my escape. He leaned closer to me and bore his stare into my eyes like some kind of Svengali trying to mesmerize a young lovely. I tugged a couple of times, attempting to reclaim my hand, but he held on fast.

"*Quanto sei bella, Eleonora*," he cooed in a soft baritone.

I gave another yank. Stuck like glue. "Ellie, please."

At length, satisfied that his spell had been cast and I was in his thrall, he released me from his grip and sat back in his chair. Then he smiled, baring a line of bright-white teeth. To be sure, Franco had some five-o'clock-shadow charm, but he wasn't winning me over. His unwelcome courting, ever intensifying with the effect of wine, struck me as somehow robotic, like a male pigeon bobbing and dancing around an indifferent female. I cursed myself again for the earlier touch of his arm. When would I learn that subtlety was far too subtle for most men to grasp? At least where women and sex were concerned.

A half hour after Franco had scraped the last smudges of *budino* from the dessert dish, and long since he'd slurped the dregs of his *caffè ristretto* from its cup, the world-weary waiter appeared above us and tapped his wristwatch, indicating he'd rather we continue our mating rituals elsewhere so he could retire for the night. Franco settled the bill with a wad of lire he'd surely appropriated from the symposium budget, then lit a cigarette and held the door for me. Outside in the street, I thanked him for the dinner. Big spender that he was, he insisted it was nothing. Then he invited me back to my own hotel room "*per un drink.*"

I declined, citing the early hour of the next morning's seminar. As we strolled back to Albergo Bardi, Franco kept up the pressure anyway. He begged as only Italian men can do, with an insistent smile and imploring hands clasped together as if praying for divine intervention, "*Dai, Ellie. Un piccolo drink.*" He dragged out the pronunciation of the double Ls of my name in typical Italian fashion. The overwhelming impression was that of being propositioned by a spoiled child who'd throw himself on the ground, kicking and screaming if he didn't get his way.

We arrived at the Bardi, and I held out a hand for shaking purposes. But Franco lunged for my lips instead. I recoiled, lost my footing, and we tumbled as one to the paving stones with my posterior cushioning the fall for both of us.

"*Accidenti!*" he exclaimed as I shoved him off my person. He rolled into the gutter and, groaning, examined the skinned palms of his hands. "*Porca miseria . . . Mi sono fatto male.*"

I propped myself up on my elbows and rubbed my smarting backside. He'd hurt *him*self? What about me? I struggled to my feet and stood over him. He looked up at me with pathetic cow eyes and begged me to take pity on him and invite him up to my room. I sensed the path of least resistance was to give in to his charms. I'd led him on, after all. So it only seemed fair to let him have what he wanted.

"Wait here for five minutes," I said, bending to whisper in his ear. "Then come up to room twenty-five."

He smiled and—I swear—would have rubbed his hands together in wicked delight if he hadn't just scraped them raw on the pavement. I straightened my skirt, stepped over him, and pushed through the door into the hotel.

I escaped to my room, number forty-one, and wondered how Big Bob Stueben of Lebanon, Kansas, would react to an amorous, and quite inebriated, Franco Sannino rapping at his door after midnight.

CHAPTER FIVE

THURSDAY, SEPTEMBER 26, 1963

The Sala dei Cinquecento was an enormous hall on the *primo piano* of the Palazzo Vecchio, what we in America would call the second floor. A magnificent, if dimly lit, echo chamber, the Sala gave off the odor of cold marble and *pietra serena*. The room was often used, I was told, for important cultural events such as the one organized by Bondinelli.

The proceedings commenced as scheduled at nine with a lukewarm welcome from the *preside di facoltà*, or department chairman—Bondinelli's' boss, as it were—of the *Istituto di Filologia Moderna* at the university. I gathered he was standing in for the *Magnifico Rettore*, who was unavoidably detained in Rome. The *preside* wasted little time in handing over the speaking duties to an old priest, who mumbled a heartfelt, often emotional, invocation into a squawking microphone. Padre Fabrizio addressed the tragic loss of his longtime friend with tears and true grief, explaining that he had served as confessor to Bondinelli for the past twenty-five years, since before the war.

"Alberto was a kind, pious man," he said in a shaky voice. He stood stooped, bent at the waist, causing the large metal crucifix hanging from his neck to pendulate and tap against the microphone each time he drew a breath or raised an arm. The resulting feedback added aural discomfort to the already mournful kickoff of the proceedings.

Padre Fabrizio wiped his brow with a handkerchief then cleared his throat. He went on to describe Bondinelli as a scholar of scripture as well as literature. He'd lived the last twenty-five years of his life dedicated to good deeds and charity unto his fellow man. In addition to tithing to the Church, he served as a board member on numerous Catholic charities, including the *Figlie della Carità di San Vincenzo de' Paoli* and another that sponsored transportation of crippled and ailing pilgrims to Lourdes and Fátima. And, many years before, a charity that provided education for orphans of the Spanish Civil War. For twelve years, he'd edited the Madonna della Tosse's weekly bulletin, *La Buona Notizia*, usually writing three-quarters of, if not all, the content, which included parish news, birth and death announcements, and the latest from the Vatican and the Holy See. He also curated the rectory's library, all at no charge.

But more moving than Padre Fabrizio's recitation of Bondinelli's charities was his own heartbreak at the loss of his friend. There were sobs and the vigorous blowing of noses all around me. Then the priest sketched out his friend's early years.

Alberto Bondinelli was born a breech baby in Lucca in 1907, exactly one hour before his mother died of complications from the delivery. The second child of a failed classics professor stationed in Eritrea to teach Italian to the natives, Alberto was raised in Florence by his maternal grandmother, a widow. The boy had an elder sister, Cecilia, to whom he was devoted. She entered the convent at the age of thirteen, following a path set by two maternal aunts a generation before. Training as a nurse, Cecilia tended to wounded soldiers in a recovery hospital in Udine, and, as the war was drawing to a close, she died in the influenza pandemic of 1918.

Speaking in a quavering voice, Padre Fabrizio described the crisis of faith young Alberto had experienced after the loss of his beloved sister. Convinced the Lord had forsaken her, his family, and him, he turned his back on God after Cecilia's death. At an age when he should have been enjoying the pleasures of an eleven-year-old boy—shooting *biglie* (marbles) in the piazza with his friends, enjoying *brutti ma buoni* cookies at holiday time, or stealing a special *caramella* from the tin box his grandmother kept not so hidden in a drawer with her napery—he brooded alone, dark and angry. Fractious, irritable, and impossible to control, Albi, as he was known to his grandmother, rebelled against all authority, most of all against the Church. And he used his large size to best advantage when delivering beatings to his classmates, innocent children of God all.

His grandmother prayed for his soul and nearly wore her rosary down to dust asking for a miracle. According to Padre Fabrizio, the poor woman sought guidance from her parish priest, who advised stern measures. He maintained that any boy who would strike his friends would do the same to his mother. Or, indeed, to his grandmother. He proposed a religious education for the boy, with an eye on the priesthood if all went well and the brothers managed to salvage his soul.

About the time his father died in Eritrea, Albi was sent off to the monastery. There he received a complete Catholic education, even as he continued to resist his tutors. Not even the personal attention and care from his parish priest could convince young Alberto of God's design. It would take many years before he finally recovered his faith.

"He never told me the story of how he rediscovered the Lord," said the priest, bringing the eulogy of his friend to a close. "He insisted that it should remain between him and God. I reminded him that he was a Catholic, not a Lutheran, and it was only proper that he should share the story with his confessor."

The crowd managed a low chuckle despite their tears. I, too, felt a tightness in my throat and had to dab my eyes. Padre Fabrizio folded the paper he'd been consulting and mopped his brow again. Then he recited a prayer in Latin and offered encouraging parting words for the success of the symposium.

"May God bless this endeavor that Alberto has organized. *In nomine patris et filii et spiritus sancti, amen.*"

Though I was looking down, the rustling of sleeves against jackets and blouses told me that I was one of only a handful present in the Sala not performing the sign of the cross. Another abstainer was Bernie, who was seated in the row behind me to my right.

Now with God safely on our side, Professor Franco Sannino—he of scraped palms and bruised ego—stepped onto the dais and took the microphone from the priest. He clipped it back into its mount, and tapped its grille three times, loosing another wave of feedback through the hall. Satisfied the mic was working, he unfolded a sheet of paper, smoothed it on the lectern before him, and donned a pair of half-lunette eyeglasses. A longish silence ensued as he scanned the document before him. I, in turn, studied him as he read. This day he was dressed in a suit and tie, and his eyes looked puffy and shot red, but he'd answered the bell. I wondered how his encounter with Big Bob Stueben had gone.

Speaking in Italian—of course—Franco introduced himself with the barest of details, assuming, I can only imagine, that everyone in the place knew who he was. Then he explained that he was saddened to have to fill in for his friend and colleague, but he was sure Bondinelli would have wanted the show to go on.

"I have here the introduction Alberto prepared, and I will read it exactly as he wrote it."

Over the course of the next few minutes, Franco reviewed and extolled the career and character of my late father, licking his boots clean, oratorically speaking. I sat on a folding wooden chair in the front row, listening to then tuning out the hyperbolic recitation of my father's accomplishments. I didn't need to hear them. I knew them all. His remarkable capacity for mastering languages, his tremendous erudition and dedication to research, prodigious talent for drawing . . . pursuit of excellence in his scholarship . . . seminal work . . . *illustrissimo letterato . . . marito affezionato, padre di famiglia*—Franco's parroting of Bondinelli's tribute melted into a sticky puddle of treacle.

My attention wandered. I gazed up at the hall's giant frescoes, which depicted crowded battlefields of knights, horses, and foot soldiers engaged in wholesale slaughter. Some Florentine victory or other over the Sienese or the Pisans, I figured, but I wasn't sure which. The wall to my left was lined with a series of six statues. At first glance, the sculptures appeared to be two nude wrestlers in the most compromising and revealing of positions. Then I realized these statues represented the Labors of Hercules. The one closest to me was the most riveting: Hercules holding Diomedes aloft—upside down—exposing his opponent's . . . well . . . his opponent's *everything* for all to see. But as our hero squeezed the air and the life out of Diomedes, the latter was maintaining an iron grip on Hercules's . . . *pisello* and the adjoining tackle, looking as if he'd only let go over his dead body. Hercules, of course, obliged him and, as the story goes, subsequently fed his defeated foe to his own man-eating mares.

"*Signorina Stone, prego.*"

Franco stood above me, extending an open hand in my direction, inviting me up to the dais. I sensed from his insistent expression and the impatience in his voice that he was either repeating the appeal for at least the third time or he was holding a grudge for my little prank of the previous evening. I'm sure I blushed.

Climbing the two steps, I joined my host at the podium as the audience clapped politely. Franco displayed the honor—a medal struck especially for the occasion—for all to see. It was a four-inch silver disk emblazoned with Dante's aquiline likeness set against the Palazzo Vecchio in the background. The poet, as always, looked cross. Or perhaps dyspeptic.

A photographer knelt before us and mimed posing instructions to me. I understood he wanted me to stand closer to Franco and to hold the open case containing the medal as if I were glad to accept it.

"*Sorrida, signorina*," he said, now giving voice to his directives. "*Un bel sorriso. Ecco, perfetto.*"

He fired off a dozen shots, reloading fresh flashbulbs as quickly as his white-gloved hand could pluck the exploded hot ones from the reflector. And he continued to offer encouragement until Franco waved him off.

Having cleared his throat with a stentorian ahem that startled a pigeon in the rafters, he closed the case—medal safely inside—and presented it to me. Then, shaking my hand—squeezing it perhaps a mite too ardently given our brief acquaintance and his own injuries of the previous night—he ceded the microphone to me. He showed no outward indication that he remembered what had happened on the hotel's threshold not ten hours before. Perhaps he'd been too drunk. In any event, he was his proper self again. He stepped back, indicating that it was my time to say a few words.

There I stood at the lectern in the magnificent Sala dei Cinquecento, staring out at the crowd—at least a hundred and fifty strong—gathering my wits to deliver the speech I'd prepared. Enunciating each word, every consonant, precise vowel, and diphthong, I read slowly the two paragraphs my tutor, Sister Michael back in New Holland, had helped me translate into Italian. It was little more than some kind words about my father and a succinct cataloguing of distinguished guests who needed to be thanked. And, with the assistance of Bernie Sanger at breakfast that morning, I'd added a few words of appreciation and sorrow for my host, the late Alberto Bondinelli. Once I'd finished and the audience had applauded dutifully, I turned to leave the stage. Pushing aside the long-standing estrangement we'd never resolved, I addressed my father in a whisper. Covering my lips with a casual brush of my fingers, I said, "None of that matters now. I love you."

With the opening ceremonies concluded, we were all directed to reconvene in the Aula Magna at the university an hour later for the actual
symposium. Franco Sannino told me he and the others were planning on
meeting for lunch in Piazza della Signoria after that. I was hardly paying
attention. Feeling wistful after the tribute to my father, I slipped out of
the hall, escaping all—even Bernie—intending to make my way to the
university on foot by myself. Instead, I wandered off through the side
streets of the city, trying to shake off my gloom.

Two hours later, swinging my purse lazily as I strolled the cobble-
stones, I found myself back in Piazza della Signoria. I was thirsty, and not
for water. I found a table on the outdoor terrace of the Cavallo restaurant
on the north side of the square, facing the Neptune Fountain. Once the
waiter had delivered my glass of whisky soda, I settled back, sunglasses
in place to shield my eyes from the early-afternoon sun to the south, and
considered the statue before me.

Ammannato's giant white Neptune, *il Biancone*, stood tall—and
equally as nude as the nearby David—in his fountain. Ever stuck in pe-
dantic mode, my father had told me the Florentines so hated the statue
that they mocked it with a little rhyme, "*Ammannato Ammannato che bel
marmo t'hai sciupato.*" (Ammannato, Ammannato, what a nice piece of
marble you've ruined.)

Franco's reading of Bondinelli's tribute, along with my own speech
that morning, steered my thoughts to my father. I'd long stopped wondering what happened in relationships like ours. The beginning, I mean, not
the dramatic denouement. That was clear to me. Maybe he'd preferred sons.
Son. Elijah. At least to grown daughters. My father and I had been closer
when I was a child, but ours had never been a "daddy's little girl" kind of
thing. At least never for very long. He liked showing me off to his friends
and colleagues as the marvel who could name any piece of classical music at
the drop of a needle. It was a silly, useless talent. But I enjoyed making him
proud when I could distinguish a lesser-known chamber piece by Dvorak
from something by Smetana. Or when I could pick Sibelius or Borodin out
of a lineup in front of his cronies at a cocktail party. But it always felt like a
test. A test that, should I fail, would cause a run on my stock. And, in fact,
that suspicion eventually spoiled the joy and pride of the exercise. It stoked
resentment and planted a nagging notion in the back of my mind that I was
singing for my supper. I doubted he'd ever felt the need to earn my affections.

I drew a sigh and blew it out, scolding myself for wallowing in melancholy over ancient history I could do nothing to change. That, too, in a beautiful spot such as Florence. Soon I'd be done with my responsibilities—the symposium—and free to pursue the rest of my Italian holiday on my own. To forge new memories that didn't stink of regret and remorse. At least that was the plan. Sitting alone in the piazza, I sank into more remembrances of things past. My first voyage to Italy with my father.

Florence aside, my favorite place of all was Venice. I hadn't even minded that the canals smelled like ripened garbage in the August heat. *La Serenissima* had delighted and amazed me as a little girl, sparking my fantasies and imagination as no other place ever had or has since. I marveled at the *palazzi* floating on the lagoon. Never mind *how* they had built a city on stilts in the water, I wondered *why*. Was the dry land not inviting enough? But Venice had indeed been built on the islands, and a ten-year-old girl could only explore—enchanted—its wonders. Each bridge and every *campo* led to new discoveries, small doors and stone wells and quiet nooks where flowers exploded in color from ancient window boxes. And Piazza San Marco, with its flights of pigeons, cafés with ice cream and pastries, and its basilica resembling—to my young mind at least—the palace of some eastern king. I gazed, entranced, at the prancing horses above the arched doorway and asked my father why that lion even higher up had wings. His long-winded answer, I recall, had something to do with Saint Mark and the Bible, but he lost me before too long. My father, you see, lacked the capacity to gauge the interest and patience of his audience, never more so than when delivering a scholarly lecture to his ten-year-old daughter. When he'd finally summed up his thesis, I asked if I could have a gelato and feed the pigeons.

"*Scusi, signorina,*" a voice from over my shoulder interrupted my thoughts. "Are you Miss Stone?"

A stout woman in her forties, shy and solicitous, waited, breath bated, for me to confirm my identity. My Italian had improved greatly thanks to ten months of assiduous study with Sister Michael back in New Holland, but there remained yawning holes in my vocabulary and familiarity with accents. Nevertheless, I sensed something different about this woman's speech, starting with the epenthetic -e- she'd tacked on to the front of *scusi*. How did I know that word, *epenthetic*? One of the bonuses of growing up with a polyglot pedant of a father who tossed such terms around the way J. D. Rockefeller used to hand out dimes. And I remembered him telling me that was why the "*Spanish*" lady who cleaned our neighbor's house called him Professor es-Stone. Ever the pedagogue, he made sure I understood that the -e- was only appended to words beginning with an -s- plus another consonant, or a -z-. Why did I need to know that? It only served to distract me each time I met someone with a Spanish accent.

"Yes," I said, answering the lady's question. "What can I do for you?"

She leaned forward at the hips ever so slightly, hands folded together. "My name is Teresa Ortega y Martín." She paused.

Spanish, as I'd suspected. "Do I know you?"

"No, let me explain. I am the housekeeper of Professor Bondinelli."

I stood and offered the chair next to mine. She hesitated, eyes darting around the terrace of the café for a brief moment, before tucking her dress against her thighs and taking the seat.

"*Grazie*," she said.

"How did you find me here?" I asked. "I mean, how did you recognize me?"

"I attended the ceremony this morning. I saw you there."

That made sense. I signaled to the waiter with a raised finger. He arrived presently, and I asked Teresa what she would have. At first she demurred, but I insisted, and in the end she ordered an *aranciata*. Once we were alone, she explained in Italian the reason for her interruption. Understandably upset by her employer's death, she nevertheless had come to tell me that Professor Bondinelli had wanted my Florence sojourn to be a comfortable one. I told her I'd been shocked to hear of the tragedy.

"How long had you known him?" I asked.

"Almost twenty-five years."

"You've worked for him for so long?"

She shook her head. "Only seven years. But I met him long ago."

The waiter returned with her soft drink. I touched a finger to my glass, and he nodded silently. I watched Teresa. She averted her gaze, not to enjoy the surrounding beauty or crowds of tourists in the piazza, but to avoid my stare. At least that's what I assumed.

"Did you see the professor Tuesday?" I asked.

"Yes, of course. I made him his breakfast and ironed his suit."

I wasn't sure how things worked in Italy. "Do you . . . live in Professor Bondinelli's house?"

She nodded. "I have a room in his home. Small, but comfortable. I cook and keep his house for him."

"Then you must know Veronica."

"Of course. She also has a room in the professor's house. A nice girl. Not so smart, but a good soul."

She wiped a tear with the cigarette-paper-thin napkin the waiter had brought with her drink. I placed a hand over hers to comfort. She wore no wedding band.

"I'm so sorry."

"He was very kind to me," she said, sobbing now. I offered her a proper handkerchief from my purse, and she buried her face in it to weep. "He was a saintly man."

A long moment later, after the waiter had delivered my refill, Teresa managed to compose herself. She produced an envelope from her bag and placed it on the table.

"*Il professore* meant to give this to you," she said.

"What is it?" I asked as I took it from her.

She jutted out her chin to indicate she didn't know. "He wanted you to have it."

I examined the envelope. Heavy bond. His personal stationery, I figured. And there was my name: "*Sig.na* Eleonora Stone" along with a one-line message, "*Da aprire dopo il simposio.*" (To be opened after the symposium.)

CHAPTER SIX

"Should I open it?" I asked.

She said that was between me and Professor Bondinelli.

Weighing the sealed envelope in my hand, I figured there was probably a single sheet of paper inside. Two at the most. I placed it on the table before me and took a healthy sip of my whisky soda. Did the scrawl on the envelope constitute a covenant between him and me? Had it been broken by his death? And since I hadn't been a party to it in the first place, was it even valid? This was silly, I thought. It was surely nothing more than a thank-you note for my taking the pains to travel all the way from New York to attend the conference. I was about to tear it open when Franco Sannino tapped me on the shoulder.

"Ellie." He gazed down at me, wagging a finger in mock reproach. "You never made it to the university hall. Shame on you."

I stammered something inadequate in reply, but he smiled, waved me off, and took the seat next to mine. He barely noticed Teresa and, in fact, ignored her after I'd made introductions.

"Don't worry about the conference," he said, checking his watch. "I'm the host. I'll grant you a dispensation."

"Is this the lunch break?" I asked.

Franco signaled to the waiter, who arrived at a trot. "*Campari soda,*" he said. Then motioning to my glass, added, "*Un altro per la signorina.*"

I was about to ask Teresa if she wanted another as well, but her glass was full. That didn't excuse Franco his lack of manners, as I doubted he'd even cast a glance her way to check. Instead he pulled a packet of cigarettes from his jacket, selected one, and asked if I'd join him. I told him no. Once he'd lit up, inhaled deeply, and sat back in his chair to observe the passersby, I repeated my question.

"Yes, this is the lunch break. The afternoon session starts at two."

"Professor Bondinelli is the host," said Teresa in a small voice, filling the brief silence that had descended upon us.

"*Prego?*" asked Franco.

"The symposium," she said to clarify. "Professor Bondinelli is the host."

Franco shifted in his seat and attempted a stiff smile. "Of course, *signora*. But as he's no longer with us . . ."

In fairness, I doubted Teresa's contribution had been intended as anything more than a statement of fact. No reproach. She didn't seem to have that kind of malice—or courage—in her. It was merely her way of participating in the conversation. Still, Franco was now painfully aware of her hitherto unnoticed presence.

"I haven't had the pleasure. *Come si chiama, signora?*"

Of course he'd had the pleasure. I'd performed the honors myself not two minutes before. Nevertheless, Teresa repeated her name and informed him again that she was Bondinelli's *donna di servizio*.

"*Condoglianze*," he said just as the waiter arrived with our drinks.

He clinked his glass against mine, then waved to a woman looking lost in the piazza not twenty feet from us. She didn't recognize him at first, but approached us anyway.

"You are Vicky, *vero?*" asked Franco.

Tall and svelte, dressed in a tapered skirt and matching jacket, she must have been melting in the heat. Yet she was elegant and quite pretty, and not letting on that she'd chosen her outfit poorly that morning.

"Yes. I'm Vicky. Victoria Hodges."

Springing to his feet, he offered her his place at the table next to me. Teresa faded even farther into the scenery.

"We meet-ed, remember?" said Franco in English. "With Alberto. Ten days ago."

She forced a smile but wasn't convinced. Not ready to accept the seat he was holding for her.

"Did we?" she asked. "Ten days ago?"

East coast accent, I thought. Hard to pin down. New York or Connecticut, perhaps. "I'm afraid I've forgotten your name."

"I am Franco. The colleague of Alberto. Alberto Bondinelli."

"Of course," she said, now only too happy to sit down. She waved a hand to cool her face and asked if he might summon a waiter. Once she'd ordered some mineral water, she turned back to Franco. "You and Alberto are staying at the house in Fiesole this weekend with the students, isn't that right?"

Franco blanched. "Well, to tell true, no. I want to say, yes. You have not hear-ed? Alberto. *Povero* Alberto. He is died."

"Died? Oh, no. When did that happen?"

"Tuesday evening. He fall-ed in the river. *Annegato. Morto. Martedì sera.*"

Vicky managed to squeeze a drop of compassion out of her heart. Yes, I was still there, observing from my place next to the new arrival. She hadn't noticed me, never mind Teresa.

"That's too sad. Max will be sick to hear this."

Franco had clearly abandoned any interest he might have had in me—at least for the time being—as the statuesque Vicky dwarfed me not only in size but in beauty as well. During my trip to Los Angeles the previous year, I'd been told on more than one occasion that I was pretty, but not Hollywood pretty. This leggy brunette *was* Hollywood pretty. Franco made a big show of bowing and scraping, commiserating with Vicky, who didn't appear especially broken up by the news she'd just *hear-ed.* His performance consisted mostly of pinched lips, pained grimaces, and squinty eyes to demonstrate exactly how grief-stricken he was. I stepped into a momentary pause in their conversation and introduced myself to Vicky. She noticed me for the first time, extended a clammy hand—it was hot and muggy after all—and pronounced herself pleased to make my acquaintance.

"Will you be at the house with the others this weekend in Fiesole?" I asked.

"Afraid not. Max and I are leaving for Lugano on the train tonight. Lugano's in Switzerland," she added.

"Is it?" I asked. "Still?"

"Yes, Switzerland."

"I see. And who's Max?"

"Max is Massimiliano Locanda," she said. "We're . . . *insieme,* as the Italians say. That means together."

"Sounds wonderful. And Max owns the house in Fiesole?"

She nodded.

I was about to interrogate her about this Max Locanda, but just then

Franco called out to a girl in the piazza, the pretty one who'd left the previous night's dinner at Trattoria Cammillo, Giuliana. Franco appropriated another chair from a neighboring table, and introduced the newcomer—whom Vicky welcomed as one might a sneeze on the neck—as Giuliana Pincherle, a student at the university.

"She will join us at the villa this weekend," he said. Vicky seemed miles away. In Lugano, Switzerland, perhaps.

Ever the gentleman—or perhaps he didn't actually remember the night before—Franco re-introduced me to Giuliana, adding that she was *ebrea* (a Jewess) as was I. That earned him a glare from me and a frown from Giuliana.

As I might have predicted, Tato was not far off. Looking unabashed, he materialized not two minutes after Giuliana's arrival.

The table was filling up fast with young people, which torpedoed my plans for a quiet hour alone with my thoughts. The crowd made Teresa uncomfortable. She rose from her chair and, clutching her purse tight, announced in her little voice that she was late and had to leave. I followed her out of the café to say goodbye.

"Is there some way I can reach you?" I asked.

She said she'd be staying at Bondinelli's as usual. That was her home. "And Signorina Mariangela is coming home for the funeral."

"Is that his daughter's name? Mariangela?"

She nodded then made a face and waved her hands at me, as if to ward off any more questions. I comforted her as best I could, putting an arm around her heaving shoulders as she sobbed. A few curious tourists stopped to gawk, and I indicated my annoyance at their staring with a scowl. They moved on. At length, having blown her nose lustily into the handkerchief I'd lent her earlier, Teresa composed herself and offered it back to me. I decided to make a gift of it to her.

Back at the table, I found that Lucio Bevilacqua had arrived and made himself at home in my seat. Brandishing a playful grin, he patted his knee, enticing me to sit. I feigned distraction and ignored the invitation, even though it left me standing in the piazza, just off the Cavallo's patio, next to Franco Sannino.

"She's Locanda's mistress," he whispered to me in Italian, referring to the pretty brunette who was trying to ignore everyone by reading her copy of the *Herald Tribune*.

"Who is this Locanda anyway?" I asked.

"I'll tell you later. She might overhear."

I squeezed past Giuliana and Tato, sidestepped Lucio, and insinuated myself in the tiny space next to Vicky.

"Hi, again," I said, interrupting her reading. "I'm Ellie."

"I know. I just met you."

"Right. So where are you from?"

"New York. Rhinecliff." She didn't ask me the same.

"So tell me about your boyfriend, Max."

She glared at me. "He's not my boyfriend. Men like Max don't have *girlfriends*."

"What do they have?"

"Why are you asking me this?"

"Sorry. Just trying to make a new friend."

Vicky leaned in and lowered her voice. "Look, Ellie. You seem nice. I'm sure under different circumstances we might be friends. But, honestly, we're never going to see each other again once I finish my glass of water. I'm off to Lugano with Max, and you've probably got a tour bus to catch for Rome or Venice or wherever is next on your itinerary. No offense, but we run in different circles."

If I was mortally offended—and I was—I didn't let on. "Of course you're right," I said. "I was just curious about handsome Italian men. Max sounds fascinating."

"We're lovers," she said. "Does that scandalize you? If so, I'm sorry. Americans are so provincial when it comes to sex."

"It's okay. I'm from New York. The city. Manhattan. Not the provinces."

Vicky studied me for a long moment, a smile curling on her painted lips. At length, she must have accepted me as a sister in crime. "Max is at the villa taking care of some business before we leave for Lugano," she said.

"Switzerland, right?" Why was I such a wiseacre?

"I came to town for my Italian lesson. I don't see the point, but Max insists. And he's paying for it."

"So is Max an old friend of Alberto's?"

"I suppose. To tell you the truth, I don't even remember meeting him." She indicated Franco with a dismissive nod in his direction. "That guy says I did, but I don't have the faintest recollection."

"Alberto never visited Max?"

"He might have. I don't know. He never talked about him to me."

Why was I quizzing this woman about Bondinelli and his friend Max? I was in Florence on my own time and shouldn't have been worrying about tracking down stories and interviewing witnesses. Still, a man had died. And of unnatural causes. Surely he'd fallen into the river accidentally. Who would want to shove an egghead professor into the Arno? And why? Or had it been a robbery gone wrong? The legions of know-it-alls who'd told me not to drink the water had also warned me about pinchers and pickpockets and kidnappers and gypsies. "Be careful! Safe travels! Keep your eyes peeled!" I'd heard it all. Were there not murders and robberies in the US? Was dying in my own country somehow more palatable than getting bumped off abroad?

This was silly. Vicky was so wrapped up in her own concerns she couldn't even remember having met a tall, horse-faced friend of her lover's not ten days before. I doubted she could tell me anything to cast light on the death of Alberto Bondinelli. She was right; we'd surely never see each other again.

I spotted Bernie staring longingly at our crowded table from about ten yards away in the piazza. He looked like a window-shopper with empty pockets. Despite his concentration, he didn't see or hear me calling to him, so I stepped off the *terrazza* and corralled him, dragging him back to join the rest of us. Vicky consulted her watch and announced she was running late. I said goodbye. She waved and left.

"Who was *that*?" asked Bernie, practically drooling on my shoulder as he watched her go.

"A geography professor," I said.

"Really?"

"No. And quit staring at her behind, you pig. Yes, she's very pretty. And taken. Locanda's lover."

"Locanda? The guy with the villa? Bondinelli's friend?"

"The very one."

"Too bad I wasn't invited for the weekend in the country," he mused.

"I can arrange it. But she won't be there. Locanda's whisking her off to Lugano." I paused. "That's in Switzerland."

Bernie gaped at me. I waved off his bewilderment just as Veronica appeared. She shimmered in and out of view like a specter. Perhaps it was because she was so quiet. Or maybe her shyness amounted to camouflage. Whatever the explanation, her sudden manifestations unsettled you the way a wet finger in your ear did. Startling and unpleasant at the same time.

With Vicky gone, I quizzed the rest of my companions about Locanda. Of course I had no reason to dig other than my native curiosity. But these people had invaded my private afternoon, so I felt some payment in return was my due. Lucio shrugged, Tato shook his head, and Veronica had already told me she'd never met him. Bernie certainly had no information about Bondinelli's friend. Franco had met him that one time ten days earlier, but he was hard-pressed even to provide a physical description. I was sure he could guess Vicky's measurements to the centimeter, but Locanda? *Niente.*

Moving on, I mentioned it was almost two and asked half-jokingly if anyone was intending to return to the symposium. There were embarrassed looks all around. The event had been organized by their friend and mentor to honor my father, after all, and no one—not even I—seemed to think it worth the few hours necessary to see it through to its conclusion. Everyone agreed that it was only proper to head back over to the university for the remainder of the conference. We settled the bill, doing the math and exchanging banknotes of frighteningly high denominations. A chorus of "*andiamo*"s followed, but in typical Italian fashion, it wasn't until ten minutes later that the group finally set out across the piazza.

I waited for Bernie on the terrace of the café. He'd run inside to use the WC, and I was left to amuse myself by monkeying with the aperture settings on my Leica. Then I heard a voice in my left ear.

"I met him." I reeled around to find Giuliana standing there.

"*Prego?*"

"I met him," she repeated. "Locanda. I didn't want to say anything with the others here."

"Why not?"

She made a pouty face but didn't answer. She was a moody one. I asked her where she'd met him.

"He was with Bondinelli. At Trattoria Sostanza near Santa Maria Novella."

"Tell me about it."

"Why do you want to know about him anyway? Do you think he pushed Bondinelli into the Arno?"

"Of course not," I said. "It's just that I've heard his name a couple of times, and no one seems to know him. Tell me about when you met him."

"They were together. Having dinner. That's all."

"Did you speak to him?"

She nodded, then she averted her eyes and gazed across the piazza as she spoke, as if she was looking for someone. "Sostanza's a tiny place. I was with my friend Filippo. Bondinelli spotted me. He called me over to his table."

"Go on," I said when she paused.

"*Niente*. He chatted about my upcoming exams, the weather, and I introduced him to Filippo. Then his companion—Locanda—said hello."

"When was this?"

"In the spring. March or April."

"And did he say anything to you?"

"Just hello, pleased to meet you. That kind of thing. Shook my hand. But he held on for a long moment. You know how it is when men do that. They won't let go. They think it's funny. He winked at me while Bondinelli and Filippo were talking."

"Anything else?"

"When Bondinelli said goodbye, I swear to you, Locanda turned white."

"Why? What happened?"

A bitter smirk crossed her lips. "Bondinelli called me by my name, *Signorina* Pincherle."

"*E allora*?"

"*Allora*, he understood I was Jewish and he reacted the way all fascists do."

Giuliana's face froze as she looked over my shoulder. I turned to see Bernie sauntering our way.

"Ready to go?" he asked.

"Just a sec. I'm talking with Giuliana."

"She's gone," he said, his eyes following her as she disappeared into a crowd of tourists.

"Damn it. She was telling me about Locanda. Then you had to scare her off. She's like a deer, that one."

"Come on, let's go. I really want to hear the three o'clock paper. 'Dante, Thomas Aquinas, and the Medieval Christian Theologians.'"

"Wouldn't want to miss that," I grumbled.

"Right up my alley," he continued. "You know who else they'll be talking about?"

"I don't know, Bernie. Albertus Magnus?"

"No, not Alber—. Well, yes, as a matter of fact, there'll certainly be talk of Albertus Magnus. But I was referring to your father. His first book, *The Twelve Lights*, was a major work and an important contribution to the field of study. Surely you've read it."

"Many years ago," I lied. "I don't remember it as well as you do."

"Of course you do. The Sphere of the Sun? In Dante's *Paradiso?* Your father's book is a masterpiece."

I shrugged an apology at him.

"Then you're in for a treat. Sit beside me at the lecture. Afterward I want to hear your thoughts on Aquinas's recounting of the life of St. Francis. That was my favorite chapter in his book."

"Let's go, Bernie," I said, reaching for my purse on the table. Then I stopped.

"What's wrong?"

I frowned. Then I crouched and searched the ground around the table. "It's not here," I said.

"What's not here?"

"One of them took it. One of them stole my letter."

CHAPTER SEVEN

"Who would take the letter?" asked Bernie once I'd explained and re-explained the sequence of events, from Teresa's arrival to her giving me the envelope to its disappearance.

"It had to have been one of the people at the table."

"That's fantastic, El. Are you sure it wasn't the waiter? Or the wind?"

"Do you feel any wind, Bernie?" The air was, in fact, quite still that day. And roaring hot. "No, it must have been one of them. Let's see, Franco was the first to show up. Then Locanda's girlfriend, Vicky. She was sitting right there at the table reading her newspaper. She could have slipped it inside with no one the wiser. Or Lucio. He even sat in my chair."

"But why?" asked Bernie. "Do you suppose there was something important in the letter? Money?"

"I doubt that. But you know, there was one strange thing about the envelope. Bondinelli had written 'to be opened after the symposium.'"

Bernie pronounced himself stumped, but suggested we confront everyone who'd been present. I wasn't convinced, but said I'd think on it. Maybe I should change my plans again and go to the country house for the weekend after all. The same folks would be there. But as Bernie and I set off for the university, I asked myself if I truly wanted to spend more time with those people. That one of them would steal a letter addressed to me was unsettling enough, but what struck me as even more troubling was why one would want it in the first place.

While the opening ceremonies had taken place in the Sala dei Cinquecento, the symposium itself was scheduled for the Aula Magna del Rettorato at the University of Florence. Located in Piazza San Marco, just a fifteen minute stroll from the Palazzo Vecchio, the Aula Magna was a cavernous room with a coffered ceiling at least forty feet high, hanging banners and tapestries, and four glowing chandeliers.

The afternoon session was well underway when Bernie and I crept inside and took seats near the door. For the purposes of the conference, about one hundred and fifty folding wooden chairs had been pressed into service to accommodate the audience, which numbered perhaps fifty or sixty souls. A long conference table with microphones had been placed at the end of the room opposite the entrance. There, three tired-looking men and one ignored middle-aged woman at the far-right end listened as a young man read his paper. The audience was, at turns, yawning, doodling into their composition books, and examining their fingernails.

"What's he going on about?" I whispered to Bernie. My Italian, though much improved and a subject of new pride for me, was not up to deciphering recondite scholarly treatises, at least not when the ushers had seated me in the middle of the third act.

"Epistolary tradition in medieval literature."

"What's that got to do with my father's work?"

"Nothing."

An elderly gentleman in the next row reeled around in his seat and aimed a reproachful glare at us. We maintained silence for the last twenty minutes of the young man's talk, though I may have wheezed a snore or two through my nose when I dozed off briefly. My body's clock was still out of kilter after my transatlantic flight.

The afternoon session consisted of a string of one academic after another pronouncing even more potent sleep incantations, some in Italian, some in French, and some in English. I nodded off once or twice more. At about half past four—I consulted my watch for at least the tenth time— Franco Sannino was wrapping up the proceedings with a valedictory oration written by Bondinelli, of course, and a thank-you to all who'd participated and helped organize the symposium. In closing, he invited the same old priest from that morning to deliver the benediction.

I made for the exit before Bernie could ask for my thoughts on *The Twelve Lights*, and returned to the hotel via the Ponte Vecchio. I was hardly paying attention, just wanting to get behind a closed door and be alone for a few minutes before the scheduled reception at the hotel. Sometimes it's that way; you simply need some time by yourself without anyone looking at you or wanting to discuss medieval theology and your past, imperfect father.

So as I rushed over the crest of the bridge, I failed to notice the man in the doorway of a leather goods shop. He stepped out, and I bounced off him like a pinball. As my father had taught me to do, I offered a proper apology in Italian—*Mi scusi*. Then I recognized him. The very same deviant who'd propositioned me two days before, practically in the same spot. He asked if I was lost. I didn't stick around to answer him, but made a beeline for Borgo San Jacopo on the Oltrarno side of the bridge.

He followed me at a discreet distance, without haste but purposefully, forcing me to take evasive action. I didn't want to lead him to my hotel, so I continued past Via de' Bardi and the Chiesa di Santa Felicita, a church my father had dragged me to see some seventeen years earlier. Something about a chapel designed by Brunelleschi and an important painting by Pontormo, he'd explained. Not the moment to worry about that. I crossed Via de' Guicciardini and slipped into a side street. Picking up my pace, I turned right—back north—onto Via dei Ramaglianti, temporarily losing my pursuer, then regained Borgo San Jacopo. There, a municipal policeman was watching a pair of foreign girls window-shop along the street. I approached him at a run and explained breathlessly that I was being followed by a strange man. Pointing back up Via dei Ramaglianti, I directed the officer's attention to my wormlike fellow about fifty yards away. But upon spying the cop, he turned the corner and disappeared into another side street.

"I don't see anyone," said the policeman.

"He's gone. But he followed me two days ago as well. I even took a picture of him."

"Can you show it to me?"

"No. I haven't had it developed yet."

The cop offered what he surely thought was an irresistible grin and told me, *francamente*, if he weren't on duty, he'd follow me too.

My dash back from Piazza San Marco, over the Ponte Vecchio, and through the back streets of the Oltrarno, had left me soaked in perspiration. So, wilted and more than a little disappointed in my fellow man, I arrived back at Albergo Bardi, confident at least that neither the pincher nor the policeman had followed me. I slid into a cool bath, a refreshing balm after a hot day in the soupy Florentine air.

As I was stepping into my slip, a knock came at the door. Cursing the interruption, I pulled on my skirt. Then, hair as wild as Medusa's, I opened the door to find Giuliana in the corridor.

"Is everything all right?"

"Can we talk?"

I stood to one side to let her in. She mumbled *"permesso"* as she entered, then made a quick study of the room. She pronounced it "not bad," and told me she was just a poor student, renting a room with another girl from the university.

"I used to live with my grandmother, but I wanted more independence. Now I have a landlady who looks through my stuff," she said. "Not to steal. Because she's nosy."

"Sorry to hear that," I said. Was that why she'd knocked on my door? To tell me about her nosy landlady?

She sat on the corner of my bed. "It doesn't bother me too much. I hid some *preservativi* (prophylactics) in my friend's drawer just to give her a shock."

I wondered what her friend had thought of the gag, but clearly Giuliana was there to tell me something else, even if she was stalling.

"You don't mind if I fix my hair while we talk, do you?" I asked.

Looking a little put out, she nevertheless shook her head.

I stood before the mirror, brushing my long wet curls. Newspaper reporting had taught me not to fill empty air with conversation. It discourages the subject from speaking. At length, Giuliana volunteered that she'd read a lot about my father.

"He was a respected, influential man of principles, wasn't he?"

"Yes, he was. Are you here to talk about my father?"

"No. About Bondinelli," she said.

"I know very little about him."

"They say he was a partisan during the war. And was arrested by the secret police."

"It sounds as if you don't believe it," I said, tugging at a particularly stubborn knot of hair.

She scoffed. "Isn't he a little too Catholic for that? I mean, sure, there were Catholic partisans, but how many with his level of fanaticism? And he was arrested by the OVRA. How did he get off without being shot? There's something fishy about that."

I paused my grooming to study her through the mirror, unsure of what to make of the information she was sharing.

"*Guarda, Ellie*," she said, using the familiar *tu* with me. "You and I are Jews. We're not like the others. We have to be careful. Do you know what Bondinelli was up to twenty years ago? Or what his friend Locanda was doing?"

Hadn't she just said Bondinelli was a partisan during the war? I opened my mouth to ask her exactly that when another knock came at the door. Giuliana blanched and whispered to me not to answer.

"Don't be silly," I said. "We're not doing anything wrong."

I crossed the room to open up. Giuliana slipped into the bathroom and closed the door behind herself. It was Bernie.

"Come on, El, you're late. Let's go."

I needed to finish dressing. He offered to help, and I shoved him back into the hallway with a promise that I'd follow right away. Giuliana emerged from the bath once he'd gone.

"What did he want?" she asked.

"To tell me I was late for the reception downstairs. As are you. What are you so worried about, Giuliana?"

"My exams. My *laurea*. Fascists. Everything. You must know what it's like in a university. You can't trust anyone."

I assured her that Bernie was an old friend, a devotee of my father's, and completely trustworthy.

"I'm not worried about him," she said, peeking through the door into the corridor. "But he might mention that I was here. It could get back to Sannino, then to the *preside*."

"What might get back to him?" I asked. "What's so sinister about Sannino anyway?"

"Nothing 'sinister.' Just the opposite."

"What? *Non ho capito*."

She didn't answer.

I tacked in a different direction. "Can I ask you something, Giuliana? By any chance did you see a letter on the table at the Cavallo this afternoon? I've lost it."

She said she hadn't seen anything, then slipped out the door and scurried off down the corridor.

The reception was hardly the event of the season. I counted twelve of the conference participants and students from the university. The rest of the attendees were professional grazers, hovering around the refreshment table and hoovering up the canapés and wine. No danger of leftovers with this crowd. Still, the mood was subdued, thanks to Bondinelli's unexpected demise. I'd arrived forty minutes late, so I didn't know if anyone had toasted to his memory or recited a weepy "poor Yorick" soliloquy in his honor.

I helped myself to a flute of prosecco. Then a waiter bearing a tray of various *crostini* presented himself. Liver pâté, chopped tomato, and olive spread. I tried the liver, which was delicious, but so rich that it nearly constituted a meal for me. That reminded me of an old French joke my father used to tell. Something about a priest mistaking a communicant's *crise de foi* for a *crise de foie*. Both terms are pronounced exactly the same, but one is a crisis of faith, the other a liver attack. I didn't find it funny.

I spied Giuliana against the wall in deep conversation with Bernie. She struck me as a paranoiac. And pinning her down to answer a few questions was proving difficult. Bernie seemed to be having more luck.

Tato, the young man who was sweet on Giuliana, approached and told me he was a great admirer of my father's work. We hadn't really had the chance to speak the night before at dinner or at the Cavallo that afternoon. After exchanging niceties about dear old Dad, we moved on to other banalities. It reminded me of my freshman year at Barnard and my first mixers with Columbia men, who served up the same three warmed-over questions every time: "What's your name? What's your major? Where're you from?" We could have used some finishing school training back then, and it was no different now with Tato. Though his English was quite good—he'd studied in London and spoke properly—no one eavesdropping on our conversation would have mistaken us for Noel Coward and Dorothy Parker.

Then I noticed I'd lost his attention. He was looking over my shoulder at something across the room. I turned to see Giuliana alone near the service table. Bernie had disappeared. Tato blushed when I asked him if he thought Giuliana was pretty.

"*Dio mio*," he sighed, apparently unable to express his admiration for her divine beauty in anything but his native language. "She's the most beautiful creature I've ever seen."

"Are you a student of Professor Bondinelli's?" I asked once he'd torn his gaze away from the object of his desire.

"No. I'm studying under the *preside di facoltà*," he said. "Better suited to my studies. Bondinelli was a bit too much of a theologian."

"Did you know Bondinelli fought along with the partisans during the war? And I heard he was arrested by the secret police."

Tato made a face that suggested surprise. Or a bad oyster. "I never heard that. I thought he was in the army. Excuse me, Ellie. I think I'll go chat with Giuliana. *Poverina*, she's all alone."

Was it my question or the draw of the beautiful Giuliana that had prompted Tato's flight? I watched him sidle up to her, dry-mouthed and sweating like a horse. Lucio Bevilacqua swooped in next to me to fill the void. Leading with a broad smile and open arms, he dropped to one knee.

"Ellie, *cuore mio*." He had a drink or two in him, I was sure. But I still found his attentions charming. Then he started in to sing. The melody—I was surprised to hear—was the popular song "Can't Get Used to Losing You," but the words were in Italian. "*Eri un'abitudine, dolcissima abitudine, che vorrei reprendere per sognar.*"

"Is a song I write for you," he said in his artless, jaggedly accented English.

"He didn't write that," said Bernie, who'd shown up just in time to hear the performance. "It's a song on the radio now."

"I figured as much."

Lucio stood and brushed off his knees. "Ellie, you know that I love you. *Mi sono innamorato di te . . .*" Singing again. "*Perché non avevo niente da fare . . .*"

I turned to Bernie for guidance, and he nodded. "Also on the radio," he said. "And Dino sings it better." He gave it some thought, then retracted his statement. "Actually, Lucio has a better voice than Dino."

I held out my right hand for Lucio to kiss, and he obliged. "If you truly love me," I said with a pout, "you'll get me another glass of wine."

He set out on his chivalric quest, actually pretending he was on horseback—clopping hooves and hands holding invisible reins—giving Bernie the opportunity to lean in close and tell me he didn't trust him.

"Neither do I," I said. "But he is endearing in a Peter Pan kind of way, don't you think?"

Bernie frowned. "Not my type."

"He was sitting in my seat at the Cavallo this afternoon, you know. Do you suppose he might have taken the envelope?"

Inspector Peruzzi and four policemen interrupted my designs on a second drink with their abrupt arrival. In fact, one of the uniformed cops bumped into Lucio as he was galloping back to me, sending half the prosecco surging like a wave into the air, only to splash back to earth on his sleeve, trouser leg, and shoes. One of Peruzzi's men called for silence, then the inspector himself announced they wanted to collect some information from the guests. Anyone who'd known Bondinelli. He instructed everyone in the room to break into groups and give their statements to the four officers.

My participation wasn't required, it turned out, since I'd never met the man. Peruzzi corralled Franco Sannino in the lobby for questioning. They sat in a couple of armchairs while I loitered nearby to listen in. The inspector retrieved his notebook and pushed his glasses up onto his forehead.

"Can you provide me with a list of everyone who attended the symposium?" he asked Franco.

"I can get you the names of the people who registered. I can't possibly know who walked in off the street."

"The registrants will be enough," said the inspector, writing in his little notepad. "Tell me again, *professore*, when you last saw Bondinelli?"

"Me? You suspect me of something?"

"Please answer the question."

"Monday morning, like I told you the other day."

From my vantage point, it appeared that Peruzzi ticked off a note in his pad. He nodded, then asked where Franco had seen him. The answer prompted another check in his book.

"But I've already told you all this," repeated Franco. "Are you suggesting that Alberto was the victim of some kind of foul play?"

"I am thorough. Nothing more than that. Now, tell me how long you knew him."

"Six or seven years," said Franco. "He was my professor. I studied with him and wrote my thesis under his direction."

"A Marxist interpretation of our great poet, no doubt," said the world-weary inspector.

"Hardly. Alberto's politics were not so radical. Mine either."

"Bondinelli was a Christian Democrat. Is that your affiliation as well?"

Franco blushed. "I don't see what my politics have to do with this, but, yes, I am a member of the *Democrazia Cristiana*."

Peruzzi recorded the new information in his pad. Then he stared at the ceiling for a long moment, as if putting the facts in order.

"I have a question for you, Inspector," said Franco. Peruzzi replaced his glasses and waited. "Did you find any signs of violence to Alberto's body? I mean, did someone do this to him? Murder him?"

The inspector declined to answer directly, saying instead that all the details would be made public at the appropriate time. Then, with a grunt, he pushed himself out of his chair, straightened up to his full height of perhaps five foot eight, and waddled off toward the reception desk.

The interviews took two hours to complete, so none of us got dinner. And, even worse, Peruzzi told us no one was to leave Florence until the drowning matter had been resolved.

"What about Fiesole?" asked Franco. "These young people and I are spending the weekend in Fiesole, near San Domenico."

Peruzzi waved a hand. "Fiesole is fine." Then he and his men decamped.

"About the weekend, Franco," I began tentatively once we were free of the police, "I've changed my plans. I won't be accompanying you to Fiesole after all."

"What? No, no. Of course you must join us. We're all going to the country. All your friends will be there. Giuliana, Lucio, Tato. Even that girl—" He turned to Lucio. "*Come si chiama?*"

"Veronica."

"Yes, even Veronica."

"I'm sorry," I said. "If I can't leave Florence, I'd like to spend some time with my old friend, Bernie."

"Bernie. *Certo, certo. Un bravo ragazzo*," he said. Then he instructed Lucio to invite him.

"You must come," he repeated to me. "In honor of dear Alberto, who wanted to conclude the symposium with the weekend in the country."

I wavered, unsure of what to say.

"*Ragazzi, venite un momento*," he called to Lucio, Giuliana, Tato, and even—what's her name—Veronica. Bernie hung back; Lucio hadn't yet delivered Franco's embossed invitation.

"Tomorrow morning," said Franco, "we'll meet at Santa Maria Novella at nine. The church, not the station. I have my car, and Lucio has his. Between us, we'll ferry everyone up to Fiesole." He paused to drive home his point. "*Mi raccomando*, don't be late or we'll leave without you."

He went on to describe the accommodations awaiting us. We would each have a room to ourselves, but the bathrooms were to be shared. And there would be plenty of food, prepared by Locanda's magician of a cook. And wine to wash it all down. Bondinelli had arranged everything.

"So it's decided," he said putting a hand on my shoulder. "You'll join us as originally planned."

I groaned silently. "Only if Bernie agrees."

"Of course Bertie will come."

"Bernie."

The hotel kitchen closed at ten, but, given the extraordinary circumstances of the police interrogations, the night clerk himself was kind enough to whip up some spaghetti with fresh tomatoes, olive oil, and garlic for Bernie and me. Sitting together on the bed in my room just after midnight, eating the macaroni and draining a bottle of Chianti along with it, we discussed the recent turn of events and what we should do. As would anyone, Bernie felt a little shy about accepting the last-minute invitation. But after considering it, we agreed it was preferable to spending our own money on a hotel and meals during our confinement in Florence. And we promised to look out for each other's wellbeing. I made Bernie swear he would never leave me alone with Franco Sannino. He agreed on the condition that I not abandon him in favor of some handsome Italian man.

Again the memory of Gigi Lucchesi reared its head. I brushed aside

Bernie's concerns as blithely as I dared and assured him I would behave. We shook on it.

"Let's make the most of this weekend," I said, clinking glasses with him. "It'll be fun. I promise. What could go wrong?"

CHAPTER EIGHT

FRIDAY, SEPTEMBER 27, 1963

At the appointed hour of nine the following morning, having slept little, Bernie and I landed up at Santa Maria Novella to meet the others. For all his admonitions the evening before, Franco Sannino hadn't respected his own instructions to arrive on time. It wasn't until almost nine thirty that he finally showed up astride one of those cute Vespas. Climbing down from his scooter, he apologized for being late.

"Where's your car?" asked Lucio, who was leaning against his own dark blue Fiat *Cinquecento* (500). I worried the car might tip over under his weight.

"It wouldn't start," he said with a shrug. "We'll have to manage with your car and my Vespa."

The general consensus was that Lucio's car was too small to do the trick.

"*Basta, ragazzi*. Stop complaining," said Franco. "I'll take one person with me, and the rest of you can go in the *Cinquecento*."

Lucio spent the better part of fifteen minutes lashing everyone's suitcases and overnight bags onto the rack atop his tiny car. At length we were ready to set out for Fiesole.

Veronica, looking more pink than white—her scratching of the previous day had left an angry rash on her neck—spared me from having to ride with Franco by drawing the short straw. She'd been provident enough to bring a scarf, so her hair would surely survive the open-air drive. That left the remaining four of us in Lucio's old blue Fiat 500, a vehicle Italians called the *Topolino*, Mickey Mouse. The description was an apt one. Barely spacious enough to shoehorn a small rodent and his girlfriend, Minnie, inside.

The bags on top of the Fiat made it impossible to peel back the canvas roof for air, meaning the windows would have to suffice for ventilation.

And even with the mountain of luggage on top, Giuliana still had to balance a suitcase on her knees in the front passenger seat. That left no room for Lucio's guitar, which he held clamped between his legs as he shifted gears and steered. The car was so small and cramped, my long curly hair, billowing ever more voluminous in the Tuscan heat and humidity, spent more time trailing out the window than it did inside.

The four of us had managed to squeeze in, violating all manner of societal norms that discouraged the rubbing of oneself against others. Bernie and I were thrust together, as it were. The discomfort wasn't merely the alternately slippery then sticky properties of shared perspiration on my bare shoulders and arms—though that was a dampness I'd rather not experience again this side of a drive-in passion pit—nor was it the poking elbows, which tickled or bruised depending on the pressure and location of the contact. More than anything else, I was tortured by the stifling heat inside the car. I stuck my head farther out the window, resigned to accept that my hair would be as tame and silky as a Brillo pad by the time we arrived in Fiesole.

When we weren't complaining about the hot air, we were rehashing the tragedy of Professor Bondinelli's drowning. Lucio said he'd known him for three years, having studied under him at the university. From the backseat, Bernie asked Giuliana if she'd been Bondinelli's student as well.

Unable to turn around due to the suitcase on her lap, she shook her head and said she was working with another professor. She'd taken some classes with Bondinelli.

"How well did you know him?" I asked.

"Not well. He was reserved. Always proper but not friendly."

"What about his youth? Do you know anything about what he did during the war?"

I couldn't gauge her reaction from the back of her head. She said no, she knew nothing about his past. I'd already heard Giuliana's incomplete version of Bondinelli's war record, even if she was denying any knowledge of it now. But I wanted to get Lucio's take on it. He seemed to have known him better than the rest of us.

"I think he lived in Tirrena," he said. "But I'm not sure. Somewhere on the coast."

"I'm always interested in what people his age did during the war. Someone told me he was with the partisans."

"Maybe. I heard he was arrested by the fascists. And he was wounded in Spain. That's where he lost his eye."

"The poor man. He lost an eye in Spain?"

"Yes. He wore a glass one."

"Did he fight on the Republican side?"

"Hardly," said Giuliana, who then remembered herself and clammed up.

"Anything else you can tell me about his past?"

Lucio fell quiet for a short moment, steering around a green Piaggio *Ape* that was chugging along too slowly for his taste. Overtaking the three-wheeler on the *viale* proved more challenging than he might have thought. The *Cinquecento* whined as Lucio punched his foot down on the accelerator, practically pushing it through the floor to the street below. Somehow it all reminded me of the chariot race in *Ben-Hur*, only without any of the speed or horsepower. I feared the car would give out before we could get around the *Ape*, but the little engine eventually delivered the goods and we passed it. With the epic duel behind us, Lucio returned to the subject at hand. He said Bondinelli had never talked about his past. In fact, his only concession to nostalgia was a photograph in his office at the university.

"An old picture of him with his late wife and two other men. Somewhere in a café."

"Any idea who they were?"

"Difficult to say."

"Could it have been taken during the war? Was there a date on it?"

"Not that I saw. Maybe on the back. He never talked about the war, though. Not to me anyway. To tell the truth, he was rather secretive about his past."

"Anything else special about the photograph?" I asked.

"*Niente*. Just some people sitting at a table in a café. It might have been springtime. And they were looking up at the camera, like someone had just called their names. Like those strolling photographers take of tourists then sell the prints to them."

It was touch and go for a while, but the *Topolino* puffed its way through Piazza della Libertà and up the winding *via* before finally breaching at the crest at Piazza San Domenico. Lucio stuffed his tiny *Cinquecento* into an impossibly small parking space between a car and a couple of *motorini*. He pulled the brake and told us we needed to wait for the motor to cool before continuing any farther. There was an *alimentari* at the corner, and so, sweating buckets, Bernie, Giuliana, and I squeezed out of the car. We staggered into the small shop, trying to recover our land legs, and bought some *Chinotto* and *Limonata*. We guzzled them down as Lucio tried to make sense of the hand-drawn map and scribbled directions he'd received from Franco. Once he'd deemed the rocket engine ready to percolate again, we piled back inside the rolling oven and headed west on Via Boccaccio.

A few hundred meters farther on, the road narrowed and high stone walls sprang up on both sides, immuring the properties beyond. Inside the tiny car, I felt mildly claustrophobic, especially since I could see little besides the mortared stones rushing past the window. I wondered how Lucio would manage if another car came at us from the other direction. Or even a bicycle. But it wasn't another vehicle that suddenly appeared on the road before us but a pedestrian. Coming out of a tight turn, we bore down on a young man walking in the same direction we were taking.

He carried a suitcase in his left hand as he hugged the stone wall to give us as wide a berth as possible. And still, Lucio, who was gesticulating as he made a point about which grew faster, the hair on one's head or in one's beard, grazed him with the right front fender as we overtook him. Had it not been for the added weight of the four passengers and our luggage on top, the Man vs. *Topolino* might have ended in a draw. As things turned out, the fellow on foot bounced off the stone wall like a pinball and tumbled into the middle of the road. The old leather valise he'd been carrying somehow got run over by our car, and, adding insult to injury, scattered its contents into the road. I shrieked.

"*Fermati*, Lucio. Stop!" called Bernie. "You hit that guy!"

Lucio shifted down to first, pulled over to the shoulder, and cut the engine. We all craned our necks to see the man we'd knocked down and were relieved to see him spring to his feet uninjured. Lucio leaned out the window and treated the fellow to the foulest Italian oaths and insults I'd ever heard. It was an education for me.

"*Disgraziato, cornuto, figlio di putt . . .!*"

I lost track after that, catching only the occasional word. But I did manage to sputter to Lucio that the man he was berating—the one who'd nearly greased the underside of his car—was none other than Tato Lombardi.

"Really?" he asked. "That was Tato?"

He popped open the door and scurried back to the scene of the collision to brush the dust off the man he'd so vulgarly excoriated a moment earlier. We all climbed out to help gather up Tato's clothes, most of which bore telltale tire marks from Lucio's car. Then, like a rescued shipwrecked sailor, he boarded our already overloaded lifeboat. It took some organizing and a couple of different combinations before we managed it, what with everyone offering opinions on how to fit him and his bag into the car. Finally it was decided Giuliana would sit on his lap in the front passenger seat, while Bernie and I would inherit the suitcase she'd been holding on hers.

Underway again, we asked Tato what had happened. Why hadn't he met us in the piazza?

"I got to Santa Maria Novella late," he said. "I thought we were meeting at the station, not the church. Anyway, I saw the car and Franco's Vespa driving away and tried to chase you down. But my valise popped open and spilled all my clothes in the street. Then a taxi ran over my things."

Perhaps the skid marks weren't ours after all.

Lucio chuckled. "Two times in one day. Bravo, Tato. Let's go for the *tripletta*."

Though it wasn't nice, we all erupted into laughter. Tato didn't seem to take it personally. And we didn't mention that not one of us had even noticed that he'd missed the nine a.m. appointment in the piazza.

"Anyway, I repacked my things and took the number seven bus up to San Domenico," he explained. "I was walking the rest of the way when you passed by and rescued me."

"Rescued?" scoffed Giuliana on his lap. "Ran over you is more like it."

Lucio shook his head, half in amusement, half in woe, and told him he needed to be more mindful of appointments, schedules, and passing cars. "You should watch where you're going. You could've hurt yourself."

We turned off Via Boccaccio, through an open gate and past a sign announcing "Villa Bel Soggiorno." The long private drive meandered up a gentle hill, guarded by two rows of mature cypress trees that waved like giant green feathers in the warm breeze. Lucio's *Topolino* crunched over the pebbled road, kicking up dust and, with each bump, treated us to a jolt to the coccyx that ran up the spine all the way to the base of the skull. I didn't mind too much, though, as I was enchanted by the view of the olive groves and fig trees on either side of the drive. And, sure that it somehow cheapened my opinion of myself, I had to admit that the beautiful property and its stunning vistas made me more curious about the man who lived there. I thought of Vicky, his . . . lover? Was that what we'd settled on to describe her relationship? I found myself wondering for a brief moment what Max Locanda looked like. Was he handsome? Or was money his best feature? What a shame it would be, I mused as we bounced through another hole in the road, if he turned out to be less attractive than Marcello Mastroianni.

"Pretty nice," said Bernie, interrupting my thoughts.

"Not bad."

"Bourgeois excess," pronounced Giuliana from Tato's lap.

"More like aristocratic excess," said Lucio.

"Same thing. I don't know why I came along. This place represents everything I despise."

"*Calmati, Giuliá,*" said Lucio. "Take some time off from the revolution and let's enjoy a couple of days in a beautiful place."

Bernie and I exchanged glances. I knew universities could be political hotbeds, but this was awkward. Giuliana may well have had a point. Why had she come if she was going to hate every moment?

"I'm going to do some reading this weekend," said Bernie, trying to ease the tension. Despite or, in fact, because of the pall hanging over the impending three-day weekend, I was glad he'd decided to accept the last-minute invitation.

"Bravo, Bernie," said Lucio. "And I'm going to sing and play the guitar. And eat and enjoy the wine. What about you, Tato? Maybe you can get your clothes pressed. With an iron this time."

"You're so mean," said Giuliana.

Bernie stifled a chuckle. I failed to swallow my grin. Lucky Tato couldn't see me. He came to life, though, assuring Giuliana it was okay. Lucio was only joking. Then he voiced his support of her argument on class struggle and Locanda's house.

"This place should belong to the people who work the land," he said.

"Usually the dummy sits on the ventriloquist's lap, not the other way around," I whispered to Bernie.

The house loomed ahead, shimmering in the hazy, late summer heat like a mirage. I only caught fleeting glimpses from the backseat. Lucio's fat head, the neck of the guitar projecting over his left shoulder, and poor Giuliana, contorted on Tato's lap, blocked my line of sight. Still, when the bumps cooperated, a large dusty-yellow building lurched into view, flanked by smaller structures on each side.

The *Topolino* squeaked to a stop on the right side of the house, where Lucio parked it against the wall of one of the side buildings, the one I could now see was a small chapel. He cut the engine, and the Fiat hiccoughed twice before giving up the ghost. The silence loosed by the little car gave way to a thrumming chorus of cicadas that buzzed all about us. Franco's gray Vespa was already there, sitting in the shade of a towering Italian stone pine.

Surrounded by long rows of boxwood shrubs, the main house stood three stories tall. I counted twelve lemon trees in great terra cotta pots, which, presumably, could be moved inside the adjacent *limonaia*—the other side building—in colder weather. Flowers spilled from boxes outside the second- and third-floor windows, open wide to catch the breeze in their gossamer curtains.

Lucio popped open his door, and Giuliana followed suit, liberating the rest of us from the torture of the hot *Topolino*.

"This place is a dream," I said to Bernie once we'd both breathed in two or three lungfuls of fresh air. "I might have to break my promise to you and seduce the old fellow who owns it."

"Too bad he's in Switzerland this weekend. But if you knew what I found out yesterday about Locanda, there'd be no *might* in your promise-breaking."

"Do tell."

"Franco heard Locanda's place in Lugano makes this one look like a garden shed. He described it as an eighteenth century *palazzo*."

"I thought Franco didn't know Locanda."

Bernie shrugged.

"So tell me about this Lugano *palazzo*," I said. "I want to know how much of my virtue I'd have to sacrifice to win him away from Vicky."

"Vicky might only be the first battle you'd have to fight. Locanda's married to a much older woman, it seems. She was the widow of a count or something."

"There goes my villa in the countryside."

"And your *palazzo* in Switzerland. Turns out Locanda's wife is loaded. He says she stashed her money in Switzerland during the war. Not sure how she held onto this place, but I heard she won't come back to Italy without her title."

"What title?"

"*Contessa* or *Marchesa*, I don't know. After the war, the new Italian Constitution prohibited most titles of nobility. Apparently she took offense and refuses to return."

"And that leaves Max free to cavort with young gold diggers like Vicky Hodges," I said.

"You didn't sound opposed to landing a sugar daddy a moment ago."

I wanted to answer with a witty retort, but nothing clever came to mind. Instead I bent over to pet a brown-striped tabby who'd wandered out of the shade beneath the boxwood to investigate the new arrivals. He welcomed the attention, curling around my legs for a couple of turns and squawking an off-key meow—as melodious as a crow—then took a seat a short distance away to watch us unload the car.

A side door of the house burst open, and a sunburned, white-haired man in a dark apron emerged like a racehorse from the starting gate. He hustled toward our car calling out a welcome. The cat hightailed it away and disappeared into the shrubs.

"*Benvenuti, ragazzi*!" called the man in a rough voice. "*Ma quanto siete in ritardo.*" (You're so late.)

The porter, Achille, as we later learned his name was, proceeded to wrestle the bags off the rack on top of the car and—God knows how—clutched them all under his arms. He trudged back to the house. I called to him to let me help, but he ignored me and hauled everything inside. Lucio took careful charge of his guitar case, and the five of us followed the porter inside.

We entered the house via a darkened vestibule of sorts, and the temperature dropped ten degrees as soon as we crossed the threshold. A stern-looking woman in her fifties shuffled into view, wiping her hands on her apron. She regarded us with something akin to horror.

"No, no, no, no!" she wailed, then explained in an accent I found difficult to comprehend that we had entered the house through the wrong door. Guests were to come in the through the main entrance. Lucio disarmed her instantly with his smile and an explanation that we were not too fancy to come in the side entrance. He charmed Berenice, as her husband, Achille, called her, with his lovable smile and a kiss of her hand. She, in turn, blushed and patted her cropped hair and smoothed her apron as if primping for a suitor. Lucio had won an admirer.

As demure as a new bride, Berenice withdrew, barking over her shoulder as she went that she was going to prepare *uno spuntino* (snack) for us.

Lucio hoisted his guitar over his shoulder and paused to regard us with impatience. "What?" he asked as if his actions hadn't been obvious. "First rule for a houseguest: be nice to the cook."

CHAPTER NINE

While Achille prepared our rooms, we sat outside on the stone terrace behind the house, enjoying *panini* with salumi, cheese, and tomatoes on Tuscan bread. Berenice also provided a liter of white and a liter of red wine for our consumption. The five of us emptied the carafes without breaking stride. We were getting the feeling this might turn out to be a pleasant weekend after all. Even Giuliana loosened up, somehow buoyed to learn that the wine had been made on the property and was the same stuff the *lavoratori* drank.

"Come on, Giulià," said Lucio with a laugh. "We say *contadini*, not *lavoratori* for farmworkers."

"*Contadini* carries a pejorative meaning," she said. "It's demeaning. These people are part of the working class."

For my benefit, Bernie explained that *contadini* technically translated as "peasants" in English, but it was commonly used in Italian to mean farmers and country folk.

"The wine is quite good," I said, hoping to steer the conversation back to less contentious topics. "In fact, I wouldn't mind some more."

No one seconded my motion. Nevertheless, a contented mood settled over us as the food and wine worked their magic. Tato and Giuliana nodded off in their chairs, and Bernie read from some book written in German. Lucio strummed his guitar without actually playing a real song. He seemed to be toying with chords and some fingering. It was the very picture of bucolic, but I still wanted another drink.

A little before four o'clock, we were shown to our quarters on the second and third floors of the house. I landed in an airy room with two single beds, a large armoire against the wall, two bedside tables and lamps, and a small writing desk. The glazed terra cotta floor tiles were the color of kidney beans, and the walls were flat white, peeling in places. But I didn't mind, especially when I saw the ceiling fan and the tall double casement window, thrown open to reveal a small balcony overlooking the *terrazza* and *giardino* where we'd been lounging behind the house. I nearly squealed with delight, but knew the idyllic setting brought with it the prospect of mosquitoes. Like a Boy Scout, however, I was prepared. I'd packed the Super Faust aerosol in my bag.

Once I'd settled in, I showed off my room to Bernie. He was bunking on the top floor.

"Looks like you got the wedding suite," he said.

"Is yours not as nice?"

"Mine's a closet under the eaves with only a tiny window."

"I've got to share the bathroom with Giuliana and Franco, if that's any consolation."

"Cry me a river. Maybe you'll tell me later there's a pea under your mattress. And I'm sharing the bathroom with Lucio, Tato, and Veronica upstairs. The bathtub's about the size of a gravy boat."

"Sorry."

Bernie gazed around the room some more. Then he noticed the fan. His face lit up. "Say, you've got two beds and a ceiling fan . . ."

"What are you suggesting?"

"Come on, El. Share the wealth with a proletarian. I'm a perfect gentleman and I don't snore."

"I'm not in the habit of sharing rooms with *perfect gentlemen*. You can visit, but no slumber parties."

"*Eccovi!* What took you all so long?" It was Franco. The late-afternoon sun cast its rays through the oak trees, dappling the right side of his face.

Having unpacked and freshened up, Bernie and I returned to the shade of the *terrazza* behind the house where we sat and admired the large park. Interspersed among the boxwood alleys and walkways, various pieces of statuary—satyrs, Dianas, Pans, Apollos, and Daphnes—populated the garden. The stone sitting benches, strategically placed in the shade of a long pergola, promised peaceful spots for lazy afternoon reading. And if books weren't your speed, there were rows of ancient, twisted, grapevines that would surely afford hours of enchanting *passeggiate*, accompanied by wistful speculation of the enjoyment their fermented harvests had once provided. Flowering plants and trees—oaks mainly—but elms and more pines, too, shaded the sun and made the temperature bearable, especially when a breeze blew. Not far off, a circular fountain, featuring a bathing nymph, bubbled happily. There was a labyrinth of shrubs laid out with a geometric precision that begged to be explored, and a gazebo perfect for a cool drink in the evening. I knew straightaway where I was going to be at seven with a sweating glass of something strong in my hand.

"We stopped at San Domenico for a *ristoro* (refreshment)," said Bernie.

"A *ristoro* for the car," I mumbled.

Franco didn't hear me. "I understand Berenice fixed you something to eat. *Ottimo*. What's her name, Veronica, isn't feeling well. She's in her room. I had a nap and a bath. Very refreshing. I hope you're all happy with the accommodations."

Franco was acting as if he owned the place. With Locanda out of the country for the weekend, I suppose Franco outranked the rest of us, but I still considered him a guest, as were we all. I was about to ask for some more towels, just to give him a small measure of comeuppance, when Vicky Hodges appeared. Looking like Venus emerging from the sea in a diaphanous cover-up over a halter top and white Capris, she shimmered through the open door onto the terrace to join us. She truly was a beauty.

"Hello," she said, though her heart was hardly in it.

Franco greeted her with a *buonasera*, then launched into his obsequious pigeon mating dance. He offered her a drink as if he were the maître d'hôtel. Clicking heels, hand-kissing, and perhaps even a curtsy were surely in the offing.

"I thought you were in Switzerland for the weekend," I said.

She pouted and told us the trip had been canceled, thanks to that awful policeman. The short one with white hair and thick glasses.

"Inspector Peruzzi?"

"I suppose that's his name. He asked Max not to leave until this drowning thing has been settled."

If Vicky had been spoiling for sympathy, she'd misjudged her audience. With the exception of Franco, who affected a positively heartbroken expression for her benefit, no one else cared. In fact, I'd say that Bernie was overjoyed to have the entire weekend to admire her beauty at his leisure.

"Remember our pact," I whispered to him. "No abandoning me.

And, since Franco is besotted with Vicky and has forgotten me, will you get me a drink?"

"Too bad about your plans," I said, sidling up to Vicky as Franco and Bernie delivered our drinks. Two Campari and sodas with ice, if you please. "But at least you get to spend the weekend with Max."

"Here he is now."

I reeled around to see who had just arrived. Tanned, handsome, if somewhat dissipated, with a longish shock of silvering hair slicked back with pomade, the man looked to be in his mid-fifties. Dressed in a navy blazer and open-collared white shirt and linen trousers, he held a smoldering cigarette between his right middle and forefinger in what was surely a practiced pose, aimed at creating the very picture of the cosmopolitan sophisticate. The paisley ascot around his neck was the cherry on top.

"Pleased to meet you," he said slowly in English, extending his right hand for me to take. "I am Massimiliano Locanda."

CHAPTER TEN

I had a beloved elderly cousin named Max. He carried himself with the air of an aging matinee idol, though a lifetime of indulgence and sloth had robbed him of his good looks. Massimiliano Locanda, younger by at least twenty years, still had some time left to seduce young lovelies like Victoria Hodges.

After a round of introductions, we all took seats on the terrace. Everyone except for our host and his lover. Locanda remained standing as he explained that the good inspector had ruined his plans for the weekend in Switzerland. He told the tale with resignation. His speech, slow and precise without being tiresome, rumbled a deep baritone that had ripened with the years, wine, and tobacco. He was of average height and weight and had the athletic build of an erstwhile tennis player. I found him terribly attractive. He commanded attention without demanding it. No one else spoke while he was holding forth. I sensed he was bored with us and wanted to leave.

He pronounced his Rs as the *erre moscia*, or soft -r-. Sounding more like a French -r- than the rolled Italian, the *erre moscia* is common among Italians of noble provenance. It's also considered a pretentious affectation by those whose sympathies lie on the opposite end of the political spectrum, to wit—I was sure—Giuliana, Tato, and Lucio. But they weren't present and hadn't met him yet. Franco, social climber that he appeared to be, was surely drooling over Locanda's pronunciation. It was ironic, to me at least, that whenever the *erre moscia* manifested itself in a person of low birth, it was considered a speech defect, not unlike a lisp, and was corrected by therapy. But for me, the distinctive -r- carried more personal significance. The torrid affair of mine that Bernie had alluded to on the terrace of the Giubbe Rosse two days earlier. The divinely handsome Luigi "Gigi" Lucchesi had also spoken with the *erre moscia*. And its resurfacing now only served to confuse my emotions about our severe but attractive host. That soft, guttural, rolling -r- was calling to me like a cooing dove.

I returned to the present, smoothed my skirt over my thighs and knees, and drew a restorative breath. Behave, Ellie, and get your mind out of the past.

"I hope Achille and Berenice took good care of you while we were out," said Vicky in English.

She poured a glass of fluorescent yellow liqueur from a service tray and handed it to Locanda. He accepted it without a word or any form of acknowledgement. *Certosa Gialla*—the liquid in his glass—was lovingly made by the monks in a monastery in Galuzzo, on the opposite end of Florence, I learned later.

Vicky had assumed the role of lady of the house. She raised her glass to welcome us to Villa Bel Soggiorno. "Are your rooms all right? Max wanted me to make sure you have everything you need."

Bernie and I nodded yes. Franco, on the other hand, went farther, giving enthusiastic voice to his approval, lavishing praise in awkward English about how satisfied he was.

"Max and I wanted to wait for you for lunch," she continued, not sure what to make of Franco's odd accent and even more peculiar turns of phrase.

Locanda slipped into the chair next to mine and crossed his right leg over the left. He sipped his drink and, with an elegant brush of his tanned fingers, flicked a spot of nothing off his white linen trousers.

"We ate at a little place past Piazza San Domenico," she said. "Nothing fancy, but the food and wine are good."

"You must have just missed us," I said. "We stopped at the *alimentari* on the corner."

"Max doesn't patronize that place." She informed me in a theatrical whisper that he didn't get along with the proprietor. "*Uno uomo malo.*"

"*Ti prego*, Vicky," said Locanda, unable to bear any more. "Don't speak, please. You don't know three words of Italian."

Vicky's Italian vocabulary, it seemed, was limited to *voglio, per piacere*, and *grazie*. And perhaps some anatomical terminology learned at the knee of her lover, Max.

I wanted to hear from him so I asked what he disliked about the proprietor of the *alimentari*.

He dismissed my question as unimportant. "Local politics," he said in a low voice. "Nothing serious."

The other guests—Lucio, Giuliana, and Tato—wandered out onto the terrace, a little timid upon noticing our elegant if unsmiling host.

More introductions were made. Lucio, hair flattened and eyes still full of sleep—surely he'd just emerged from a nap—plopped himself down on a bench and began tuning his guitar. The magical one that, heretofore, hadn't managed to produce a single song. He plucked and tightened, plucked and tightened, plucked and tightened the E-string, searching for the perfect pitch. Then he plucked and tightened one turn too far, and the string snapped, its recoil delivering a stinging bite to his left hand. He yelped, waggled his injured fingers vigorously, and treated us all to more of his unvarnished vocabulary. "*Porca Mad . . .*"

Giuliana, Tato, and I chuckled at Lucio's expense for a few moments before Franco lectured him to watch his language in front of the ladies. And our host.

"It's a very bad oath," he said, turning to me. "The worst swear words in Italian invoke the Madonna. Not like in English where you find sex and scatology more scandalous. A very prudish race the Anglo-Saxons."

"I'm not an Anglo-Saxon," I told him. "I'm Jewish,"

He was nonplussed. "Of course you are. Your father was a famous man in academic circles. Everyone knows he was a Jew."

"Even Professor Bondinelli?"

"Of course."

"And he didn't mind? I mean since he was a devout Catholic?"

"My dear Ellie, what are you saying? Alberto loved all people and all races. He was a true Christian. Like me."

Perhaps it was time to change the subject. I cracked a nervous smile and turned to Locanda to ask what leisure activities he would recommend at Bel Soggiorno. He seemed confused by my question, and Vicky rode to the rescue. Despite my better instincts and intentions, I was disappointed that he'd opted out of engaging in conversation with me, no matter how insipid my request had been.

"There's no television here. Max won't have it," she said. "I have some pencils if you like to draw. I tried to learn, but I'm no good at it."

"I saw a *bocce* court on the side of the house," said Franco in Italian. "The balls are in the little shed next to it. And there's an archery kit near the *limonaia*. That might be fun."

"What need do you have for bow and arrows here?" I asked.

Franco shrugged. "For target practice. Or sport."

"And the occasional boar," added Vicky, ever a font of information.

"Are there boars on the property?"

"You find them everywhere in Tuscany. They're quite nasty and can be dangerous. The horns, you know."

"Tusks?" I asked.

She blushed and corrected herself. "Tusks, right. It's just that they're so long and sharp, they look more like horns."

"What is this *tuskses*?" asked Franco, showing off some of his lubberly English.

Though my Italian had improved greatly over the past months and during my brief stay in Florence, I certainly didn't know the word for tusks. And I doubted any of my Italian friends would know the English word either. So I looked to Bernie for help. He was reading his German book at the far end of the terrace, ignoring the rest of us.

"Bernie," I called. "How do you say 'tusks' in Italian?"

"What? Tusks?" he asked. "Like elephants, walruses, boars?"

"Yes, boars."

"They're called *zanne*. *Zanna* in the singular."

"Of course, *tuskses*, *zanne*," said Franco, tapping his forehead as if the word had been rolling around inside his cranium like a stray marble all along.

I thanked Bernie, called him a human encyclopedia, then turned back to Vicky. I asked again if there were really boars on the property.

"Lots of them," she said.

I must have looked terrified, because our host finally chimed in to reassure me in flawless English. "Do not worry, signorina. Boars are mostly nocturnal. But one must always be careful not to disturb them when they're sleeping during the day."

"Where do they sleep?" I asked, not quite sure if I'd batted my eyelashes or not. Those -r-s would be the ruin of me.

"In the leaves, tall grass, wherever it's cool and quiet."

Franco was hanging on our every word. Not that he understood even half of what we were saying. Certainly not the parts in English. Nevertheless he hovered above us, reacting with rubbery facial expressions, nodding when appropriate—or inappropriate—and throwing his head back with exaggerated mirth whenever he sensed an attempt at humor had been made.

"Try not to step on one," said Locanda dryly. "But if you were to cross paths with a full-grown boar, you would be glad to have a bow and arrow handy."

"How about *pallavolo*?" asked Franco from left field. "Do you like *pallavolo*?" I assumed he was asking me, as I was the one inquiring about leisure activities on the property, but I quickly realized he was more interested Locanda's thoughts than mine. I felt like a distant also-ran in Franco's estimation, what with Max's leather moccasins needing licking. But whether the question had been addressed to me or to our host, I didn't know the word anyway. After ten or fifteen seconds of charades all around to arrive at the meaning, Franco finally—reluctantly—looked away, searching for a capable translator. We all turned to Bernie, whose nose was still planted in his book.

"*Bernardo*," called Franco, "*Come si dice 'pallavolo' in inglese?*"

"Volleyball," he answered without looking up.

Everyone was suitably impressed, with the exception of Massimiliano Locanda. He'd taken advantage of the diversion to rise from his chair and vanish in a puff of smoke. Franco asked Vicky where he was going.

"Probably to take care of some important business," she said. "He's very private. Doesn't like to socialize much."

Besides Franco, the others didn't seem to mind that he'd left. I, however, was curious. Locanda had never signed on for a weekend of entertaining us. Indeed, he was supposed to be in Switzerland. He'd only agreed to lend the place to his friend Bondinelli. I imagined that a group as unremarkable as ours paled in comparison to the people he might have rubbed elbows with in Lugano. Still, despite his lack of manners, he was attractive in a brooding way. Like the hero in a gothic romance. I wondered if his insane wife might not be locked in the attic above our rooms at the villa.

"Your boyfriend's a smart one," said Vicky, grinning at me. "And kind of cute in an eggheaded way. Hold onto him."

"Do you mean Bernie? Oh, no. We're not together. He's just an old friend. He was my father's student."

Her conspiratorial smile faded. "Then you're with that guy?" She indicated Tato with a bob of her head.

"What? No."

"That one? What's his name?"

"Lucio? No. I'm not with anyone. I'm with me."

"Really? After our talk the other day, I thought you might be interested in a fling on your Italian holiday. You should loosen up, Ellie. You might just find a rich guy."

"Sorry," I said, surely blushing at the suggestion. "I'm not here in Italy looking for Rossano Brazzi."

"Suit yourself," she said with a sniff. "But remember, Max is mine."

She turned on her heel, crossed the terrace, and took a seat near Bernie, who—what do you know—put down his book and engaged her in conversation.

"*La Vicky* is very beautiful. *Bellissima*," said Franco from behind me. I wondered how much he'd overheard. Or understood.

"I'm sorry?"

"The Vicky," he explained in English. "Is a very beautiful female."

I'm sure I frowned despite my best efforts to refrain. "Do you mean to say *woman*?"

"Yes. *Una femmina*. A female. A woman."

Lucio had threaded a new string into his guitar and resumed tuning it, still stubbornly refusing to play anything that resembled an actual song. While I chatted with Franco, Bernie was keeping Vicky busy, quizzing her on everything from her hometown to her canceled weekend in Switzerland. His interest was as transparent as Franco's sycophancy toward Locanda. Men. They claim women are the foolish sex, but they're the ones who lose their heads at the bat of an eyelash, abandon their dignity whenever a shapely figure walks by trailing a river of perfume. Predictable and pathetic. Except, of course, when I'm the subject of their foolishness.

"It's a shame you're stuck here with us," I heard Bernie say to Vicky. "I'm sure you wanted to see Max's place in Lugano."

"Oh, I've been there before," she insisted. "It's an eighteenth-century palace."

Bernie's eyes shifted nervously. "Do you mean a *palazzo*?"

"What's the difference?"

With great difficulty, Bernie tried to explain that while *palace* was technically the correct translation, the connotation in English was more regal and grandiose than the Italian word, at least when describing noble houses.

"It's a bit of a false friend."

"I don't understand," she said. "Is a *palazzo* a palace or not?"

"Back home," he said, "palace makes us think of the king's residence. Like Buckingham Palace. Here, a *palazzo* is a beautiful residence, but not necessarily quite as grand as the queen's house."

Vicky frowned. Bernie sighed.

"Never mind," he said. "It sounds like a nice palace."

"It is. Max took me there once. It's eighteenth century. That's the 1700s. So romantic." She gushed, pronouncing the words with relish, as if you scored points for having been debauched in eighteenth-century *palazzi* by married men thirty years your senior. "*Che cosa romantico!*"

Bernie looked confused, Giuliana snorted, and Lucio broke another string. A G-string, this time.

"That's not quite right," said Bernie, and I cringed for him. She was never going to get this. "You can say '*Che romantico*,' to mean 'how romantic,' but not '*che cosa romantico*.' Unless, of course, you make the adjective feminine, too, as in '*Che cosa romantica!*' That means 'What a romantic thing!' Otherwise, '*che cosa*' is for questions only."

Vicky looked skeptical. Surely she'd lost confidence in Bernie's knowledge of Italian after the palace-*palazzo* fiasco. In fact she proceeded to argue her usage with a man holding a doctorate in Italian language and literature.

"I had a lesson yesterday with that nice Professor Crocetti in Florence. He's an excellent teacher and quite expensive. Max says he's the best. He taught me '*che cosa romantico*.'"

"No, no, no," said Giuliana, shaking her head. "I'm sure your Professor Crocetti never taught you that. Bernie is right."

"*Eh, sì*," added Lucio. Then Tato agreed as well.

Vicky pouted. "Italian is so hard. Why do I have to learn it? Everyone speaks English. At least they should."

Franco comforted her with an indulgent smile and told her, "No to worry. You speak much cutely."

"Anyway the *palazzo* in Lugano is romantic," said Vicky, ignoring his praise. "Bigger and even nicer than this place."

She excused herself on the pretext that Max would be needing her any moment.

"I don't know about the palace in Lugano," I said to Bernie, "but this place'll do."

"No, El, 'palace' isn't really . . ."

"Get yourself a sense of humor, Bernie."

Before too long, Lucio had restrung his guitar, this time using a B-string—called *si* in Italian—to replace the G *(sol)* he'd snapped.

"Will that work?" asked Bernie.

"Not ideal, but a little less tight, and voilà. The *si* becomes *sol.*"

"Play us a song, Lucio," said Giuliana. "*Una bella canzone.*" Then with a glance to the *salone* door, she made a request. "Play '*Bella ciao.*'"

At first Lucio resisted, doubting our host would approve. I asked what was objectionable about it and, again, it fell to Bernie to explain.

"'*Bella ciao*' is an old song, dating back to the last century. It was adopted by the partisans during the war as an anti-fascist anthem of sorts. It has strong leftist connotations."

"It's a fine song," added Franco. "Part of our struggle to liberate Italy from the foreign occupiers." He paused. "But perhaps better not to sing it here."

"Why not?" asked Tato.

After some more prodding, Lucio finally relented and produced a real song from his guitar, jury-rigged G-string and all. Everyone, save Franco Sannino and me, sang along. I didn't know the words, and he probably worried he'd lose his seat in the first pew in church if he did. The chorus was simple and catchy, and I was able to join in before too long.

The first verse tells of a young man who wakes one morning to find the invader in his land. He bids farewell to his lovely girl, "*bella ciao.*"

Una mattina mi son alzato
O bella ciao, bella ciao, bella ciao, ciao, ciao
Una mattina mi son alzato
E ho trovato l'invasor

The second verse is a plea for the partisan to take him away with him to fight.

O partigiano, portami via
O bella ciao, bella ciao, bella ciao, ciao, ciao

O partigiano, portami via
Ché mi sento di morir

The next verse begs the girl to bury him in the shadow of a flower on the mountain should he die. The song ends with an evocation of the flower of the partisan who died for freedom.

Questo è il fiore del partigiano,
O bella ciao, bella ciao, bella ciao ciao ciao,
Questo è il fiore del partigiano
Morto per la libertà

But Lucio never quite finished the song, which hardly surprised anyone. Achille arrived at a gallop waving his hands to silence the music. He said nothing, only gestured. Behind him Berenice was frowning at Giuliana and Lucio. A spirited if half-whispered argument ensued, with hand gestures, red faces, and pointing to the house. Achille remained silent, watching intently as Berenice lectured the singers. Giuliana took the lead for the young people, insisting that there was nothing wrong with singing a patriotic song. Tato stood at her side though, in truth, I doubt she even noticed he was there. She was incensed, making no attempts to lower her voice, as Berenice had done to avoid alerting the master to the fuss in the garden.

But just as she'd shouted something about fascists and oppression, a pair of shutters on the second floor opened and Max Locanda leaned out.

"Berenice," he barked. His voice sailed through the garden and, I fancied, bounced off a hill about five hundred yards away and echoed back. We all stared up at him, no one daring to speak.

"*Sissignore?*" she answered.

"*Lasciali stare.* They may sing whatever songs they like."

And, with that, he disappeared back inside the window and pulled the shutters closed again. Berenice apologized for the interruption and, smoothing her apron, cleared her throat before grabbing Achille by the elbow and shuffling back into the house.

"Again," said Giuliana to Lucio. "Come on. Play it."

His lips curled into a grimace. "*Non lo so* . . . I'd rather not. I'll play something else," he said without looking anyone in the eye.

Then he started strumming "*Volare*" and everyone groaned. Giuliana threw her hands into the air and, muttering to herself, stomped off into the house. Tato followed.

"That was awkward," I told Bernie once Lucio had abandoned his version of "*Volare*." We'd grabbed a far corner of the terrace for ourselves and were engaged in a private powwow over fresh drinks.

"I'll say. Giuliana takes no prisoners. Locanda did the right thing under the circumstances. It would be rude of a host to dictate what guests can and can't sing."

"Maybe," I said. "But what kind of host do we have here? I mean his servant feels the need to silence a song that celebrates the defeat of foreign invaders."

Bernie nodded. "And don't forget he married the *contessa* or *marchesa*—whatever she is. Maybe she has real reasons not to come back to Italy. Besides her title, that is."

"What kind of reasons?"

"I don't know. Maybe she was the president of the Mussolini Fan Club or something."

"I'm curious about her, the wife. Did you say she was older than Locanda?"

"That's what I heard. But why would you be interested in her?"

"It's just the way I am, Bernie. Since I'm curious about Locanda, I'm doubly curious about his wife. And her late husband, for that matter. He's the one who provided this place after all."

"Good luck," he said. "I've got more important things to do. Like finish this book I'm reading."

We sat in silence for a long moment. Then I interrupted Bernie again.

"Why would he marry her?"

"Sorry?"

"Why would a handsome young man like Max Locanda marry some old widow?"

Bernie chuckled. "Locanda? A young man?"

"Back when," I said. "When he married her."

"I don't know. Maybe because she was rich, owned this little pied-à-terre, as well as an eighteenth-century *palace* in Switzerland."

CHAPTER ELEVEN

Bel Soggiorno was an idyllic spot to be sure, but tension had already surfaced among the guests and hosts. And, of course, the lingering grief for the passing of Bondinelli was never far from our thoughts. Not that anyone was weeping over his demise, but an ever-present sadness lurked in the corners and empty moments of the villa.

And there was something unsettling about Bondinelli himself. Something that didn't quite make sense. I'd heard of his good works, his generosity, but of a dark side as well. Questions about his past. The contradictions and intrigue. His parish priest clearly loved him. Giuliana suspected something sinister in his war story, and Locanda was playing his cards close to the vest. Then there were his devotees, Veronica and Teresa, the most unlikely of companions for a fifty-something professor. Living in his household, they certainly would have known him better than the others, yet they seemed distant. Admiring and grateful perhaps, but not intimates. I wanted to know more about this man I'd never met. This man who'd died mysteriously, practically in broad daylight in a bustling city full of tourists.

It was nearly nine, and I was freshening up before dinner when Giuliana knocked at my door. I expected a repeat performance of insinuations against the late professor. But, instead, she'd come to tell me Veronica was quite ill. Franco happened to be passing through the corridor on his way down to dinner at that moment. He asked us what was wrong.

"It's Veronica," said Giuliana. "*Sta molto male.*"

"Who?" he asked.

"Veronica," repeated Giuliana. "The girl on the back of your Vespa this morning. The one with the rash."

"*Oddio,*" said Franco, practically gasping. He touched his brow as if to take his temperature. "What's wrong with her? Is she contagious?"

Giuliana didn't know anything except that she had a fever and a rash on her neck.

"Go find Achille and ask him for some aspirin," she told Franco. "Ellie and I will go check on her."

We found Veronica in a small, hot room on the third floor. Lying on her back, bathed in sweat, half out of her nightclothes, she scratched her neck with what was left of her gnawed-off fingernails.

"Veronica," I said, rushing to her side. "Are you all right?"

"I'm hot," she moaned.

I poured her a glass of water from the bottle near her bed. She sat up and managed a few sips. I asked if she was hungry, but she shook her head.

"I'll be all right. It's just this heat."

Achille arrived with a small box of Bayer aspirin. "*Ecco, signorina,*" he said, dispensing three tablets into Veronica's hand.

"Take these *compresse,*" said Giuliana. "You'll feel better."

Perhaps feeling guilty about their indifference to Veronica's illness, Franco, Vicky, Tato, and Lucio—still carrying his guitar, by the way—appeared at the door to inquire after her health.

"Is there anything we can do?" asked Lucio.

"We don't need a song, thanks all the same," I said without turning. I was concentrating on Veronica's ferocious itching. "Please, Veronica, don't scratch. It only makes it worse."

Giuliana urged the others to wait downstairs on the terrace. "*Poverina.* She doesn't need an audience."

"Leave us Lucio," I said. "Giuliana and I will move Veronica to my room where it's cooler. Lucio, put down the guitar and pack her things back into her suitcase, please."

Veronica looked confused, and I wondered if it was my Italian or some kind of delirium. I repeated myself in English this time, and she practically sprang from the bed. I lent her a gentle hand on the elbow to guide her, even as I sensed the worst had passed. She jumped at my touch. This girl doesn't have a fever, I thought. She's got sunburn.

Achille herded the others out the door. I called after him but he didn't stop. Stepping into the hallway, I shouted again, but he ignored me.

"What's wrong?" asked Giuliana once I'd returned to the room.

"It's that porter. I wanted to ask him to inform Locanda and call for a doctor. But he won't even acknowledge me when I speak to him."

"You're joking, right?" she said. "He's completely deaf, you know."

Once in my room, Giuliana and I soaked a towel in water and took turns applying it to Veronica's forehead, neck, and arms. After five minutes, she asked us to use something called *amamelide* instead.

"It's soothing, and I like the smell."

We started over with a new towel doused in the substance, which I recognized immediately as witch hazel. I'd never liked the odor, even less so under the present circumstances. But, coupled with the wind roaring from the ceiling fan on the highest setting, it seemed to give her some temporary relief from the heat. The room, in fact, felt easily fifteen degrees cooler than the steam bath she'd been occupying upstairs. Despite our most diligent attention and the anti-inflammatory properties of the liniment, Veronica continued to complain of the itching rash on her neck and another one on her arm. Berenice, summoned by Achille, arrived with something called *borotalco*, advising that we should clean and dry the rash then apply the powder, which, after a sniff, I realized was nothing more than talcum. Giuliana and I handled the ministrations, and, twenty minutes later, Veronica, powdered like a freshly diapered baby, felt well enough to eat some *panzanella* Berenice had prepared for dinner. We gave her another aspirin and lots of water.

After a short while, Achille returned with a young man wearing a rumpled black suit. He introduced himself as *Dottor* Pellegrini, the junior associate of Locanda's physician, Francesco Gherardi. Achille had informed the signore after all, even without my suggestion. We learned that *Dottor* Gherardi was visiting relatives in Arezzo for the week, so the house call fell to young Pellegrini. He might have looked like a schoolboy, but he came highly recommended, this according to Vicky, who'd shown up at the door to get an update on Veronica's condition.

Pellegrini shooed us all out of the room—my room—so he could check on the patient, who kept insisting she was feeling better thanks to the cooler temperature.

Dinner was on hold until the young doctor had finished his examination, so we all waited downstairs in the *salone*, fortified with another round of *aperitivi*, which threatened to send Franco to the showers early. He wasn't much good after two glasses of wine, and he'd already downed three. I hoped he wasn't gunning for a rematch with me after his performance of Wednesday night. Two out of three falls, as it were. Bernie was staying close, and I took the opportunity to remind him to keep an eye on Franco's alcohol intake and his designs on me.

After about ten minutes, Achille announced that dinner would be served shortly. Locanda sauntered into the room and poured himself a bit of the *Certosa*. I screwed up my nerve and asked him if the doctor had gone.

"Yes," he said. "He'll telephone me in the morning with his diagnosis. Your friend is resting comfortably."

CHAPTER TWELVE

By the time we sat down to eat, dinner had been delayed more than an hour and, as it was past ten thirty, we were famished. Still, despite the scare of Veronica's illness, coming on the heels of Bondinelli's sudden demise, the mood was surprisingly lighthearted, the way mourners take comfort in each other's company after the catharsis of a wake or funeral. We all managed to smile. Even laugh.

The place settings were laid out on an ancient refractory table that measured about twenty feet in length. Our host sat at the head of the table, a heavy cudgel that resembled a sledgehammer stood on its head by his side. I risked a peek and saw that the hammer was resting on a block of wood. I couldn't fathom what that was for.

When pressed to share the history of the table, Locanda claimed he'd rescued it from a monastery near Avignon. And, in spite of its rough texture and well-worn edges—or perhaps because of them—the table inspired both a healthy respect for the functional simplicity of the piece, as well as a curiosity of what conversations, intrigues, and meals had been consumed on its planks over the centuries.

I studied the rest of the room. The bare floors, tiled in an ornate antique pattern, suggested a huge bordered carpet with eight-pointed stars and smaller flowers inside. A dappled mirror, its glass heavy and dark, hung on the north wall above a battered filigreed credenza. Sconces on either side illuminated the area with a faint, flickering electric light. Bright lighting, I was coming to realize, was not a prized feature in old Italian homes. An octopus of a crystal chandelier overhead provided little more than a glow from ten of the twelve working bulbs. Completing the picture was a gothic triptych that may or may not have been wildly valuable, depending on its provenance. Still, the lack of guile in the room's trimmings led me to believe everything was genuine. They exuded sincerity and plain honesty while showing their age and wear.

In fact, all of Villa Bel Soggiorno presented itself in an unselfconscious manner, indifferent to the changing styles and tastes of passing time. Beyond the electric lights, powered by occasional cloth wires climbing the walls like veins carrying blood—and of course the ceiling fan in my room—the house looked as it must have done two or three hundred years before. It showed its share of warts, for sure, the antiquated, dripping bathrooms, rambling somewhat desultory architecture, and occasional musty zones for starters. But in its entirety—the gardens, views, ancient stone, and worn furnishings—Bel Soggiorno was the most genuinely elegant home I'd ever seen.

Now at the refractory table, for reasons unclear to me, Locanda lifted the sledgehammer to his right with both hands and let it drop hard on the block of wood, producing a minor seism that shook the room. The thud silenced everyone.

"Don't mind that," said Vicky. "It's to call the servant. He can't hear but he can feel that."

And, in fact, a moment later, Achille arrived at a trot. Locanda gave some silent signal that meant nothing to me, but the porter got the message. He ducked back out of the room only to return straightaway with a huge platter of steaming spaghetti.

Once we'd all served ourselves the first course and dusted our dishes generously with pepper and *Parmigiano* cheese, the conversation ceased and we attacked our hunger using our flatware as weapons and napkins as shields.

"I'm worried about her," said Tato between forkfuls of spaghetti *aglio e olio*. "That rash is spreading. I hope it's not contagious."

"Rashes are not appropriate dinner conversation," said Locanda in a soft but stern voice.

I eyed him from my seat. Slouching in his chair in a languid, patrician manner, cigarette burning between his fingers, he'd barely touched his food. I wondered about the etiquette of smoking during a meal, but this man clearly did things his own way. He reached for the glass of wine before him—a Gavi—squinted at the pale liquid, and raised it to his nose. He sniffed, frowned, then put the glass down. He thumped the sledgehammer again.

"*Mi dica, signore*," said Achille, who had been preparing some plates on the sideboard nearby.

"*Sa di tappo*," said Locanda, flicking a finger under his nose. "It's corked."

Achille nearly threw his back out bowing and scraping and apologizing to the master. He promised to bring a new bottle immediately and began snatching the glasses from the other diners, whether they objected to the wine or not. Scarcely a minute later, he'd wrenched the cork from another bottle, poured himself a splash, and tasted the wine. Nodding smartly, he offered a few drops to Locanda in a fresh glass, of course, and our host pronounced the replacement acceptable with a slow blink and curt bob of his head. Achille filled our glasses again and withdrew.

I watched Locanda the whole time. Now, with the drama over, he took a bite of his spaghetti and a sip of the Gavi. Then his gaze crossed mine. He'd caught me staring at him. I looked away and struck up a conversation with Bernie across the table, asking him if he'd heard any baseball scores recently.

"Baseball?" he asked. "I don't follow sports. And how would I hear about baseball here?"

"There's the *Herald Tribune*," I offered.

As noted before, Locanda sat at the head of the table to my left. Vicky was on his other side. She glared at me. I must have been too obvious in my contemplation of our host, her lover, because she seemed to have discovered a new antipathy for me. To counter my attentions, she began fawning over Locanda, offering to serve him food, fill his glass, and rub his arm, which probably didn't need rubbing at all. But she performed all these tasks with great care, much to the visible annoyance of her man. He grumbled at her to stop—"*Vittoria, basta.* You're annoying me." He even twitched when she attempted a loving touch of his cheek with her long fingers. He asked her if there was food on his face.

Franco sat to my right and, as I'd anticipated, his inability to hold his drink had emboldened him to undertakings of awkward seduction. His hand strayed into my airspace at regular intervals, probing the vigilance of my defenses, as he soaked up more wine like a blotter. Throughout dinner, he insisted on monopolizing my attention, all the while addressing my breasts by my name. I fired repeated nasty glares at Bernie, who was marooned at the far end of the table, engrossed in a conversation with Lucio about some stupid school of Italian poets from the twelfth or thirteenth century. Or maybe they were discussing the weight of a bowling ball on Neptune, I really couldn't be sure. All I knew was that he'd broken his pact to keep me free from Franco's attention as promised. I vowed to have my revenge on Bernie Sanger later.

With no knight in armor to protect me, I inched away from my neighbor, unwittingly approaching Locanda on the other side until my elbow was practically planted in the center of his plate. I might as well have thrown gasoline on the flame of Vicky's wrath. She fumed and stroked Locanda's arm all the more vigorously to counter my perceived advances. No one was happy, except perhaps Bernie and Lucio, who were becoming fast friends over their fondness of astronomy, physics, and—presumably—inter-planetary bowling. And, of course, Tato, who was never more content than when beholding Giuliana's beauty.

A word about language. My Italian, though functional and much improved over the past year, was nevertheless plagued by frequent gaps in vocabulary and nuance, all of which hindered fluent, trouble-free communication with my new acquaintances. To greater or lesser degrees, the Italians suffered similar difficulties with English.

Franco Sannino, for example, spoke English with the naïve lack of awareness of, say, a provincial who's never visited the capital but thinks his Sunday best is the latest rage in fashion. He knew a good number of words, of course, and got his message across, but not without first mesmerizing whosoever was listening with his bumbling attempts at natural English accent and correct grammatical constructions. His usage was precious, at times comical, but always compelling. Even worse were his comprehension skills. As a result, our exchange of ideas never qualified as deep. In our interactions, he and I tended to stick to Italian.

Locanda spoke with great precision in both languages. While it was clear he was not a native speaker of English, he displayed remarkable fluency and command of idiomatic expressions. Mostly we communicated in English unless others less gifted in the language arts were present.

Bernie and I spoke English, of course. But his Italian, as noticed by all, was remarkable. Fluent and versatile. His accent was precise, thanks to years of study and a natural propensity for language. He quickly became the resource everyone relied on whenever a difficult phrase or an arcane term needed translating.

Lucio spoke English the way a drunken sailor might recite the *Rime of the Ancient Mariner* after a cursory glance at the text. The pauses, ums, restarts, and protracted searches for the simplest words would have sent even the most patient interlocutor running for the exit. A greeting as basic as hello could, and usually did, lurch into an auto wreck of limping syntax and twisted morphology. I'm not sure how I managed to understand him, but the light always seemed to blink to life in my head at the last moment and I got it. I think . . . We mostly communicated in Italian. He only seemed interested in singing me love songs anyway. And swearing a most entertaining blue streak whenever things went wrong.

After that first dinner at the villa, Vicky Hodges's eyes did most of the talking between us, so it didn't actually matter that we shared the same mother tongue. But her Italian was atrocious. I pitied poor Professor Crocetti who'd been sentenced to giving her lessons.

Veronica and Giuliana both spoke reasonably good English, but they preferred Italian most of the time. Tato had studied in England, and his command of the language was excellent. Since the group was mostly Italophone, however, Italian dominated as the lingua franca during our time at the villa.

As the diners savored the spaghetti, a fierce debate broke out between Lucio and Tato over the match between Italy and Chile at the previous year's World Cup tournament, now known notoriously as the *Battaglia di Santiago* (Battle of Santiago). The disgraceful behavior culminated in the ejection of two Italian players from the game. When one of them refused to leave the field, he was dragged off by the Chilean police. Lucio and Tato's disagreement escalated, though I couldn't understand why, since they seemed to be on the same side. To wit, that the Italian team had been treated unfairly by the English referee, and Italy surely would have gone on to win the tournament if not for the cheating by the host country. And of course the aforementioned English referee.

Achille appeared and removed their plates, even as they held their forks aloft, still loaded with food. Poor Giuliana. With Lucio and Tato on either side of her, buffeting her with their raised voices, breath, and flying spittle, she bore the brunt of the misery caused by the ridiculous argument. I begged them to be more considerate and leave talk of sports and politics outdoors. Lucio and Tato apologized, promising each other to settle the matter later in private.

Thirsty from having shouted himself hoarse, Lucio asked Vicky in English to pass the wine. He needed three tries to make himself understood. And with Vicky temporarily distracted, I had the opportunity to cast a few more glances Locanda's way. It was obvious that he was still an attractive man. In his day he must have been a lady-killer. And that led me to wonder again about his past. He was of a generation that had come of age under the fascist regime after all. What had he done in the war? And during the *Ventennio*, Italy's twenty-year-long fascist era? He would have been in his mid-twenties and -thirties at the time. Had he belonged to the party? Served in the army?

He was a distant, almost indifferent host. It wasn't that he was begrudging of the largess he bestowed on his guests, nor demanding of acknowledgement of the same. Rather he seemed not to care about them at all. He was quiet, not inviting anyone inside his private world, not even his lover, Vicky, who now ate in silence beside him. It was as if he were trying to fade into the surroundings as the evening grew late.

"Do you think Veronica is all right?" I asked the others. "Maybe I'll go check on her."

Franco dismissed my concerns. "She'll be fine in the morning."

I dabbed my lips, pushed back my chair, and excused myself. Upstairs in my room, Veronica was asleep under the whirling ceiling fan. Her breathing was regular, not strained at all. I put a hand on her forehead to check her temperature, which felt normal to me. Confident she was on the mend, I returned to the table downstairs just as Achille charged into the dining room.

Bearing a tray laden with two fresh carafes of white wine and three bottles of *acqua minerale*, both *naturale* and *frizzante*, he moved quickly, efficiently, head-down and lips pressed tightly together, as if concentrating on a task as exacting as threading a needle. After distributing the water bottles evenly among the diners, he wiped his perspired brow with the back of his hand, huffed a couple of deep breaths as he surveyed the table for anything missing, then scampered back to the kitchen to receive the marching orders from Berenice for his next task.

A moment later he re-emerged, this time carrying a large platter loaded chest-high with plates of food. Berenice followed on his heels to supervise. Once the dishes had been doled out, she announced the menu in her thick Tuscan accent—-h- for -c-, -th- for -t-. I noticed, for example, that she addressed our host as *Signor Lohanda*. The second course was a *lombatina di vitello ai ferri* (grilled loin of veal), boiled *fagioli*, and *patate arrosto alla ghiotta* (roasted potatoes in meat drippings).

"Has anyone heard from the police today?" asked Bernie as we ate.

Franco, feeling ever more talkative under the influence of the wine, volunteered that he'd spoken to Inspector Peruzzi that morning to give him the address of Bel Soggiorno and the list of the guests. I wondered if he'd remembered Veronica's name.

"Anything new?" asked Bernie.

Franco took a bite of his veal, and before he could answer, his eyes rolled back in his head and he moaned in bliss. "*Che buono questo vitello.*"

"The inspector?" prompted Bernie.

"Sorry. Nothing certain yet. He won't rule out an accident, but he thinks it might have been a deliberate act. I told him that was crazy, shocking. *Pazzesco. Allucinante.* Alberto had no enemies. Perhaps not a lot of friends, but no one hated him. No one."

"Really?" I asked. "How can you be sure?"

Franco shrugged. "Who would want to kill Alberto?"

"I knew him better than anyone here," piped up Locanda, surprising us all. "He made some enemies over the years."

Franco gulped, and it wasn't the veal he was swallowing. "I'm sorry?"

Locanda plucked a half moon of potato with his fork, daubed it in the veal drippings, and slipped it into his mouth to chew. "Alberto was not always so pious. He was once a hard man."

Franco couldn't quite accept the description of his mentor. Lucio sat mouth agape. I glanced around the table to gauge reactions, and noticed Giuliana shared none of their shock at the pronouncement. She took a bite of veal and a sip of her wine and waited to see how the next act would play out.

I decided to end the awkward silence. "Tell us about his youth," I said. "After he returned from his education in the monastery."

If Locanda had been reluctant to speak to any of us before, he granted us a rare privilege now.

"Alberto was a troubled soul," he began, and all other conversation ceased. "I knew him from a very tender age, of course, but he returned from his time with the brothers as a different boy. He'd lost some of his physical brutality. Not all, but some. He was just eighteen, after all, and not a full-grown man yet. But his more violent urges seemed less . . . dominant."

"Max, *amore*, you're not eating," said Vicky when he paused to take a breath. "Let me cut your veal for you."

"No," he said simply and quite rudely. Then he continued. "I chanced to meet Alberto in a bookshop in Via del Castellaccio, near the university. I was shopping for some books for my classes, and ran into him doing the same. I greeted him, tried to embrace him. But he turned away. It was a jolt to me, I confess. Alberto and I had been friends as boys. Until he was sent away."

He took a sip of wine and ran his tongue over his teeth, upper then lower, as if to dislodge a bit of veal or potato. Vicky was still flushed in reaction to his recent censure and made no moves to wipe his lips with a napkin.

"What did you say to him?" I asked.

Locanda took another bite of the veal, chewed on it for a long moment, then resumed.

"I asked after his health, of course, when he'd returned to Florence, and things of that nature. He told me he was back for good from the friars who'd been instructing him for nearly six years. Of course I was overjoyed at the news and the luck of finding an old friend again. I invited him for a coffee, and we left the shop. But not before he slipped two expensive books under his coat."

All chewing stopped.

"You mean he stole the books?" asked Lucio.

Locanda nodded, pushed his plate to one side, and sat back in his chair. I couldn't be sure who at the table was most upset or surprised by the news. Franco was inebriated, but he managed to summon some indignation, announcing that he, for one, didn't believe it.

"Believe what you will," said Locanda, clearly indifferent to Franco's outrage.

"It's fantastic," added Lucio, shaking his head. "Amazing. Bondinelli was such a righteous man."

"Sanctimonious hypocrite," said Giuliana, nearly spitting her words. *"Bigotto."*

Tato, who'd turned white, grasped her hand in attempts to silence her. His eyes darted back and forth between the object of his desire and Franco Sannino, who might well do irrevocable harm to her academic career. For her part, Giuliana appeared satisfied with having had her say. She fell quiet, offered nothing more on the subject, but didn't retract her statement either. In fact she sat as still as a statue, and the only movement I could detect was the steady rise and fall of her breathing and the hint of a budding smile on her lips.

Franco tried to argue with her—convince her that Bondinelli had been a just man—but his faculties weren't completely engaged and he would have lost the debate in a first-round knockout if debates were settled that way.

"What do you say to that?" I asked Locanda, wanting to know if he'd defend his friend. "Was he a hypocrite?"

He shrugged then explained in his well-marinated voice. "Alberto's life was a long road with many unexpected turns and detours. He was a wicked boy after his sister, Cecilia, died. Then he was a tortured boy at the hands of the friars."

He had our attention.

"Tortured? Do you mean . . . ?" asked Lucio.

"They beat him, punished him, deprived him, damned him. And, yes, even worse. Crimes against a young boy. Alberto told me that day we went for coffee. The day he stole the books."

Alcohol has a way of nudging those who are less resistant to its effects from laughter to tears in a trice. And so it was with Franco Sannino, who wiped his eyes and hung his head.

"This is too much," he said. "Poor soul. He was a good man who suffered much." Then he aimed a glare at Giuliana. "He lost his sister and was abused. And still he found God and righteousness. You should never have said those things about him."

Lucio intervened, urging calm all around. "Now is not the moment."

Tato, also eager to help, tried to pat Giuliana's hand, but she yanked it away.

"*Ragazzi*, please," said Locanda. "I shouldn't have said anything. This is not a conversation for the dinner table. We'll change the subject."

But I was intrigued. Locanda had been poised to say more about Bondinelli's life and that meeting for coffee after the book theft, but Franco's drunken tears interrupted him. How I wanted to pose one last question about which detours the late professor's road had taken after serving his time with the friars. There was, after all, a lot of his life still unaccounted for. But, as Lucio had said, now wasn't the moment.

Sitting on my hands in the tense silence that followed Franco's outburst, I considered Giuliana from across the table. I couldn't decide which I wanted to know more, the subsequent chapters of Alberto Bondinelli's contradictory history or why she hated him so.

CHAPTER THIRTEEN

After dinner, which had turned to ashes on at least a couple of guests' tongues, we were invited to repair to the *salone* for coffee, *digestivi*, and conversation. I said I'd be right along, and gathered Bernie by the elbow, dragging him to a darkened room down the corridor.

"El, I'm spoken for," he said once we were alone behind the closed door. "But if you truly can't resist me, I'm willing to let you have your way with me."

"I didn't shanghai you for fun and games. Besides, after thirty seconds with me, you'd be spent like a burnt matchstick. A puff of breath away from breaking in two." And I blew a gentle kiss at him.

I reached for the light switch, but Bernie stayed my hand.

"Leave it off or someone will see the light. Why did you drag me in here anyway?"

"I wanted to discuss that painful dinner we just sat through."

"It was uncomfortable, I'll grant you that."

"Why would Locanda say those things about Bondinelli?"

"He's a strange one. Sour and tight, like a lemon. And without any sentimentality that I can detect. It's odd that he chose to tell that story at dinner. About his old friend who'd just been fished out of the river."

"Maybe they didn't like each other after all."

"Yet he offered his home to him for this weekend jamboree."

We both shrugged.

"He is a little spooky," I said after a short moment had passed. "But he's got some kind of charm."

"Yeah, like a cobra."

"Vicky seems to like him. She must be a third his age."

"A third? Really?"

"Okay," I said. "That's an exaggeration. More like . . . thirty-eight percent his age."

Bernie shook his head. "I don't get it. What's a gorgeous girl like her doing with a fossil like him?"

"Lots of American girls find Italians sexy."

"I get that. But usually the newer models. Not old jalopies like Locanda."

"I wouldn't exactly call him a jalopy. He's quite attractive in a debauched, blackened-soul, Don Juan kind of way. You're jealous, Bernie. Don't worry, you'll be old and used up one day soon."

I glanced around at our surroundings for the first time. Books crammed into shelving along the walls; a mammoth desk, piled with folios and correspondence, squatted like a bull in the center of the room; and a long secretary overflowing with documents and sundry papers loomed large against the opposite wall. A marble bust surveyed all from its vantage point in the corner. I couldn't rightly say in the semi-darkness, but it looked like a Roman emperor or senator.

"This must be Locanda's study," I said, wading deeper into the room.

"Wait, El. What are you doing? You can't go snooping around in here."

"Why not? We're alone. For all the others know, I dragged you into a dark corner because I couldn't resist your charms."

"Come on. Be reasonable. We'll get caught."

"Don't worry, Bernie. I won't touch anything," I said as I wandered over to the secretary. "I'll bet he's got all sorts of secrets squirreled away in here."

Bernie stuck close to the doorway, a sentry, listening for any approaching footsteps as I peered at the items lying in plain view. Old files, some with official stamps and ribbons, and stuffed folders occupied the space alongside various knickknacks and photos. There were small cast-iron statuettes of dogs, horses, and even a Leaning Tower of Pisa. It was all dry stuff, but I shuffled through a couple of old letters, which were addressed to someone named Rodolfo Locanda, *Ing.* The long-winded Italian sentences were indecipherable, and not because of the dark.

I gathered up a few photos lying loose on top of some recent newspapers. The first one showed a group of men in suits meeting around a long table. Another was a blown-up shot of a balding man making a point at a lectern. Then there was an old torn envelope, the kind studios used to send photographs. The tear showed a black-and-white picture inside. I drew it out to have a look. Four people—three men and a young woman—sitting in a café. One of the men bore a strong resemblance to the bald lecturer in the other photo. And, come to think of it, the bust in the corner, too. The last picture was of a pretty young blonde woman in a stylish studio portrait with the name *Fotografie F.lli Manfredi Firenze* stamped in fancy script in the lower left-hand corner. I compared her to the young woman in the café. Looked like a match to me, but she was wearing a hat in the group photo, so I couldn't be certain.

I held the café picture up to catch a faint light coming through the window. Hard to see much of anything. Whoever had snapped the photo must have been a few feet away from the terrace where the four people were seated. A photo like so many others. Just people smiling vaguely at a camera. It reminded me of the picture Lucio had described. The one in Bondinelli's office. Could it possibly be a print of the same one?

Bernie screamed my name in a whisper from his post near the door. "Someone's coming!"

I ditched the photos where I'd found them and darted across the room. Throwing my body against Bernie's with a thwack that nearly knocked the wind out of him, I wrapped my arms around his neck, and—standing on my tiptoes—planted a sloppy, wet kiss on his lips just as the door opened and the lights flickered to life.

"*Cosa fate qui?*" It was Locanda. He wanted to know what we were doing in there. And he didn't look his usual jovial self.

I released Bernie from my embrace, noting the smudge of red lipstick I'd made sure to leave on his mouth, chin, and half his cheek, and assumed a shamed expression. I could only assume I was sporting similarly clownish maquillage on my own face. Hastily adjusting my brassiere, which didn't need adjusting, I smoothed my skirt and croaked an apology.

"We took a wrong turn," I lied, knowing it was ridiculous but altogether understandable under the circumstances. Who wants to admit to getting caught petting heavily in someone else's study? "We were looking for the *salone*."

Locanda's fierce gaze ranged from me to Bernie, who stood frozen, flattened against the wall in terror, then back to me. At length, he had the good manners to blush. Or perhaps the redness was the result of the extreme pique setting his blood aboil. A moment later, his glare softened into an uncomfortable frown. He grunted that the *salone* was at the end of the hallway. Then, choking out a half cough, he excused himself for the interruption and stepped back into the corridor, pulling the door closed behind him.

"That was close," I said, exhaling the breath I'd been holding since Locanda burst into the room. I wiped my mouth with a handkerchief I'd retrieved from the pocket of my skirt, then turned to my partner in crime. "Here, let me clean you up."

I squared up in front of Bernie, took stock of the state of his appearance, then set about scrubbing my offending lipstick from his face. He complied, standing there motionless as I performed my ministrations. I realized he hadn't uttered a word since Locanda's inopportune appearance.

"What's the matter?" I asked. "I didn't break your ribs or anything, did I?"

He shook his head and moistened his lips with a dab of his tongue. Then another, as if the first attempt hadn't sufficed. His eyes, saucer-sized, peered back at me from behind his smudged glasses. Blinded by wonton abandon, I must have mashed my forehead against the lenses, leaving them a clouded mess. He removed his specs and, squinting, polished them on his shirttail.

He finally managed speech. "That was . . . um . . ."

"Unexpected?" I asked.

"I was going to say nice. Really nice."

Uh-oh. That hadn't been the idea at all. I kicked myself now for using Bernie's lips to deflect the suspicion that rightly should have fallen on me for snooping through Locanda's things.

"Don't get any ideas, Bernie," I said. "We're pals. You know that. I was just trying to throw Locanda off the scent."

"I know that," he said, replacing his glasses on his nose and assuming an indifferent attitude. "It's just that it was more pleasant than that dinner we just sat through."

"Agreed. And speaking of that, what did you make of Giuliana's outburst? She left little doubt of what she thinks of Bondinelli."

"She a feisty one."

"I saw you chatting with her last night at the reception. I think she likes you. Maybe it's the Jewish thing."

"I think she's taken by Tato."

"I have my doubts. He's her little lapdog for now, but I don't see her settling for someone without her convictions. And, again, I mention the Jewish thing."

"I'm not interested," announced Bernie, his eyes sparkling at me in the low light.

I knew I had to tread carefully after throwing myself—literally—at him. I asked him for a favor.

"Do you think you might corner her at some point and find out what she knows about Bondinelli? Why does she hate him so?"

"I can try. But what is it exactly that you suspect, El? Do you think she had some grudge against Bondinelli strong enough to do him harm? If not, I don't know why you're snooping. The same goes for rifling through Locanda's stuff in here."

"It's not something I can easily describe, but I'll tell you that I'm curious by nature. And thorough. Nosy. And obsessed with sharp corners and fully explained answers. I cannot abide unfinished business or loose threads."

Bernie aimed his freshly cleaned glasses at me, one lens catching a flicker of light from the window as he did. "You think someone murdered Bondinelli, don't you?"

"Not sure. We'll have to see about that."

"Okay," he said, pushing the door open and inviting me to pass first. "For you, El, I'll do it. But I can't help wondering what the hell we've gotten ourselves into with this weekend in the country."

I peered into the hallway, checking that no one else was lurking, and, finding all clear, stepped outside. Bernie followed.

CHAPTER FOURTEEN

In Italy, it's common to enjoy a *digestivo* after dinner, dessert, and coffee. By the time Bernie and I had repaired to the *salone* to join the others, it was past midnight. Everyone was there, including our host, the keeper of our dirty little secret—at least for the time being—as it was clear the others suspected nothing. They'd already fortified themselves with fresh drinks and were engaged in their post-prandial colloquies and cigarettes. Despite my best efforts to appear casual about the recent smudge I'd applied to my own honor in Locanda's eyes, I'm sure I came across as on edge.

I chanced a glance at him to gauge how he intended to handle the embarrassing indiscretion he'd witnessed. A cool customer, he was seated at the periphery of the circle, the beautiful Vicky on one side and another sledgehammer on the other. His paramour looked bored. She stared at the opposite wall and its imposing fresco, which had a crack down the center. The colors had faded, but one could make out a bucolic setting populated by fat little cherubim and three nymphs bathing in a stream. Nearby three hunters stalked a stag, the implications being that they might well stumble upon the naked maidens. Enchantment and romance were in the offing to be sure. I conferred quietly with Bernie and, after a moment's debate, we agreed that, given the age of the house, the painting was probably sixteenth-century and of pedestrian authorship at that. Still, it was a remarkable work to have in one's drawing room.

With that detail settled, I turned my attention back to Locanda. His cigarette fumed in the ashtray on the table to his right, as he thumbed through a slim tome that, for all I knew, might have been poetry, a bartender's guide, or even a pocket book version of the *Kama Sutra*. From time to time, he reached for the glass next to the ashtray, raised it to his lips, and took a sip. Whatever was absorbing his attention, it was clear that he wasn't interested in making eye contact with me or my partner in crime.

Bernie and I were seated on one of the divans, opposite Lucio who was, as always, toying with his guitar. Giuliana remarked that it was late and that the dinner had lasted too long. No one challenged her assertion except Lucio, who felt we'd rushed through the delightful meal due to the late start caused by Veronica's illness. He maintained that anything less than three hours at the table was uncivilized.

Achille had placed a tray of liqueurs, mixers, and even some watery ice cubes in the center of the room. At Locanda's urging—no more than a distracted wave of his hand in the direction of the drinks, really—Bernie and I stood to help ourselves. I returned to the divan and sank into the worn cushions and pillows with my *Fernet Branca*. Bernie, on the other hand, was interested in an ancient bottle of cognac, but his courage didn't go so far as to pour himself any, especially in light of recent developments. He settled instead for some moscato. Making polite conversation, I asked Lucio what he was drinking. He said it was *grappa* and held his glass out to me.

"No thanks," I said. "Maybe later if my lighter runs out of fluid."

He offered a suit-yourself grin and took a swig that twisted his face into a grimace.

"*Buono,*" he announced in a hoarse voice, his eyes watering. Then he resumed tuning his guitar.

Giuliana was drinking water. Tato had some white wine, while Locanda and Vicky were enjoying what I believe was *genepì*, a botanical liqueur related to absinthe. Now, with the late arrivals armed with beverages and seated comfortably, everyone was present and accounted for. Except, of course, Veronica, whom no one seemed to miss. As if on cue, Lucio decided to serenade me with another love song.

I didn't dare look, but I felt Locanda's eyes on me as Lucio crooned, "*Tu sei sempre nel mio cuor.*" What must my host have been thinking of my morals? First he'd found me affixed to Bernie's lips with more suction than a primed toilet plunger could manage, and now another young man was, by all appearances, seducing me with Italian love ballads.

In the end, Lucio held to form and, having strummed the barest beginnings of an actual song on the guitar, he stopped, apologized for the pitch of his B-string, and set about tuning the instrument again. I sensed it would be hours before he was satisfied.

With the plinking of his guitar tuning, Lucio effectively strangled all conversation in the room. Giuliana yawned and announced she was turning in. Tato begged her to stay up a little longer.

"The weekend is short," he said. "Let's enjoy it to the fullest."

"How do you propose we do that?" I asked.

He racked his brain for a short moment, searching for some acceptable activity that everyone might enjoy.

"What if Lucio sings us another song?"

A groan rose from the assembled, and Giuliana pointed out that the guitar player didn't seem to know any songs. Lucio said nothing to contradict her. In fact, he just kept plinking away, tuning and plinking, plinking and tuning.

"*E la radio*?" said Franco.

"Off the air," answered Giuliana. "And there's no television either."

"Then I'll tell you all a story."

More groans with less effort to disguise the disappointment.

"*Va bene*," he conceded. "I'll save my story for another time. Tonight Lucio will put down his guitar and entertain us with a tale of his own devising. Each evening, one of us shall be king—or queen, as the case may be—of our little group and tell a story. We must obey and listen attentively to our sovereign's tale."

While the gang didn't exactly cheer and hoist Lucio onto their shoulders, there seemed to be a willingness to grant him a chance. He was quick with a joke, after all, and quite handy with words, if not songs. He agreed to take on the challenge with one proviso.

"*Amici*, I will keep my guitar," he announced with a playful air that suggested feigned offense. "And you will see that I hold in store for you a wonderful surprise. I shall make my guitar sing to add beauty and drama to the story I am about to tell."

Someone groaned again. Lucio ignored the affront. Instead he chewed his lip for a moment, searching his memory for a good story to tell. Soon enough, his face lit up, and we knew he'd found one.

"Tonight I shall recount a parable that will give you cause to consider your own actions in life and the meaning of redemption in the afterlife," he said. "Your hearts will be gladdened by the power and generosity of God."

"*Uffa*, I'm going to bed," said Giuliana. "There is no God, and I have no desire to listen to your bourgeois fables. Religion keeps the worker in ignorance of his oppression."

"Come on, *Giulià*," whined Lucio. "You know I'm a Communist like you. *Siamo tutti comunisti qui*. It was just for fun that I introduced the story that way."

"Speak for yourself," said Franco, throwing a glance in Locanda's direction. "I am not a Communist. And I doubt our host is either. Or our American friends."

Locanda, who'd remained aloof and silent throughout the discussion, offered a languid blink. "I no longer concern myself with politics. There's no need." He indicated the house around us all with a lazy wandering gaze. "But, *vi prego*, no political arguments here."

The motion passed unanimously. And the idea of Lucio recounting an amusing story was preferable to his incessant tuning of the guitar, so everyone climbed onboard. Everyone except Vicky, who showed little enthusiasm for the exercise, as she understood practically nothing of Lucio's—or anyone else's—Italian.

We all refreshed our drinks and adjusted our seats to give Lucio a proper audience, and he, having taken another gulp of *grappa* and cleared his throat, settled into a large armchair and began strumming an ancient air on the guitar. Something out of a medieval village fair. Despite a slight slurring of his speech and the occasional suppressed belch, he turned out to be a fine raconteur. Basing my translation on memory, I believe I've managed to reconstruct the tone of his tale here. He began.

"There once lived in France a pair of moneylending brothers by the name of Francese." He paused to wink at Giuliana. "*Vedi?* My villains are capitalists." Then he returned to his story. "Although small in physical stature, the Franceses were known far and wide as hard businessmen and unscrupulous usurers, who showed little sympathy for their clients, no matter the misfortunes that may have driven them to seek loans at exorbitant rates. Following a particularly cruel drought that wiped out the harvest and led to hardships throughout the land, many townsfolk found themselves in dire need of money to survive the winter. With great reluctance, the distressed citizens approached the brothers, hat in hand, to make a bargain with the devil.

"The usurers knew well that there was no trick to lending money. Handing out *écus* and pieces of gold was easy. The rub was recovering the principal amount and its high interest when the loan came due, especially since they lacked the size and strength to enforce their business agreements. Without the second half of the transaction—the restitution—the brothers realized, they would be bankrupt and in the poorhouse in no time. They were not in the business of philanthropy, after all, even if they tried to project a public image of piety and Christian charity. So when the snows began to melt and the good weather returned, they devised a plan to collect the payments from their impoverished debtors."

Throughout his narration, Lucio continued to strum and pluck his guitar in a most pleasant and competent manner. The man could play after all.

"In the capital there lived a wicked man named Venereo Ruttonaccio," he said. "Reputed far and wide as the hardest, most ruthless brigand in the land, Ruttonaccio stole from the collection plate at church, extorted money from local merchants, and made a habit of having his wicked will with innocent maidens and maids alike, as well as with ladies of ill repute. He happily burned down homes for a fee, robbed travelers on the highway, drank to excess, and brawled with fellow drunkards in the most disreputable inns of Paris. Ruttonaccio took the Lord's name in vain several times a day, but saved his most potent oaths for the Madonna . . ." This time Lucio glanced at Giuliana and threw her a high sign to urge forbearance on her part; he was not advocating piety. "He kept poor hygiene, throwing off an odor that suggested a strong bovine lineage in his blood, and never once in his life had he failed to kick a stray dog whenever presented with the opportunity. Indeed, he did so sometimes even when not presented with the opportunity. On more than one occasion, he was said to break into burghers' homes with the sole goal of seeking out the guard dog in order to give him a swift kick in the rump. Oh, yes, I nearly forgot. He also sang off key."

Lucio punctuated this last statement with a sudden and violent rasping of his fingers across the strings of his guitar, producing a loud, dissonant chord. Everyone laughed.

"Where was I?" he asked after swigging from his *grappa* again. Tato, noticing the nearly empty glass, snatched it and refilled it as Lucio resumed the ancient air on his guitar and, along with it, his tale.

"Faced with the task of collecting from hundreds of impoverished debtors, the Francese brothers traveled to the capital to seek out this Venereo Ruttonaccio and engage his services to do the necessary. The blackguard set his price, which was high. The moneylenders negotiated a more advantageous fee by offering the terrible man room and board in their house while he extracted the money from the poor *contadini*—*Oh, Scusami, Giulià* . . . the poor *lavoratori agricoli.* The trio shook hands and sealed the deal.

"Over the next fortnight, Ruttonaccio terrorized the debtors who had no means to repay the loans, never mind the usurious interest. He threatened violence, slaughtered lambs as a warning, and even poisoned the well of one unfortunate borrower. And his tactics bore fruit. The poor farmers and townsfolk scrounged to find the money to pay the scoundrel, some resorting to stealing, while others borrowed from different opportunistic usurers. More still sold their sons and daughters into servitude to raise the funds. All the while, the Francese brothers kept their distance from their collector in attempts to maintain their good Christian reputations.

"But soon after he'd begun his collections, Ruttonaccio fell ill and took to his bed. His head pounded as if possessed by a thousand demons, his tongue swelled as large as an eggplant—the same color, too—and he burned with fever. In his agony, he cursed the *lavoratori agricoli* he'd visited, for he believed they'd infected him with the horrible, festering contagion that had laid him low. After three days of suffering, he called the Francese brothers to his side and told them he feared he was not long for this world. On the one hand, the brothers were sorry to lose such an effective debt collector, but on the other, they secretly rejoiced that they would not have to pay him his fee if he expired.

"While the brothers lived a sinful life of moneylending, a practice prohibited by the Church, they nevertheless took pains to present an image of piety in their town, at least to the richer folk. They attended Mass every day, including twice on Sundays. In fact, they often marveled to each other about how much business they routinely conducted inside the walls of the church. God was good for commerce, said they. And for that reason, they came to understand the danger that Ruttonaccio's imminent death posed for them. If word were to get out that a sinner had died under their roof without the sacrament of the last rites, the brothers would be shunned by the local bishop and all the town's most respected communicants. To remedy this potential undoing of their social standing, they summoned their local priest, Father Fabrice, to perform extreme unction for their moribund houseguest.

"The sick man rebuffed the priest, feigning unconsciousness. After two more days of worsening health, reasoning with the last of his failing wits—for the fever was working its magic on his mind—Ruttonaccio decided that his last act on earth would be to thumb his nose at the priest, the Church, and, indeed, God Himself. He summoned Father Fabrice to return and listen to his last and—in truth—his first confession.

"'When was your last confession, my son?' asked the priest at his bedside.

"'It was the very day I fell ill,' said the sick man, feeling no shame for his lie. Indeed, he secretly relished his brazen dishonesty. 'One week ago. But I have not unburdened my soul since that day. For that I am deeply aggrieved for the offense I have given to God.'

"Father Fabrice assured him that the omission was understandable under the circumstances and hardly offensive to the Lord. He then asked Ruttonaccio how he had spent his life.

"'Verily I must confess that I have led a spoiled existence,' said the sick man. 'Born into a rich family, I inherited my father's considerable fortune at a young age. But rather than spend my days in honest toil, I gave away all but a small portion of my riches to the poor, and occupied myself in good works, devotion, and prayer because those kindnesses gave me joy. A most selfish act on my part.'

"The priest disagreed and declared that this was a most admirable way to live a just life. Then he asked Ruttonaccio for his confession.

"Knowing that in order to fool the priest he would need to summon all his failing wits, Ruttonaccio asked for absolution of sins so minor that Father Fabrice came to believe that he was indeed a saintly man. The priest assured him that performing the sign of the cross too slowly was not a cardinal sin. Neither did expressing admiration for his neighbor's cow for the prodigious amounts of milk she produced qualify as the sin of coveting.

"'But, Father,' protested Ruttonaccio, 'I am a sinner. I have not always honored the Sabbath. Once I asked my servant to sweep the hall on a Sunday.'

"'Why, pray, did you do that, my son?'

"'A group of tired and sick and hungry pilgrims chanced upon my house on their journey to Rome. I offered them succor and forced my poor servant to work on the Sabbath.'

"Father Fabrice was moved by what he perceived as the exemplary holiness of a man who considered such insignificant transgressions sins.

With a great gladness in his heart, the priest absolved Ruttonaccio of all shortly before he died."

Pausing for another sip of *grappa*, Lucio wet his whistle before continuing.

"As a final gift to the saintly man, Father Fabrice arranged for Ruttonaccio to be buried in a crypt in the church. He eulogized the good soul to the entire congregation, extolling his virtues and good deeds, and urged the faithful to pray to Ruttonaccio to intercede with the saints on their behalf whenever they were in need. The locals followed his advice, especially the debtors who'd not yet repaid the Francese brothers. To those poor souls, the demise of the fearsome collector was a miracle, as the moneylenders lacked the courage even to visit them thereafter to demand repayment of the loans.

"A movement grew in the land. The poor prayed to Ruttonaccio for relief from their pecuniary woes. In time, the local priest took notice. He recounted Ruttonaccio's virtuous life to the bishop and presented evidence of certified miracles of financial salvation attributed to the dead man by the poor of the region. Soon, the bishop was pleading the case for sainthood with the Holy Father himself.

"In due course, Ruttonaccio was beatified as the patron saint of impoverished victims of usury. To this day, the faithful pray to this most holy saint in times of financial difficulties, thus proving the old adage that a life well lived is its own reward. The end."

With that, Lucio plucked a few happy notes on his guitar, and concluded his tale. Tato applauded vigorously, Giuliana somewhat less enthusiastically, but with a satisfied smile on her lips all the same. Franco frowned, perhaps reacting to the ambiguous moral of the story, perhaps from too much drink. Locanda seemed unmoved. Vicky snored. She'd long since fallen asleep. Bernie leaned in to whisper in my ear.

"Entertaining," he said. "But he lifted it straight from the first story of the *Decameron*. That was the tale of Ser Cepparello."

"Did you expect anything less?" I asked. "He lifts all his love ballads from the radio. Why wouldn't he steal from Boccaccio?"

I had certainly read some of the *Decameron* over the years. My father had been a renowned scholar of Italian literature after all. But I confess I didn't remember the Ser Cepparello story. Still, I didn't begrudge Lucio for appropriating it. He'd changed enough details—probably due to a faulty memory—to make the tale his own. Yes, I told, Bernie. I'd quite enjoyed it. The clever way Lucio turned the themes to fit his twentieth-century political ends impressed me. But why had he changed the names?

"Were the moneylenders named Francese in Boccaccio?" I asked Bernie.

"Franzesi, or something like that, I believe. Why?"

I ignored his question for the moment and asked about the priest in the story instead. "What was his name in the *Decameron*?"

"I don't remember. I think he was just referred to as a friar. But what difference does it make if Lucio changed some names?"

I huffed an annoyed sigh, not aimed at Bernie, but at the unanswered question. "Lucio's confessor priest was named Fabrice. Remember the opening ceremony of the symposium at the Palazzo Vecchio yesterday morning? Bondinelli's priest—his confessor—offered a tribute to him. And his name was Fabrizio. Why would Lucio change the name like that? Was he implying something sinister about Bondinelli?"

Bernie considered my question for a moment before leaning in even closer to whisper again. "Are you suggesting that Lucio—that wooly-headed sweetheart of a guy—was equating Bondinelli with a maggot like Ruttonaccio?"

CHAPTER FIFTEEN

SATURDAY, SEPTEMBER 28, 1963

Veronica slept through the night. I can attest to that since she snored like a well-fed porker from the time I retired at about two a.m. till the cock crowed outside our open window at 5:43 sharp. Lying there in my hard bed, puffy-eyed and dry-mouthed, I swore I would convince Berenice to take an ax to that damn rooster's neck and serve his remains for dinner that evening, burnt to a crisp if possible.

Holding a pillow over my head didn't do much to dampen Veronica's snoring. It might have done more good had I squashed it over her face for about three minutes instead. Unable to sleep, I got up and took consolation in the knowledge that I was the first to rise and had the bathroom to myself. By seven, I was bathed and ready for the day.

Downstairs in the dining room, however, I arrived second. There, alone, sitting before a bowl of *caffellatte* at the head of the table, his legs crossed elegantly, Max Locanda was smoking a cigarette and reading the paper.

"*Buongiorno*," I said.

He lowered his newspaper and regarded me over his eyeglasses. He said nothing for a long moment, choosing instead to study me as one might a rara avis. At length, he offered a lukewarm hello and asked if I'd slept comfortably.

"Very well," I lied. Had I known then the verb for *to snore* in Italian—*russare*—I might have given him the real story.

He took a sip of his coffee and then, snapping his paper back into its reading position, buried his nose in the news.

"What shall I call you?" I asked from behind the curtain of newsprint.

He lowered his newspaper again and fixed me with a penetrating stare. "*Prego?*"

"What shall I call you?" I repeated. "*Signor* Locanda? *Dottor* Locanda? *Cavaliere?*"

Okay, the last one might have been a tad insolent on my part. Or perhaps not. I'd met a few *cavalieri* in my day, and they'd taken their honorific seriously.

"Call me Max," he said, unfazed by my effrontery. "Massimiliano is a waste of breath. Too many syllables."

"*Va bene.*" I cleared my throat. "Max."

Though I'd agreed to call him by his first name—and a diminutive at that—I was not about to use the familiar *tu* with him. A dusty Florentine memory of my father rose like a cloud from somewhere deep in the past. On our long-ago Italian voyage, the ten-year-old me had once used *tu* when addressing a friend of my father's, the ancient Professor Dagoberto Lucón. Dad corrected me in front of the old man and told me never to use *tu* with someone so senior to me, except perhaps with close relatives.

"But he called me *tu*," I said in my defense.

"He has that privilege. You do not. When you're as old as he, you may use *tu* with young girls. But for now, you must show Professor Lucón the respect he deserves and use *lei* with him."

Then he winked at the old man before concluding his lecture to me. "After all, you don't want people thinking you're Professor Lucón's girlfriend."

I didn't think it was funny, and I doubt Lucón did either, if a red face and averted eyes meant what I thought they did.

"I prefer Ellie," I said to Locanda, even though he hadn't asked.

After a moment's pause to digest my name, he informed me that he would stick with "signorina." His response silenced me. In fact, it felt like a tight slap in the face.

The niceties over, he folded his newspaper once and for all and put it down. Somewhat reluctantly, it seemed, he indicated the chair opposite him, a signal that I was to join him.

"I expected you young people would sleep in this morning," he said once I'd taken the seat. "After so much wine last night."

"You should know that I have a horror of men who keep track of how much I drink."

It was a weak attempt at banter, especially after the "signorina" remark. Why was I trying to engage him in conversation anyway? Yes, I wanted to draw him out, confirm or disprove my suspicions about him. Clearly he was a womanizer, or he wouldn't be carrying on so shamelessly with a woman thirty-eight percent his age. But how much of my interest was personal? I couldn't possibly be attracted to a man of his years and temperament, could I? Still, I had to admit he had magnetism. I pushed that thorny thought to one side. This was about him, not me. At least as long as I was lying to myself.

My comment—the one about men monitoring my alcohol intake—prompted a frown from him, more due to surprise, I thought, than outrage at my manners. Then he realized perhaps that I was attempting to flirt, or at least joke, and his expression softened somewhat. I figured he was unused to young women telling him where to get off. He drew a last puff on his cigarette and stubbed it out in the ashtray before him.

"May I confess something to you, signorina?" he asked, using the formal *lei* with me. I was relieved to know that my instincts—as well as my father's advice—had been right. Use *tu* with your familiars, classmates, friends, and dogs. Not with aging Lotharios like Locanda or relics like Professor Lucón.

"Of course you may."

"I find your friends tiresome," he said.

"Tiresome?"

"*Esatto.*"

"And me? You don't find me tiresome?"

Again I'd surprised him with my candor. And again he recovered his aplomb forthwith, or at least disguised his discomfort by summoning Berenice. No sledgehammer was necessary for her. He tinkled a small bell on the table instead. She appeared, wiping her hands on her apron.

"*Il signore desidera?*"

"*Un caffè per la signorina,*" he said softly. "And something to eat."

Berenice nodded and withdrew.

"The weather will be hot today," he said. "Not as hot as August, but you might find it uncomfortable at midday."

Oh, God. He was discussing the weather with me.

Berenice breezed back into the room with a great bowl of coffee and milk for me, along with a *tartina* of bread, butter, and *marmellata*.

She asked Locanda if *la signorina* Vicky was on her way down to join him for breakfast.

"Yes. Bring her the usual," he told her. "Whatever it is she eats in the morning."

Berenice huffed, then observed with the supercilious air of an offended cook that Vicky didn't eat anything. "*Quella ragazza non mangia proprio niente.*"

Locanda wasn't in the mood for a lecture from his servant. "Bring her some tea then," he snapped, and she headed back to the kitchen.

We were alone for the moment. My native curiosity prodding me to action, I took advantage to ask him some questions before his lover appeared.

"I'd like to offer you my condolences. I'm sorry for your loss."

"My loss?"

"Your old friend, Alberto. Professor Bondinelli."

He mugged an expression that didn't quite communicate sorrow, but something akin to fatalistic acceptance instead. I waited for him to speak. He just sat there in silence.

"I understand you'd known him for many years," I continued.

"*Già,*" he said as if he'd only just remembered his late friend. "Since we were children."

"Then you knew his sister, too? The one who died from influenza?"

He nodded. "Not well. She was older."

"Cecilia was her name, I believe."

Again he nodded but offered nothing more. *Muto come un pesce,* (mute as a fish) I thought, remembering a favorite locution of my father's. He'd used it as an admonition for discretion as well as a way to tell Elijah and me to shut up.

Perhaps a direct question would get Locanda talking. I asked him if he was one of the boys Alberto used to beat up.

"Who told you Alberto was a bully?"

"His priest mentioned it at the symposium."

"Rather indiscreet of him," he said, lighting another cigarette. "But no, Albi never struck me. I was a year older than he, and a little stronger at the time." He smiled. "If I remember rightly, we acted as a team."

"You mean you both beat up the others?"

"We were young children then."

"The child is the father of the man," I said.

"Boys are violent creatures. They lack the restraint that comes with maturity. It's unfair to expect them to behave like civilized adults."

"And when he was sent away to study with the friars, did you stay in touch?"

He shook his head. "No. He was gone for five or six years. I saw him only once or twice in that time. We both changed a lot during those years."

I asked him how so.

Locanda made a face, as if annoyed, and asked me why I was so interested in his friendship with Alberto.

"I'm sorry," I said. "It's just that I never met him and I was curious."

"It was the twenties," he said at length. "I can tell you that for many years we found ourselves on opposite sides of the era's political struggles."

"Then you were ... I mean, I assume, given your age, that you were ..."

"A fascist? Why do you assume that?"

I stumbled over my words, fearing I'd insulted him. "Just that I understood that Professor Bondinelli was with the partisans during the war. If you were on different sides, well, I figured you meant the fascists."

Max took a drag of his cigarette and regarded me for a long moment. "Now you're talking about the war. I said the twenties, not the forties. A different time altogether."

I was thoroughly confused. "I ... *Scusi*, but I don't understand."

"Alberto was indeed with the partisans during the war. At the end of the war, that is. I, alas, like almost all males of my generation, found myself in the military. And then in a prisoner-of-war camp. So, yes, we were on different sides then as well."

"What about during the twenties?"

"We hadn't seen each other in many years by that time. He'd been with the friars. But we ended up at university together."

"That's when you saw him steal the books?"

"Yes. The friars gave him an excellent grounding in Christian theology and history. But the ... brainwashing didn't take. Alberto was fiercely anti-clerical in those days. And he wasn't above pinching a couple books."

"His priest suggested he was rebellious."

"He claimed to be an atheist. I recall he joined up with a secretive society of anarchists. At least they thought they wanted to be anarchists. Just teenaged Communists suffering from some existential crisis of faith. Communist faith."

"And what groups did you join?"

"I wasn't much for joining."

"Surely you belonged to some group or another while at university."

"I worked at one of the student newspapers," he said.

"Then we have something in common. I'm a newspaper reporter back home."

He smiled a weak, dismissive smile. "I wrote opinion pieces. No reporting."

Vicky entered the room, and Locanda rose to greet her with a "*carissima*" and a kiss on both cheeks. "What took you so long? I've been dying of boredom without you."

That stung.

Vicky practically glared at me. I fancied she was sizing me up as one wrestler might another before busting a folding chair over his head. Taking the seat next to her lover, she asked me what I was doing up at the crack of dawn.

"I couldn't sleep," I said. "The rooster and Veronica . . ."

"Who's Veronica?"

"The sick girl. The one with the rash."

"Oh, right. I wanted to sleep in myself, but Max offered to take me into town to shop."

She batted her eyelashes at him, and, marooned, I felt superfluous and unwelcome at the same table with the happy couple. I debated whether to gulp down my coffee or abandon it. I had more questions for Locanda, of course, but this was not the moment.

Berenice returned with a cup of tea for Vicky. Placing it on the table, she cast a dirty look at the steaming *infuso*. Or perhaps the target of her disapproval was Vicky, not her breakfast beverage. Berenice withdrew again, and Vicky proceeded to squeeze some lemon into her tea—I preferred milk—stir it absently, and take a sip. Then she eyed me again. She couldn't quite disguise her expression, which was one of those nettled, annoyed-by-my-proximity-but-not-sure-how-to-send-me-packing looks. I sympathized. I, too, wanted to shake the dust of that room from my heels, but if I was being polite, I couldn't exactly tap-dance my way off stage vaudeville-style.

"I suppose you have plans with the others," said Vicky.

"No. I thought I might explore the grounds today. Maybe do some reading."

"There's not much to see here. Just olive trees and old, useless grapevines."

"I think they're quite beautiful in their retirement," I said. "In a knotty, arthritic way."

Vicky wasn't convinced but let it go. "If Max would put in a pool like I told him, we could escape the heat with a swim."

"That's all right. I'll find plenty to keep me busy."

I thought of the library and its trove of photographs. Was I actually brazen enough to mount a second invasion of his study? I wanted to tell myself no, but . . .

"If you're interested in swimming," said Locanda to me, "there's a little stream over the hill. It's a pleasant, private spot for a dip."

"I loved to swim when I was a girl."

Vicky pursed her lips, squeezing them into a meaty mush of lipstick, presumably indicating what she thought of what I had or had not loved to do as a girl.

And then something unsettling happened. Until that moment, notwithstanding his sexy young girlfriend, Max Locanda had behaved like a humorless, cold-blooded prig. Aloof and reserved, bordering on rude at times. I had been waiting for him to show some overt sign of debauchery, but he'd defied my expectations from the start, never more so than when he surprised Bernie and me in our passionate embrace. He seemed more a prude than a Casanova. But just when I'd resigned myself to having misjudged my host's character, his true self shone through. As Vicky peeled an orange, Locanda fixed me with a penetrating stare and, without the slightest hint of shame, addressed me in Italian.

"If you're not shy, signorina, know that here at Bel Soggiorno we have no objections to guests swimming *in puris naturalibus.*"

I nearly choked. Vicky took another unenthusiastic sip of her tea, unawares, as Locanda stubbed out his cigarette and smiled.

He urged Vicky to finish her tea and hinted at a little something bright and shiny from Torrini's if she was a good girl. She cooed, replaced her cup in its saucer, and gathered up her skirts.

"*Sono pronto!*" she said, jumping to her feet.

"That's *pronta, cara,*" corrected Locanda. "With an A."

A brief contretemps ensued, with Vicky pouting and whining that she'd heard him say *pronto* with an O hundreds of times. Why was it wrong when she said it?

"Because, *amore*, you are a woman. Feminine, *'pronta.'* I am a man, masculine, *'pronto.'*

"It's silly," she said with more drama than the situation merited. "I see how a woman is feminine, but how can you tell with words? Like that," she said, pointing to an apple in a basket on the table.

"*Mela*," answered Locanda. "*La mela*. It's feminine."

"What's feminine about an apple?" she whined, practically weeping. "How am I supposed to know?"

Locanda smiled indulgently. "It's very simple. You turn it over and look underneath."

That didn't go over well. Now in tears, Vicky stomped from the room, and Locanda, drawing a sigh, followed.

CHAPTER SIXTEEN

The beauty of Tuscany lies in its tranquil landscapes. I can't describe it in its winter vestments since I've never seen it, but I remembered its hot summer haze of seventeen years before. And in the cooling autumn, it was redder and golder, no less lazy, but more inclined to welcome. If only a few degrees more temperate than the sizzling month of August, late September still managed to paint the panoramas and skies and cypress trees in a different palette, one that suggested work was nearly done and rest was coming.

With my awkward breakfast behind me, I wandered out through the *salone* to the *terrazza*, then into the garden for a solitary stroll. The others, save Locanda and Vicky, were surely still in their beds, sleeping off the indulgences of the night before. I had the grounds to myself.

A canopy of green-and-white ivy climbed the long sturdy pergola leading to a copse of trees and a gentle hill. I meandered down the shady corridor, stopping to admire wildflowers and spy on a gecko resting on a bed of pebbles. A few steps farther, a bee buzzed over a meager bunch of yarrow, what the Italians called *Achillea millefoglie*. This was perhaps the last hurrah of the season for the little white flowers, which, thanks to my late mother's gardening passions, I knew would have thrived better in direct sunlight.

The pergola's cover of ivy provided the day's last moments of cool until dusk. I could sense the gathering heat settling over the land just yards away in the open sunlight. An idyllic escape, peaceful and redolent of smoky cypress and earthy mushrooms. The kind that spring up overnight at the feet of mossy trees. At the end of the path, I emerged from the shade and was greeted by Diana, goddess of the hunt. Frozen in stone in the tall grass, she stood straight, her waving garment draped off one shoulder to expose a breast and her entire right side. She clutched a bow in her left hand. A sleek hound heeled beside her. I approached her tentatively, studying her weathered concrete features, mottled by moss and lichen, and noticed that both her nose and quiver of arrows had been broken off somewhere in time. I thought of Locanda's warning of boars on the property and wondered if the huntress was on their trail. Silly thought. Then I worried for real that there might be *cinghiali* in the area after all. Max had said they were primarily nocturnal, but the last thing I wanted to do was stumble over a sounder of sleeping boars. There were plenty of leaves and tall grass on the ground, after all. And I'd seen lots of berries, chestnuts, and roots for them to eat. They could be anywhere.

I took leave of the statue and stepped carefully through the broken cypress twigs and needles, away from the trees, the earthy odors of decay and hints of skunk, making my way down the grassy hill.

I reached the bottom and wandered through a shady glen about a hundred paces until I came to a small brook, most probably the one Locanda had mentioned at breakfast. The water trickled through the creek bed, which wended its way through the grass, heading—I could only imagine—to the Arno far below and eventually to the Ligurian Sea. A leaf floated by on the swirling current, and I followed it on foot, thinking of Arturo Bondinelli yet again.

He was indeed a puzzle, having died mysteriously without a clear identity left behind. And even though I was spending the weekend among people who'd worked with him, grown up with him, lived with him, they couldn't tell me with any degree of certainty who he'd been. Was he short-tempered, demanding, hypocritical? What were his politics? A Christian Democrat, yes, but that didn't necessarily tell me anything of substance about him. Then there was Giuliana, the girl who purposely approached me to tell me about the professor's past. She claimed he'd been a partisan during the war, but just as quickly she cast doubt on his character and past sins. And, of course, she refused to repeat her insinuations in the presence of anyone besides me. Until, of course, her outburst at dinner the night before.

I recalled Lucio's late-night story. Had he actually been pointing a not-so-subtle finger at Bondinelli, mocking his reputation and legacy for the amusement of those who knew him best? But why do that? Why not just accuse him openly? And did his clever little roman à clef even matter if the professor had fallen into the river by accident? Or if he'd thrown himself off a bridge to end it all? But why would a man who, by all appearances had achieved peace with himself, resort to suicide just one day before the opening of the symposium he'd been planning for more than two years?

And so, effortlessly, my thoughts turned to the third dark possibility, namely that someone might well have pushed Bondinelli into the Arno. If true, such a scenario cast Lucio's story in a more sinister light. Because if someone had indeed murdered the professor, why shouldn't I harbor doubts about Lucio who'd mocked him as a fraud and a false saint?

Strolling alongside the creek, I drew a sigh, wishing I'd never accepted poor Bondinelli's invitation in the first place. But since I had, and since the tragedy had occurred, I knew I couldn't ignore it until it had been explained to my satisfaction. That was surely one of the reasons I wanted to dig through Locanda's study. Not that I believed him capable of murdering his old friend, but he had known him longer than anyone else. Longer even than Padre Fabrizio. No, I wasn't sure how Bondinelli had come to die in the Arno, but I couldn't stop myself from wanting to find out. And the first step for me was to pin down Lucio on the meaning of his tale.

The stream continued to burble on its merry way. At some point during my rumination, I'd lost the floating leaf. I stopped in my tracks and, throwing a glance behind me, checked to see if anyone had followed me through the woods and down the hill. As far as the eye could see, the countryside was mine. A thought occurred to me.

Then I scolded myself. Was I really thinking of taking a dip in the inviting stream? Even with Max Locanda's explicit permission and encouragement to swim *in puris naturalibus?* I settled instead for removing my shoes and splashing through the water barefoot. After a half hour or so, as the sun climbed high in the morning sky, my toes had gone pruny and cold. I dried my feet, slipped back into my shoes, and set off up the hill toward the villa.

It was just past ten when I washed my hands and face in the small bathroom on the second floor. I'd managed to slip in between the late risers, some of whom had performed their ablutions, and others who hadn't yet answered the cock's crow and were still sawing wood in their beds.

I took some fruit, a brioche, and a *caffellatte* to Veronica in my room. She said she was comfortable, with no fever at all, but the itch would not relent.

"Hand me the bottle of *amamelide*. It's the only thing that helps."

She slathered the witch hazel on her arms and neck, then, having first claimed she wasn't hungry, changed her mind and wolfed down her breakfast.

"I want to read now," she informed me as she'd wiped her lips with a napkin. "You can take all this away."

She lifted a thin volume from the bedside table, *Le vite dei santi*, the Lives of the Saints. It was a children's book with bright illustrations on the cover. She seemed quite well recovered to me, except for the rashes, so, despite wanting a brief nap myself, I left her alone in my room.

Besides some chatter and the clanging of pots and pans coming from the kitchen, Bel Soggiorno was quiet at half past ten on a Saturday morning. The dining room was empty and the tables cleared. I feared the late risers had missed their chance at breakfast; Berenice had a schedule to maintain, and she didn't strike me as the type to indulge *dormiglioni*. Sleepyheads. Perhaps Lucio could charm an orange or a coffee out of her, but the smart money was on no more food before *pranzo*.

I wandered out onto the back *terrazza* looking for signs of life. Deserted, if you didn't count the three sparrows nosing around for crumbs left over from the previous evening's cocktail hour. As I was in exile from my own room, I resigned myself to an early siesta in the *salone*. I was still tired from the late night and the noisy tag team of Veronica and the rooster. Back inside the house, I intended to stretch out on one of the divans, but a glance through the door down the corridor gave me other ideas. I knew Locanda and Vicky were in Florence to buy her something bright and shiny to satisfy her magpie proclivities, but I wondered if any of the guests were about. A quick inspection revealed no one, so I chanced it. I slipped into Locanda's study.

Yes, I knew I was doing wrong. Over the years at the newspaper, my intense curiosity had found a home, and it had only become more demanding of me for professional reasons since. There were, of course, no professional reasons for me to be snooping through Locanda's things, but I rationalized my transgression with a promise that I only wanted to see if there was a typewriter I might be able to borrow. Okay, that was disingenuous of me.

In the light of day, the room presented few obstacles to a cursory examination. I could see everything Locanda kept on his large desk: letters, bundles of documents, an old telephone, an adding machine, and a half-drunk glass of water leaving a ring on the leather-bound blotter. The glass ashtray overflowed with cigarette butts. On the edge of the desk were a little wooden stand of office stamps and well-worn red, black, and blue ink pads, as well as five chewed-up old pipes in a revolving rack. They must have tasted grand, I thought. Circling around behind the desk, I noted some fountain pens lying jumbled like pick-up sticks alongside pencils of varying length, thickness, and sharpness. Some of the pens had blackened nibs while others were stained blue. There was an ink blotter with a silver handle shaped like one of those spouting fish you see in fountains. The metal had been blackened and blued and tarnished by what looked like years of use. I could see no dictionary, but that was hardly surprising. My father had taught me that Italians didn't need dictionaries for spelling guidance.

"Italian is spelled exactly as it's pronounced," he'd said. "Right down to the double consonants. If you can hear it, you can spell it."

The desk's large side drawers were locked—yes, I tugged at each of them—but the center one slid open on command. Inside were more pens and pencils, erasers and paperclips, as well as stationery. And a small triangular enamel pin with the letters GUF above a red-white-and-blue fleur-de-lis. I thought it might be French, given the colors and the heraldic device, but I didn't know why it might be in Locanda's desk drawer. I glanced at the door to ensure I was alone, then picked up the pin. On the verso was the inscription, "*Stabil.ti Artistici Fiorentini* (Florentine artistic works)." I shrugged, replaced the pin, and slid the drawer closed.

The correspondence on his desk looked to be run-of-the-mill business mail. I didn't know how Locanda supported his comfortable lifestyle, though I'd assumed his elderly wife in Switzerland kept him in silk ascots and fancy cigarettes. A cursory peek at two or three letters revealed words such as *olivicoltore*, *ettari*, and *vendemmia* (olive grower, hectares, and harvest), indicating his business might well be olive oil production.

I made my way over to the secretary against the wall. This was where I'd found the photographs and assorted newspapers the night before. Someone had straightened up the disorder, but everything was still there. I shuffled through the photographs once again, stopping to examine the group photo in the café. The faces were clearer in the light of day. The young woman was quite pretty, that much I could see. Knowing no one in Italy, I had little chance of recognizing any of the people in the café. But since this was Locanda's house, perhaps he was in the photograph. Then again, maybe not. This was his wife's house after all, wasn't it? I squinted at the blurry photo and thought he might be one of the three men, but there was no way of telling for sure, given the intervening years and the soft focus.

I left them as I'd found them, and moved on to the paintings and photographs on the walls. The Tuscan landscapes, drab watercolors, and dusty old framed photographs of whiskered bald men merited only the barest of glances. Some nineteenth-century portraits of Thoroughbreds and jockeys, however, struck me as out of place. On closer inspection, I ascertained that they were oil originals, most of which were unsigned. Two bore brass plates on the frames identifying the artist as John Alfred Wheeler. Perhaps Locanda's wife's late husband had been a horseman. The paintings predated Max's birth by at least twenty years. But who knew? Maybe his wife was old enough to have placed a wager on some of the illustrious horses.

Next, a bank of tall bookshelves held leather-bound volumes that showed almost no wear at all. Most likely bought by the yard, I guessed, unless the *marchesa*'s late husband was interested in eighteenth-century tomes on physics, French philosophical thought, histories of indigenous peoples of the Americas, and legal references, some in English and French, others in Italian, and more still in German and Latin. A mishmash of disciplines and traditions, with the only common denominator being the beautiful bindings. Not much to see here. Until I noticed a nook of sorts between the bookshelves and a corner of the room. There was a leather armchair flanked by a standing ashtray on one side and a small decorative folding table on the other. A brass floor lamp completed the scene. A lovely spot to read, I thought.

Then I gasped. There on the wall behind the armchair, arranged in rows of threes and fours, each with a different idea of alignment, hung ten or twelve framed glossy photographs. Soldiers in black shirts bedecked with various insignia and tasseled fascist fezzes perched atop their heads. A casual observer might have been tempted to return the broad, beaming, straight-toothed smiles the men were brandishing like swords. They looked so satisfied, hale and hearty, heroic even. But I knew from the uniforms that these were bullies on the prowl, searching for any pretext to bash some heads. The *Camicie Nere*, also known as *squadristi*, were the all-volunteer paramilitary arm of the fascist party. They represented the most fanatic, dogmatic adherents of Mussolini's lictorian movement. Staring at their smug posturing, I felt sick. I wanted to tear the frames off the wall and smash them under foot. Of course, I couldn't do that, so I studied them more closely instead.

The lowest of the three rows of photographs was a collection of four portraits of a bald middle-aged man in full military regalia. I figured him to be sixty or sixty-five. He looked somehow familiar to me, though I couldn't see how. Then I remembered the photograph from the café. Was he one of the men? And who was he? Locanda's predecessor, I assumed. His wife's late husband?

That thought blunted some of my disgust at staying under the same roof with a person who celebrated fascists with a portrait gallery in his inner sanctum. I'd been raised to hate fascists and, indeed, taught there was no dirtier word than "fascist." But if these photographs had belonged to his wife's husband, then perhaps Locanda had no authority to remove them. Or did he have the authority and had simply chosen not to? Hadn't Bernie told me the *marchesa* refused to return to Italy after the war? Would she even know if he took down the offensive photos?

I mulled that over as I leaned closer to view the bald man's features. Then I heard a commotion coming from somewhere beyond the closed door of the library.

Stealing along the wall, I reached the door and cracked it open to listen for footsteps. No one seemed to be approaching the library, but there were three or four voices in the front hall. I heard two men, a woman, and what sounded like a young girl. A teen, perhaps. Another woman was weeping. I slipped out into the corridor, assumed as innocent a demeanor as I could muster, given my upset at having discovered the photos, and strode toward the source of the commotion.

As I emerged into the front hall, I spied five people. The first I recognized was Locanda, who, I'd assumed, was in Florence with Vicky to buy "a little something bright and shiny from Torrini's." But there he was, very much present in casual attire, and I realized how lucky I'd been that he hadn't surprised me again in his library. Behind Locanda, Achille stood awkwardly, surrounded by four large valises and a couple of vanity cases. Next to him was Berenice, who, I could see now, had been the person wailing. A second woman, her back to me, faced Locanda, whose fierce glare frightened me, never mind her. And in the middle of it all was a girl, also back to me. Outfitted in a plain cornflower-blue sailor dress, she stood with her light-brown hair drawn back into a simple *coda di cavallo*, ponytail. A leather camera case was strung over her shoulder.

Uninvited, I nevertheless intruded on the scene, circling around to see the two people I'd been unable to identify from behind. I was startled to discover the woman whose comforting arm was holding the girl to her side was none other than Teresa Ortega y Martín, Bondinelli's *donna di servizio*. She nodded subtlety, almost imperceptibly, to acknowledge me. The girl looked miserable. No more than fourteen or fifteen, she stood there gaping up at the stern man before her. Her eyes were clear, though her nose appeared red and chapped. Tall and gangling for her age, skinny, with an overbite, she wasn't quite pretty yet, but I was sure she would grow into her frame and might well wind up a statuesque beauty. I knew instantly that she had to be Bondinelli's daughter. He'd stood nearly six and a half feet tall, after all. And Teresa's presence at her side clinched the deal in my mind. But what I couldn't fathom was what she was doing at Bel Soggiorno. There was no connection between her and Massimiliano Locanda beyond the long-standing friendship between him and her father. Then I overheard the girl say two words that only deepened the mystery. Or perhaps shed light on it. "*Zio Max*."

CHAPTER SEVENTEEN

She'd called him Uncle Max. But how? Had she meant "uncle" as in a close family friend? Surely he wasn't her flesh and blood. Locanda would have mentioned it, wouldn't he have?

"What do you want, Signorina Stone?" he hissed at me once he became aware of my presence.

"I heard raised voices and weeping," I said. "I came to see if I could help."

Barely containing his prickly animus, he told me I wasn't needed. "Everything is in order."

"Why is Berenice crying?" I asked.

"*Povera bambina*," she answered, and her wailing started anew. "*Povera piccola Mariangela*."

I was confused. It was one thing for Locanda to know his late friend's daughter, who might well have called him "*zio*," as children are wont to do with close friends of their parents'. But how would Berenice have known this girl?

Before Locanda could dispatch me with a swift kick in the seat of my pants—and I was sure he was itching to do just that—footsteps descending the stairs drew his attention away. The *dormiglioni* were emerging with perfect timing, if inconveniencing and thoroughly annoying their host had been their goal.

Locanda was fuming now. He turned his attention back to the girl just as Lucio, Giuliana, and Tato reached the ground floor.

"Mariangela, go with Berenice. She will show you to your room. I'll come to see you as soon as I finish some important business."

"What about Teresa?" asked the girl. "I want her to stay with me."

Locanda ran a hand through his hair, and I had to wonder if he intended to rip the silvery mane out of his head. His house was already packed to the rafters with unwelcome guests, and now the inconvenient appearance of a young girl seemed to inspire a desire to give someone—anyone handy—a thorough drubbing. But with so many witnesses present, he couldn't very well wrap Achille in a half Nelson or strangle the life out of me. So his own head of hair suffered the brunt of his ire.

He drew a deep, restorative breath. "Everyone, please go about your business," he said in a softer voice.

Thanks to the liberal application of brilliantine, a couple of locks of his hair were left jutting out from his head at awkward angles, and I struggled to suppress a snicker. The look was quite clownish, at least until I realized he was aiming a murderous glare at me. I swallowed my mirth.

"Signora Teresa, please go with Mariangela to her room. Berenice will make up a bed for you in the servants' quarters."

On a silent signal from Locanda, Achille gathered up the luggage and lumbered off behind the women and the girl. Lucio, Giuliana, and Tato averted their eyes and wandered off toward the back *terrazza*. I wanted to follow, but not before having a word with Locanda.

"I am busy," he said in English, dismissing me with a wave of his hand. I scurried after him. "This won't take long," I said.

He reeled around to confront me, and I nearly ran into him in my haste. His eyes, wild and piercing, stopped me in my tracks. I took a step back and summoned my nerve.

"I need to talk to you about what I saw in your study last night."

He stewed as he weighed my words, staring me down for a good ten seconds. Then he nodded curtly and set off down the hallway. After a few steps, he realized I hadn't moved. Stopping yet again, he turned and motioned to me with a jerk of his head.

"*Viene o no?*"

Shifting into gear, I followed him down the corridor. When he reached the library door, he shoved it open and entered with no thought of ceding the way to the lady.

"*Si sieda,*" he told me once we were inside, indicating a chair before his desk. I gulped, feeling like a truant schoolgirl hauled up before the principal. We both took a seat. "Now tell me what this is about."

"I'm leaving," I said.

"*Come?*"

"I said I'm leaving Bel Soggiorno immediately. I cannot in good conscience stay in this house."

His anger seemed to dissipate. "Of course," he said. "Once Achille has settled our new guests into their rooms, I'll have him drive you back to town."

"Thank you," I said, dissatisfied with his reaction. I waited.

"Is that all?"

I answered reluctantly that, yes, that was all.

He nodded and rose from his seat behind the desk. And then he paused. Though he'd done his best to hide it, he was as interested in hearing my reasons for leaving as I was in telling him. "Did you say that you saw something in this room last night?"

"I did. And I'll be happy to share my reasons for leaving with you if you'll answer one question for me."

He settled back into his seat and tented his fingers under his chin. "I am happy to answer your questions whether you tell me why you've decided to leave or not."

He was trying to play it cool, but I was convinced he was curious. Still, I could use his arrogance to my advantage if he wanted to play it that way.

"That girl," I began. "Mariangela. She's Professor Bondinelli's daughter, isn't she?"

He nodded.

"Poor thing. She must be devastated."

"She's holding up well. Is that your question?"

I fidgeted. He projected a strong suggestion of menace in all his interactions, even when he was the one being questioned, but he was even more intimidating when engaged in a one-to-one chess match, which, I was sure, was what was happening at that moment. He made a game out of normal conversation, as if there were points to be won by gaining the upper hand or divulging as little information as possible, even if it were as innocuous as the existence of a fourteen-year-old niece. So, if he was bent on keeping his mouth shut, I was forced to ask him.

"No, that's not my question," I said. "The girl, Mariangela. What is your relationship to her?"

He knitted his brow. "It's not really any of your affair, but she is my niece. My sister's daughter."

"Then Professor Bondinelli was your ... brother-in-law?"

"*Mio cognato, sì.*"

Why, I asked myself. Why had he hidden that detail from me? From anyone? What difference did it make if Bondinelli had been married to his late sister? It didn't appear there'd been a falling out. By all accounts, the two men had still been chummy when the professor died. And I'd had a substantial conversation with Locanda that very morning about his late friend's—his late brother-in-law's—life, and he hadn't seen fit to mention that Bondinelli had been married to his sister.

"You're wondering why I didn't divulge that Alberto was my brother-in-law," he said.

"Of course I am. Why were you hiding it?"

He frowned. "I wasn't hiding anything. It wasn't important. I had no intention of meeting any of you people here this weekend. I was supposed to be in Switzerland, after all."

"But . . ." I began then fell silent. I didn't know what to say.

"My sister, Silvana, was married to Alberto. She died seven years ago."

"I'm sorry."

He offered a fatalistic shrug, then continued. "I wasn't expecting the girl here today. She was at school in England. I knew she was coming back to Florence, of course. There's the funeral to arrange, after all. But I thought she would go to her home in the city."

"You weren't expecting her?" I asked. "You're her only living relative."

"That Spanish woman, Teresa," he said, ignoring my question. "It was her idea to bring the girl here."

"Are you not close to your niece?"

"I have little in common with a fourteen-year-old girl."

A girl of twenty-two—thirty-eight percent his age—was another matter, I wanted to say, but kept that to myself. Instead I sat in silence, trying to figure out this odd, standoffish man. For his part, he seemed content to wait for me to pick up the ball. At length I complied.

"Max," I began, though it pained me to use his first name, "I'm struggling to understand all this. First, you kept secret the fact that Alberto Bondinelli was your brother-in-law. And, by extension, you hid the fact that his daughter was your niece. Then you say you aren't close to her, a fourteen-year-old girl. An orphan. Have you no heart? Don't you care about her? About your friend Alberto?"

He pondered my question for a long moment, rocking absently in his chair. "No," he said finally. "No, I suppose I don't have a heart. I certainly don't wish them any harm, but I don't really care about them either."

"How?" I asked, the horror surely visible on my face. "How is that possible? She's just a girl with no one in the world."

Locanda swiveled his chair to face his desk directly. He straightened some pens and letters, and shook his head.

"I don't know how, signorina. Frankly, I wish I cared, but I don't. I've always been this way."

I gaped at him, noticing for the first time his blue eyes. He stared back at me, emotionless, cold, terrifying.

"You have no convictions? There's nothing you love?"

"I care for my comfort. My enjoyment. Nothing more."

His answers only convinced me that my sudden decision to leave Bel Soggiorno was the correct one. This man had no goodness in him, and I did not want his hospitality. First, I thought, I would find Bernie and drag him away with me. I was confident Giuliana would follow us, too, and, if she left, Tato wouldn't be far behind. As for the others, they could do as they pleased, but I was decided. I considered Locanda lucky that I didn't slap his face before I left.

"You are judging me harshly," he said. "But before you leave with your mind set against me, I ask you to consider this. I do not choose to feel this way. It's how I have always been. Since my earliest memories. The sadness of others has never moved me. I was indifferent to the death of my parents. I wanted to feel something. Or, at least I thought I should. But there was nothing. It intrigued me. For years I asked myself why. I spoke to a priest about it once when I was a boy. He gave me some ridiculous penance to perform and assured me I would see the light. But I didn't."

I wondered how he'd felt about his sister's death. He hadn't mentioned her. But I didn't know how to ask him that. Didn't want to ask him. Was it possible to be indifferent toward the world? No pity or compassion for others? No love or hatred either? I just couldn't fathom it. And his trove of fascist photographs led me to believe he'd once believed in something. Something horrible. And perhaps that he was nostalgic for it now.

Unless the photographs weren't his at all. Yes, I had decided to go, but I hated leaving questions unanswered. I could not abide unwashed dishes in the sink, a sloppily made bed, or newspapers strewn willy-nilly on the floor. Unfinished crossword puzzles drove me mad until I filled in the blanks. And so, though I'd decided to leave Bel Soggiorno and forget the soulless wretch of a man who roamed its halls, I wanted to know about his past sympathies. His feelings about the thugs who'd bullied their way to power, stripped citizenship and rights from the Jews of Italy, and led the country into a cowardly and disastrous war against the democracies of the world. So I asked him.

"Last night, before you surprised Bernie and me in here," I began with a voice hoarser than I'd expected. "Last night I saw something in here that upset me."

He frowned. "You didn't appear to be upset when I found you in here. Quite the contrary."

As I was already lying about the timeline of when I'd become perturbed, I sidestepped his observation.

"The photographs on the wall over there," I said instead, indicating them with a nod. "The ones behind the chair."

He turned his head to the right and focused on the wall of the nook. "What about them?"

"Why do you display them? Are those pictures of your wife's late husband? Or are you a fascist yourself?"

He seemed confused by my question, never mind by my barely concealed disgust.

"My wife's late husband?" he asked. "What nonsense are you saying? Are you unwell? Why would I have his photographs in my house?"

"Because this was his house. You married his widow, didn't you?"

Now he laughed. The first time I'd seen him laugh. He muttered something I couldn't make out, then addressed me with all the haughty indignation he could muster.

"I don't know where you got such an idea, but this is my house, Signorina Stone. It was my father's house before me, and his before him. And since I have no children and no other close relatives, it will pass to Mariangela when I die. She is my sole heir."

Damn Bernie and his specious gossip. I surely blushed. But, just as soon, I regained my composure. The history of Bel Soggiorno's ownership only proved I'd been right to judge Locanda.

"Then those are your photographs?" I asked to accuse. "The ones of the *Camicie Nere*?"

"If you put it that way, yes, I suppose they belong to me." He paused to consider the pictures again. "That is to say, they belonged to my father. He hung them there, and I never thought to remove them."

"But why wouldn't you take them down? After the war and the defeat? Why would you keep them there?"

"Because, as I've just said, I didn't think of it. I didn't care either way. I still don't care. *Che importanza hanno queste cose?* It's history. I live in the present."

We sat in silence for a short time, long enough for Locanda to fish a cigarette from his vest pocket and light up.

"Is that why you want to leave Bel Soggiorno?" he asked, his face mostly obscured by the curtain of blue cigarette smoke, irradiated by the sunlight behind him in the window.

"Yes. I was raised to care about such things. In my home, 'fascist,' '*Camicie Nere*,' 'Nazi,' and '*Braunhemden*' were foul words. *Parolacce*. We were taught to spit after we said them."

Locanda scoffed. "In my home they were paeans, worthy of anthems and hymns. We were raised in different eras, different countries, and different realities, you and I. You were a little Jewish girl in America with an assumed, Anglicized name. I was the scion of an industrialist. An authoritarian, a fascist ideologue."

"And that's why I must leave."

"Do as you please, but I don't understand your haste. You say you discovered the photographs last night in this room. At the time, your emotional turmoil seemed amorous, not ethical. So, if your conscience is so decided against staying in this house, why didn't you leave last night? Or this morning?"

His lingering, inquisitive stare triggered no small measure of paranoia in my mind. Was he on to me? Did he know I'd been snooping in the room again? But if he thought he was dealing with a faint-of-heart panicker, he was mistaken. I knew just how to wriggle out of this tight spot and drive him to distraction at the same time.

"You're right," I said, smoothing my skirt over my knees. "I didn't notice the photographs last night."

He smiled in triumph. "Then you admit you returned here to look through my belongings this morning?"

"No," I said, my chin jutting out in feigned defiance. "I returned here to retrieve an article of clothing I lost in my haste last night."

The smile vanished. The cigarette he'd pinched between his lips for dramatic effect—a stab at intimidation or something of the sort—dipped like a pump jack. Only it didn't rise again. A bit of ash dropped into his lap, and, once he'd recovered from the shock at my shameless confession, he leapt to his feet and furiously brushed off his trousers.

His devotion to hedonism notwithstanding, Locanda was scandalized by and uncomfortable with the detour our conversation had taken. Still he managed to ask in a halting voice if I'd recovered what I'd lost.

"The strange thing is that I couldn't find it," I said. "I looked everywhere."

He cleared his throat and retook his seat. "You were standing over there when I came in last night. Is it possible you lost it under the little table near the door?"

"Under where?" I asked, switching to English.

Right over his head. Despite his excellent English, my last salvo was perhaps a word too far. He never caught on. But I fancied I'd lit the fuse to his lust. His gaze ranged up and down my person in a manner it hadn't done heretofore. Not even when he'd suggested I swim in the stream *in puris naturalibus*. Still, he wasn't ready to proposition me.

"I'm sure someone will find the article of clothing eventually," he said, and stubbed out the cigarette he'd been smoking. "Are you truly decided on leaving?"

"I don't see how I could justify it to my conscience if I stayed."

"Do as you wish, signorina, but I am not a fascist. I never was. I performed my patriotic duty during the war and served in East Africa."

I was intrigued, even as I scolded myself for listening to him.

"What did you do in the war?" I asked.

"I flew biplanes," he said with touch of red in his cheeks. "I was a trainer."

"The Air Force?"

"Yes. The *Regia Aeronautica*."

"Biplanes? Really?"

"That's what we had. And they weren't so bad. I was stationed in Ethiopia. We did all right at first. We had air superiority and good airfields. But then we ran out of fuel, and the British eventually got around to destroying nearly every craft we had. Within three months, we'd lost nearly half of our fleet. And eight months later, our last plane was destroyed."

He uttered a sad laugh. "Imagine an Air Force without aeroplanes. We surrendered. Best thing that could have happened to me."

"You didn't fight to the last man?"

"No," he said as if that weren't obvious. "I told you I had little passion for fascism. I was happy to lay down my arms and survive. And I learned English. Jolly well, too." He added the last bit in English. Not quite up to BBC standards, but it wasn't half bad.

I pursed my lips and drew a sigh through my nose. His arguments were persuasive, but thoughts of my father and the rigid principles he and my like-minded mother had instilled in Elijah and me tugged at my sleeve. I could no more enjoy the hospitality of a man who lived in a villa housing a fascist shrine than I could play center for the New York Knickerbockers. It was a physical impossibility, even in light of Locanda's defense of his own beliefs or—more accurately—lack thereof. His argument had softened my opinion of him, though I hated to admit that to myself. Why should I condone the moral bankruptcy of a man who refused to take a stand against an ideology that had oppressed its own people, including its Jews, revoked their citizenship, and legislated out of existence their rights to live and work in society? And then, for good measure, helped their Nazi overlords deport ten thousand of them to death camps in the East? How was I supposed to break bread with a man who felt no revulsion at a movement whose atrocities included the "Pacification" of Libya? Or the mustard gas and concentration camps of the Second Italo-Ethiopian war? And, of course, even as a young girl and in the years that followed, I remembered my father quoting our American president's famous speech decrying Mussolini's cowardly attack on France in her most desperate hour. "The hand that held the dagger has struck it into the back of its neighbor" became a lesson against perfidy and dishonor and fascism for my brother and me.

Max Locanda's experience was different from mine to be sure. He was a grown man in May of 1940. An aviator in the Italian Air Force. I was a four-year-old girl with an Anglicized Jewish name, as he'd pointed out apropos of nothing. But with the knowledge and first-hand experience, how could he stomach such photographs in his house? How could he look upon them every day without revulsion, or at least regret?

These were the immediate reasons for my departure. Another was the unsettling draw this man exercised on me. On others. On everyone, it seemed to me. No, I wasn't attracted to him in the same way I'd fallen for handsome men in the past. But his severe stare, the commanding presence, and piercing eyes provoked a vague worry in my mind. A worry that I might be susceptible to his powers of persuasion. Not necessarily sexual, but that was there as well. I just wanted to get away and never worry about ending up in his thrall.

"Shall I call Achille to pack your bags?" he asked, calling me back to the present.

CHAPTER EIGHTEEN

I checked my watch: half past noon. Achille had already lugged my bags down the stairs and was now resisting Bernie's efforts to take his own valise to the car. I waited as they wrestled for the honor. The prospect of a guest carrying his own luggage offended the porter, and Bernie—never more egalitarian and, indeed, self-sufficiently American than in that moment—felt it his duty to bear his own burdens. I made my way down the stairs, intending to say goodbye to the other guests. They'd gathered on the *terrazza* outside the *salone* to smoke and gossip about the new arrival at Bel Soggiorno. Lunch was an hour away still. I greeted them from the doorway.

"Why do you have your purse?" asked Lucio. "Going somewhere?"

"*Me ne vado*," I said. "I've come to say goodbye."

"Why are you leaving? We're all enjoying a nice retreat from the modern world. You must stay."

I lied that I had previous commitments on my itinerary that I couldn't avoid. We sat and chatted for a while, exchanged addresses and assurances to stay in touch. Lucio promised he'd visit me in Nuova Olanda and we'd get married. Or at least have a torrid love affair. Tato and Franco stood to the side and listened and smiled. Giuliana, however, looked positively alarmed. She sat beside me and, once Lucio had gone to retrieve his cigarettes from a table across the *terrazza*, grabbed my hand and asked in a low voice if I was leaving Florence.

"Not for a few days," I said. "Bernie and I are going back to Albergo Bardi."

That seemed to satisfy her. She let go of my hand and drew a breath.

"I need to speak to you," she whispered. "I'll come see you at the hotel Monday when we get out of this prison."

"What is it? What do you want to tell me?" I asked, thinking Bel Soggiorno hardly qualified as a prison. It was idyllic, if you didn't count the fascist ghosts.

"Not here," she said, just as Bernie appeared in the doorway of the *salone*.

"Ready?" I asked him.

"There may be a delay," he said, and I caught sight of Locanda behind him. There were two more men beyond, inside the house.

"*Signore e signori, buongiorno*," announced the short, stocky man in a dark suit as he stepped outside. It was the police inspector, Peruzzi. He noticed Lucio in the corner of his eye. "Please, young man, put out that cigarette until I've finished. This won't take long."

Lucio complied, though not without a sigh of exasperation.

"Do you have news on Professor Bondinelli?" asked Franco, all serious and self-important, as if he were investigating the case along with Peruzzi.

"Nothing new," said the cop. "Except that we've released the body to the family. For the funeral."

Franco touched his forehead, an affected acknowledgement of what should have been obvious. "Of course, the girl. Has the funeral date been set?"

Peruzzi scowled. "Professor Sannino, please stop asking questions for a moment. I've come here to inform you all of an important if unfortunate development."

Franco blushed, swallowed his tongue, and kept all subsequent queries to himself. We all waited for the news. I looked to Locanda in the doorway to the house. His stare was focused on my person, by all appearances intent on boring a hole clear through me. His regard flustered me, and before I'd realized it, I touched my chest as if to shield myself. The man standing beside him was Pellegrini, the young doctor who'd visited Veronica the night before.

I turned back to Peruzzi and adjusted my seat in hopes of putting Giuliana between me and Locanda's eyes.

"I believe you met *Dottor* Pellegrini last night," resumed the inspector. "He examined the patient, Veronica Leonetti, and has now arrived at a diagnosis. Doctor?" he said, inviting Pellegrini to come forward.

"*Grazie, ispettore*," he said, stepping outside. He cleared his throat.

"*Oddio*," whispered Giuliana in my ear. "It must be bad news for Veronica."

"I have consulted with the police," said the doctor, "and given the gravity of the situation, we have decided to place this house under quarantine. At least for a couple of days, until we can be sure the contagion has been contained."

"What contagion?" I asked, risking Peruzzi's censure.

"*Rosolia*," said Pellegrini.

My Italian let me down. "*Rosolia*?" I asked. "What's that?"

The doctor had no idea how to translate, nor did Peruzzi. Everyone looked to Bernie.

"Rubella," he said. "German measles."

"What does that mean for us?" demanded Lucio.

Peruzzi repeated the good doctor's prescription: temporary quarantine. Lucio fairly shook with rage, or perhaps shock, and then he retrieved his stubbed-out cigarette from the ashtray and relit it.

"I'll smoke whether you like it or not," he told the cop. "Go ahead, arrest me. Your objections to smoking are not law."

Peruzzi rolled his eyes but said nothing.

"Quarantine?" I asked. "For everyone? Even the people who arrived an hour ago?"

"I'm afraid so," he said.

"Even for the people who were about to leave," said Locanda, again unsettling me with his gaze.

"Yes. No one is to leave the property. That means all of you and the staff and the girl and her guardian. The Spanish lady."

"*Dio mio*," said Franco. "She rode on my Vespa yesterday. She put her arms around my waist because she said I drove too fast. Am I going to be sick?"

Pellegrini mugged ignorance. "Perhaps," he said. "Unless you've already had *rosolia*. Have you already had *rosolia?*"

"*Non lo so*," said Franco in desperation.

"I had *rosolia* when I was seven," I said, aiming a glare at Locanda. Had I? I was fairly sure. "So may I leave?"

"Me too," said Bernie. "I was eight or nine."

Pellegrini nodded. "Of course, *signori*. If you can provide a certificate from your physician, you are free to leave."

My current physician was Fred Peruso, who was also a good pal and the county coroner back in New Holland. But I wasn't going to tell the young doctor that. "My family physician is in New York," I lied. "And he died fifteen years ago." That part was true, but I was aiming for an exemption, and I figured he might be swayed if I placed enough hurdles in the way of obtaining a certificate.

Bernie's prospects were equally unlikely. For one thing it was the weekend. For another we were four thousand miles from home. It would take at least a day or two to get confirmation from the US, and that was if he would accept a telegram or telex. In English. If he actually wanted a certificate, we'd need at least two weeks by mail to prove our cases.

And we weren't the only ones troubled by the sentence. Tato and Giuliana slumped in their chairs, looking miserable, and muttering what a disaster this was. Between puffs on his crooked cigarette, Lucio was spitting a geyser of new, more colorful *parolacce* under his breath. The object of his rancor was clearly the policeman, at least until he'd exhausted his bile. Then, turning to the doctor for new inspiration, he produced fresh oaths that, I had to admit, demanded respect for their remarkable creativity if not propriety. But he'd saved his best work for last: to wit, Veronica, the Typhoid Mary of our jolly throng. Had she been present and heard his words, she surely would have suffered a seizure and collapsed in a convulsive, insensate heap of self-soiling, thumb-sucking stupor. Good thing she was up in my room—now hers alone—enjoying a nap and snacking on the chocolates I'd intended to take home for my editor, Charlie Reese.

As we sat there on the *terrazza*, all wondering what the next few days or weeks held in store for us, Vicky strolled in from the garden.

Upon noticing the dour expressions on our faces, she asked in English what was going on. Locanda waved her over and explained quietly in her ear.

"What? I've got to stay here? With your boring friends?"

And, with that, Vicky supplanted Veronica at the top of Lucio's list of people he'd rather kick than kiss. She'd also ensured an empty seat on either side of her at dinner. Locanda told her rather rudely to go to her room.

"Here's what you can expect if you contract *rosolia*," said Pellegrini once Vicky had flown off on her broom. "The symptoms are often mild. But if they are not, you'll experience low-grade fever, rash, and itching. Headache, swollen glands, and general malaise are common. These will pass in a matter of three days. But as many as half of infected subjects suffer no symptoms at all. So don't worry and enjoy Signor Locanda's hospitality."

He paused. His face betrayed a niggling doubt. "That is don't worry unless you're a woman and you're pregnant. The risk of severe birth defects in the child is real." He thought some more. "And, of course, if you're an adult male, there's a remote chance of sterility. But aside from those complications, there's really little to worry about."

Lucio exploded. "*Sterilità*? *Porca Mad* . . . ! How will I give my *mamma nipotini*?" And just like that, Vicky was forgotten, and he heaped his invective onto Veronica once again.

Locanda had heard enough. He nudged the doctor to one side and urged everyone to calm down. "It's not certain that it's rubella," he said, much to the dismay of the young doctor. "My trusted friend *Dottor* Gherardi will settle all this in a couple of days. Wednesday at the latest. In the meantime, *calmatevi per dio*. Act like adults."

Cowed by the rebuke, the guests grumbled among themselves as Peruzzi and Pellegrini took their leave. When asked by Lucio why they were free to come and go, they'd both assured him they'd already had rubella. I asked Bernie as discreetly as I could if the police had the authority to quarantine us. He wasn't sure.

"I'm sure there are public heath statutes we could research," he said. "But that would involve going to a library in Florence. Or consulting a lawyer. And the police could keep us here for the investigation anyway, I suppose. Let's just enjoy the hospitality as the doctor said."

"I told you why I wanted out of this place, Bernie. Do you think I can just relax and pretend I didn't see what I saw?"

"Come on, El. He said it was his father's stuff. You can't expect everyone to share your values."

"I studied history at Barnard. Ten thousand Italian Jews were deported by the fascists and Nazis. Ten thousand, Bernie. You should be as outraged as I am."

He nodded. "Of course. But we have no choice at the moment. We're not condoning Locanda's politics. We're trapped here with the others."

I huffed. "Says you."

"*Il pranzo è servito*," announced Locanda.

Slowly, reluctantly, everyone wandered inside for the midday meal. Our host stood fast at the doorway, then addressed Bernie and me.

"I will have Achille take your bags back to your rooms," he said, almost as an apology.

"Put me in Veronica's old room on the top floor," I said coldly. "She can have mine."

CHAPTER NINETEEN

The table had been set for nine places. Veronica was absent, having requested her meal be served in my—scratch that—*her* room. She was milking this German measles thing for all it was worth. The others, still shaken, had already taken their seats. But there were still three empty chairs: one on Locanda's right and two at the end of the table. The pair of chairs in left field were for Bernie and me, I was sure. The empty place next to the host was earmarked for Mariangela, his fourteen-year-old niece.

We slipped into our seats, Locanda eying us as we did. Then the final guest entered the room. The girl, escorted by a watchful Teresa, shuffled to her spot next to her uncle without a word.

"*Grazie*, Teresa," said Locanda in a low voice. "You may have your meal in the kitchen. Berenice is expecting you."

"I want Teresa to stay," said the girl.

"That's not possible," answered Locanda, and the poor woman withdrew. Mariangela craned her neck to watch her go. Then she rose from her seat.

"Where are you going, Mariangela?"

"To the kitchen," she said. "I want to be with Teresa."

"*Siediti e non fare la sciocca.* You'll eat with us."

The girl bowed her head and retook her seat. I lost my appetite.

The first course was the *minestra*. Berenice had prepared a *tortellini in brodo*, which she doled out herself. At least she served Mariangela, cooing over her and petting her hair. The girl submitted to the fawning without a word. The rest of us passed the tureen around the table and helped ourselves. No one bothered to comfort us. Locanda's ill humor, coupled with Peruzzi's quarantine, had sucked the spirit out of our mealtime conversation. Gone were the repartee and bonhomie that had characterized our previous meals, replaced by a clinking of spoons against bowls and disjointed, uninspired banalities.

"*Ottimi*," said Franco with no real conviction as he chewed his tortellini.

"*Davvero*," concurred Tato.

"I heard the weather might cool down," added Bernie.

"Is there any salt?" asked Vicky.

"One doesn't add salt to Berenice's cooking," said Locanda a mite more sharply than the beauty was probably used to.

Not even pretending to show interest in her food, Mariangela sat motionless, eyes cast down toward her lap where she'd folded her hands. She looked miserable, poor thing, and I wanted to talk to her, listen to her sorrows, comfort her in some way. The indifference of her uncle's welcome was a cruel offering. No wonder she wanted Teresa.

I'd had enough.

"Mariangela, my name is Ellie," I said in English across the table. Everyone fell silent. Even the spoons ceased their mirthless tune. "I've been admiring your dress. It's quite pretty."

She was still wearing the simple blue sailor dress, so my compliment surely struck her as odd. In fact, what I really wanted to say to her was how sorry I was for her terrible loss. I wanted to wrap her in my arms and hug her and give her the barest minimum of compassion her uncaring uncle should have provided. That we were all seated at the dining table and hadn't been fittingly introduced—or at all—prevented me from offering proper condolences at that moment. So I complimented her on her dress instead.

"My frock?" she asked, lifting her gaze for a moment to see who'd spoken. Her English was perfect, with a prim little British finishing school accent. She thanked me then returned to the silent contemplation of her hands.

Locanda glared at me, clearly trying to communicate his displeasure with me. Too bad, I thought. He couldn't exactly send me away given the quarantine.

"I saw you have a camera case," I said to Mariangela. "Do you enjoy photography?"

More awkward silence from the others, and another disapproving look from Locanda. But the girl was intrigued.

"Yes," she said. "My father gave me a camera last year. I've been learning about film speed and exposures."

"My father gave me my camera, as well."

She seemed to be debating whether to proceed and ask a question. Finally she did. "What kind of camera?"

"A Leica M3. I got it for my eighteenth birthday. How about you?"

"An M3? That's a wonderful camera. Last year my father gave me a Braun Paxette. Nothing like yours. It's secondhand but in excellent repair."

"I'd love to see your Braun later if you don't mind. I'd be happy to show you mine. I have a new lens I've been wanting to try out, but I haven't had much of a chance yet."

"I'd love that," she said before catching her uncle's eye.

"I have some Kodachrome, too. I'd be happy to give you some if you're interested."

Her face lit up, surely for the first time since she'd received news of her father's death.

"I've never used Kodachrome before," she said. "It's very expensive."

"Mariangela has schoolwork to do," said Locanda, interrupting us. "And her father's funeral to prepare."

When the meal ended, I took advantage of Locanda's absence to approach the girl. I expressed my deepest sympathies and told her how sorry I was not to have met her father. She put on a brave face—no tears—and thanked me again. She seemed to want a break from the mourning, as she leaned in close and whispered that she'd really love to see my camera if I didn't mind.

"Are you free this afternoon?" I asked. "We can go for a walk through the grounds and take some photos."

Mariangela glanced over her shoulder toward the doorway and, seeing no uncles in the vicinity, turned back to me and nodded. "Four o'clock at the Diana statue."

The perils of sharing a bathroom with others should be obvious. Having to wait one's turn when it's least convenient to do so. And discovering exactly how much or little zeal your friends apply to their personal hygiene or, indeed, to the fixtures they use and leave behind for others to clean. And let's not even think about the hair.

I was emerging from the WC on the third floor, when Giuliana, looking dead serious and even more paranoid, found me. She steered me to my new room down the corridor and shut the door behind us.

"Are you going to tell me this time?" I asked once we were seated on the bed. "Or is this going to be more of your mysterious suggestions that you'll deny later on?"

"You must understand, Ellie, I'm in a difficult position. If I want to finish my *laurea*, I have to be careful. And what I'm going to tell you about Bondinelli is *una bomba*."

"I'm listening."

"You know I told you about his war record?" she began. "That he was with the partisans? Well, that's true. But there's more to it than that. I know for a fact that he was a member of the fascist party throughout the thirties. He joined the *Corpo Truppe Volontarie*, the *Dio lo Vuole* division."

"What's that?"

Giuliana pursed her lips impatiently. "The *Camicie Nere*. The worst of the fascists, willing to fight republicanism and socialism and communism in the service of *Il Duce*. Despicable beasts. Bondinelli even fought in Spain on the side of the Nationalists."

I thought of the photographs in Locanda's study and wondered if Bondinelli might have been in one or two of them. He was the son-in-law of the man who'd tacked them up on the wall, after all. I hadn't looked too closely at the men in the pictures, but then again I wasn't sure I'd be able to identify young Alberto Bondinelli anyway. Not only hadn't I met the man, I'd only ever seen one photograph of him, the small black-and-white picture Franco had shown me. All I knew was that he was quite tall, about six-five, had a prominent set of teeth, and wore a dyed beard that called to mind Lenin. Not much to go on. Still, I thought, a second examination of the Black Shirt photos in the study might be worth the effort. I wondered if Locanda would object.

"A lot of people were fascists back then, weren't they?" I asked Giuliana. "Even our host was in the Air Force."

"The *Camicie Nere* were different," she said with a sneer. "You had to be a particular type of *stronzo* to join the Black Shirts."

I asked Giuliana about her sources. I was a reporter, after all.

"You don't believe me?"

"I'm only trying to understand how he could have been a fascist—a Black Shirt—one day, then the next, he was a partisan fighting the Nazis."

Giuliana shook her head slowly and told me I was naïve.

"He was a fascist," she said. "If he joined the partisans it was to spy on them, don't you see? To betray them."

I must have looked incredulous when, in fact, I was horrified, because Giuliana asked if I wanted proof of her accusation.

"Of course I do. But what proof do you have?"

"A witness," she said. "A member of my own family. And just the other day I found newspaper clippings in the library. Articles and opinions written by Bondinelli for the university paper in the twenties, the *Goliardia Fascista*."

"Locanda told me he'd worked at a student newspaper at the university as well. I wonder if it was the same one."

"I wouldn't doubt it. He's just another oppressor like all the rest. And a decadent *borghese* living off the sweat of the working classes."

"And they were friends back then," I mused. "But who is this witness? Can I meet him?"

"Let me think about it."

"Just one question," I said. "This all happened twenty years ago. Longer, too. Why are you telling me this? What do you expect me to do about it now?"

She considered her answer carefully before responding. "You'll think this spiteful of me, but I want his reputation ruined. Not ruined, I misspoke. I want the truth about him to be known by all. Especially in the academic community."

"I still don't see how I can help you with that."

"The proceedings of the symposium are going to be published. Since you are the daughter of the man in whose honor the symposium was held, you can make sure Franco expunges Bondinelli's name from the record."

"You won't mind if Franco takes the credit? It would surely fall to him if Bondinelli's name is removed."

Before she could answer, a knock came at the door. I asked who was there, and Bernie called from the other side. Giuliana reached out and grabbed my arm before I could get up to open the door.

"Franco Sannino is DC," she said. "A Fanfani DC man, but he's no anti-Semite fascist like Fanfani was during the *Ventennio*. And he didn't betray any Italian Jews. At least not that I know."

CHAPTER TWENTY

O nce again, Bernie's timing was perfect. Giuliana still wasn't ready to trust him. Or perhaps one shared confidence was all she could permit herself. The result, at any rate, was the girl slipping away with a vague suggestion that we should talk again.

"What was that about?" asked Bernie after she'd gone.

"Just talking about this quarantine," I lied. Perhaps I'd tell him the truth later on, but Giuliana had asked me, albeit tacitly, to keep her information to myself. "It's terrible news for Veronica."

"Could be worse."

"How?"

Bernie shrugged. "She could be pregnant." A significant pause ensued. "She's not, of course. But that would be worse, I'm sure you'll agree."

"And what about the rest of us?" I asked.

"Are you pregnant, El?"

"Of course not. And I remind you that I've already had German measles. I was referring to being locked up here for several days more."

"And I thought you were lying about having had German measles."

"Why would I lie about that?"

He shrugged. "I don't know. To get out of this place."

His words gave me pause. I sat for a moment recalling something I'd seen in Locanda's desk.

"What is it?" he asked.

I set my jaw and frowned. "Do you know what GUF is?"

"Goof? As in a mistake?"

"No. GUF. In Italian. G-U-F. I found it on a pin of some kind in Locanda's desk."

"Jesus, El, were you snooping around again in his study?"

"Do I really need to answer that?" I asked. "There was an old enamel pin with the letters GUF and a fleur-de-lis. Come on, UNIVAC. Any ideas? Something French perhaps?"

Bernie shook his head. "No, don't be fooled by the fleur-de-lis. It's also a symbol of Florence. I suspect GUF was a collection of fascist student groups, The G and U might stand for *Gruppi Universitari*. And the F must be for Florence. Or maybe . . . *fascisti*."

"I see. Then Locanda was more of a fascist than he wanted me to believe."

"A couple of generations of Italians were brought up that way, El. It's hardly surprising that he was one of them."

"What about Bondinelli?" I asked.

"I thought his history was different. He was a partisan in the war, wasn't he?"

Giuliana's parting shot had left me thinking. She clearly had an ax to grind against her late professor. I wondered when exactly she'd come into possession of the information. Surely recently, otherwise she would have raised some kind of alarm earlier. Or would she have? Perhaps she felt proximity to him might provide an advantage, whether for revenge or blackmail or something more nefarious still. I caught myself. This was my first real suspicion that Bondinelli's drowning might have been something other than an accident.

I shook the thought from my mind. Giuliana was a zealot to be sure, but capable of murder? I didn't see it. For one thing, why would she share her damning information with me? That could only sow doubt in my mind. Why not just keep her mouth shut? She'd said she wanted the truth about Bondinelli's past to be known, but that was hardly reason enough to jeopardize your perfect crime.

No, I thought, blackening Bondinelli's name seemed as far as she wanted to go. It all felt petty to me. Or at least futile. I understood, of course, the passion that drove her to desire such an outcome, to punish someone she felt was a monster, but the stakes were so small. In the grand scheme of things, what difference did it make if Alberto Bondinelli's name graced the cover of a collection of scholarly papers that no one would read? I couldn't say, but it mattered to her. I wanted to ask her about it again. And to meet her so-called witness.

"How do you develop Kodachrome?" asked Mariangela as she wound the film I'd given her into her Paxette.

"You don't," I said. "It's not like Tri-X or even Ektachrome. Prints are one thing, transparencies are another. You need professional developers for Kodachrome."

"What's so great about it anyway?"

"I'm no expert, but I know it stores well. Preserves colors. And many professionals swear by the look. But they're transparencies. Not prints. It's fairly subjective, I suppose. Ektachrome can shoot a lot faster, if you're working with low light."

Camera loaded and ready, Mariangela crouched and focused on something in the scrub flora at the edge of the wood. She clicked three quick frames, rose to her full height, and told me she'd captured a small lizard. I congratulated her and said we'd get the roll developed right away.

"What about the quarantine?" she asked. "And the funeral? My uncle says we should do it Thursday or Friday."

My heart sank. She was doing her best to distract herself from the adult responsibilities that awaited her. What fourteen-year-old girl should be tasked with her own father's funeral arrangements?

"There's time to think of that later," I said. "Let's finish off that roll of film."

Mariangela wandered off away from the trees, camera at the ready, and proceeded to snap the occasional photograph of a dragonfly, a white pinecone, a far-off hill, and the sun sinking to the west.

"Here, let's try this," I said, pulling the 135mm Elmar lens from my bag. "See what you can do with some more magnification."

I helped her screw the lens onto her camera, and pushed her out of the nest. With new extended range, she finished the roll of Kodachrome in no time. The sun was low and throwing that magical, late-afternoon light across the land. I couldn't bear to watch her temporary respite from grief end, nor could I justify her missing the opportunity for such beautiful color slides, so I gave her another roll and told her to have a ball. She took her time now, concentrating on the golden hills and lonely farmhouses in the distance. Once she'd finished off the second roll, we both switched to Tri-X, just to see if we could manage the countryside in black-and-white.

"It's wonderful," she gushed. "Everything is so big and clear with this lens. I can't wait to see the slides."

"I'll take the film into Florence tomorrow and drop it off for processing. And before you ask about the quarantine, I've already had German measles. When I was young."

"But the policeman warned everyone to stay here. Besides, tomorrow is Sunday. The shops will be closed."

"Something is bound to be open near the Ponte Vecchio. For the tourists."

"It sounds risky. I saw a police car at the end of the drive. To make sure no one leaves."

"Have you had German measles?" I asked, deflecting her concerns. I intended to fly the coop and I didn't want any more attention than necessary.

Mariangela shook her head. "Chickenpox, but not German measles."

We sat in the grass, rewinding the last of our exposed film, polishing our lenses with tissues, and snapping our cameras back into their cases.

"Is it true that your father was . . . murdered?" she asked.

"Where did you hear that?"

"Teresa told me. She heard it from my father."

Not a topic I relished discussing, but since she'd lost her own father, I thought we might find some solace in our shared grief. "Yes, it's true."

"How did you manage? I mean, how did you deal with such a horrible thing?"

I looked off toward the southwest, where the sun was disappearing behind Bel Soggiorno, creating a glowing corona above the rooftop. It lasted barely thirty seconds, only long enough for the last slice of the sun to sink from sight. Then the aura vanished like a candle's doused flame, and the colors of the sky changed temperature in an instant. Once warm and red, they now radiated clear and blue, edging ever bluer with each passing moment. I glanced at my watch: just past six. There would be light for another hour behind the house and the hill it stood on, but Mariangela and I sat enveloped in the gathering gloom of day's end.

"It was sudden," I said. "He'd been in the hospital. In a coma. But I always assumed he'd come out of it. When he died I wasn't prepared. I felt guilt and shame."

My words were of little comfort to the girl. Realizing how selfish I was, I tacked in a different direction.

"It was hard, but it gets better. We have no choice but to mend. Nothing can replace our loved ones. We simply heal and carry on as best we can."

She bowed her head and nodded solemnly. I thought she was terrifically brave, especially for a fourteen-year-old.

"You must feel the same way," I continued. "Tell me about him. What kind of man was he?"

She lifted her head and blinked at me. "He was a strict father." She seemed to search for the right words. "Not soft, you know? He loved me, I suppose—no, I'm sure—but everything in life was duty and sacrifice for him. Even this camera he gave me. He said he wanted me to use it to learn from the world. To see the beauty and the ugliness through its lens."

"Did he dote on you? Was he affectionate?"

"No, that wasn't his way. As I said, he was a good man, but . . . proper. Like a headmaster. Or a priest."

Probably not one to dandle his daughter on his knee. Not so unusual, after all. He sounded somewhat correct and preachy, but wanting to instill values in his child. So he wasn't the warmest of men. At least he seemed a decent sort. Nothing like the portrait Giuliana had painted of the late professor. I recalled, too, Lucio's thinly veiled critique in the story he'd told the night before. And Locanda, dear old friend that he was, had informed us all of Bondinelli's theft of school books and other sins, including how he'd bullied his friends as a child.

"I know this is a sad time for you. You can come find me to talk whenever you like. About photography or your father or anything."

"It's strange," she said, fiddling with her camera. "My father was a serious man, but not harsh or mean. I never heard him shout or tell a joke or have a drink. A couple of sips of wine with dinner, and he added water to it at that. He made sure I had everything I needed in life, sent me to my wonderful school in England, but . . . but he never hugged me. Not like you'd expect anyway. Not like a dad. He was a father."

"It's all right, you know," she continued. "That he wasn't all loving and kissing with me. Sure, that might have been nice. But he was a good man. As if he had a higher purpose in life. More than being *babbo*."

I recognized some parallels between Bondinelli and my own father, though they were different enough. Mine, too, had been strict and principled, and could freeze you with his disapproval. But he could be tender and loving, something Alberto Bondinelli apparently was not.

"He was interested in making the world a better place," she said. "Spreading Christian values. That's a noble thing, isn't it? He believed in helping others. Everyone. Anyone, even strangers. Even non-Christians. He taught me to honor the poorest, least fortunate among us. As Jesus did."

I felt sorry for Mariangela. She was mature and clever beyond her years, able to weigh the pros and cons of her aloof father's qualities and accept the good for what it was worth. What she wasn't saying was that she wished a touch more of her father's love for God's children had been reserved for her.

"He sounds like a great man. We mustn't judge people too harshly for their emotional shortcomings."

"You sound like Teresa," she said with a weak smile. "She's always defending him, telling me he loves me dearly but it's not his way to make a show of it."

"Tell me about her," I said, walking straight through the door she'd opened. "She's Spanish, isn't she?"

"Yes, from Guadalajara. Not far from Madrid."

"How did your father meet her?"

"I think it was through a Catholic charity. My father devoted much of his time to good works."

"Father Fabrizio mentioned a charity for orphans in Spain."

"You've met Father Fabrizio?" she asked.

"I heard him deliver a eulogy for your father at the symposium two days ago. Why do you ask?"

She frowned. "No reason. He's my father's priest. His confessor."

There was more to this. "He seemed like a nice old man. Is there something you don't like about him?"

"He's a priest. That's all."

"And you don't like priests?"

"I have nothing against them except when they try to push me into a confessional booth to share my most embarrassing personal secrets."

I wondered if Mariangela realized how much she had in common with her late father. She was a young rebel, pushing back against the control of her religion. Would she find her way back eventually to the Church, as did her father? Or, perhaps, without his steady hand, would she forge her own secular path?

Aware that I might have been crossing a line, I asked her if she was a practicing Catholic. She shook her head and said no.

"That's my father's world. Teresa's, too. Not mine. I don't believe in everything they preach. I'm not convinced all sins are wrong."

That sounded reasonable to me, but I hadn't been raised Catholic. Or even Christian. I lived my life according to my own moral code, which didn't always align neatly with the expectations of society. My landlady, for one, regularly registered her objections to my drinking. My "loose" behavior, she said, was its inevitable result.

"You shouldn't let those men get you tipsy," she'd once told me in her most supercilious tone. "Alcohol is a sedative, after all. The dentist gives you Novocain before he tells you to open wide. It's the same with men and alcohol, dear."

"Teresa's very loyal to your father," I said to Mariangela. "He must have been good to her."

"I suppose. They didn't speak often, other than to plan meals or the household budget. And church, of course. Teresa's one of those who never misses Mass, not on Monday or Wednesday or Sunday."

"Is she married?"

"A widow. Her husband died in the civil war."

Had he been on the Nationalist or Republican side? I calculated the odds in my head. Difficult to say, but if she was a seven-day-a-week communicant, I was putting my money on Nationalist. Not that it mattered. I was just curious.

"And she looks after you?"

Mariangela nodded. "She's been like a mother to me since *mamma* died. I love Teresa. She's my family."

The two of us lay back on the grass and contemplated the darkening sky and its ghostlike, nearly transparent moon as we listened to the squawking crow of a pheasant somewhere nearby. The temperature was dropping with the falling light, and I suggested we head back to the house.

"Just a little longer, Ellie," she said. "If you don't mind. I don't want to go back there yet."

I propped myself up on an elbow and regarded her. Unaware of my attention, she continued to stare at the sky, eyes wide and alert.

"She was very pretty, my mother," she announced.

"So I've heard. Do you have a photo of her?"

"No, but I can show you one tomorrow. My favorite one of her."

Another bout of cloud-gazing followed before I asked about her uncle. "Do you know him well?"

She shook her head back and forth in the grass but said nothing.

"I suppose he was close to your father."

"Not particularly," she said at length. "I don't see him often. That's why it was strange that he arranged for me to come here."

"*He* arranged?" I asked, recalling his claim that he hadn't been expecting Mariangela to show up.

"Yes. He phoned my headmistress and dictated all the details. The train tickets, Channel crossing, even a car to collect me at the station. He sent Teresa to take me to my father's office before bringing me here."

This all struck me as odd. Locanda had appeared put out when I'd come across him and Mariangela in the front hall of the house. Had he been upset by her arrival or the presence of others to witness the awkward reunion? He was something of a stick in the mud, after all.

"Why did he send you to your father's office at the university?" I asked.

She drew a sigh. "He said I should gather up what I wanted there and be done with it. There might not be time later on. He's always been organized that way."

"Did you find anything you wanted?"

Still flat on her back, she attempted a manner of shrug that looked more like shoulder-scratching against the ground. "Just a couple of photographs. One of my mum."

"What was she like?" I asked, hoping I wasn't coming on too strong.

Again the itchy shrug. "I barely remember her. I mean, of course, I remember her, but I was only six when she died, so my memories are more feelings than things. She was very pretty. She smelled nice. And she was gentle and loving. The opposite of my father."

A voice from behind startled us. "Who was the opposite of your father?"

CHAPTER
TWENTY-ONE

Mariangela and I pushed up off the ground, faced her uncle, and brushed the grass from our clothing. He smiled—after a fashion.

"You look as though you've seen a ghost," he said. "It's only me. Come back to the house. It's time for *aperitivi*. Mariangela, you will bathe and change for dinner."

We trudged back up the hill, through the trees, under the pergola, and across the *terrazza*. The others had gathered there, drinks already in their hands, but the alcohol clearly hadn't cast its spell yet. Long faces and silence all around. I felt bad for Bernie, who'd agreed to this weekend idyll only in exchange for my promise not to abandon him. And he looked abandoned. Sitting alone on the periphery of the group, he smoked a lonely cigarette and sipped something green from a small glass. His face lit up at the sight of me. And, strange to say, so did the faces of the others.

"*Urrà!*" shouted Lucio. "*Ecco, è tornata la Ellie!*"

I wasn't sure I deserved such a hearty welcome, but I accepted the accolades and backslaps with the good grace and magnanimity of a monarch. And as I did, Locanda led Mariangela into the house. I watched them disappear.

"What's going on?" I whispered to Bernie.

"The mood here is dismal," he said in an equally low voice. "In desperation, everyone started asking where you were. Just for something to talk about."

"Thanks, chum. I missed you, too."

He apologized, insisting that I was actually the life of the party.

"Can I get you a drink?" he asked.

"Sure. But I want to change first. Give me ten minutes."

The lavender soap I'd picked up at the Farmacia Santa Maria Novella provided a refreshing cleanse of my face and hands. I daubed on some lipstick, brushed my unruly hair, and changed my skirt and blouse. Ready to face cocktails and dinner, I climbed down the narrow steps to the second floor, then set off down the corridor toward the broad flight of stone stairs leading to the front hall below. I passed Veronica's room—my former room—and stopped in to see how she was faring.

I found her in bed, propped up against four pillows. A food tray with two dishes and a carafe of water sat balanced in her lap as she shoveled white rice into her face from a heaping bowl in her hand. The rich aroma of butter filled the room. She waved me in and invited me to sit on the edge of the bed.

Something looked different. Something felt different. I'm not the tallest girl on the team, but still, I found it odd that I actually had to give a little hop to reach the mattress. A glance across the room to my old bed solved the mystery. The pillows were gone, pressed into service to prop up Veronica in her bed. But that wasn't all she'd appropriated. My bed was missing its mattress as well, and I realized I was sitting on it at that very moment. She'd piled my mattress on top of hers.

"Are you feeling any better today?" I asked her as she spooned another mouthful of rice and butter into her mouth.

"*Non c'è male,*" she said once she'd swallowed and washed it down with a couple of gulps of water. "I still have this rash. And that oaf Achille knocked over my witch hazel when he brought me *uno spuntino* this afternoon. Broke the bottle. I yelled at him, but he's *sordo come una campana,* deaf as a bell. Now I have nothing to soothe the itch."

"You should be nice to him, poor man." I leaned in for a closer look. "The redness is fading. Maybe just some calamine. I have some in my room."

But she refused and kept on eating.

"No fever?" I asked. "Are your glands swollen? Do you have a headache?"

"*No, niente.* I feel fine except for the itch."

I told her I'd look in on her later that evening.

"Ellie," she called as I slid off the bed to the floor. "Ask Berenice to send up some *dolci. Panna cotta* or *torta della nonna.* And coffee would be nice."

A light rain had started to fall, so the gang came inside with their drinks. In the *salone*, I spent the cocktail hour filling in Bernie on my conversation with Mariangela. He thought it strange, but not necessarily significant, that Locanda had planned everything for his niece's return.

"And you probably misunderstood him when he told you he wasn't expecting her."

I fumed. "Bernie, I'm a trained reporter. But even if I weren't, I still know the difference between expecting and not expecting."

"Sorry," he said and offered to fetch me another drink.

I'd fixed my eyes on Lucio across the room. "Not just now. I want to ask Lucio about something."

"Padre Fabrizio?" asked Bernie.

"Exactly."

Lucio sat slouching on one of the divans, staring into space, a Campari soda in his hand. His guitar leaned against the wall behind him, and I fancied he was miffed no one was clamoring to hear him play. Compounding his sense of oblivion, I was sure, was the fact that he'd already taken his turn as storyteller the night before and there was likely no chance for a return to the spotlight. I thought I could use that to my advantage.

"*Salve, Lucio,*" I said, taking a seat next to him. He returned the greeting. "I enjoyed your story last night, *amore mio*. And your guitar playing."

That brought a grin to his lips. And he treated me to a long-winded explanation of where he'd poached the tale and how he really did know lots of songs on the guitar.

"But I'm a perfectionist. If the guitar is out of tune, I can't finish."

Then he fetched the instrument and launched into a new serenade to me, loud enough to silence all the other conversations taking place in the room.

"*Non dimenticar che t'ho voluto tanto bene,*" he began, practically pouring himself into my arms.

"I know this song," I said. He paused, somewhat miffed at the interruption. "Nat King Cole sang it, but half in English."

He picked up where he'd left off. "*Or di questo amor un sol ricordo t'appartiene . . .*"

Lucio was one of those men who, like small boys, can't contain their urge to entertain in social gatherings of any kind. They know they'd be better off reining in their enthusiasm, but the temptation to dominate the stage, sing a song, or play the clown, is just too great. The performance often ends in disappointment, if not disaster, and regret and tears are the result. Yet, at the slightest hint of an invitation to perform again, they dive in headfirst and repeat the cycle. Lucio knew, I was sure, that no one wanted to hear him sing just then, least of all me, but he was powerless to stop himself. Until Franco spoke up.

"Please, Lucio. *Basta* with the songs. We're not in the mood."

I decided to take control of our tête-à-tête when Lucio, burning red from Franco's censure, gulped down his enthusiasm with a Campari chaser.

"If you really love me, Lucio, you'll tell me something," I said in a low voice only he could hear. He liked the attention and the flirting. Recovering from the humiliation in an instant, he was almost ready to start singing again. I headed him off. "I want to know why you chose that story last night."

"*Boh*. It's a story I read in school. I thought it would be fun, especially to tease Giuliana a bit about politics."

"And maybe our host, too?"

He blinked slowly and raised his eyebrows, a not-so-subtle sign that I was welcome to my conclusion.

"And . . . Professor Bondinelli as well?"

His eyes popped open. "*Cosa?*"

"Your debt collector, Ruttonaccio. That was your little revenge on Bondinelli, wasn't it?"

Lucio's gaze darted across the room, first falling on Franco then Locanda. He whispered to me. Hissed might have been a more apt description. "Why would you say that?"

"Because you changed the name of the priest in the story."

"I can't talk about it here," he said. "Come to my room later."

I smirked at him. "I'm not that naïve. Let's step outside for a smoke instead. We can talk there."

We strolled to the far end of the *terrazza*, far from the open doors and the people inside. As the misty rain was still falling, we stood beneath the canopied pergola.

"Okay, so I made a little joke about Bondinelli. You shouldn't mention it. If Franco heard you, it could spell trouble for me."

"Don't worry," I said. "Your secret is safe with me. *Acqua in bocca* (mum's the word). But tell me why. Was Bondinelli really a horrible man with a saint's reputation?"

Lucio took my assurances of confidentiality to heart and, after another glance toward the *salone*, leaned in closer to me. We were nose to nose like a couple of lovers, but at least he felt safe to speak this way.

"He was my professor," he began. "But that doesn't mean I liked or respected him. Of course, those who didn't know him thought he was a saintly man, with all his charities and humble nature. He spent half his life on his knees in a church praying. That's what the public saw."

"But you knew the real Bondinelli?"

"Not at first. I never would have agreed to study under him if I'd known."

"What *do* you know?" I asked. "That he was a thief, a fornicator, blasphemer, a man who kicked dogs?"

Lucio frowned. "No, none of those things. That was just for fun in my story. But worse. He was a fascist."

"But many young men joined the fascists in those days, didn't they? Even Benedetto Croce was an early supporter of the fascist government." I remembered my father lecturing a colleague once about the great Italian philosopher's politics. Another of those useless pieces of information one acquires when growing up the daughter of an academic.

"But *il Croce* later saw the evil," insisted Lucio. The class clown also had a passionate side. "He changed his mind on the fascists in less than two years. Bondinelli took the opposite route. He was an anarchist who came to embrace the fascists as their power grew. He even married the daughter of a fascist industrialist. Did you know that? Did you hear that girl call him '*zio*' this morning?"

"Yes."

"Our charming host's father was a powerful supporter of Mussolini's in the early days. He used his riches to fund rallies, propaganda, and arms for the fascists. He was awarded the *Ordine dell'Aquila Romana* medal during the war. They didn't hand those out for good penmanship."

"Did you know any of that before this weekend? Or last week?" I asked.

"Of course not."

Then where had this information on Locanda's father come from?

When had Lucio had the time to do so much research? I asked him. At first he hemmed and hawed, then admitted he'd helped Giuliana with some digging at the library the previous Monday.

"Has she always hated Bondinelli?"

"No. That's a recent development. She was never particularly fond of him. She objected to his DC politics, of course, but nothing more. It was only last week that her attitude toward him changed."

"Did she tell you why?"

"No details. Just that she suspected he'd been a Black Shirt."

"Do you think Bondinelli committed crimes?" I asked. "Or was he just like so many others of his generation?"

"Have you heard of the *leggi razziali*?" he asked as he lit up a cigarette. "The racial laws of 1938?"

"*Sì, so qualcosa*," I said. "They denied citizenship to Jews. And the right to work."

"*Esatto*. Thousands and thousands of citizens lost their jobs, their property," he said in an angry whisper. Then he began counting the items on his fingers. "Their right to serve in public office, travel privileges, even marriage to Italians. The fascists expanded those laws as the years went on. They became more restrictive, more severe, and ended with the deportation to concentration camps. These were Italian citizens, Ellie. People whose families had lived here for centuries. They were a small number, a tiny part of Italian society, and well integrated. The fascists passed those laws against their own citizens to appease their racist Nazi allies in Germany. It was a disgrace for Italy and all Italians. I feel that shame even now."

"And Bondinelli? What was his connection to the racial laws?"

Lucio took a quick drag of his cigarette, then explained, smoke oozing from his mouth and nose as he spoke.

"Jews were not permitted to work in public education. No universities. Hundreds lost their positions here too, in Florence. And when those men were thrown out . . ." he tossed his cigarette aside, "others were ready to take their places."

"Are you saying Bondinelli got his job at the university because . . ."

Lucio nodded solemnly. "He took the position previously held by a Jew. And he's had that position ever since. Twenty-five years."

I asked Lucio why he cared so much. He wasn't a Jew, after all. He seemed baffled by my question, and explained that he was a Communist and a believer in the brotherhood of man. It was nothing personal about Bondinelli. Finally, he insisted, he cared because he was an Italian. Just as the deported Jews had been.

CHAPTER
TWENTY-TWO

While Locanda seemed to have adapted to, or at least accepted, the new reality of having his erstwhile secret niece in our midst, the others clearly felt uncomfortable after they'd witnessed his boorish behavior upon her arrival. They surely would have rather shared drinks with the Borgias than spend another awkward minute in his icy company. But that option was unavailable to us. We were stuck, trapped in a beautiful sixteenth-century villa on the outskirts of Fiesole, perched high above the city of Florence. Sentenced to wait out the quarantine, we had no choice but to enjoy the hospitality of a man who made us feel supremely unwelcome. Of course he was generous with his food and liquor, but a good host—even if he's a poor man with little to offer—never makes his guests feel uncomfortable.

For me, the quarantine had removed all impulses to avoid Locanda or, for that matter, to suffer his intimidation. I didn't want to be there, after all, and had informed him of my intentions to leave before the fateful diagnosis had been delivered. That fortuitous order of events gave me a certain moral high ground, at least to my mind, and it freed me from the discomfort the others were experiencing. They were guests of a boor while I was a prisoner.

As we were being seated for dinner, I caught Mariangela's eye and patted the chair on my left, a signal for her to sit with me. Her uncle frowned weakly, but said nothing. This wasn't a battle he wanted to fight. If I was willing to babysit his inconvenient niece, then so be it. He would devote his attention to Vicky, or to his wine and meat.

"Do you like music, Ellie?" Mariangela asked me over the antipasto, a sampler of *salumi*, olives, and cheeses.

"Of course," I said, then butchered the Shakespeare quote, "The man that hath no music . . . Is fit for treasons, stratagems, and spoils." I got the treasons, stratagems, and spoils, but the rest was a mess. Mariangela smiled.

"I like music, too. I've got the biggest crush on Paul McCartney."

"Paul . . . Sorry, who?"

"Paul McCartney. Don't you know the Beatles?"

"Beetles? I know the Crickets. Buddy Holly and the Crickets. Of course he died in a plane crash a couple of years ago."

"Not Beetles as in insect," she said with a giggle. "Beatles, B-E-A, not B-E-E. They're the coolest band in England. You have to crawl out from under your rock, Ellie."

I laughed. "Sorry."

"I can't decide which song is my favorite, 'Please Please Me' or 'She Loves You.'"

"It's a tough choice," I said.

"Oh, what am I saying? Of course my favorite is 'She Loves You.' It just came out last month."

"I'd love to hear it sometime."

"What kind of music do you listen to?" she asked, letting me off the hook.

"Mostly what people call classical music," I said. "My father drummed it into me from a young age."

"Some of it's all right, I suppose. We have music appreciation class at school."

"The important thing is to cherish music in some form or other. I know a man who once heard Mongolian horse herders playing some stringed instrument at a cultural exchange concert back in the thirties. He remembers it to this day as a thing of beauty. He said all authentic music is beautiful. Are the Beatles authentic?"

"Authentically dreamy. Who is this man?" she asked in a conspiratorial whisper. "A boyfriend of yours?"

The memory of a lost love tickled me, the way a stray finger grazes your neck and sets your skin atingle. It was a bittersweet memory. Perhaps more sweet-bitter. "No, not a boyfriend," I said. "His father, actually. I'll never forget how his eyes sparkled when he recalled that Mongolian music. Probably never heard it again."

"I don't know anything about that," she said. "But you should hear the Beatles. I brought two records back with me. If there's a record player here, we can listen together."

"I'll ask your uncle."

Her eyes grew. "You're not afraid of him? I am."

Before I could answer, Vicky broke the reigning silence among the others by inquiring in a strong voice when Max thought the quarantine would end. She wanted to go into town.

"My dear," he said with more indulgence than I thought him capable of, "do you know the origin of the word 'quarantine'?" (What were the odds?) "Quarantine derives from the word *quaranta*. Forty. Traditionally quarantines lasted forty days."

"Forty days?" she gasped. "That's impossible. I'll go crazy."

"Would a week be better?" he asked.

"Of course."

"Then let us say one week. At the most. I hope this will be resolved before that. My physician, *Dottor* Gherardi, is due back day after tomorrow. He will provide guidance then. *Nel frattempo . . .* how do you say that, *giovanotto?*" he asked Bernie.

"In the meantime," he answered, mouth full of the saltless bread Achille had laid out.

"*In the meantime,*" continued Locanda, now addressing all of us, "let us enjoy the good food and wine." He aimed his gaze at me. "And each other's company."

"Has anyone checked on Typhoid Mary today?" asked Vicky, and not out of any real concern for the sick girl.

Only Bernie and I got the reference, which meant that he had to explain Vicky's comment to the others. Strange how a bit of sarcasm, no matter how clever, loses all its humor when someone has to translate it, supply footnotes, and place it in historical context. But that was our Bernie, ever clueless about the patience and intellectual curiosity of others. Exactly like my father.

"I looked in on her before coming down for cocktails," I said. "She seems fine today, except for the rash. But even that looks better than yesterday. And she's eating like a horse."

"How long is the rash supposed to last?" asked Tato.

"Didn't the doctor say three days? For all the symptoms. Veronica first started scratching Wednesday, before we went to dinner at Cammillo. She wasn't feeling well. Bernie took her home in a taxi."

"So that's . . . *giovedì, venerdì, sabato,*" said Bernie, counting the days. "Three nights have passed since she first started itching. Seems right to me. Ellie, you said the rash was improving. That's consistent with rubella."

"Yes, but her fever was gone yesterday, if it ever was a fever. She might just have got some sunburn on Franco's Vespa. And she never had swollen glands or a headache. Does that make a difference? Does one always have all the symptoms?"

No one was sure.

"The boy doctor said symptoms can be mild," offered Lucio.

"I, for one, am worried about this *rosolia*," said Franco. "Remember she was on the back of my Vespa. I'm not sure I've caught it, but I've been itching all day. Ever since that doctor told us."

"Do you have a rash?" asked Locanda, joining the conversation. His tone dripped with impatience.

Franco had to admit he did not. "No rash, but I feel like scratching, especially when everyone is talking about it."

"*Psicosomatico*," said Locanda. "Fever? Headache? *Ghiandole gonfie?* Swollen glands?"

"*No, niente.* I feel fine. It's a nervous itch, I suppose."

"Anyone else?" he asked the others. "Does anyone have a rash?

The response was a unanimous no.

"*Bene.* Then I suggest you enjoy your meal and wait for *Dottor* Gherardi's return. And if it turns out to be rubella, just be glad the symptoms are usually mild."

Still, concern hung in the air. Heads bowed and forks clinked as the diners resumed their meals. I tried to gauge the worry on each guest's face. While no stroll in the park for grown men, German measles was known to cause devastating side effects in unborn children. I figured it was unlikely that any of us was pregnant. But if one of the four young women in the house were, or even suspected as much, the concern would show on her face.

I studied them one by one and concluded that Vicky was in the clear. She frowned, all right, but also yawned and made no attempts to conceal her boredom. Whether she'd already had the German measles or she knew for sure that she wasn't pregnant, I couldn't say.

That was not the case for Giuliana. Her demeanor was too cloudy. She might well have been twisting herself into knots at the prospect of carrying a child who, in all likelihood, would be born with serious birth defects. But in fairness, I had to admit that she'd worn the same dark expression even before anyone suspected a rubella outbreak.

And, of course, it was ridiculous to think Mariangela might be pregnant. She was in love with some singer named Paul McCartney, but I doubted the two had even been in the same city, let alone had the opportunity to meet and conceive a child together.

I certainly wasn't pregnant, which only left Veronica herself. And while she certainly was eating enough for two, I wasn't buying that she was with child. Her strong religious beliefs, for one thing, and her *winning* personality, for another, rather reduced the odds.

Relatively certain that none of the women in the house was pregnant, I turned my attention to the men. Locanda clearly had no concerns. He'd probably contracted German measles at some point over the years. Bernie had stated he'd had rubella when he was a boy. Franco was worried, but he struck me as a hypochondriac. Lucio wasn't sure if he'd ever had the disease, nor was Tato. And *Dottor* Pellegrini had said the risk of sterility in adult men was slight, so perhaps they could rest easy. A rash and a little discomfort might not be the worst bargain in exchange for a brief vacation in a lovely villa.

The first course arrived on the rough but steady hands of Achille. He distributed the noodles, which, that night, were *maltagliati* in a Bolognese sauce. As was the case with every dish Berenice prepared, the macaroni was delicious and perfectly cooked.

The mood brightened as the wine flowed. A simple Chianti, but what could be more authentic in Tuscany? Franco led the charge on the wine, and I resolved to keep an eye on him. I'd already witnessed his fresh behavior when he'd had too much. Even Locanda seemed to be making an effort to be cordial. He engaged Giuliana, of all people, in a civilized discussion of the finer points of olive cultivation. Giuliana's grandfather, who'd owned a small machinery business, once manufactured olive and grape presses for local cultivators. I wondered if Locanda remembered that he'd met her once with Bondinelli. Her beautiful face was not one easily forgotten. Nor was her Jewish name.

"Perhaps I know the company," he said. "We bought a lot of presses over the years."

"The company was Dalla Torre Fratelli," she answered. "It was my mother's father and his two brothers."

Locanda's mien darkened, as if he was sweeping the corners of his memory to find his bearings. Or was he? "I remember the name," he said. "They went out of business. Didn't they have sons to carry on?"

Giuliana stiffened in her chair. "They . . . lost the business," she said. "In 1938."

Locanda understood. Lucio, I noticed, was listening in as well. To his credit, our host expressed his sympathies for what had happened to her family, indeed to all those who lost their rights. I couldn't say if he meant it. After all, he had told me that very morning that he simply didn't care, was indifferent to the suffering of others.

If nothing else, Massimiliano Locanda was smooth when he decided to make the effort. Without batting an eye, he turned the subject to John XXIII, who'd died in June. The late pope's record of protecting Jews and refugees across much of Eastern Europe during the war met and exceeded Giuliana's standards for approval. She praised John as a fine man of conscience, even if he was the leader of the richest religious sect in the world. She didn't exactly utter the old familiar opium-of-the-masses line, but we all knew where she stood on that score. Still, I thought Locanda had won a small measure of appreciation from the dogmatic Giuliana simply by bringing up the pontiff's name.

After dinner, we repaired to the *salone* as we had the night before. This time, however, I neither visited Locanda's study nor did I throw myself at my friend Bernie. Instead I stuck close to Mariangela who, at her uncle's insistence, was not permitted the company of her beloved Teresa in social situations.

Sitting together on one of the divans, we chatted at leisure. I watched Franco filling a king-size portion of brandy into a snifter across the room. Should I say something to him? To our host? Locanda was in his own world, languid in his chair, staring at nothing in particular.

"Ellie," said Mariangela, calling me back. "Tell me about your job at the newspaper."

I tried to make it sound more interesting than writing articles about spelling bee champions and the city's pothole patrol. In fact, I'd investigated a few high-profile murders in the preceding three years in the small burgh of New Holland, New York. Unsure of how much detail to give to an impressionable girl of fourteen, I left out the gory details and salacious behavior of the people who committed such terrible crimes. We talked cameras instead. I told her again how I'd received my Leica M3 as a gift for my eighteenth birthday, omitting the crushing codicil my father had tacked on to the gesture, effectively spoiling what had started as a precious moment. I believe his exact words were, "My hope is that you'll spend more time with this camera than you do with the bottle."

Once all takers had filled their glasses, Lucio pulled out his guitar, and the groans commenced straightaway. Mariangela asked if he knew any songs by the Beatles, but Lucio was as square as I was. So he began his usual picking and strumming that ended up dying on the vine before a true song could mature. Then, slurring his words as he did, Franco reminded us all that it was the storytelling hour. I thought back to the night before, trying to recall if Lucio had used any profanities that might offend the sensibilities of a young lady such as Mariangela. No dirty language per se, but he'd talked about fornication, and his story might be interpreted by some—perhaps most—as blasphemous. Still, following my conversation with Mariangela that afternoon, I figured she was mature enough to handle it. The decision, of course, was not mine to make.

Locanda, in fact, took that moment to inform the girl that it was time for her to go to bed. There was no argument, no pleading for a stay of execution, no whining. She stood, bade goodnight to all, then bent down to kiss me on both cheeks.

"*A domani, Ellie*," she said, speaking Italian to me for the first time. How I envied her perfect bilingualism.

CHAPTER
TWENTY-THREE

"Whose turn is it tonight?" asked Franco.

"*Tocca a me*," announced Giuliana firmly. "My turn."

Vicky rolled her eyes and announced she was tired and turning in for the night. Bernie slipped into the seat next to me on the divan just as Tato sprang to his feet and offered to replenish everyone's glasses. Giuliana shook her head in reproach.

"I just want to help," he said.

"Help, yes. But don't act like a servant."

Once everyone had a fresh drink, Giuliana settled into an armchair and smoothed her cotton skirt over her knees. She cleared her throat and drew a breath. Then Lucio interrupted, asking if she would mind if he accompanied her on the guitar.

"Do what you want," she said to dismiss him and began. "Inspired by Lucio's clever tale last night, I've decided to follow his example. I will recount a story that hides some meaning—I trust—skillfully and in a most pleasant manner to afford you all enjoyment. So, to begin . . . In Paris there once lived a rich Jew."

Even if no one groaned, I sensed some irritation from Franco Sannino and possibly Locanda at her fixation for Jewish topics. I saw no signs of exasperation on the faces of the others.

"Boccaccio again," Bernie whispered in my ear. "This should be interesting."

"Abraham was an honest merchant and a good and moral man of fine standing," continued Giuliana. Lucio plucked an air that I instantly recognized as Mahler's Titan Symphony, third movement, the Jewish-sounding theme. A jaunty bit that you can't help but want to dance to. "He was respected throughout the city and counted as his closest friend a man named Giannotto, a trader who prided himself as a devout and righteous Christian."

I can't fathom how he managed it, but Lucio produced a phrase from his guitar that called to mind a fugue or, perhaps, church organ. His guitar-playing talent took a backseat only to his zeal for guitar-tuning. If he ever succeeded in tightening the strings just right, he might set the world on its ear and play Carnegie Hall. Or perhaps be the Victor Borge of the guitar if only he could finish tuning the damn thing.

Giuliana pressed on. "One fine day, Giannotto called Abraham to his home to confess a fear. The good Christian's greatest worry was that Abraham, upstanding man though he was, would be damned to the eternal flames of hell if he did not accept Christ as his one and only God. Touched by his friend's concern, the Jew nevertheless pointed out with alacrity that Christians believed their God was a trinity, incorporating the Father, Son, and Holy Spirit. Giannotto, while vexed by this correction—and from a Jew no less—indulged his friend and suggested that he maintain an open mind and investigate the merits of Christianity. Over the course of the ensuing months, Giannotto and Abraham debated the finer points of the world's three great religions, always with the Christian extolling the virtues and truths of what he maintained was the one true faith. Finally, the Jew announced to his dear friend that he would consider converting to Christianity, but only once he'd completed a trip to Rome, where he intended to seek an audience with the pope himself. If, he told Giannotto, the pontiff could convince him of the superiority of the Christian faith, he—Abraham—would gladly accept Christ as his savior and embrace the Christian way.

"Now this plan greatly worried Giannotto. He knew only too well of the wicked indulgences and sinful behavior of the pontiff and his cardinals, and realized his friend would never choose the Christian path if he were to base his decision on the behavior of the Vicar of Christ and his court in Rome. Indeed, Giannotto was convinced that were his friend already a Christian, he would most assuredly reject the faith and convert to barbaric idolatry—or worse, godlessness—after witnessing the depravity of the highest officials of the Church. Accordingly, Giannotto endeavored to discourage Abraham from ever embarking on such a pilgrimage. He reasoned that the journey was long and dangerous, with brigands and highwaymen lying in wait to rob and cut the throats of prosperous travelers such as he. Instead, he urged his friend to stay in Paris where he—Giannotto—would resolve all his doubts and demonstrate the superiority of the Christian religion."

Bernie whispered in my ear again. He pronounced himself impressed that Giuliana had so far stuck to the script Boccaccio had penned centuries before.

"I was sure she'd turn this into an October Revolution, or something similar," he said.

Giuliana continued her tale. "But no matter Giannotto's rhetorical skill, Abraham would not be swayed by his friend's arguments. And so, in good time, he set off for Rome to seek out the pope and his prelates in order to find the true essence of Christianity and decide if it was deserving of his conversion.

"Upon his arrival at the Vatican, however, Abraham observed behavior so sinful and vainglorious that he nearly abandoned his quest. Indeed, each act performed, every enterprise undertaken by the Vicar of Christ and his cardinals seemed to defy all the tenets and prescriptions of the Christian faith, at least as far as Abraham understood them. If there were seven deadly sins, these princes of the Church committed them all at least thrice daily. They practiced simony, engaged in fornication and sodomy, indulged their gluttonous appetites, and drained more wine barrels than the most dissolute drunkards Abraham had ever observed in the taverns of the darkest quarters of Paris."

"This is a pretty damning portrait of the Church," I whispered into Bernie's ear. "Is she still following Boccaccio's story?"

"To the letter," he said. "I'm surprised. Looks as if she's going to bring it home properly."

Giuliana geared up for the finish. She took a sip of her wine. Lucio strummed away.

"So horrified was this Jew of Paris," she began, "so convinced was he that these charlatans were undeserving of the title of holy men, be they Christian, Jew, or Mohammedan, that he instantly determined that all religion and all gods were false and instruments of oppression of the people."

"Uh-oh," said Bernie. "Here it comes."

"So filled with righteous rage was Abraham that he drew his dagger and plunged it into the neck of the pope, whose blood spewed purple, gushing like a fountain of evil, depravity, and wickedness over the land."

"Oh, my!" I gasped.

Bernie was white. Tato's mouth hung open, and Franco looked to be in full apoplexy. Lucio stopped playing his guitar, and not because it needed tuning.

"Abraham withdrew his weapon from the neck of the stuck pontiff," continued Giuliana, her voice gaining volume and passion. "The bourgeois pig collapsed on the marble floor, vomiting blood and bile in plenty, while the Jew turned his wrath on the cardinals cowering nearby in horror and shame. He sawed their heads off one by one with his dagger, exhorting the masses to follow him into battle as his did. 'Rise, brothers, and with your scythes slaughter your oppressors as you slaughter your swine! Unite, workers, and establish with me a new dictatorship of the proletariat, free from religion and its bloodsucking hypocrites!'

"Word of Abraham's heroic deeds spread quickly throughout Rome, Italy, and all of Europe. The Church, decapitated and exposed for its true villainy, died the death of a scurvy dog and the workers built their social- ist paradise atop the ashes of St. Peter's Basilica. The end."

Stunned silence said it all. The notices were sure to be bad, but Gi- uliana had achieved her goal. She beamed from her seat in the armchair, gauging the success of her tale by the shock on the faces of the audience. She seemed particularly interested in Locanda's reaction, but his poker face revealed nothing. Perhaps because he didn't actually care if class war- fare arrived and blood flowed in the streets. As long as it wasn't his blood, the revolution could proceed.

Franco was the first to speak. He coughed and proclaimed that he hoped the next day's story would be less violent. And less political.

"Our host asked us to leave political arguments outside, after all," he said, nodding cross-eyed toward Locanda.

"I wasn't arguing," said Giuliana. "I was only telling a story. There's plenty of violence in stories."

I thought how lucky it was that Mariangela had been sent to bed and missed Giuliana's tale of blood and gore. Bernie might have anticipated it, but the rest of us had been taken by surprise.

"Your tale was a provocation," insisted Franco, who was holding his glass at a precarious angle that sloshed waves of amber liquid onto the floor at regular intervals. "You were deliberately trying to upset our host."

Locanda, who, I'd noticed, hadn't been paying attention to any of our discussions, now lifted his head and claimed he wasn't upset.

"Tell whatever stories you like," he said.

Neither Giuliana nor Franco was happy with that answer, perhaps confirming the latter's position that the former had been trying to provoke a reaction.

"We all came here for a pleasant few days to enjoy a well-deserved thank-you for our contributions to the symposium," said Franco. "And to remember our dear colleague and mentor, Alberto Bondinelli. But you chose to ruin our collegial mood with your slanderous lies about my church. Everyone's church except yours."

"That's not true," she said in her defense. "Lucio and Tato are atheists like me, and Ellie is Jewish."

"To be absolutely accurate," I broke in, "Bernie is also Jewish."

"You two did not insult my religion," said Franco. "This girl did." He pointed at Giuliana. "And I won't stand for it. Don't forget you still have your exams to pass."

"*Calmatevi*," urged Lucio, putting down his guitar and rising to his feet in attempts to restore order. "Franco, you can't threaten a student because you don't like her politics. And in front of witnesses."

Franco's scalp nearly blew off the top of his head. His eyes had turned blood red. He reeled to the left then to the right, looking for someone to back him up. "Didn't any of you hear what she said about the Church? About the Holy Father? It's untrue and a poorly constructed story besides. She should fail her exams for such a poor rhetorical performance."

"Excuse me, Franco," said Bernie. "That's not true. Her story was taken from the *Decameron*. Would you fail Boccaccio?"

Now Franco found himself backed even farther into a corner. He hadn't recognized the tale as Boccaccio's, which was a humiliation for a professor of literature. That realization, along with the effects of too much wine, fueled his rage. He lashed out in a different direction.

"Then she should fail for plagiarism."

"This is a social situation," said Lucio. "Not an exam. You can't fail her for a story she told at a party."

I stood, crossed the room, and placed a hand on Franco's shoulder. "Let's all try to calm down," I said, eyeing the others as I spoke. "Perhaps we've all had too much to drink . . ." (Like fun I had.) "Come, we're all friends and colleagues here. Let's not let a story and politics interfere with our enjoyment. And let's also remember Professor Bondinelli. He would be sad indeed if he knew we were arguing this way."

"*Me ne strafotto del Professor Bondinelli,*" announced Giuliana, and everyone—every last person in the room—choked. Her language was so vulgar, so unexpected, that even her story seemed tame in comparison. "He was a terrible man. A usurper and a fascist killer."

Tato took her by the arm and yanked her toward the door. Her protests, punctuated by more, uglier oaths and accusations against the late professor, echoed from the corridor, growing ever fainter, as Tato put distance between her and us. Her outburst shocked everyone present, even Locanda, who raised an eyebrow and pursed his lips. The profanity had one positive side effect, however. It knocked Franco out of his funk. He was sobered, if not sober, and his anger evaporated. He shook his head as if to clear the cobwebs from his addled brain, and apologized to the group.

"I'm very sorry," he said, face white now. "Somehow I think this is partially my fault."

Bernie, Lucio, and I exchanged knowing glances. Locanda, too, seemed to agree with our assessment, if his roll of the eyes meant what I thought it did. Franco started hiccoughing.

"You mustn't drink so much," I said. "It's the wine that makes you aggressive."

He nodded sheepishly.

"You're a sweet man," I continued. "Except when you drink."

"I'm ashamed," he said, tears welling in his eyes.

Here it came. The comical, overly dramatic Italian man weeping like a child. He draped himself over me, wailing and hiccoughing that he'd been wrong and would apologize to Giuliana the next morning. He mumbled incoherently about his mother, then about me. I wasn't sure exactly what I had to do with anything, but he was stroking my hair and soaking my shoulder with his tears. Bernie recognized the direction the breakdown was headed. If he didn't act promptly, Franco would have a whole different set of sins to atone for in the morning.

"I'll take him to his room," said Bernie, pulling the pulpy mass of a man off my person.

Lucio joined Bernie, and they each took an arm over their shoulder to bear Franco away. They only lost the handle on their cargo once, dropping him to the floor with a thud. Wrestling him to his feet again, they disappeared down the corridor.

I found myself alone with Locanda. The room had gone eerily quiet, and I wanted to get out of there.

CHAPTER
TWENTY-FOUR

"Have another drink," he said, rising and making his way to the tray nearby. It was an order, not an offer to refill my glass. "After that performance, I confess that I am ready for one."

"Whisky," I said, handing him my glass. Whether he'd offered or ordered, I didn't care. He was the host and the man.

He took the glass and poured some Scotch into it. "I know very well what you drink, signorina."

The moment was supremely awkward. After our last conversation that morning, the ice was going to be difficult to break. I wished Bernie and Lucio would hurry up and dump Franco into his bed and come back to rescue me.

We stood there, Locanda and I, staring at each other, not quite sure what to say or do. Finally, he motioned to a nearby chair, another order for me, or perhaps a just a suggestion. I took the seat, and he did the same in his usual armchair.

"Interesting evening," he croaked at length.

"Is Alberto Bondinelli in any of those photographs of the *Camicie Nere*?" I asked, ignoring his small talk.

"*Quali fotografie?*"

"The ones in your study. The ones your father hung and you never thought to take down."

He frowned and sipped his drink, Cynar. "I'm not sure," he grumbled. "I've never looked at those pictures closely. Why would I want to?"

"I can't pretend to know what motivates you. But I'm curious to know if he is in any of those photos," I said, thinking back to my conversation with Giuliana earlier that day.

"*Perché?*"

"Because I heard a rumor that he was a member of the Black Shirts. I'm a reporter and like to confirm information."

"Are you writing a news article?"

"No. Are you avoiding my question?"

"Absolutely not. We can go have a look at the photographs. *Subito*, if you like."

I took him up on his offer, and, leaving our drinks behind, we made our way down the corridor to the study. He pushed open the door and flicked on the dim light. The little reading nook was to the right of the entrance. Locanda switched on the reading lamp on the table, illuminating the space so we could examine the photographs on the wall.

"*Ecco a lei*," he said. "Take your time."

"I don't think I would recognize him. After all, I never met him. And the one photograph I've seen is recent."

"I'll help you then, shall I?"

He removed a pair of eyeglasses from his vest pocket and slipped them on his nose. Then, bending at the waist for a closer look, he examined the photographs one by one. He grunted at one picture, chuckled to himself at another, then stood up straight and removed his glasses.

"So? Is he there?"

"Yes, Alberto's there. In two photographs. This one," he said, pointing to a group picture of a squadron or kindle of Black Shirts—whatever the collective noun was for the bastards. Perhaps an unkindness, as in ravens, or a murder, as in crows. "And this is him, too." He pointed to the last photograph at the bottom.

It was a group of four men in fezzes holding rifles across their chests. Each man grinned at the camera. Except for one. The tall one. The thin one with fierce eyes and a tight grip on his weapon. He was cleanly shaven in the photograph, and I doubted I would have picked him out on my own. His focus was singular, intense, and all business. No smile in his dark eyes. A mission, perhaps, a conviction. It seemed to me that he would have rather been elsewhere, but he was willing to submit to being photographed because someone—his commanding officer perhaps—had ordered him to do so. I saw no humanity or joy, could detect nothing but a vacant stare from a hollow soul. And I'd seen that man before. He was one of the four people in the photograph from the café. The one I'd seen the night before, when Locanda had surprised Bernie and me in the study.

"There's another photo I'd like to see," I said, crossing the room to the secretary against the wall.

Locanda followed. I shuffled through the prints I'd examined that very morning.

"There," I said, holding the photograph out for Locanda to see. "Is this Bondinelli?"

He unfolded his glasses again, and threaded them behind his ears and onto the bridge of his nose. He took the picture and studied it for a few seconds.

"Yes, that's Alberto. But how did you know he was in this photograph? Were you snooping in my study?"

"Oh, please," I said, snatching the picture from his hands. "You know perfectly well I was."

He pulled the eyeglasses off again and held them to his cheek in a pensive pose. Perhaps he hadn't known perfectly well after all.

"Then you were not in here to kiss your friend Bernie last night?" he asked in an unsure voice. "You did not lose your . . ." he cleared his throat. "You lied about having lost your . . . *mutandine*."

I said nothing to confirm his statement and glared at him instead.

Locanda frowned and huffed his indignation. "You come into my house as a guest and search my possessions? Why?"

"Because I'm incurably curious," I said. "I wanted to know why the man who invited me here died before I'd even had the chance to shake his hand. I wanted to know who he truly was. I wanted to know why you, his friend, had nothing nicer to say about him than he used to steal books and beat up his childhood classmates. And I wanted to know why you would hide the fact that such a man had been your brother-in-law and father to your niece."

Locanda bristled. "You didn't know Mariangela was my niece until today."

"That's beside the point. A couple of hours difference. Yes, I glanced at a couple of photographs you'd left lying around in plain view. But you're hiding something. You must be. Why else would you lie about your relationship with him?"

"I don't have to answer to you or anyone else in my own house," he said, taking a step toward me.

This was the first time he'd ever made me feel threatened. It wasn't that he was fuming or frothing at the mouth. Just the opposite. He was calm, as if he'd made a decision of how to handle the situation. I backed away from the secretary, but he cut off my escape.

Then a noise came from the doorway, distracting Locanda and startling me. We reeled around to see who was there and saw a barefoot ghost, framed by the doorway, standing there in a fluttering gown of gossamer. The light from corridor shone behind the figure rendering her face a dark hole beneath a wild bird's nest of hair.

"Oh, my, God," I said, clutching my chest. "Veronica, it's you."

She stepped inside the room, and the eerie illusion caused by the light faded away. "I came down for something to eat," she said. "I heard voices."

"Everything is fine, signorina," said Locanda, edging a few inches away from me. "You must be feeling better. *Brava*."

"Yes, thank you. I feel fine. I'm just hungry."

I took advantage of the small talk and the presence of a witness to slip past Locanda who, though he'd given me some breathing room, was still too close for my comfort. I joined Veronica at the doorway. Her expression told me she thought she'd interrupted something, though she wasn't sure what.

"I'll ask Berenice to fix you something to eat," he said. "Why don't you go back to your room to rest?"

"*Grazie*," she said, unsure, perhaps, if it was safe to leave me with him. Or maybe she thought we'd been up to some kind of naughtiness and she should exit stage right.

"Wait," I said. "Veronica, may I look at your rash?"

She submitted, standing close to the light near the armchair.

"It's much better," I said. "Does it still itch?"

"A little. Not like before."

"Splendid," said Locanda. "I'm sure tomorrow you will be able to join us all for meals. Go on upstairs now and I'll send Berenice."

Veronica left the study and retreated down the corridor, disappearing into the darkness at the far end. With my witness gone, Locanda joined me in the doorway. We stepped into the corridor. Then, producing a keychain from his jacket, he shut the study door and locked the room.

"Shall we finish our drinks in the *salone*?" he asked as if nothing had happened. "I'll join you once I've roused Berenice from her bed to serve that silly girl something to eat."

"There you are," said Bernie from the same seat he'd occupied during Giuliana's bloody story. Lucio was there as well, pouring himself some more white wine. "Where were you?"

"Caber tossing," I said.

"Caber . . . what?" he asked. "Like throwing telephone poles in a field?"

"It's a joke."

Then Lucio chimed in. "Now you will marry me, Ellie?" he asked in English. "Please. I love you. *Ti amo!*"

"Max and I were just looking at some photographs in his study," I said, answering Bernie's question and putting Lucio's plea to one side for the moment. There would be time to fall into his arms later if the mood struck me.

Locanda returned, took up his orphaned drink, and we settled into a reluctant, uneasy peace, the four of us. It didn't last long; I wanted to put as much distance as I could between me and our host. It was late, nearly one, and I announced I was punching out for the day. Bernie stood and said he, too, was turning in. He took my elbow and said he'd "walk me home."

"Maybe I'll invite you in to see my etchings," I said. Turning to Lucio, I added, "*Buonanotte, amore mio.*" He rose and kissed me on both cheeks.

"*Vengo da te?*" he asked with an adorable smile.

"You will not come to my room, Lucio," I said. "Bernie's going to be there, after all."

He chuckled and wished me goodnight.

My eyes darted from him to Locanda. I didn't want to say anything to him, but in polite company I had little choice. "*Buonanotte.*"

He returned my good wishes, stiffly, but he was playing the same game as I was.

Halfway down the corridor, I spotted a shadow on the tiles. I stooped to investigate.

"What's that?" asked Bernie.

"A keychain," I said, turning it over.

"Looks like the key to a Vespa," he said, stating the obvious. The small leather fob was emblazoned with a metal badge reading "Vespa."

"I think this belongs to Franco," said Bernie. "He must have dropped it when we hauled him off to bed. I'll give it to him in the morning."

"Or in the afternoon," I said as we continued on our way down the corridor. "He might sleep in tomorrow. And don't worry. I'll return it to him."

CHAPTER
TWENTY-FIVE

Sleeping under the eaves, I heard the rain as soon as it began to fall. Heavy at first, like a spigot had opened up full blast, then lighter, and finally steady. The showers brought cooler temperatures, even if the wet air grew thicker as a result. Still, lying beneath the sheets, instead of on top of them, was a refreshing change. My Super Faust kept me safe from the *zanzare*, which should have made for the soundest sleep I'd had to date in Florence. And yet I was troubled.

I dreamt disturbing dreams, all of which involved either Bondinelli or Locanda. They appeared as riddles and threats. To my horror, one manifested himself as an incubus. Despite his lack of civility and basic kindness, Locanda had managed to invade my slumber and my bed. His presence in my subconscious discomfited me as I wasn't sure if he'd been ready to slap, strangle, or kiss me earlier that night in his study, when Veronica interrupted our intense moment. Either way, he was now in my dream engaging me in undertakings I'd heretofore only enjoyed with men of less advanced years.

I awoke. If ever there was an inspiration to reach into my suitcase and retrieve the bottle of Dewar's, this was it. I huddled on the bed, emptied my little water glass into my mouth, then filled it again with whisky. The rain continued to fall. The roof dispatched its duties, keeping the water outside and me inside, comfortable and dry.

Pushing impure thoughts of Locanda to one side, I concentrated on Bondinelli instead. He'd seemed such a polite and proper man in his correspondence with me. Nothing in his letters suggested a former Black Shirt. In fairness, he'd given me no clues as to his feelings on Jesus or war orphans in Spain either. But the people who had known him had provided me with varying opinions on his character. If the ugly portraits of Bondinelli were to be believed, he was someone my father would have throttled. That set me to wondering. Abraham Stone had been no fool when it came to judging people. He'd prided himself on his ability to detect dishonesty, claiming he could smell it on a person before he'd said more than three words. And he'd told Bernie that Bondinelli was "a nice man," even as he disparaged the late professor's scholarship.

I didn't know what to believe. On one side, Lucio and Giuliana brooked no dissent when they claimed the late professor had been a usurper and a monster. Even his oldest friend, his brother-in-law, Max Locanda, had told us of Bondinelli's brutality as a young boy. His theft of textbooks seemed quaint in comparison, yet there was that story as well. Should I really cast stones, though? In my youth, I'd stolen liquor with my best friend, Janey Silverman, from her uncle's store on Fifteenth Street, and I'd reformed. Perhaps not from the thirst for drink, but from the larceny.

But, of course, I'd seen with my own eyes photographs of young Bondinelli in his *camicia nera* and fez. Were those things enough? Did they provide me with the evidence to dismiss any other version of his life? Was his worth lost to me based on that one undeniable fact? Or, in the Christian sense, was there scope for change and redemption?

I considered the other side of the coin. There was Bondinelli's daughter, his student Veronica, and his *donna di servizio*, Teresa. They'd described him to me respectively as a good father, a brilliant scholar, and a saintly man. Then there was Padre Fabrizio, Franco Sannino, not to mention my own father. All had vouched for Bondinelli's character. What was I to believe?

I rose and poured myself another glass of whisky, then peered out the tiny window at the black night. Even the rain was invisible in the dark, except for the drops that somehow found their way to the windowpane. I slipped back between the sheets and asked myself why it even mattered who Bondinelli had been. There was no talk of a crime. By all accounts, the professor had fallen into the Arno and swallowed too much of the foul green water. Tragic, yes, but I'd never met him. Should I mourn or cheer or be indifferent? Forget it, I told myself and sipped my Scotch.

Later, I nodded off again, and this time I dreamt of Franco Sannino. He was drunk, of course, and in need of a mother to make love to him. Or feed him or something, it was all a little blurry in the morning. I did recall that I'd begged off in no uncertain terms, but he'd seemed intent. I didn't know what his mother might have looked like, but I resolved there and then in my bed, as the rain drummed on the terra cotta tiles inches above my head, that I would make sure I was never alone with him again, at least not when drinks were being served.

CHAPTER
TWENTY-SIX

SUNDAY, SEPTEMBER 29, 1963

I was up with the cock. The one I'd forgotten to ask Berenice to behead and fricassee the day before. He crowed in the steady rain, and I could have sworn he was perched on the sill of my window as he called to the rising sun. As it turned out, he was actually cock-a-doodling in the courtyard below. With no other projectiles handy, I started flinging pennies from my purse at him. Just to frighten him off at first. But after three or four near misses, I zeroed in on him and winged him with my very last coin. He leapt into the air, flapping his wings and squawking as if he'd been shot, before shaking it off and strutting a couple of steps to his left. There he squared himself, gathered his strength, and commenced to crow again. If I'd had a gun, that rooster would have been no more than a puff of singed feathers and a red stain on the ground.

I bathed and dressed instead and made my way downstairs to the dining room a little past seven. Berenice had laid out the breakfast dishes, flatware, and linens. There was a pitcher of fresh orange juice, milk for coffee or tea, and some brioche. Noise from the kitchen—a clattering of pots or pans and a hissing of steam—told me hot food and coffee were being prepared.

I poured myself a glass of juice and took a seat at the table just as the shuffling of feet behind me caught my attention. Craning my neck, I watched as Teresa and Veronica entered the room and headed for the kitchen. Mariangela brought up the rear.

"*Buongiorno*," I said, startling them. They hadn't noticed me.

The three of them joined me in the dining room. Teresa appeared ill at ease, probably because Locanda had made her feel like the help, not a guest. Veronica had bathed and dressed for the first time in two days. The rash on her neck was all but gone, a mere shadow of its former self. More pink than red now, and no longer angry. Mariangela looked lovely in a white dress.

"You're up early," I said.

Mariangela made a face. "On our way to church."

"Church? But you can't leave the property."

"There's the chapel outside. Next to the *limonaia*. Teresa insisted we have a Mass. It's Sunday, after all. We don't have a priest, but we'll make do. Will you join us?"

I declined as politely as I knew how.

"Lucky you," she mumbled so the Italian and Spanish ladies wouldn't catch on.

"*Vieni, Mariangela,*" said Veronica. "It's getting late."

They left me there in the dining room, and presently Berenice appeared with a bowl of *caffellatte* for me. She was about to withdraw when I asked her to wait.

"Were you here at Bel Soggiorno when Signor Locanda's father was alive?"

She nodded with a frown. She mostly frowned. Not from annoyance or anger. It was her normal expression.

"I've been here since 1920," she said. "*Il colonnello* took me in when I was fifteen. I was an orphan. And a war widow. *La Grande Guerra.*"

"A widow? At fifteen?"

She gaped at me, as if she didn't understand the question, and I realized things must have been quite different in the Italian countryside forty years earlier. I tacked in a different direction.

"*Il colonnello*? Was he a military man?"

She offered a phlegmatic expression that didn't quite qualify as indifference, but neither did it rise to the level of a shrug. "*Insomma . . .*"

I fixated on her answer, because she hadn't said anything more than the one word. How to describe *insomma*? It literally means "in short" or "in sum." In some contexts it can mean *basically* or *all right* or *well*. But that's not how she meant it. Italians sometimes use that word to express a lack of enthusiasm in response to a question, especially when uttered with the exact facial expression Berenice had used.

"Was he not a soldier?" I asked to clarify.

"He had a commission," she said. "But he wasn't a soldier. Not before that."

"I see. It was a reward. *Una ricompensa.*"

"*Insomma.*"

He must have pleased the fascists to earn such a handsome rank.

"How kind of him to take you in," I said.

"*Gentile?*" she asked, repeating the word I'd used. "*Regala mori.*"

I didn't know the expression and asked Bernie later on. He, too, was stumped. Finally, Lucio explained that it was a Florentine saying that meant "No one ever gives anything for nothing." Or, in American parlance, "There's no such thing as a free lunch."

"I was a hard worker," she continued. "A good cook and *una bella ragazza.* I wasn't always so fat, you know."

"Did you know Professor Bondinelli?" I asked, steering her away from observations of her former beauty and current corpulence to the question I'd been leading up to.

"I didn't see him much in recent years," she said. "But during the last war and after, when he was courting Silvana, he came here often."

"Silvana was the signore's sister?"

"*Sì, poverina.* Died seven years ago."

"How?"

"*Polmonite.* Pneumonia."

"So sad." I paused for a moment out of respect for the departed soul before asking how Silvana and the professor had met.

"He was a friend of the signore's. He must have met Silvana when she was a girl. In the thirties, I remember, because the professor still had his eye. Then he courted her before the war. And during, of course."

"It must have been an uncertain time. Not a good moment to fall in love."

"Oh, no. Signorina Silvana wasn't in love with the professor. No, no. She was in love with someone else."

"Why didn't she marry the other man?"

Berenice rubbed her hands on her apron. "*Perché, perché?*" she replied, seemingly asking the ceiling for the answer. Or the heavens. "For the oldest reason. Because he died."

CHAPTER
TWENTY-SEVEN

Berenice didn't remember the young man's name. In fact she'd never met him. He'd never come to the house. But it was the war, and dying was hardly unusual.

I asked if he'd been a soldier, but she knew nothing beyond that Silvana's father did not approve.

"*Giulietta e Romeo*. Now I must get back to the kitchen."

"*Un'ultima domanda*," I said. "What's the name of the rooster?"

"The rooster?"

"Yes, the one who makes all the noise every morning."

"We call him Ermenegildo. Why do you want to know?"

"I'd like to have him for dinner tonight, if that's possible."

She uttered a little laugh. "*No, no, no, signorina*. Ermenegildo is twelve years old and is still going strong. The signore likes him, so his neck is safe for now."

"*Buongiorno*," came a voice from the opposite end of the room. Good God, it was Locanda.

Berenice excused herself and scurried back to the kitchen, leaving me alone with him. He took a seat opposite me at the table, a newspaper under his arm and a cigarette between his fingers.

"Where's Vicky this morning?" I asked. "Sleeping?"

"I have no idea where she is," he said.

"What?"

He looked at me as if I had two heads. "She's left. What is it you don't understand?"

"For one thing, what's happened to her? Is she all right?"

"*Non ne ho idea*," he said as he opened his paper. "She's probably pouting about something or other somewhere. Like a cat, she'll come back when she's hungry."

"But she doesn't speak Italian," I said. "And she's not supposed to leave the property. Where would she have gone?"

"*Non lo so*. She's an adult who acts like a child. I can't be nursemaid to her whims."

Berenice reappeared with a coffee for Locanda.

"*Vuole qualcosa?*" he asked me.

"Nothing for me," I said.

He dismissed her, and asked me what my plans were for the day. I told him I hoped to spend some time with Mariangela to teach her some photography tricks. Truth be told, I half expected him to forbid me from seeing her. But he barely reacted, beyond sipping his coffee and making a face.

"*Troppo amaro*," he said. "How many times must I tell Berenice to taste the coffee before serving it."

"It seems fine to me."

"Of course it does."

"Max," I said, stirring him from his practiced detachment. "How did your sister and Bondinelli meet?"

After a suitable period of pique, he considered my question. He said it was in thirty-five or -six. Silvana was young. Fifteen or sixteen.

"She was born in 1920?"

He nodded. "Alberto was much older than she. He didn't court her until later. They met, they fell in love, and they married."

"I understood it happened quite differently. Your sister, Silvana, was in love with someone else when she met Bondinelli."

"It's possible, yes. So?"

"Did you know the other man?"

"The one she loved? If she loved another? No. I was a prisoner of war at the time."

"But surely you heard something later on. It's been twenty years, after all."

He smiled one of those condescending grins, as if he thought I was a naïve little girl, hopelessly out her depth.

"Do you think married couples discuss past love affairs? Do you think they recount them to their brothers? To their fathers? I doubt that. I arrived home in September of forty-five, finally set free by the British, and I never heard a word of any of Silvana's former love affairs."

"So she and Bondinelli were engaged by that time?"

"Oh, no. Not for another three, four years. But why are you asking me questions about my sister? What interest could you possibly have?"

He'd finally caught on. This was always the dicey moment when I had to convince my interviewee of the benefits of answering my questions, even when I couldn't justify them to myself.

"I apologize," I said. "Of course it's none of my business. And yet . . ."

"Yes?" he asked.

"And yet, your sister had a lover. Or a betrothed. *Un fidanzato*. Why did she change her mind? Why did she choose Bondinelli?"

He considered my question for a long moment, then told me that I already knew the answer.

"He died, of course," he said. "I'm not sure who told you, but I believe you were aware of that."

I'm sure I blushed. "I meant to say why did she agree to marry Bondinelli."

"It's no mystery. She couldn't marry a man who was dead, could she?"

"Of course not. But I'm still wondering who this mystery man was. I can't ask Mariangela, and I doubt there was anyone else present at the time who might have known him. Maybe Achille? But how well?"

"You are a curious girl, signorina," he said. "And I don't mean that as a compliment. You ask personal questions about things you have no right to know. I find it tiring. You annoy me."

If Locanda thought he could put me off by telling me I asked too many questions, he didn't know me very well.

"I annoy you because I ask questions you don't want to answer."

"You annoy me because you do not understand hospitality. I have welcomed you into my house, and you treat me with disrespect."

"There's no disrespect in asking. If my questions make you feel uncomfortable, don't answer them."

He studied me for the longest moment, surely wondering what to make of me.

"What is it you want? What is it you hope to accomplish?"

I took pity on him. I truly didn't want to cause him pain or be ungrateful in his house.

"As I've already told you, I want to know why Professor Bondinelli died," I said in answer to his question. "Did he fall into the Arno by accident? Did someone push him into the river? Or did he take his own life?"

"Alberto never would have taken his own life. He was a Catholic. He feared God. It's impossible."

"Then what?" I asked. "Did he wander down to the riverbank and fall in? After fifty years of living in Florence? Or maybe a thief hit him on the head and threw him in the river. For the riches he was carrying on his person?"

"I have no idea. But you didn't even know him. Never met the man. Why do you care?"

"He invited me here. I was his guest. It's only natural that I care about what happened to him."

"No, signorina. There is more that you refuse to say. I believe it has to do with your father."

"What? My father?"

He nodded. "You lost your father under criminal circumstances and now you see conspiracy everywhere. You want to put right the in-justices of the world to soothe your soul. Alberto's death is a convenient exercise for your nosy nature. Signorina Stone, you are a *ficcanaso*. A busybody."

I wanted to slap his face. Or at least tell him off properly in Italian, but I sat there frozen in my seat, my language skills not up to the task of delivering one of my usual biting ripostes. Instead—I'm ashamed to admit—I wept. Running from the room, covering my eyes as I went, I ran like a child for the comfort of solitude. That beautiful space where one is free to mourn, to wallow in pity away from the prying eyes of others. For me, that day, that space was outside in the rainy garden. I stood there in my gloom, staring at the ground, wondering how I could break the quarantine and get away from Bel Soggiorno. I knew I could go on foot, if I trekked over hill and dale, avoiding the policeman stationed at the Via Boccaccio entrance to the property. But did I really want to lug my suit-case through the rain? And it would easily be a mile or two before I cleared the property and reached the road undetected. I kicked the wet ground in frustration and, in the process, spied two of the pennies I'd thrown at the rooster, Ermenegildo, earlier that morning. Then the brown tabby who'd welcomed us to Bel Soggiorno two days prior appeared and distracted me. Soaking wet, he stared up at me and uttered another caw-like meow. I squatted and held out two fingers to him. He, in turn, sniffed my hand and commenced to twirling around my ankles.

"*Come ti chiami?*" I asked him.

"His name is Benito," called Locanda from the doorway. Then he ran toward me with an umbrella as a peace offering, scaring off the cat in the process.

"I refuse to call him by that name," I said. "To spite you I'll call him Antonio, after Gramsci."

Locanda chuckled. "Fine. I, too, will call him Antonio." A pause ensued. "Signorina. Ellie," he said finally. "Come inside. Don't stand in the rain. *Venga dentro*."

I looked into his eyes, bloodshot, a touch yellowed, with the skin around them leathered and brown. And he studied me, the rain beating down on both of us, because he hadn't opened the umbrella. His face was softer than I'd seen, his expression almost human.

"*Mi dica*," I said. "Tell me about her."

His expression hardened a bit but only for a second. Then it softened again. He clearly didn't want to talk about her, but I was sure he had to.

"She was a lovely girl, my sister," he said. "And she was heartbroken when Marco died."

"That was his name? Marco?"

"I think so. I don't know his family name."

"Why did your father object to him?"

"What does it matter now? He died. Silvana's heart broke to pieces. She became depressed, morose, inconsolable. My father had her committed to a sanitarium in France. But she swore she'd kill herself if he didn't bring her back home. She even tried suicide once, and my father relented."

"And that's when Alberto came onto the scene again?"

We must have looked comical, the two of us, standing in the rain with a closed umbrella at hand and the open doors of the house just steps away. The absurdity of our nose-to-nose didn't strike me until later, when we shared some brandy in the *salone* after we'd dried out and changed clothes.

"Where have you been?" I asked Bernie in the corridor near the bathroom upstairs.

"I slept in," he said. "I see you're dry now. Changed your clothes?"

That sounded odd. I balked at responding for a moment, wondering what he'd meant by it. "Yes, I got caught in the rain."

"I saw you with Locanda outside. You didn't get caught in the rain. You walked right out into it."

"What's your point, Bernie?"

"Nothing. I just want you to be careful."

"Are you implying something happened between me and him? Because nothing did. He told me about his sister and Bondinelli. That's all."

"It sure looked like more than that. El, he's a slippery one. Don't let your guard down."

"See you later for cocktails," I said, pushing past him toward the stairs.

"Where are you going?"

I didn't answer. I couldn't. Not without blushing crimson. I was, in fact, headed to the *salone* where I was to meet Max for that brandy.

He held a large leather-bound album on his lap. And though it was only a few minutes past ten, he poured us each a snifter of Cognac to counter the chill from our soaking. We settled into the divan's cushions to watch the rain through the doors.

"Has Vicky surfaced yet?" I asked.

He shook his head and took the minutest sip of brandy, barely wetting his upper lip. "I assume she's gone down to Florence. Victoria is a big girl with plenty of money. She managed just fine alone in Italy before she met me."

"How do you mean?"

"Her family is wealthy. Money is no problem. Not that she ever spends her own. Men are always ready to feed the starving little *trovatella*."

I didn't know the word, and he couldn't translate it. After a brief back and forth, I came to understand it meant *waif*. By that time, of course, the moment had passed, and the feathery cough of a laugh I produced hardly convinced anyone.

"How long have you known her?" I asked.

He seemed to count in his head, all the while looking at anything but me. "Five months," he said finally. "I met her in Milan where she'd just had an argument with her companion. A man of questionable connections. Handsome and rich, to be sure, but not likely to stay out of jail."

"She was lucky you came along to rescue her."

Now he looked directly at me. "I doubt she needed rescuing. Anyway, she'll find another rich man, I'm sure."

"I'm sorry."

"*Dio mio, perché?* Don't be sorry," he said. "Not for me. I told you, I am not sentimental. Whether Vicky is here or somewhere else, I truly do not care. She was an amusement. *Un divertimento.* Nothing more."

Even if his love affair with the beautiful young creature had failed to achieve its happily ever after, I couldn't help thinking that not caring about anything must have been a sad way to go through life. I wondered if he really meant it or were these merely sour grapes?

"I've had disappointments, too," I said.

"*La* Vicky is not a disappointment. Just a little story that ended."

"Was it like that for Silvana?"

That caught his attention. "You mean with Marco?"

"Yes. Did she get over him? Did her heart heal?"

"It took a couple of years, but with the help of her friends and family, she came back to life."

"And Alberto helped?"

"Of course. He cared for her as if for a kitten. He suffered her moods, her rudeness, her anger, never once losing his patience. She experienced wild bouts of depression, and she drank too much. It was Alberto who cured her. He simply would not allow her to slip away."

"Did she share his passion for the Church?"

"No, not for the Church. But for God, yes. I believe she found comfort in God."

"And your father? Did he approve of the match?"

"*Assolutamente,*" he said firmly. "He encouraged it. My father always liked Alberto, from the first time he met him when he was a child. And then they were in Spain, in thirty-six and -seven."

"In Spain? Together?"

He gazed indulgently at me over the top of his eyeglasses. "I'm sure you've heard of the little *contretemps* that went on in Spain in thirty-six." I nodded. "Franco—the *generalísimo*, the *caudillo*, not the idiot who's staying here at Bel Soggiorno—invited the Italians and Germans to help. Both my father and Alberto were dispatched to Spain. One was more involved in diplomacy with the Nationalists, while the other was in the thick of the fighting."

I didn't need to guess which was which.

"Yes, both served in Spain. It created a strong bond between them. Naturally my father approved of Alberto as a husband for Silvana, even after he left the Black Shirts."

"He left the Black Shirts?"

"As you know, he was gravely wounded in Spain. Lost an eye. His military career was over. He was discharged from active duty after that."

Max opened the leather-bound tome he'd been holding in his lap and flipped through the pages. It was a photo album. A few of the white mounting corners had come unglued and slipped out of the book onto the floor, as did one photograph. He retrieved the photo, but left the little corners for someone else to sweep up.

He examined the pictures in silence but with great interest, even running his fingers over the edges, as if caressing some memory ressurected from long ago. Turning the pages with care, he seemed to have forgotten I was there. For my part, I couldn't quite make out who or what was in the photographs. But then he turned the album toward me and offered a better view.

"This is me," he said, pointing to a small, wrinkled photo of a toddler with curly locks of blonde hair. He was dressed in a military outfit of some kind. "And here's another of me with Father and Mother."

"You were quite the handsome little man," I said.

He dismissed my flattery. "Kind of you, but who can tell in such small, dark photographs?"

He turned the page again, hesitated, then tried to close the album. I asked who it was that I'd glimpsed in the large photograph in the middle of the page. He opened the book again and showed me. It was a little blonde girl of about four standing in her Sunday finery holding the hand of an adolescent boy, also dressed for some special occasion. Or perhaps just church.

"Is that Silvana?" I asked. "And you?"

He nodded, his blue, bloodshot eyes focused intently on the image. "She was eleven years younger than I."

"A beautiful girl. I'm sorry."

He snapped out of his reverie. "No reason to be sorry," he said. "Think of it this way: She lived one hundred percent of her life. We all do. Whether we die at birth or at ninety-nine, our lives are complete. A whole."

I'd never thought of life as a total made up of one hundred percentage points. And as I considered that thought then, I wondered if such an out-look made death easier to accept. Perhaps for deep thinkers, but for those experiencing the loss of a loved one, I wasn't so sure. My brother Elijah's sudden death had kicked me like a mule. Thinking of his short life now as one hundred percent complete and whole gave me no solace. No, this philosophy struck me as cold and soulless.

"How did Alberto take her death?" I asked.

"Like a sheep. With docile acceptance of his God's will and wisdom."

"That sounds quite different from his reaction to his sister's death."

"He had no God at that time. Religion provides strategies for coping with death, but I've found those lacking as well. If your deceased loved one is with God, then why be sad at all? Death should be reason to celebrate."

I refused to believe sorrow could be tempered by divine recompense or mathematical completeness. I had to admit that I was glad death sad-dened me. How hollow life would be without mourning its passing.

"I have one last question," I said, thinking back to something Padre Fabrizio had said in his eulogy. "What happened to change Alberto? If we assume the death of his sister, Cecilia, was the first moral crisis on his spiritual journey, then what was the second? What brought him back to God?"

"I have no idea. But it happened in Spain, I'm sure of that. He re-turned a changed man."

I napped in my room for three hours, catching up on the sleep Ermene-gildo had denied me, and missed the midday meal. The patter of the rain on the tiles above my head lulled me into a comfortable slumber, which was punctuated by pastoral dreams of bubbling creeks and butterflies and sunflowers. And then more dreams, of food and drink and laughter. Fi-nally, I dreamt of Max Locanda having his wicked will of me on his desk in the library for the second time in barely twelve hours.

I awoke with a jolt. It was past four, and I realized cocktails were only a short way off. I'd had a head start, of course, swilling brandy with Max in the *salone* before noon. Now, lying in bed with only a sheet covering me, I stretched and yawned, at once trying to forget the disturbing dream and curious about its conclusion. I told myself it was Bernie's suggestion that had prompted the erotic vision. That and the brandy, which I rarely drank. Or the lack of a proper night's sleep. Yes, I found many culprits to blame for the appearance of the incubus in my unconscious imagination. The sole innocent party was me.

How was I going to face him now, after yet another explicit encounter? Even if it had only been in my mind. A while later, as I brushed my unruly hair, I urged myself to give him no reason to suspect any embarrassment or discomfort in my demeanor when I saw him next. That, of course, would be in a few minutes when I went down for cocktails. I rolled on some lipstick and applied a touch of blush to my cheeks, then steadied my nerves with a gulp of whisky from my bottle of Dewar's. Feeling right again, I made my way downstairs.

"We missed you at lunch," said Bernie, who poured me a drink in the *salone*. It was still drizzling outside. "I was worried you might have come down with German measles.

"I told you I've already had German measles," I said, taking the glass he'd offered, whisky and soda.

We chatted alone for a while as the others arrived one by one and settled in. Even Veronica joined us that night. She looked her old self again.

"Have you noticed no one else has shown any symptoms?" I asked Bernie.

"Come to think of it, you're right. You'd think at least one person might have developed a rash or a fever by now."

I studied our companions from across the room. "I don't think it's German measles at all," I said. "Veronica had a rash, but none of the other symptoms."

"Didn't she have a fever that first day?"

"It was a hot day, and she's a delicate flower who'd spent an hour in the sun on the back of Franco's Vespa. She said she felt fine that night except for the itching. And she never had swollen glands or a headache."

"Still, the doctor gave his diagnosis."

I sipped my drink. It was washing away the last of the sleepiness from my head. I took another, larger sip, then emptied the glass and held it out to Bernie who promptly refilled it.

"You drink too much," he said, handing me a fresh whisky and soda.

"One more word about my drinking and you'll be wearing this." I showed him my glass.

Poor Bernie. He looked crushed, and I felt bad. He only had my best interests at heart, after all. But, as previously noted, I had a horror of people monitoring my alcohol consumption, and no one was going to tell me when to stop. Especially when I was only on my second. Well, that is if you ignored the belt I'd downed in my room and the two brandies that morning. Damn it. Now I was the one counting.

"I don't trust that doctor's judgment," I said, changing the subject. "He's young and inexperienced. And not confident in his own diagnosis. He can't wait for that other doctor to return to confirm his opinion."

"But how do you explain the rash?" he asked.

"Lots of things can cause a rash. Eczema, rheumatism, sunburn. Once, a new brand of soap gave me a rash. Never mind where, Bernie, you pig. The point is it wasn't German measles."

"Has Veronica been using a new soap?" he croaked, and I regretted having mentioned my rash.

"How should I know? But ever since Achille broke her bottle of witch hazel, the rash has been improving."

Bernie was distracted. "Looks like someone's arrived," he said as the aforementioned Achille appeared to announce someone. "It's the cop. Peruzzi."

"Let's hope he's here to lift the quarantine."

CHAPTER
TWENTY-EIGHT

We joined the others in the center of the room as the barrel-chested policeman waddled in.

"*Buonasera*," he said to one and all. "I'm happy you're all here. I have some news to share about Professor Bondinelli's death."

The circled tightened around him.

"We are now convinced that Bondinelli was the victim of a crime."

The consensus among the convened was one of shock and curiosity in equal measure. Franco Sannino stepped forward and more or less demanded to know what the police had discovered. Peruzzi didn't exactly roll his eyes, but one sensed a dearth of patience in his expression.

"We are not ready to divulge the evidence that has persuaded us that this was a crime and not an accident," he said. "But I can assure you that in a day or two, we will make our case known."

"Surely you didn't come all the way up here to speak in riddles," said Franco. "There must be something more you can tell us."

Peruzzi nodded. "*Infatti*, there is a question I'd like to ask all of you who knew him."

We waited.

"If you would be so kind as to join me in the corridor, one at a time, to answer my question in private, I would be most grateful."

Over the next five minutes, everyone, with the exception of Bernie and me, was invited to file out of the room and answer the inspector's question. Not having known the dead man, we couldn't possibly provide the answers he was seeking, and so we were excused.

The first to speak with the inspector was Lucio. He returned to the *salone* under orders not to discuss the question with anyone until Peruzzi had finished with the rest. Franco went next. Then Tato, Veronica, and finally Giuliana. Lucio asked Locanda why he wasn't being questioned.

"I've already discussed the evidence with the inspector," he said. "I answered his question last night on the telephone."

While Giuliana—the last interviewee—was out in the corridor, the others exchanged notes on their encounters with the cop.

Franco began. "Did he ask you about the wallet, too?"

They all agreed.

"What about the wallet?" I asked.

"He asked if we'd ever seen it."

"And? Had you?"

"Not that I can recall," said Lucio. The others professed ignorance as well.

"To tell the truth, I have seen his wallet many times," said Veronica. "I live in his house, after all."

"What did Peruzzi make of that?" asked Franco.

"Nothing. He just wanted me to describe it."

Moments later, Giuliana returned to the *salone* with the inspector following close behind. He stopped in the middle of the room and—as usual with his eyeglasses perched halfway up his forehead—wrote some notes in his pad.

"*Allora*," he said once he'd finished. He scanned the group and pointed to three of them, Franco, Tato, and Giuliana. "*Voi tre*, I'd like to know why you lied to the police about your activity on the day the professor died."

The three exchanged terrified glances. Amazing how much adults resemble schoolchildren when called out by a policeman.

"Lied?" asked Franco in a hoarse voice. He cleared his throat and tried again. Same result.

"You told me you last saw Professor Bondinelli on Monday and only spoke to him by telephone on Tuesday, the day he died."

"Did I say that?"

"Yes. Would you like to amend your statement now?"

Franco didn't dare move. He just stood there, stooped, head immobile, his eyes large with fright, the way a dog freezes when terrified by his master.

"So where and when did you see Professor Bondinelli last Tuesday?"

"I remember now," he said, convincing no one, least of all Peruzzi. "I was so upset when you told me the news about Alberto, I must have forgotten. I was at the university that morning. All morning. I saw Alberto in the office. He was talking to the secretary, Signora Vannucci."

"Was that before or after noon?"

"A little after. I was thinking how hungry I was."

"*Bene.* And you, Signor Lombardi," said the inspector, turning to Tato. "You told my adjutant that you were with Signorina Pincherle in the university library for five hours Tuesday afternoon. That is not true. Will you please tell me where you were?"

Tato stammered his answer, claiming to have spent part of that day in the library with Giuliana. But he also visited the department offices and saw Bondinelli around 2:45.

"Was he alone?" asked the cop. I was sure he already knew the answer.

Tato didn't want to say it, but in the end he had no choice. "Professor Bondinelli was speaking to . . . Signorina Pincherle."

"*Bene,*" said the inspector. "Now, Signorina, do you wish to give me a different account of your whereabouts last Tuesday?"

"No," she said.

"No?" Peruzzi was as surprised as everyone else.

"I was in the library all afternoon and did not see the professor."

Peruzzi studied her, bemused by her stubbornness. A frown creased his face horizontally at the brow and the lips, creating the illusion of a wadded-up pillow. At length he spoke again.

"What do you say to Signor Lombardi's claim that he saw you speaking with Bondinelli?"

"He's lying," she said.

Tato nearly erupted into tears. Surely he hadn't meant to implicate his beloved Giuliana, but it was done. I thought he might fall to his knees and beg for her forgiveness.

"And Signora Vannucci, the secretary? She also told me you met Professor Bondinelli in his office last Tuesday. And when you left he appeared quite distracted. Upset. Agitated. The word she used was . . ." he flipped open his notepad and read, "*innervosito.* Rattled."

"She's a liar. I wasn't there."

"Well," said the cop, returning the pad to his breast pocket, "if you weren't in the library with Signor Lombardi, and you weren't in Professor Bondinelli's office, where were you?"

She looked across the room to the person standing behind me. I reeled around to see who. It was Lucio.

"I was with Lucio Bevilacqua in his apartment. We meet there often for our *appuntamenti*."

The collective gasp from the assembled nearly sucked me off my feet.

"Is this true?" Peruzzi asked Lucio.

"I-I'm not sure," he said. "What day was this?"

"*Martedì scorso.*"

Lucio didn't answer right away, and I doubted it was because he didn't recall. Nevertheless, he stuck to that story, claiming Giuliana might well remember better than he.

Peruzzi stayed cool. He informed them that he would be interviewing other witnesses at the university who were sure to corroborate Signora Vannucci's account.

"I urge you both to reconsider your statements. Lying to the police is a crime. And, a bit of friendly advice: you would be wise to take extreme care in your *appuntamenti*. Remember there is a *rosolia* quarantine. This is not the time to . . . *fare un bambino*."

That was on the nose. But neither of the two could very well protest since they had volunteered this scandalous alibi themselves.

Peruzzi let his last warning hang in the air for a moment then explained that, in light of the quarantine, he could not take them into custody for more questioning. But he intended to return the next day, most certainly with new evidence to prove Giuliana had spoken to Bondinelli the previous Tuesday.

"Won't you stay to dinner?" Max asked the inspector. His face was a stone, but after our time together, I was better able to read his moods. His blue eyes, I noticed, betrayed the slightest hint of a wicked smile.

CHAPTER
TWENTY-NINE

eruzzi declined Max's kind invitation and was out the door moments later. At dinner, the conversation was slow to get off the ground. There were plenty of sullen looks from the four guests who'd been caught in lies by the police. And Giuliana's sticky entanglement with Lucio had been exposed. She, for one, didn't seem to mind, even if it had broken poor Tato's heart.

Of course he was in love with her, but nothing I'd seen indicated that his feelings were reciprocated. Did she owe him fidelity if she wasn't his girl? Clearly not. Still, the way she'd made the revelation—in front of everyone and with no warning or attempt to soften the blow—struck me as particularly cruel.

Finally, as the silence soured into a pall, Veronica piped up and addressed the situation everyone else had been avoiding.

"The inspector wanted to know if I'd ever seen Professor Bondinelli's wallet," she said, chewing on a healthy portion of *lardo*. It was one of the featured specialties of the antipasto Berenice had prepared, though, I confess I couldn't stomach it.

"We already know that," said Franco. "The question is *why* did he ask us about the wallet?"

Veronica had no answer for that. Max Locanda cleared his throat quite vigorously.

"We shall not discuss this at the table," he said, his eyes indicating his niece ever so subtly. Everyone got the message, even the brick dropper Veronica and the petulant Franco Sannino.

A few minutes later, in an ill-advised attempt to kick-start the conversation, Franco inquired into Vicky's whereabouts. Was she indisposed? I wanted to kick him under the table, but he was too far away. Max, however, seemed prepared for the question and, adopting his coolest tone, announced that she had run off.

"Run off?" asked Franco. "But what about the *rosolia*?"

"Clearly her departure is a violation of the quarantine," said Max, and the subject was dropped.

Dinner continued in silence until I posed a question to break the ice.

"Those Vespas look like fun to drive. Can anyone tell me how you start one of them?"

As conversation openers go, it was a beauty. Most of the people around the table regarded me as if I'd asked if the Queen of England had any tattoos. But Franco couldn't resist showing off his expertise on the subject

"There are different Vespa models, of course," he began. "Mine is the GS 150. *Motore monocilindrico*, two-stroke, with four gears. It rides like a dream."

"Yes, but how do you start it?"

"Nothing easier. First you turn the key, then, if the engine is cold, pull the choke. Turn the fuel tap to the middle position and shift the gear to neutral. You'll need to set the throttle to the slow running position, then lean the Vespa to the left to give yourself plenty of room to start the thing. Now you start it by kicking hard on the pedal on the right-hand side. And voilà, you've started it."

Lucio interrupted. "You forgot to tell her not to flood the *carburatore*. And she has to close the choke once she's started it. Don't you have any idea how to start a motor?"

"I was going to tell her that," said Franco, close to flinging his plate at Lucio in anger. "Stop interrupting me and listen."

Despite the technical jargon, which Bernie translated for me after dinner, I figured I could manage it. My brother, Elijah, had shown me how to start and ride his motorcycle in the months before he was killed in a road accident. I pushed that memory to one side.

The lesson—and the bickering between the two men—continued, touching on the finer points of shifting gears, accelerating, and braking. The discussion lasted halfway through the second course. They were talking to each other more than to me.

After the *dolci*, fruit, and *caffè*, we wandered back into the *salone* for our nightly ritual: drinks and a story. Mariangela and I chatted for a few minutes about the new song she'd mentioned earlier.

"It's called 'She Loves You,' and I think it's even better than 'Please

Please Me' and 'From Me to You.' Don't they play the Beatles on the radio in America?"

"I don't think so," I said. "I've never heard any of their songs."

"I have the 45, but I haven't seen a record player here. Maybe they'll play it on the radio. We can listen for it tomorrow if the reception's good."

I wasn't sure they'd be playing the Beatles on Italian radio, but maybe the BBC. I told her I'd be happy to try. Then Max appeared in the *salone* with Teresa on his heels. He dispatched Mariangela with instructions to make sure she went straight to bed.

"*Domani, mi raccomando*," she said to me and followed Teresa upstairs.

For a speaker of English, *mi raccomando* is a curious admonition. It's a reflexive verb with its "*mi*" referring back to the speaker himself. Yet it's actually a warning or an exhortation for someone else to do some task. In this case Mariangela was warning me not to forget about our appointment the next day.

With only adults left in the room, Bernie wasted no time posing a question to the group. He wanted to know what was so important about Bondinelli's wallet.

I waited to see if anyone else had an idea. As no one volunteered, I offered a theory.

"There are two possibilities. One, the wallet is missing. Or, two, the wallet has been found."

"*Brava*," said Lucio. "*Hai scoperto l'America.*"

I frowned at his sarcasm. Italians are fond of telling you you've discovered America when you state something obvious.

"I believe that the wallet has been found," I continued, choosing to ignore his remark. "On dry land."

"Dry land?" asked Bernie.

"I mean not in the river. Not with Bondinelli's body."

"Why would you think that?"

"The inspector told us the police no longer suspect Bondinelli's death was an accident. That tells me the wallet was not on his person when he drowned in the river. If it had been in his pocket, the police would naturally suspect accidental drowning. Or possibly suicide."

Franco objected to this last idea. I assured him I wasn't suggesting suicide, only that the police would have to consider it or they wouldn't be doing their job.

"On the other hand, if the wallet's been found somewhere on dry land, the police would naturally suspect foul play. Robbery or even murder. A thief would have relieved him of his wallet before pushing him into the river."

"What if the wallet is still missing?" asked Lucio.

"If it's missing, why would the inspector ask you if you've ever seen it? No, they've found it and want to know if any of you stole it from him."

"Does he suspect one of us robbed Alberto and pushed him into the river?" asked Franco.

"Maybe. Or perhaps he's simply trying to eliminate suspects."

"Ellie is right," said Max, interrupting us. "I spoke to the inspector last night by telephone. He told me the police had recovered the wallet. He wouldn't say where, but it had been emptied of all cash."

"How do they know it was his? Was there identification inside?"

"They found two pieces of identification. An ATAF bus pass, monthly . . ." he paused. "And a Società Filomatica Dantesca membership card."

Giuliana scoffed. "He carried that around? When or where would he ever need to present it for identification?"

Max ignored her question.

"No *carta d'identità*?" asked Bernie.

"Not in the wallet," said Max.

Franco pointed out that the missing ID card ruined my theory, but Max promptly contradicted him.

"I'm afraid not. The police found it in Alberto's vest pocket."

I felt green. "Do you mean . . ."

"Yes, soaking wet and still on his person when they pulled him from the river."

"Why didn't you mention the phone call to anyone before?" asked Lucio.

"What an absurd question," said Max. "The inspector asked me to say nothing. The police believe someone stole Alberto's wallet and pushed him into the river."

A sobering realization descended on the group. An accidental death was tragic enough. But murder added a whole new sinister twist to Bondinelli's drowning. No one said a word for a long moment. Then Max urged us to make the best of what was left of the evening. Our moping wasn't going to bring Alberto back.

"I suggest one of you tell another story," he said.

I doubted anyone was in the mood for story hour, but I was wrong. Tato stepped forward and announced he was prepared to do the honors.

"Brace yourself," I muttered to Bernie, who again had taken a seat by my side. I was happy for his company; things were becoming quite tense among the guests at Bel Soggiorno, and I preferred to keep my reliable friend close.

"Yeah," he said, "I'm expecting fireworks."

"I'll lay you odds five to one he doesn't finish the story."

Bernie regarded me as if I had two heads. "I'm not taking that bet. Do you think I'm an idiot?"

With no action riding on the outcome, we settled in to listen to the evening's entertainment.

"Aren't you going to accompany me on the guitar?" Tato asked Lucio. To be accurate, he didn't so much ask as sneer.

"Tato, try to understand. We didn't mean to hurt you."

"*Silenzio*. It's my turn to tell a tale. You've had yours. With the story-telling and with Giuliana."

Lucio groaned. Giuliana didn't react at all.

"You all must listen," concluded Tato, then he began his story. "There once lived in our fair city a beautiful but perfidious young widow named . . . Giuliana."

"Oh, come on!" she said. He'd finally succeeded in getting a reaction out of her.

"*Sst!*" he answered with the Italian version of shush! "I am king and you will listen. As I was saying, there lived in our fair city a duplicitous, wretch of a whore named Giuliana and her black-hearted lover, Lucio Pugnalaspalle."

A roar of protests arose from the crowd, and Franco, who hadn't touched a drop of alcohol that evening, stepped up to the plate to lecture Tato. "Either you speak respectfully of Giuliana and Lucio, or you will say nothing at all. We shall not listen to such insults."

Sensing he might lose the crowd, Tato promised to steer clear of foul words in his story. We were all skeptical, but it was agreed that he'd have one last chance to finish his tale.

He nodded and continued.

"I will now amuse you with the story of a young scholar returning to Florence after years of study in Paris. One day, near the Feast of the Nativity, as he crossed the Ponte Santa Trinita, deep in reflection of the lessons of philosophy and rhetoric and astronomy he'd acquired abroad, he happened upon the ravishing widow Giuliana, who was in the company of her maid. Just as the poet Dante Alighieri, who was said to have espied the virtuous and angelic Beatrice on that very same bridge, our scholar, whose name was Tato Lombardi, fell hopelessly and completely in love with the beautiful widow."

"Real subtle about the names," whispered Bernie.

Santa Trinita. Again that bridge troubled me. This time I intended to get to the bottom of the mystery. I raised my hand. "*Una domanda.* You mentioned the Ponte Santa Trinita. Was it really there in Dante's time?"

Tato bristled at the interruption but confirmed that it had been. Bernie, the human encyclopedia, added that a famous painting by Henry Holiday depicts the scene when Dante encountered Beatrice on the bridge.

"I've always thought Dante looks like a hood in that painting," he said with a chuckle. "Watching the pretty girls go by. Beatrice's body language is definitely telling. She refuses to greet him. And, of course, the stone bridge is an anachronism. It was made of wood in Dante's day. The current bridge was built in the seventeenth century."

"But I don't remember a stone bridge from my first visit after the war," I said.

"I think I know why you're confused," said Bernie. "The Germans destroyed it when they were retreating from Florence in forty-four. It was a tragedy. So many bridges blown up just to prolong the war. So many treasures razed to the ground."

"And they built a temporary bridge after the war, didn't they?" I asked.

Bernie nodded. Max chimed in to say he remembered it well. "Made of wood and steel. A Bailey bridge, built by the Royal Engineers. Later they pulled the stones and debris of the original bridge out of the river and rebuilt it."

I knew that bridge had been made of wood when I'd last seen it. I wasn't losing my mind. "And when was the reconstruction completed?"

"Fifty-seven or fifty-eight," he said.

"Excuse me. May I continue my story?" asked Tato. "I am the king today. You must do as I say."

Happy that my memory still qualified as top drawer, I apologized and yielded the floor. Tato cleared his throat and resumed.

"As I was saying, the scholar saw his beloved on the bridge. But unlike Dante's Beatrice—the lady to whom the poet owed his salvation—this Giuliana, though beautiful, was *una troia, una disgraziata, una zoccola che tromb* . . . with my best friend!"

I've purposely left the offending slurs in Italian, as they are words I do not favor.

We all might have suffered a few moments more of Tato's story—just to see how far he intended to go—its violent profanity and all, had he not lunged at Lucio's throat mid-sentence, swearing he was going to kill him for his betrayal. Franco and Bernie tackled him before he could lay a hand on Lucio, who vaulted the divan and was hiding behind our host. Max, by the way, had made no move to intervene. Veronica ran from the room screaming. Giuliana blinked the slowest blink I'd ever seen, a sure sign of her exasperation and humiliation. But she still said nothing.

Tato didn't put up much of a struggle. In fact, before ten seconds had passed, he went limp, abandoning all resistance and aggression, and was apologizing to everyone in the room, Lucio and Giuliana included, for his outburst.

"Forgive me," he said, tears in his eyes. "I'm so sorry."

We helped him to his feet, brushed him off, and—keeping a close eye on him lest he charge Lucio again—watched as he shuffled, head bowed, out of the room and up the stairs.

"Do you think he'll be all right?" I asked.

"We were never together," said Giuliana. "We're friends, nothing more. I never gave him any reason to believe . . ."

"*Ego te absolvo*," said Franco, making the sign of the cross in her direction. "That poor *ragazzo* is brokenhearted and all you can say is it's not my fault? Have some pity, Giuliana."

"I'm going to check on him," I said, making for the door.

Lucio stopped me. "No, I should go. He's my friend after all."

The tension in the room eased slowly, almost as if a valve had been opened. We all sat down and drew a breath. Then a sip of our drinks or a drag on our cigarettes. Giuliana slipped out of the room without a good-night, leaving Bernie, Franco, Max, and me. At length, Bernie spoke.

"He was trying to tell a story from the eighth day," Bernie said in English to me. Franco and Max were well within earshot and were welcome to listen in.

I must have looked confused.

"*The Decameron*," he said. "Tato was following the precedent set by Lucio and Giuliana. And I think we all noticed he changed the names."

"How did that story go?" I asked. "Tato didn't get very far."

"The part about the scholar returning from Paris was pretty faithful to the original. And the beautiful young widow. I don't recall their names off hand. The rest is a tale of how the widow tricks the scholar in the cruelest, most selfish manner in order to prove to her lover that he has no reason to doubt her devotion to him."

"What does she do to him?"

"She convinces the scholar that she loves him and will give herself to him, but instead she leaves him locked in her courtyard on a frigid snowy night. Then she and her lover watch for hours as he nearly freezes to death."

"How awful."

"Yeah, the poor guy spends the entire night in the icy snow while the two lovers ... um ... well, you can guess what they do—several times—in the warmth of her bed."

"And that's how it ends?" I asked. "Not a very good story."

"No, the scholar realizes how foolish he's been and plots his revenge. Months later he gets the chance when the widow's lover leaves her for another woman. The scholar hatches a plot involving black magic that he promises will win her her lover back. She buys it, and somehow he gets her to take off all her clothes and climb a high tower where he strands her totally naked in the blazing hot sun."

"I see. Nice symmetry there. A little obvious and rather unlikely, but I suppose it works. Does that mean Tato is planning his revenge on Giuliana?"

"If I am any judge of human behavior, I'd say no." This was Max tossing in his two cents, also in English. "That young man will beg to have her back again. And she might accept him. Once Lucio finds another."

"You don't believe in their love?" I asked with a wink and gob of sarcasm heaped on top besides. "Giuliana's and Lucio's, I mean."

Max clicked his tongue. "They are young and finding their way in life. Their love affair is just a pleasant diversion until they grow older and more serious."

How sad, I thought, that love affairs were so frivolous. Then I stopped myself. It was different with me. I wasn't looking to grow old and serious, so I could permit myself some frivolity.

I realized that Franco might be at a disadvantage with the change in language, but he seemed to be following. Still, to get my mind off my own thoughts, I told him in Italian he'd behaved admirably this evening, not like the night before. I kept that last bit to myself. He blushed and said he'd been ashamed by his behavior and promised to monitor his drinking more carefully.

"I'm also embarrassed for having lied to the police. Yes, I saw Alberto that day, but we barely said hello. I don't know why I lied."

I climbed the long stairs to my room and wished Bernie goodnight. He lingered just a touch longer than necessary, which told me all I needed to know. He wouldn't have turned down a chance to see my etchings. But I wanted no part in ruining a good friendship. Sure, he was tall and good-looking in an offbeat way, but an hour or two of pleasant diversion would surely lead to an awkward tomorrow. Perhaps if he hadn't been so close to my father, I might have invited him into my room, just on a lark. But I liked Bernie too much to stoke a fire I had no intention of tending. I kissed him on the cheek and pushed him off toward his room down the hall. He made a pit stop at the bathroom.

I waited and listened until I was sure Bernie had performed whatever exigencies nature had required of him, then I slipped into the bathroom to do the same. Back in my room, I undressed and slid between the sheets. That's when I noticed the envelope propped up on the bedside table.

CHAPTER THIRTY

I recognized the letter immediately as the one Bondinelli had addressed to me. The one that had disappeared from the table in Piazza della Signoria on Thursday afternoon. Rising from the bed, I covered myself with a robe. Those old Italian country houses had no closets, but there was an armoire standing against the wall. It was too small to hold a grown person, of course, but I opened it just the same. Nothing besides my clothes inside. Then I peeked under the bed. All clear. Confident the room was free from unwelcome guests, I locked the door with its church key, slipped between the sheets again, and took up the sealed letter. I opened it with my fingernail. Written in an elegant hand, it read:

Friday, September 27, 1963

Carissima Sig.na Stone,

I trust your stay in our beautiful city has been a satisfying one. By now the symposium has ended, the visiting scholars have left to return home, and we are all happy with the achievements of our little conference. It was a supreme honor for me to present you with the medal honoring your distinguished father. As you know, I met him a few times many years ago, and his memory is still fresh in my mind.

The purpose of this letter is to thank you for your participation in the symposium. Florence is a long way for a young woman to travel alone without a husband, and I understand you've spent the past ten months perfecting your Italian. Complimenti! You have earned full marks. I shall be forever grateful to you for your wholehearted enthusiasm and good will, both of which helped make our symposium a success.

Finally, I'd like to divulge a secret. You may not realize that you and I have more in common than a passion for medieval literature and your father's work. In fact, dear Eleonora, you and I share a name. Or at least we once shared a name for a time. I do not wish to say more in writing for fear it might be discovered by someone else, but I shall be happy to explain it to you over the weekend in Fiesole, when we will have time to chat at our leisure.

Remember that this is something I've never discussed with anyone. I know I can count on your discretion.

It was a pleasure to meet you in person, and I look forward to seeing you at Villa Bel Soggiorno.

Tante grazie e distinti saluti,

Prof. Alberto Bondinelli

I sat on my bed, letter in hand, perplexed by the riddle I'd just read, never mind the absurd suggestion that I had some kind of passion for medieval literature. What on earth did he mean that we had once shared a name? Had he called himself Eleonora at some point in his ever-changing life? Had I been Alberto once upon a time? Or was it our last names?

Unable to answer any of those questions, I read the letter again. Then once more. I took note of the date: Friday, September 27, 1963. That meant one of three possibilities: one, he'd written it two days after his death; two, someone else had forged it; or three, he'd post-dated the letter. I immediately discounted options one and two, settling for number three.

I could understand why an organized man might write a note of thanks in advance. He'd left the information vague enough for that scenario to be believable. Yes, I was convinced the letter had been composed in anticipation of a successful symposium, at the latest the previous Tuesday, but possibly months earlier. Why not?

The thank-you was generic, but the tantalizing mystery was anything but. He'd intended to fill me in over the weekend, but that, of course, was not in the cards. Was the secret of the name tragic? Scandalous? Amusing? And why did he want to keep it a secret? I couldn't fathom a guess. I wondered if anyone else at Bel Soggiorno could fill in the blanks.

MONDAY, SEPTEMBER 30, 1963

Ermenegildo crowed at 4:39 a.m., well before the sun rose at ten past six. I had no pennies or anvils to toss out the window, let alone a sniper's rifle, which is what I really needed. I considered sacrificing a small painting on the wall, but resisted, knowing that it wasn't mine to fling at the bird. Had it belonged to me, the dark, little picture of a marketplace—frame and all—would have ended up around the rooster's neck like a lace ruff collar. I tried to get back to sleep, but after an hour of listening to Ermenegildo exercising his considerable voice, I threw in the towel and repaired to the bathroom down the hall. By half past six I'd made my way downstairs, fully intending to rummage through the larder in search of milk and bread for breakfast. But that wasn't necessary. Berenice was already on the job.

"*Buongiorno, signorina*," she said. I returned the greeting. "Why are you up so early?"

"Why?" I asked. "Because you refused to chop off Ermenegildo's head."

"You Americans like eggs for breakfast, don't you? Sit down and I'll fix you some that *povero* Ermenegildo never had the chance to fertilize. We don't let him near the hens."

She offered up a lascivious grin, and I wished she'd hadn't. I didn't need to think about my tormentor's sex life, his frustrations, or his off-limits harem.

"I believe Teresa, the Spanish lady, is staying in a room near yours," I said to change the subject. "Tell me about her."

"What do you want to me say? She's quiet, reads her Bible. She's clean."

"She's devoted to Mariangela."

"*Certo.* Why shouldn't she be? That girl is a love."

"Does Mariangela take after her mother?" I asked.

Berenice cracked two eggs with one hand and dropped them into a hot skillet on the stove. She frowned. "*La piccina* is a love, but, *poverina*, she's not a beauty. Not like her mother. Maybe she's an ugly duckling—*un brutto anatroccolo*—and will turn out to be a swan."

"Was the *signore* very fond of Silvana?"

Berenice stirred the eggs in the pan, perhaps mulling over my question. Then she sniffed and said he'd loved her as a brother loves a younger sister.

A voice came from the kitchen door. "What are you talking about?" It was the ugly duckling herself.

Berenice burned her hand on the skillet. I did my best to maintain calm. "We were talking about how beautiful your mother was," I said. "And how much your uncle loved her."

After a *colazione* of eggs, bread, and *caffellatte*, Mariangela and I took advantage of the warming sun—the rain had stopped well before the rooster had crowed, not thrice but thirty, forty, fifty times?—and embarked on a stroll through the garden. We took a different route that morning, eschewing the pergola and its long alleyway, opting for a path that took us east through a wooded area of olive trees. The temperature was pleasantly cool at that hour, more so given the rain of the day before, but I sensed the sun would mount its revenge later that day. The girl was carrying one of those navy blue BOAC flight bags with a shoulder strap.

"What have you got there?" I asked.

"I brought some fruit and water," she said, sitting down cross-legged in an open dry spot. She produced a bottle of San Benedetto *acqua gassata* as if pulling a rabbit from a hat, then pouted. "Oh, drat. I forgot the bottle opener."

In college, I'd learned a few tricks for removing crown tops from bottles. Those usually were filled with beer, but water would work just as well.

"Here, give me the bottle and your bag," I said, taking a seat next to her on the ground.

She handed them over. I slid the end of one of the straps to the far edge of the metal fastener that connected it to the bag, then I positioned the bottle cap against the rectangle.

"See, this metal doohickey here? If you hold it tightly against the heel of your thumb and push . . ."

The cap popped off into the grass before I could finish explaining.

"*Brava*, Ellie," said Mariangela.

"Actually, almost any edge will do. As long as you catch it under the crimps, you should be able to pry it off with a swift tap."

"You're so clever."

"Yes, I had a first-rate education."

We each peeled and ate a tangerine, washed down with mineral water from a couple of dented metal cups Mariangela had squirreled away in her bag.

"It's all so strange," she said. "Losing my father, I mean. I can't quite convince myself it's real."

"It will take time. People react in different ways to death."

"I feel so wretched. I haven't even wept once. Is there something wrong with me?"

"Of course not. You're simply trying to understand. There's no training for this. You're doing just fine. You know, I reacted much the way you describe when my mother died. Somehow I couldn't cry any tears."

"I'm sorry to hear that, Ellie. Were you not close to her?"

"Quite the opposite. I loved her and cherished her and respected her. She was the sweetest person in the world."

"Then why didn't you cry?"

I kept the answer to myself. Tried to answer it to myself before sharing with Mariangela. Though I'd long felt my stoic acceptance of my mother's passing was due to how devastated I'd been by my brother's death just months before, I was no longer sure that was the case. I still couldn't offer a reason. We'd shared a healthy bond as mother and daughter, with none of the heartache and rancor and reproach that characterized my relationship with my father. His death had scarred me more than hers, and Elijah's had torn out my heart. Why, then, had I not wept at her funeral? Why had I thrown up a wall of impassive calm when I lost her? I didn't know. I simply didn't know.

"I did it to punish my father," I said. "We had . . . a stormy relationship. Let's leave it at that."

Perhaps I did know after all.

I immediately regretted having burdened a child with my sad story. I apologized to her, but she told me not to fret.

"Goodness, Ellie. You lost everyone. I'm so sorry. You've no reason to apologize to me."

We reflected on that for a while as we sipped our water. It was time to change the subject.

"What else do you have in there, Mary Poppins?" I asked, referring to her bag.

"This," she said, producing two records, both 45s with bright labels reading "PARLOPHONE" in all capital letters. "This one is 'She Loves You.' It's the Beatles' best song ever. And this one is 'Please Please Me,' which is really fabulous. Better than any other song besides 'She Loves You.' And there's 'Ask Me Why' on the B-side. That's the third greatest song ever, but not like 'Please Please Me.' Remember I told you we were going to listen to the songs?"

"Do you have a record player in that bag as well?"

"Of course not. But I asked Berenice this morning, and she said there's one in the house somewhere. We'll listen when we go back."

"So nothing else in the bag?"

"Just my camera kit and this," she said, pulling out a framed black-and-white photograph. I recognized it immediately. It was a copy of the one I'd seen in Max Locanda's study. The one from the café. Mariangela pointed to the woman. "There. That's my mum. And, of course, that's my father." She indicated the tall man sitting two seats away.

"Who's this?" I asked, referring to the bald man on Bondinelli's right.

"My grandfather. I don't remember him. He died when I was small."

We'd arrived at the last man in the photo. "And who is this?"

"I don't know, but, here, Father wrote the names on the back of the frame."

She flipped the picture and, sure enough, beside the sticker identifying the framing house, there were three names written in black scrawl with a fourth scratched out: "R. Locanda, S. Locanda, P. Sasso."

"That's strange," I said. "He's only identified three people here."

"He must have removed his own name," said Mariangela. "He was a very modest man."

"Still, he's written the other names, including his father-in-law's and his own wife's."

"But they weren't married yet, don't you see? The date is there. April twenty-first, 1944. So it makes sense that he noted down the names."

I wasn't so sure. Something seemed off about the explanation, but then again I couldn't stand to see a crossword puzzle clue go unsolved. I bought her idea that he might not have included his own name, but why would he have scratched it out? And more than anything, I was disappointed that the names on the back of the frame did not include Marco, Silvana's one-time love.

"So you don't know this P. Sasso?" I asked. "Your parents never spoke of him?"

As an answer, she offered one of those precious, awkward, adolescent shrugs along with a rubbery face of lips and eyes stretching the boundaries of their natural resting positions.

"Would you mind if I borrowed this photo? Just for a day or two. I'd like to study it a bit more."

"I can't imagine why, but be my guest."

We made our way back to the house a couple of hours later, still well before the noonday meal was to be served. Lucio, Franco, and a subdued Tato were milling about on the *terrazza*, smoking cigarettes and talking about anything except what had happened the night before. Mariangela and I had little time for chitchat. We were on a quest to find a record player or a gramophone or a hi-fi. I hadn't seen anything remotely resembling any of those in the house, but Mariangela wasn't one to give up so easily. Having badgered Berenice for information, she finally discovered her uncle's BSR portable record player atop a dusty, forsaken piano in a sitting room beyond the dining hall. It was one of those machines that looked like a miniature suitcase orphaned in the baggage room at a train station. We lugged it up to Mariangela's room on the second floor and placed it on the dressing table near her bed. Despite an aging needle and a fraying power cord, the BSR sparked to life when we plugged it into the wall. We pulled up a couple of chairs, and Mariangela slipped a record onto the turntable.

"Now just listen, Ellie. How I envy you, hearing this for the first time."

A spirited harmonica opened the song. Unusual, I thought, for pop music, but not unpleasant. A nice beat, then the energetic harmonies of two or three voices followed. The Beatles had a different sound, I had to admit. Sweet and melodious, but with more of an edge than your average hit parade offering. I appreciated the bridge, one of my favorite parts of song structure—along with the intro, verses, refrain, and coda. I suppose one could point out that those are all the parts of a popular song, and I wouldn't disagree.

In the case of Mariangela's "Please Please Me," the totality was, on first listen, a catchy little tune sung by voices with some character and personality. Not bad, though I wasn't yet ready to swoon.

Mariangela played the song three more times before suggesting we listen to the flip side, a song called, "Tell Me Why."

"This one is good, but not as good as 'PPM.'"

I gathered PPM was her shorthand for "Please Please Me."

This song began with a muscular intro of drums and guitar, then dived right into the refrain. Again, good harmonies from the singers and a roughness to the lead's voice. The melody, like the first song's, was memorable and pleasing, even if I didn't quite understand the words. "Tell me why you cried and why you lied to me." I struggled to determine who was the villain and who was the aggrieved. But then, maybe that made it a better song after all. Not the tired old theme of "you are mine" or "be true to me" or anything by Pat Boone.

"What are you thinking, Ellie?" asked Mariangela. "Don't you like the song?"

"Of course I do. In fact, I was just thinking how much better it is than the music I normally hear on the radio."

She beamed at me and said now was the moment. "I've saved this for last. I'm going to play 'She Loves You,' and you're going to flip." She placed the new record on top of the other one and cued it up.

Despite the repetitive "yeah, yeah, yeah" that made the song instantly memorable, this was clearly the number with the most potential for success. As in the other tracks, there were harmonies. They were having fun with this song.

"That's Paul there," she said, pointing to the spinning record as it played.

I couldn't really distinguish any single voice standing out, but Mariangela seemed sure. The arrangement, vocals, and overall performance all seemed more professional and polished, at least to my mind.

"*Che chiasso infernale è questo?*" came a voice from the door as the song played for the fourth time. It was Max Locanda.

Mariangela plucked the needle off the record, loosing silence in the room.

"She was playing her favorite song for me," I said. "And it's not an infernal racket. It's the Beatles."

"The Beetles? *Gli scarabei*? What is this 'yeah, yeah, yeah' nonsense?"

I fired a silent glare of reproach at him. His niece had just lost her father. She was an orphan. I'm not sure how a fierce scowl managed to communicate that specific message to him, but I believe it did. His expression softened somewhat.

Now that the music had stopped, he stepped into the room and asked if that was his record player. The girl stared at the floor, too frightened to say anything at all. I thought the best strategy was to leverage my new-found friendliness—if it could be called that—with Max and plead ignorance at the same time.

"We don't know whose it is. Berenice found it. And since it was collecting dust on a piano, we didn't think it would be missed. Surely you won't deny us a little amusement."

"No, of course not," he said. "But I wish you were amused by more pleasant noise."

"What if we turn down the volume?" I asked.

He could find no argument with that and reluctantly agreed.

Then he noticed Mariangela's BOAC bag, which she'd tossed on the bed earlier. The photograph from the café was peeking out. Max nodded at it and asked if that, too, was his?

"No," I said. "It's from her father's office at the university."

He picked it up and examined the faces. "This was forty-three or forty-four. Piazza della Repubblica. My father used to frequent that café."

I joined him to study the photograph as if for the first time, even though we'd already discussed it in detail in his study the day Mariangela arrived. I glanced at her. She was still seated at the dressing table next to the record player. If Max knew she was there, he made no attempt to acknowledge her. She watched us silently. I fancied she was searching for a secret, perhaps how I managed to talk to her uncle without trembling.

"My father was looking particularly nasty that day," said Max. He reconsidered his statement. "Every day, really."

"And you're sure you don't know who this is?" I asked, pointing to the fourth man.

"*Non lo so.* I never laid eyes on him."

I took the frame from him, stared at the picture for a brief moment, then turned it over to reveal the names on the verso.

"Look here," I said. "There's your father's name, your sister's, and this other name. P. Sasso. Do you suppose that's his name?"

Max squinted to see, his brow knitted into a tight frown. "Alberto didn't write his own name, so I suppose that man is P. Sasso."

"Perhaps he didn't feel the need to identify himself in the photograph. Or he changed his mind and scratched it out here." I pointed to the offending blotch on the back of the frame. "It could be anything. The name of the café or some other note. Perhaps he'd misspelled something and decided to cover it."

My answers didn't satisfy him. The frown remained fast in place as he looked up at me.

"You must be right. But what does it matter? This man must have been a friend of one of them. Maybe he knew my father or Alberto."

I didn't want to add his sister's name to the list, and clearly neither did he. Not in front of Mariangela. He took the photo back from me for one last look. Then he placed it on the bed and said lunch would be served in a half-hour.

"Go ahead and listen to your music," he said to the girl. "But not too loud, *ti prego*."

Before heading down to lunch, I gathered up the photo Mariangela had said I could borrow and took it to my room.

CHAPTER THIRTY-ONE

After lunch, whose main course featured spaghetti—or something resembling spaghetti but thicker—served with a delicious meat ragout of *cinghiale*, most everyone retired for a siesta or a stroll in the garden. Only Franco refused to budge from his spot in the *salone*, where he was engaging me with questions about my youth in New York. Had I ever met a real mafioso? Did all Americans chew gum? And other such nonsense. At length, once he'd smoked a couple of cigarettes and succumbed to the magic of Berenice's heavy meal, he yawned and said perhaps he'd take a nap after all.

Once he'd climbed the stairs, I waited a full minute before grabbing my purse and darting out the door. The gray Vespa stood against the wall where Franco had parked it three days before. He'd ridden it like a cowboy from Santa Maria Novella to Fiesole, the fetching Veronica seated behind him, holding on for dear life, like some kind of itchy ingénue in a bad movie. I didn't care about any of that. I only wanted to get the thing moving and drive it down to Florence without anyone catching on.

Fearing discovery, I wheeled the scooter behind the house and down the path I'd walked that morning with Mariangela. I'd noted how isolated the way had been and, figuring it would eventually reach Via Boccaccio, I thought I could escape Bel Soggiorno without the policeman at the head of the drive any the wiser.

I walked the Vespa at least two hundred yards into the olive grove to the south of the house. Confident no one would hear me there, I climbed aboard, inserted the key as Franco had explained, and switched the fuel tap to the on position. Then, having pulled the choke, I lifted myself up onto the kick-start pedal and gave it every ounce of my weight as I pushed down against its resistance. To my surprise, the thing roared to life on the first try. And after one or two stalls as I learned to handle the clutch,

I got the hang of it. Before I'd reached Via Boccaccio, I was shifting and accelerating like a pro.

I made it to Piazza della Libertà in twenty minutes. There, I parked Franco's Vespa in front of a bank and found a phone booth. The directory inside yielded no Pincherles. Not one. My clever idea was butting up against a major roadblock. But if my years of reporting at the *New Holland Republic* had taught me anything, it was that closed doors sometimes have a transom overhead or a window off to the side. There was always another path you could try, a different tack, to get around an obstacle. So, standing in a phone booth in Piazza della Libertà, I thought back on what I knew about Giuliana. I recalled a discussion she'd had with Max Locanda about olive and grape presses a couple of days earlier. She'd said her mother's family had been in the machinery business once upon a time.

"The company was Dalla Torre Fratelli," Giuliana had told him.

I flipped through the directory and came across only one listing, under the name Sra A. Dalla Torre on Via Laura.

The elderly neighbor woman at the Via Laura address said the signora wasn't in. She was never in during the day. Instead, she directed me to the nearby synagogue. She said Signora Dalla Torre spent most of her time helping out there. Then she lowered her voice to tell me there wasn't actually much the old lady could do.

"It's more a kindness for her sake than the other way around. She wants to feel useful."

"What kind of work does she do there?" I asked.

"She helps with reading to older congregants. And with donations of books and food. Sometimes she polishes a piece of brass. Other times she watches the little children at the *shul*. But her hearing's not good. Mostly she sits and chats about the old days. Before the war. Before the *Ventennio*."

Tempio Maggiore was only a short distance from Via Laura. I approached the synagogue from the north. It loomed large ahead on my left, its green copper dome, flanked by a tower on each side, was visible long before I'd come close. The view from the street took me by surprise. The great synagogue rose before me like a pink Moorish palace. Less than a hundred years old, it nevertheless projected a weighty history. It had been built in the 1870s and was one of the largest synagogues in Southern Europe. Florence counted fewer than 1,500 Jews, yet this magnificent house of worship stood in disproportionate grandeur to its congregation's size. A true monument to faith and tradition. I wondered how it had survived the German occupation during the war.

A porter met me at the gate. He knew Signora Dalla Torre and directed me through the garden to an entry on the northeastern side of the apse. He said I might find her there.

I pushed through the little door, announcing myself as one does in Italy, *"Permesso?"* An elegant lady in a black dress sat alone in the room. She looked up at me from a chair beside the window where she was reading, and closed the book in her hands. Her eyes were sharp and intelligent. She seemed a matron of society or a quick-witted doyenne, ready to charm or reduce you to size according to her whim.

"Buongiorno," she said. "May I help you?"

I explained that I was looking for Signora Dalla Torre.

"I am Alide Dalla Torre," she said, striking me as neither feeble with age nor hard of hearing.

Her bearing was so dignified, so proper, that I felt a wretch with my hair all tangled from racing down the hill from Fiesole on Franco's Vespa. I introduced myself and explained the purpose of my visit. She was happy to hear her granddaughter's name.

"Giuliana came to visit me last Tuesday," she said with a bright smile. "Such a good girl. I raised her when her parents passed away ten years ago. Are you a friend of hers?"

"Yes. She told me about you. She said you know Alberto Bondinelli. I was hoping you could tell me about him."

I was playing a hunch, of course, figuring she was the witness Giuliana had mentioned. But I was mistaken.

She looked perplexed. "Who?"

"Alberto Bondinelli. Giuliana's professor. He died last week."

Still no sign of recognition from the signora.

"Giuliana has many professors. I don't recall her ever mentioning this Bondinelli. And Giuliana said I knew him?"

I wriggled and lied, claiming I must have misunderstood.

"Why do you want to know about this man?" she asked.

"He invited me to Florence for a symposium in honor of my father. But he died before I could meet him."

"I'm afraid I can't help you. I never met the man. What does he have to do with me?"

"I'm not sure. That's why I came here today."

Then I told her that Bondinelli had once been a Black Shirt, wounded in Spain fighting alongside the Nationalists, and left the service before the war began. He later joined the partisans to fight the fascists and their German overlords.

"But you said he was a professor."

"Yes. He was hired after the racial laws of thirty-eight."

"In thirty-eight my son-in-law, Giacomo—Giuliana's father—was a professor of philosophy at the university. When the fascists passed those laws, he was dismissed. If what you tell me is true, this man—Giuliana's professor—effectively took her own father's position."

This news nearly bowled me over. It cast doubt over every opinion I'd formed about Giuliana to that point. Her antipathy toward Bondinelli was personal, not ideological or political. I found myself wondering if she might not have been capable of violence against the man who'd profited from the injustice done to her father. And, of course, Giuliana had concealed the detail about her father's having lost his job, even as she railed against the man who, for all intents and purposes, had taken it. That sparked in me a suspicion bordering on certainty. Giuliana had good reason to hate Bondinelli. She'd spoken to him an hour or two before his death. Something unpleasant had taken place during their last meeting, as the department secretary claimed the professor was distraught after the encounter. I wondered if they'd met again before his tumble into the Arno.

Alide Dalla Torre fretted, smoothed her dress, and moistened her lips with her tongue.

"I can't believe that this man changed. *Il lupo perde il pelo ma non il vizio*," she said. ("The wolf loses his pelt but not his wickedness." I was unfamiliar with the expression but took it to mean, "A leopard can't change his spots.") "I find this story incredible. This man was a fascist, then a partisan? No. *Non ci credo*."

I explained that I was as confused as she. "Since I arrived in Florence, I've heard terrible stories about his character. But I've also heard loving praise of his goodness."

"What does Giuliana say?"

"She believes he was an evil man. But, according to her friend, she only recently came to that conclusion."

Signora Dalla Torre knitted her brow and considered me carefully. "Why have you come here to ask me this? Where is Giuliana?"

"She's under quarantine," I said. "For *rosolia*. She can't leave the house where she's staying for a few more days."

I assured her that the diagnosis was probably incorrect. No one was exhibiting any symptoms at all. This seemed to satisfy her, though she worried her granddaughter might fall sick. We chatted a while longer and, at length, her nerves settled. She seemed to like me well enough despite the upset I'd caused by reminding her of the ugly past. She asked me about my family, my husband.

"I'm not married," I said.

"Don't wait too long. You won't be young and pretty forever. I tell Giuliana the same thing. She's so beautiful, that girl. She should get married."

Then she asked if I'd like to see the synagogue.

I lent Alide Dalla Torre my arm as she escorted me on a private tour of the treasures, from the frescos to the mosaics. She explained how the architects, for the first time in Christian Europe, had been freed from long-standing requirements to hide Jewish places of worship in nondescript buildings. They designed a synagogue worthy to stand as a monument beside the great churches and cathedrals of Florence. The Jewish Emancipation, she said, was the period after the Enlightenment when European Jewry gradually achieved some measure of acceptance in the Christian world, including citizenship and the rights that came with that status. It went hand in hand with the Haskalah, the so-called Jewish Enlightenment, which espoused, inter alia, the integration of Jews into gentile society.

"My father told my brother and me about the Maskilim," I said. "He wanted us to belong to Western society, but also to know and appreciate our Jewish heritage."

"Are you a Jew?" she asked. "I didn't realize."

I nodded, stopping short of explaining that I wasn't a religious Jew. Or even a believing one. What would I have accomplished with such a declaration?

Instead I turned the subject back to her granddaughter. "You said you last saw Giuliana Tuesday."

"Yes, we had a short chat. A little before noon. She said she had an appointment at the university. It's very close by, you know."

"And she has no other living relatives?" I asked, still trying to reconcile Giuliana's statement about a witness, as it clearly wasn't her grandmother.

"No. They're all gone. We're the only ones left." Then she reconsidered. "Wait. There's her uncle. Her father's sister's husband. Not a blood relative, but he's still alive."

Alfredo Levi lived at 28 Borgo Pinti, minutes away from the synagogue on Franco's Vespa. I leaned the scooter against the wall of the building on the narrow street and rang the bell. After a long moment, a buzz unlocked the heavy arched door, and I slipped inside a dark vestibule. A few trash bins stood lopsided on my left, mailboxes and a wood-and-glass entrance on my right, leading to a set of stairs. I checked the names. A. Levi was in apartment four.

When I reached the top landing, the door to number four creaked open a couple of inches. An elderly man peered out and asked who I was. His right eye—the one he was aiming at me through the crack, was clouded with cataracts that glowed eerily in the low light. I wondered if he could even make out my shape.

"I'm a friend of Giuliana's. Your niece. Her father, Giacomo, was your brother-in-law, wasn't he?"

He let the door fall open. A small but sturdy man of about eighty, A. Levi stared back at me with his milky eyes. From where I stood, I could see that the apartment was dark and close, with old furniture, tarnished silver pieces, dusty lace doilies, and threadbare rugs and chairs. Nothing had changed for decades, I was sure.

"Who did you say you were?" he asked.

"My name is Eleonora Stone. American. Visiting Florence. I'm a friend of Giuliana's."

The man made no indication he'd even understood me, let alone be-lieved or trusted what I'd said. Then he asked me to come inside, address-ing me as Giuliana.

I considered my options. I could try to explain that I wasn't his niece, but that might have been more trouble than it was worth. And—for all I knew—he might ask me to leave. I opted instead to say nothing. He closed the door behind me and shuffled over to a well-worn chair, where he dropped into the cushion with a plop reminiscent of a baseball landing in a catcher's mitt.

"It's nice to see you, Giuliana," he began. "Twice in one day. *Brava ragazza.*"

"I visited you earlier today?" I asked.

"You cooked Sunday dinner for me."

"Sunday? But today's . . . Never mind. I've come back to ask you a question. Do you know a man named Alberto Bondinelli?"

The old man wiped his mouth with his rough hands. "No. Who is he? Your boyfriend?"

"No. He's . . . He was . . . I mean he's my professor. Are you sure you've never heard the name?"

He shook his head. "Thursday," he said.

"*Scusa, giovedì?*" I used *tu* with him; if I was playing the part of Giuli-ana, I might as well play it all the way.

"Sorry, I meant Friday. Friday I have my driver's test. For my license."

Oh, dear, I thought. This wasn't going well. The poor man didn't know what day it was. And, for some reason, he wasn't even curious as to how his niece had suddenly acquired an American accent.

"Last Sunday I was tired," he said now. "I slept for a couple of hours, and you kept me company. Then you cooked me dinner. We had a nice visit. I'm glad you've come back again today."

"It was nice," I said, sensing we'd reached the end of any useful con-versation.

"No. I don't eat much these days," he said, confusing me again. "Just a *minestra* and some bread."

"What did I do to occupy myself while you slept?" I asked. "Did I read a book or listen to the radio?"

"You wanted to look at some of Gabriele's things."

"Gabriele?"

"Your cousin. Don't you remember?"

"Of course I do. Tell me about Gabriele. Where is he?"

"Where is he? He's dead. You know that. He died in the war. Captured and shot by the Germans."

I didn't know what to say. Lucky for me he'd primed the pump and was happy to talk without further urging.

"It was in La Chiusa, near Calenzano. Northwest of here. Not far. Some of the boys came out of the woods and ambushed a German soldier. In those days, the SS killed ten Italian civilians for each German to discourage hostilities against them."

"Ten to one?"

"Oh, yes. Ten for each one. The OVRA grabbed Gabriele on the street, rounded him up with some of his friends here in Florence. He was dead an hour later, shot by the Germans."

"That's right," I said. "I'd forgotten. Poor Gabriele. He was a hero."

The old man's eyes shifted a touch. He wiped his lips again, then smiled. Yes, he smiled. "I'm not sure if Gabriele was involved in the attack on the German soldier," he said. "At least not that one."

"Was he with the partisans?"

His smile broadened, his lips parted, and I saw that he was toothless. But he was grinning. "He was with the CLN. The *Comitato di Liberazione Nazionale*. Mostly Communists and Socialists. *Bravi ragazzi*, all of them." He paused, looked confused. "I told you that, Thursday."

"*Già*, Thursday," I said. "Sorry. Tell me more about Gabriele and the *bravi ragazzi*."

"He led his own *squadra* of three partisans. Here in Florence."

With great difficulty, he pushed himself out of the chair and waved to me to follow him down the corridor. "Come, Bianca. I'll show you something."

He shuffled along, the fingertips of his right hand grazing the wall as he went, perhaps for balance or maybe guidance. I followed, taking in what details I could, wondering who Bianca was. The low light prevented any careful study, but I noticed the unswept stone floor, the faded, crooked photographs mounted on the walls, and the three doors squaring off the corridor up ahead, one on each side and one in the middle. Alfredo reached the door on the right, found the handle with no trouble despite his cataracts, and pushed his way inside. The heavy shutters—the *persiane*—were closed tight outside the two windows, shrouding the room in darkness, like a mausoleum. He flicked on a light. A single bed—its mattress rolled up on the springs—stood between the windows. A large bookcase, an armoire, a desk, and a couple of wooden chairs completed the furnishings. The walls were bare except for one picture frame over the bed.

"*Vieni a vedere, Bianca,*" he said, urging me to come forward. "Can you see it?"

I gazed up at the frame. Behind the glass was a certificate of some kind with an official stamp and fancy signatures.

"Read it to me," he said, his toothless smile splitting his wrinkled face in two.

"*Repubblica Italiana, Ministero dell'Assistenza Post-Bellica,*" I said. "*Partigiano.*"

The old man could barely contain his excitement. His hands twitched, not from any neurological disorder or physical infirmity, but from giddy joy.

"Go on. What comes next?"

I read the name, "LEVI, Gabriele," followed by the date and place of his birth. And then his parents' names, father and mother, Alfredo and Bianca.

"And then?"

"Then, '*Caduto*,' (Fallen)" I said, "April twenty-first, 1944, at Florence."

And that was it. Aside from the signatures and the stamp, there was nothing more to read. Alfredo's twitching hands fell still. And his smile melted back into his face. The milky eyes drooped, the short-lived happiness gone, having left a hollow hunger in its place. A father's pride could hide the heartbreak for only so long—for a brief moment in front of a young stranger, or his niece or late wife—but then no more. The mask fell to the ground, and he was a lonely, demented old man again.

"We're so proud of Gabriele," I said, but he'd moved on to some gloomy corner of his memories by then.

He showed me to the door. I thanked him for the honor of viewing his son's certificate of recognition and asked if he needed anything. "Something from the *alimentari* or the *farmacia*?"

"I have plenty to eat," he said. "The neighbors do the marketing for me. But..."

"What is it? What can I get for you, *zio*?"

"They won't buy me cigarettes. I wouldn't mind a packet of *Nazion-ali*."

I'd noticed a *tabaccheria* a few doors away in the street below. Not sure I was doing the right thing, given his age and infirmities, I bought him three packages of cigarettes all the same and climbed the stairs once more to deliver them. Alfredo Levi greeted me as if I'd been gone a week. And as if I were Giuliana.

"Come back Sunday," he said. "You and I will talk while you look through Gabriele's things again."

"Again? What am I looking for?"

"No. Thursday. Wait. No. You took that photo you found. To remember him. Of course I said yes. But now I want to see it. Show me the photo."

I rummaged through my purse looking for a photograph of some kind. He could barely see, after all. Where was the harm? I found one of me with my late brother, Elijah, tucked inside my billfold. I held it out for the old man to examine.

"How handsome I look," he said from his toothless smile. "Bianca not so much. She's a good wife, but not very pretty."

I told myself not to take it personally; his cataracts surely rendered the photograph a total blur.

"*A presto, zio*," I said, taking his broad hand in mine. He pulled me in for a kiss on each cheek.

"*A domenica*," he replied. "*Mi raccomando . . .*"

CHAPTER
THIRTY-TWO

B y now I felt completely at ease with the Vespa. Shifting gears, braking, and handling became second nature after a few miles of navigating the streets. I had two last errands to run in the city before heading back up to Fiesole. First, I zipped down Via della Pergola, then zigzagged my way through the *vie* until I reached Via del Proconsolo. From there, I rode through a couple of side streets and arrived at Piazza dei Cimatori. Lifting the Vespa up onto its kickstand, I locked the steering column and dismounted. A young man whistled at me, but I ignored him, heading instead straight into the American Express Office.

"I'd like to make a phone call to the United States," I informed the clerk behind the granite counter.

"There's a wait," he said. "Probably twenty-five or thirty minutes."

With no other choice, I agreed, cashed some traveler cheques, and took a seat to read the *Herald Tribune* I found abandoned on the bench. An income tax reduction had been approved in the House of Representatives. That sounded good. In other news, a crazed man had crashed his pickup truck through the White House gates and demanded to speak to President Kennedy, shouting as he did that the Communists were taking over North Carolina. I thumbed through the rest of the paper but could find no corroborating evidence of an invasion of the Tar Heel State. In sports, the Colt .45s beat the Pirates in eleven innings—that was Thursday. The *Herald Tribune* was notoriously late with news and scores from home.

My phone call still hadn't gone through, so I continued flipping through the paper. Someone had started then botched the crossword puzzle, in ink no less, which made solving it more annoying than it should have been. The comics bought me another minute—*Miss Peach* and *Johnny Hart's B.C.*—were mildly amusing. Then, just before five, the clerk called my name and pointed to a booth against the wall.

"*Numero tre.*"

I closed the door behind me and picked up the receiver.

"Hello, Fred?" I asked. "It's Ellie Stone."

"Eleonora," his voice crackled down the line. "I thought you were in my old country."

"I am. And this call is costing me a fortune."

"Missed me, did you?"

I'd first encountered Dr. Federico (Fred) Peruso a few years before in his professional capacity of Montgomery County coroner. We'd become friends over a couple of dead bodies in New Holland, New York, and, at some point—about two years earlier—I'd asked if he'd take me on as a patient. Now I needed his help enough to spend a minor fortune on a transatlantic phone call.

"Save the wisecracks for when I get home," I said. "You have my medical records, don't you?"

"Of course. What do you think I read for laughs in the evening?"

I warned him again about the jokes. "I know I requested them from my old family doctor's practice, but I never followed up with you."

"You can climb down off the roof," he said. "I remember receiving them a year or so ago. What do you want to know?"

I explained about the suspected rubella outbreak and wanted to know if I had indeed already had German measles.

"I remember the chickenpox, but I'm not a hundred percent sure about rubella."

After giving him the details of Veronica's illness, as well as everyone else's symptom-free status, I asked him for his opinion.

"Your doctor over there is an idiot," he said. "No fever, headache, or swollen glands. Only a rash? Sounds like she rubbed something irritating on her skin."

It hit me. An explanation for Veronica's rash that carried no other symptoms.

"Fred, could witch hazel cause a rash?" I asked.

"I suppose it could. Almost anything—especially irritants—can cause contact dermatitis. Depends on the person and his allergies or how much of the stuff touches the skin."

I told him about her fondness for splashing witch hazel all over, and he agreed it was a possible suspect.

"Can you send me a certificate of some kind to spring me from quarantine?" I asked.

"Where are you calling from?"

"The American Express office in Florence."

"Sounds like you've already managed to spring yourself," he said.

"I'm AWOL at the moment. Can you help me out?"

I gave him the address for Villa Bel Soggiorno, and he promised to send me a wire as soon as possible.

"Thanks, Fred. For a coroner, you're a lifesaver."

The phone call set me back 9,973 lire, which at sixty-two lire to the dollar came to more than fifteen dollars. I nearly wept as I paid the clerk. I comforted myself and my pocketbook with the knowledge that I'd incurred no other expenses in the past three days while a prisoner at the villa.

After the American Express office, my last stop in the city was the shop across the little piazza, the *cartoleria* where I'd left my film the previous Wednesday. I collected my prints and slides and dropped off Mariangela's film, both the Kodachrome and Tri-X. The same man assured me everything would be ready Saturday. Not much room for haggling, I thought. I thanked the shopkeeper and, as I was heading out the door, spotted an English-language copy of the *Decameron* on a shelf next to a row of guide books. I simply had to have it after the stories I'd heard at Bel Soggiorno.

With the new book safely tucked into my purse, I climbed aboard my borrowed Vespa for the ride back up the hill. I ran out of fuel about halfway up Via San Domenico and cursed Franco for not having filled the tank. I considered myself blameless in the matter, of course. A nice man of about forty on a *motorino* stopped to inquire what was wrong. I told him I was out of gas.

"Did you try the *riserva*?"

Who knew there was a reserve tank? Franco and Lucio hadn't mentioned it. What a couple of lousy teachers they were. The nice man turned the little switch below the seat and helped me get the thing running again. I thanked him, offered some money, but he refused. Instead, the little creep patted my bottom when I climbed back aboard the scooter.

CHAPTER THIRTY-THREE

Turning off Via Boccaccio at the same path I'd taken on my outbound journey that morning, I glided through the olive groves, climbed hills and wound through meadows, before finally coasting to a stop on the gravel near the *limonaia*. I left the Vespa in the very spot I'd found it. Well, stolen it.

Safely back at Bel Soggiorno, I wasn't yet sure my unauthorized visit to Florence had yielded the identity of Giuliana's witness, but I had a theory. I turned one bit of new information over and over in my head. It might have been a coincidence. Or perhaps not. One thing was certain, I intended to get a straight answer from Giuliana.

"Where have you been?" It was Max.

He was alone, for which I was thankful, and I assumed a man of his moral profile would keep my secret whether I asked him to or not. I also noticed Peruzzi's car parked not thirty feet away in front of the house.

"Just admiring Franco's Vespa," I said.

He smiled. Actually smiled. "*Bugiarda*. You went down into Florence, didn't you?"

I don't normally cotton to being called a liar, but, in fairness to Max, his characterization was an accurate one. Still, who did he think he was? I had a good mind to stomp off in a huff.

"I don't know how to drive one of these things," I said, challenging him to repeat his accusation. "How could I go all the way to Florence? I don't even know about the reserve fuel tank."

"*Bugiarda*," he said again. "You quizzed that idiot Franco on how to operate it the other night. But where did you get the key?"

"What key?" I asked.

"The one in your hand."

The back and forth might have gone on for hours if Franco himself hadn't appeared with a glass of wine in his hand.

"There you are," he said to Max. And, noticing me, he flashed a bright smile. "*Ecco la Ellie!* Where have you been? The inspector wants to talk to everyone. *Vieni a prendere un drink con noi.*"

He was imbibing again, using *tu* with me, and already one or two sheets to the wind. I'd seen the effect alcohol had on him. He'd wept on my shoulder the last time he'd overdone it. Still, his arrival provided me with an escape from Max's scrutiny. Hiding the Vespa key in my right fist, I took Franco's proffered arm with my left hand and, tossing a flirtatious bob of the head at Max, I made good my exit, slipping the key into Franco's coat pocket as I did. Max followed us inside, through the house, then out onto the *terrazza*.

Peruzzi glared at us, three tardy students showing up late for school. We separated, hoping to dodge his attention. I sidled up to Bernie, who was holding a *bocce* ball, of all things. He noticed my puzzlement and motioned to a couple of iron balls about twenty feet away. Clearly they'd been playing *bocce* when the inspector showed up. Not sorry I'd missed that.

"I have news on the death of Professor Bondinelli," announced Peruzzi.

I caught Max's attention and mouthed the words, "*Dov'è Mariangela?*" He jerked his head toward the door to indicate she was safely inside. The inspector continued.

"We have learned several important details concerning his movements that day. And . . ." he surveyed our faces as he paused for dramatic effect, "we have made an arrest for his murder."

Just as in any locked-room mystery worth its salt, the assembled rogues, suspects, and acquaintances gasped on cue, as they had done the day before when Giuliana announced her affair with Lucio. The inspector raised a hand, indicating we should hold our reactions for the end. He retrieved the notebook from his pocket, pushed his eyeglasses up onto his forehead, and proceeded to read us the details.

"Thanks to the professor's *donna di servizio*, we know that Bondinelli left his residence Tuesday morning at nine ten or nine fifteen and headed to his office at the university. Furthermore, we have witnesses who saw him arrive there at approximately nine thirty. According to colleagues who spoke with him, he was in excellent spirits, happy and planning to attend to some final preparations before the symposium."

Peruzzi paused to lick his thumb and turn the page.

"Professor Sannino spoke to Bondinelli a little after noon and, according to witnesses at the university, he saw him earlier as well. We have no reports that the two men met after that.

"Which brings us to Signorina Pincherle," he said, turning the page yet again. "Despite her statements to the contrary, we have three witnesses who claim they saw her speaking to Professor Bondinelli in his office at the university at approximately two forty-five on the afternoon of Tuesday, September twenty-fourth."

Giuliana tapped her foot, fuming, but kept her mouth shut.

"The question of your false declaration is something we will address later," he said to her. "For now, let me continue with the order of events. Shortly after his meeting with Signorina Pincherle, the professor left his office. That was a few minutes after three. Witnesses described his mood as *turbato*, *agitato*, *innervosito*, and *sconvolto*. Devastated."

Peruzzi stashed the notebook in his jacket, returned his eyeglasses to their customary position, and, head down as he studied the stone surface, embarked on a brief turn around the *terrazza*. We all waited for him to finish with the dramatics.

He stopped his perambulation and regarded us. "Where did he go?" he asked, expecting no response. This was a question he himself intended to answer for his audience. "After some excellent investigation by my men, we discovered that Professor Bondinelli came here, *proprio qui*, to Bel Soggiorno."

Nicely done, I thought. He'd set the scene perfectly before delivering the punch line.

"But why did he come here?" he continued, feigning befuddlement. "Whom did he meet?"

A long silence ensued. No one dared speak, so I did.

"Well?" I asked. "Why did he come here?"

Peruzzi frowned at me. I must have been throwing a wrench into his grand summation. Nevertheless, he answered me.

"Professor Bondinelli came to see Signor Locanda but, not finding him at home, spoke to the porter, Achille, instead. Unfortunately he did not reveal the motive for his visit, but the porter's description of his emotional state is consistent with that of the witnesses from the university. He was extremely upset."

"What time was that?" I asked, wanting to update the timeline I was tracking in my head.

"To the best of Achille's recollection, it was between three thirty and three forty-five, which is adequate time for Bondinelli to rush home from the university, jump into his car, and drive up here from Via Bolognese."

"You said you've arrested someone for his murder," said Franco.

"Yes, I was coming to that. As you know, I came here yesterday to question some of you about the professor's wallet. When we didn't find it on his body, I decided to launch an exhaustive search for it on both sides of the Arno. In cases of robbery, it's rare for the thief to hold onto the wallet. He usually empties it and tosses it away. Often into the river, but that was not the case here. My men fanned out and questioned shopkeepers, local residents, *spazzini* (garbage collectors)—everyone—asking if they'd found or seen an empty wallet. We had little luck at first, but eventually our hard work paid off. We located a man known to us as a petty criminal, *un piccolo deliquente*, who harasses young women, especially tourists. He lives in Coverciano, on the east side of the city. He spends his days drawing caricatures outside the Uffizi when he's not bothering foreign women."

"And he's the one who killed poor Alberto?" asked Franco.

"He denies it, of course," said the inspector. "But he had the wallet. He says he got it from an old beggar woman on the Oltrarno. Can't remember where. An obvious lie. None of that matters, of course. We are sure that he robbed Bondinelli and threw him into the river at the Ponte alle Grazie."

"What time do you think that was?" I asked, again trying to complete my timeline.

Peruzzi beamed, clearly pleased with the information he was about to share. "From our interviews, we know that Bondinelli left Bel Soggiorno around three forty-five. Furthermore, we know he returned to his home on Via Bolognese at approximately four. He worked in his study for a period of time, perhaps an hour. Then he left in a hurry a few minutes after five. It is our theory that he went from his home directly to the Ponte alle Grazie and was robbed, murdered, and pushed into the river there."

"And when exactly did the young couple spot the body in the water?" I asked.

"Very close to six. The call to the police was recorded in the log at 6:04."

"And, of course, you've tested how long it would take a body to float west from the Ponte alle Grazie to Santa Trinita."

"Of course. We consulted a *limnologo* from the university in Pisa. And also meteorologists. Even the local rowing club and fishermen on the Arno. They provided us with their best estimates based on the conditions of last Tuesday evening. We also performed a test with a dummy approximating the height and weight of the professor. We are confident that the current transported the professor's body from the Ponte alle Grazie to Santa Trinita in approximately half an hour, give or take five minutes."

"What's a *limnologo*?" I whispered to Bernie.

"Limnologist. Someone who studies inland bodies of water," he said.

Well, that was thorough of the police. But I still had my timeline to straighten out, so I asked Peruzzi for a final estimate on the time of death.

"*Dunque*," he began in typical Italian fashion, "we have the eyewitness reports of the two young people on the bridge who spotted the body in the water at approximately five fifty-nine that evening. Working backward from there, we have established with reasonable certainty that Professor Alberto Bondinelli entered the water upstream between five twenty and five thirty."

Sensing the presentation was at an end, Franco stepped forward and congratulated the cop. "Meticulous work. *Complimenti, ispettore.*"

Peruzzi accepted the plaudits gladly. I still had a question for him.

"What's the name of the man you arrested?"

He disliked my interrupting the ovation, but he pulled himself away from Franco's attentions to answer me.

"He gave us an assumed name at first. Paolo Notte. Quite unlikely. I sensed he was lying and, in short order, we discovered it was a nom de guerre he'd used during the winter of 1944. He claims to have been a partisan fighter, but the only record we could find showed he was an army deserter. Abandoned his post in Rome in September 1943, following the armistice. Just as our forces were ordered by Badoglio to resist all alien invaders."

"Except the Americans and the English," added Max from the periphery of the group.

Peruzzi coughed. "Yes, of course. Except the Americans and English."

"So he deserted the army and ended up a partisan," I said.

"He ended up with a partisan nom de guerre. We have our doubts about his valor in the fight against the occupiers in the north."

"So what is his actual name?"

Peruzzi didn't need to consult his little notebook. This arrest was a feather in his cap, and he'd committed the name to memory. "Leopoldo Migliorini. A small man of little consequence. A failure in life. Even as a caricaturist, he was *carente di talento*. I was unable to recognize any of the famous people he'd drawn. His Alberto Sordi looked more like Garibaldi." He chuckled at what must have been a memory of the comic actor.

"Now we know what happened to our dear Bondinelli," said Franco with a sigh.

I caught the wicked scowl Giuliana fired in his direction. Though she might not have realized it, her face betrayed the emotions roiling inside her. I can only assume that she objected to the words "our dear Bondinelli" in his description. Whatever the spark, the result was a sneer so malevolent and Medusa-like Franco might well have turned to stone had his eyes met hers.

"For me he was not dear," she said to all present.

Lucio chided her, insisting that it was wrong to speak ill of the dead. She countered that Lucio was a coward still clinging to the Catholic guilt the priests and nuns had beaten into him as a child.

"You call yourself a Communist and an atheist, yet you still believe in bad luck, fate, and a moralistic logic to the universe. You're no more enlightened than the little old ladies who spend their days walking the Stations of the Cross, jiggling their beads, and hoping for the answer to their prayers. Pure superstition."

"*Calma, Giuliá.* I'm not one of those. I just think the poor man is dead—murdered—what good does it do to say such things about him now?"

She stamped her foot and demanded the inspector tell her when she could "get out of this prison."

"Now that you know who killed him, let us leave. No one has German measles, as you can see. Why keep us here any longer?"

"While the investigation was continuing I had some authority to restrict your movements," said Peruzzi. "I can no longer keep you here now."

"In that case, I'm leaving." Giuliana turned on her heel and headed for the house.

"One moment, signorina," said the cop. "I strongly urge you to reconsider. Stay until tomorrow when *Dottor* Gherardi returns and gives us his opinion."

Giuliana glared at him. "Can you force me to stay?"

"No. I cannot. But there is one last consideration. You are free to leave this house and risk contamination of those you come into contact with. But if you do so, I will arrest you at the gate for making false statements to the police and impeding an official investigation."

Giuliana bristled. Her anger nearly erupted into tears of rage. She stormed back into the house and up the stairs to her room.

"Where the hell were you all afternoon?" asked Bernie once Peruzzi had left. "Everyone was wondering."

"I did a little sightseeing, that's all."

"Sightseeing? Did you go down to Florence?"

"Yes. I borrowed Franco's Vespa."

He grinned. "You little thief. How did you even manage? You've never driven one of those things before."

I ignored his question. How hard was it to drive a scooter anyway? I'd seen scores of girls, women, and men doing that very thing all afternoon. Bernie needed to pull his nose out of his books and give it a try.

"As usual, your confidence in me knows no limits," I said.

"Come on, El. I didn't mean anything by it."

"Get me a drink and all is forgiven."

While Bernie tried to win back my good graces by plying me with alcohol, I noticed Lucio sitting on a bench, head buried in a newspaper. I joined him.

"Giuliana sure was angry," I said.

He lowered the paper and shrugged. "She's rather dogmatic."

"I'm glad she's decided to stay. I may not agree with everything she says, but I admire her passion. What are you reading, *amore mio*?"

"Today's paper," he said. "There's an article about Professor Bondinelli in the *cronaca nera* section."

"May I see that when you've finished?"

"Take it," he said, handing me the paper. Then he had second thoughts. "Wait. Give me back the sports pages."

I only wanted the *cronaca*, so I left him the rest. There was a two-column piece on the death of the professor. The accompanying headline and photograph stopped me in my tracks.

FIRENZE:

CARICATURISTA ARRESTATO

PER L'OMICIDIO DEL PROFESSORE

The grainy photograph showed a startled man, face white from the harsh flash, flanked by two policemen. The caption below the picture identified him as Leopoldo Migliorini, and he was the same man who'd followed me on Thursday as I returned to my hotel from the symposium. The same man who'd propositioned me on the Ponte Vecchio the previous Tuesday, the very day Alberto Bondinelli died.

I recalled the timeline Peruzzi had shared with us. He'd stated that the police were convinced that Bondinelli had died between 5:20 and 5:30 on Tuesday, September 24. That was the day I'd arrived in Florence. In fact, it was approximately the time I'd run out to take some photographs of the sunset on the Ponte Vecchio. My memory is quite strong, and it wasn't about to let me down as I sat there on the *terrazza* behind Bel Soggiorno waiting for Bernie to return with my drink.

"What's that you're reading?" he asked, bearing the cocktail he owed me.

"Lucio showed me this article in the paper about Bondinelli's murder. See?"

"So that's the guy? Leopoldo Migliorini. He doesn't look the type to knock over a man as large as Bondinelli. And he was a trained soldier, too."

"He didn't kill Bondinelli," I said in a low voice.

"How do you know that? Peruzzi was sure it was this Migliorini guy."

"He couldn't have robbed and murdered Bondinelli at five thirty last Tuesday evening because he was busy pinching my behind on the Ponte Vecchio at exactly that time."

"You're sure? There are lots of men who go around bothering foreign women."

"Yes, I'm sure. You don't forget your first pincher. And I have a picture of him."

"So what are you going to do? Tell the police?"

"Of course. This man may be a pervert, but he's no murderer. At least he didn't murder Alberto Bondinelli."

"I suppose you can tell the inspector tomorrow when he shows up with the doctor."

"I'd rather tell him right away."

"Why's that?" he asked.

"Because I'm afraid we might be sharing a house with the person who actually killed Bondinelli."

CHAPTER
THIRTY-FOUR

The dinnertime repartee hardly qualified as scintillating. No one this side of Dullsville was going to invite us to a soirée. It wasn't that we were an uninteresting bunch, but rather we'd pretty much exhausted all topics of conversation over the past three days. I had plenty of new information I could have shared, of course, but only if I'd been willing to come clean about my escape to the city. And I wasn't.

After the antipasto, Achille served up Berenice's dinner, which featured grilled *petti di pollo* with sage, accompanied by sausage and beans *all'uccelletto*.

"I know *uccelletto* means little bird," I said to no one in particular. "But why do they call this dish *all'uccelletto?*"

No one seemed up to the task of explaining, so I turned to Bernie.

"Because they prepare it with garlic and sage, the same herbs they typically use in fowl and small game recipes."

"How do you know all these things?" I asked.

He shrugged. "I thought everyone knew that. It's delicious, isn't it? Kind of like a Tuscan pork and beans."

When dinner ended, the general mood was no better. Tato sulked, surely wanting to retire early to lick his wounds alone in his gloom. Lucio and Giuliana looked to be angling to sneak off somewhere, though not together. She slouched in an armchair, examining her fingernails, which were ragged and unfinished, while he sat on a divan with his guitar. He'd propped it upright beside him on the cushion, like a person, and draped an arm over its shoulder, as if they were on a date. Franco was working his way to the bottom of his glass, another evening of losing his temper and his keys was likely in the offing. Max had sent Mariangela off to bed after the dismal dinner, and he was sitting alone nursing some Cynar and a cigarette. He cast the occasional eye my way, and I wondered again where Vicky had gone. Bernie and I, like an old married couple, occupied space next to one another, nothing needing to be said. We were content. Veronica just watched.

"I'm going to bed," announced Tato.

"You can't go," said Veronica, jumping to her feet. "It's my turn to tell a story."

The groaning was loud and all the ruder for its volume and energy. Poor Veronica almost melted from the humiliation. But she wasn't so easily put off when she set her mind on something, be it a second helping of dessert or your spacious bedroom with ceiling fan.

"Everyone has to stay for my story," she said, accusing us all of wanting to abandon ship.

Giuliana and Tato found common ground. They had no intention of sticking around for her tale, she out of sheer boredom, and he out of embarrassment for his own performance of the night before. But Franco, who still had some of his wits about him, pointed out that it was a requirement that all residents of Bel Soggiorno participate in the group activity.

"Who decided that?" demanded Giuliana.

Franco had no answer, but insisted all the same. I suggested it would be impolite for anyone to beg off.

"Let's listen to her story. She's been sick in bed for three days, after all."

The grousing that followed didn't quite equal the discourtesy of the previous groan, but it was blunt enough to feel a lot like insult on top of injury to me. Veronica, however, brushed the protests aside without a second thought, and told everyone to replenish their libations and settle down because she would brook no interruptions once she'd begun her tale. A stampede to the drinks tray ensued. Then, with everyone amply provisioned, Veronica spoke.

"I intend to recount for you a story to prove the greatness of God and the awesome power of what His love can inspire and bring to pass in the hearts of men and women."

"Oh, Jesus," Bernie whispered, then took a large swig of his drink for strength.

"There once lived in Barbary a young girl by the name of Alibech," continued Veronica.

Bernie spat his drink across the room, spraying Lucio and his precious guitar.

"Bernie, please," said Veronica.

He apologized to her and to Lucio. We were spared our fate for a short moment while Lucio dried himself and his date with a napkin. I took advantage of the commotion to quiz Bernie.

"What got into you?" I asked in a low voice.

"Sorry, but it's the story. It's . . . I can't even . . ."

"What about it? She's barely started."

"You'll see," he said, and Veronica was ready to resume.

"As I was saying before I was so rudely interrupted," she announced with a glare aimed at Bernie, "there once lived in Barbary a young girl by the name of Alibech. She was a fair and clever girl, barely fourteen years of age, the daughter of a rich and powerful man."

I surveyed the crowd for clues to substantiate Bernie's horror, and I got them in spades. Lucio wore a look of bemused alarm. Giuliana's eyes had grown to twice their size, but she was all ears. Clearly relishing what was to come next, she was smiling for the first time since I'd met her. Tato squinted in disbelief, and Franco's jaw hung open as if he were catching flies. Max Locanda actually sat forward in his seat, the better to hear what came next.

"Now, living in that part of the world, it was natural that Alibech was a heathen. But there lived in the town a community of Christians who took great pains to glorify their faith and praise their God. In good time, young Alibech came to hear these accounts of the glory of Christendom and, being a girl with a lively and curious mind, she declared her intention to learn what she could about the Christian religion, its tenets, and its God."

I nudged Bernie, mugging a confused expression. So far the story seemed innocuous enough and perfectly in keeping with Veronica's strict Catholic beliefs. He sank deeper into his seat and shook his head.

"Alibech sought the counsel of some prominent local Christian citizens to ascertain the best path to serve God and thereby gain His glory and everlasting grace. The advice she received told of sacrifice and simplicity. The best and purest way to serve and please God, they told her, was to abandon earthly riches, leave all possessions behind, and embrace a life of penance, worship, and asceticism.

"'How, pray, might I best achieve such an austere and holy existence?' the girl begged them. And they answered that she should exile herself into the desert and seek the guidance of a saintly monk. And so, with great dispatch, Alibech set out into the wilderness in search of the holy man they had extolled as the most selfless servant of God, an ascetic monk known as Rustico."

Lucio frowned. Giuliana snorted a laugh. Bernie muttered under his breath.

"After many days of fruitless wandering in the desert, her determination waning in the face of the futility, Alibech came upon a grubby little hermit living alone in silent existence in a wretched hovel. The holy man, surprised by the appearance of the fair young girl, asked her the purpose of her quest. She fell to her knees, clutched her hands together in supplication, and replied that she was on a mission to discover the best way to serve God.

"'Please, good brother, will you teach me?'

"Now Fra Rustico was a dutiful monk who wished at all times to serve his lord God. But, often doubting his own constancy, he asked himself if he was worthy to receive divine providence. And so it occurred to him that this comely young girl might well provide the test he so desired to prove his merit in the eyes of the Lord. If he were equal to the task of resisting her untouched feminine charms, he would surely have earned his place at the right hand of God. And so, with a mind to show his steadfast resistance to temptation, Fra Rustico agreed to take in this earnest soul in search of God's grace.

"The haggard monk, who subsisted on a meager diet of figs, dates, and nuts, prepared a litter upon which the girl could take her rest. As evening fell, he beheld her pulchritude and verily admitted that her beauty presented a forbidding trial of his resolve. He prayed for strength to resist temptation.

"'I shall demonstrate my worth to God and guide this child to the righteous path of His service at the same time,' Rustico thought as he lay down beside her. 'Let this be a trial of my constancy.'

"Well, as you may have surmised, Fra Rustico's will was strong, but his flesh was weak. Before ten minutes had passed, he had debated and lost the battle with himself. He decided to gauge her knowledge of human sin with the most basic questions and, in short order, came to understand that the girl was indeed as simple and pure as he had imagined. Now he beseeched her to do as he did to serve God."

"Here it comes," said Bernie to me.

"Fra Rustico knelt on the floor of his cell and folded his hands in prayer. Alibech followed his lead.

"'My dear child,' said the monk, 'I tell you that the greatest service one can do for God is to resist the devil in all his disguises.'

"'Forgive my ignorance, Fra Rustico, but how might a girl such as I resist the devil?' she asked. 'I am most eager to do so but require your instruction.'

"'If you are wholly committed to resist Satan, we must first send him back to hell whenever we cross his path. I shall show you now how to put the devil in hell.'

"Then, to illustrate his lesson, he loosened his ragged cloths and dropped them to the floor, leaving himself as naked as a newborn babe. He instructed the innocent girl to do the same, and she readily complied with his wish.

"Now kneeling side by side, they began to pray. But Alibech, being young and ignorant of the shape of the unclothed male body, found her attention drawn away from prayer and toward Fra Rustico's . . ."

"Stop!" called Giuliana. Though she'd been amused by Veronica's choice of story earlier, she clearly thought better of it now. "Do you have any idea what this story is about?" she asked.

"What? I . . . Of course I do. I'm trying to tell you all a story of a young girl's conversion to Christianity."

Giuliana waved her hands in frustration. "By putting the devil in hell? Don't you know what that monk is about to do?"

"He's going to show her the devil and then explain how to put him back in hell."

"And what, do you suppose, is the devil he's going to show her?"

Veronica shrugged. Giuliana leaned in, cupped a hand over her ear, and whispered something. Veronica's eyes nearly popped out of their sockets. Blushing crimson, she turned to Giuliana and shook her head.

"No! That can't be. It's . . . sinful! And disgusting. His . . . is the devil? Then what is hell?" She stopped and covered her mouth. "Oh! Oh, no."

"Oh, yes," said Giuliana, and Franco, Lucio, and Bernie all confirmed Giuliana's interpretation with apologetic nods.

Veronica grappled to comprehend man's unrelenting urge to debauch, defile, and deflower—even saintly men of dubious stamina due to meager diets of figs, dates, and nuts. All attention was on Veronica and her botched interpretation of Alibech and Rustico's tale. In fact, there was no interpretation needed at all. The story, as recounted to me later in full by Bernie, was quite clear. And explicit. Lifted again straight from the *Decameron*. Fra Rustico had tricked young Alibech into believing that his erect member, its head held so high in sinful pride, was indeed the devil. And, as he'd taught her—the best way to serve God was to put him back in hell, which—of course—was to be found, more or less, in the corresponding region of the girl's anatomy. Somehow, Veronica had failed to grasp the game. Maybe, like Alibech, she was an innocent herself. Lucio, Franco, and Teresa had all told me she was not a bright girl, after all.

Later, after Veronica had excused herself and slunk off to bed, we marveled that she could have failed to understand what the monk was up to. None of us could say for sure why, but the unfinished story broke the tedium of the day and reignited the warm jollity that had characterized the group of friends before we'd all been trapped in the villa. Even Tato laughed and embraced his old pal, Lucio—the one who'd stolen his girl and knocked him down with his car just three days earlier. All thoughts of betrayal were water under the bridge.

Franco, too, though a little tipsy, was in good spirits and happy to share his impressions of Veronica's tale. Even Max found Veronica's misreading of the story amusing.

We, the remaining comrades, enjoyed a few more drinks and stories not, I'm glad to say, from the *Decameron*. It was one of those nights you recall fondly later on. Muted conversation, so as not to disturb those who'd already turned in, and occasional bursts of laughter followed by shushes and fits of not-so-sorry guilt. And then giggles, softer but naughtier because we knew we shouldn't be unkind in our mirth. Yet even then, in the low light of the *salone*, in the first hours of the first day of October 1963—cigarette smoke choking the room like a cloud—I knew I'd cherish this moment in the years to come. Friends, laughter, and no intention of ever growing older, wiser, or more sober.

But then, as it had to be, the hour grew late and the will to carry on flagged. First it was Franco who yawned and, blaming advancing age for his fatigue, threw in the towel and exited with no curtain call. We soldiered on a short time longer until Lucio and Tato accepted that slumber was the undeniable sovereign of the night and must be obeyed. We teased them in good humor for their weakness, but they went off all the same.

Bernie was next to go, bleary-eyed as he shuffled away, leaving only Giuliana, Max, and me. Was this a dance marathon? What was the prize for the one who outlasted the others? Or were we simply enjoying a long, slow waltz? No prizes, no applause, only sore feet in the morning.

"What happened to that girl? *Come si chiama? La* Vicky?" asked Giuliana apropos of nothing, effectively splashing cold water on the spell we'd fallen under. But that was Giuliana. Always defiant and combative, uncompromising in her passions and opinions. "Where is she?" she asked Max.

"I don't know."

"You must have an idea where she might have gone."

Max frowned. Clearly he didn't enjoy answering to others, least of all young women. "The female mind is a mystery to me."

"Was she upset? Why would she leave without a word?"

Max rose from his seat, crossed the room, and refilled his glass. What he didn't do was answer Giuliana's question.

"Did she take her things?" asked Giuliana. "Or maybe she just disappeared somewhere for a few days to collect herself. *A riprendersi.*"

"Collect herself how?" asked Max from the drinks tray. "She's a spoiled girl with more beauty than brains. Better lost than found."

"But..."

Max had heard enough. "*Basta.* This is none of your affair."

If nothing else, Giuliana suffered the sin of pride, a shortcoming that hindered her fondness for battle. Even in the wrong, she would scrape, scratch, and spit. But in this case she was his guest. Even if she was there against her will, she was accepting his bourgeois hospitality, eating his delicious food—*earned on the backs of workers*—and drinking his expensive liquors and wines. Somehow she bit back on her rage, and her tongue, and offered a weak explanation that she was merely worried for Vicky's safety. Max, true to form, said nothing, and Giuliana bade us goodnight.

My wristwatch read 2:15. Ermenegildo would be up screeching through that scrawny neck of his before too long. Thoughts of the crowing rooster aside, the hour was late, and there I was alone with Max Locanda. Still standing at the drinks tray, he filled a glass with whisky and presented it to me.

"I probably shouldn't," I said. "Look at the time."

He urged me to have one last drink to wash away the distaste of *la Giuliana*'s memory. "And why not? *La* Vicky's, too."

He sat down beside me and offered his glass as a toasting partner to mine. Then, formalities observed, he took a healthy sip and exhaled a long breath. Was it fatigue, relief, or contentment that inspired him to let down his guard? Or did he feel at ease with me now?

We sat in silence for a short moment until Max put a question to me in English. "This Bernie fellow," he began. "Are you in love with him?"

I turned in my seat to look him in the eye. Still no hint of anything going on behind the mask. Just those cool, blue eyes.

"No, I . . ." How was I supposed to answer that?

Max continued, in Italian again. "I suspected that you invented the story of losing your underwear in my study, but I'm not sure why. Either you were kissing Bernie for real, or you were trying to convince me that you were."

I sipped my drink to buy time. If this had been a chess match, I'd have been down to my king and, at most, one pawn. "No, I'm not in love with Bernie."

Max nodded solemnly as he considered the implications. Then he spoke, slow and measured. "You asked me before where Vicky has gone. Everyone, in fact, is wondering, even Giuliana. What if I told you I sent her away because of you?"

If ever there was a moment to spit my drink across the room, that was it. Unfortunately I had nothing in my mouth when he said it.

"What are you saying?" I asked, incredulous.

"Don't be alarmed." He was still using *lei* with me, which meant we hadn't crossed into the dangerous territory of *tu* and unwelcome familiarity. "I only wanted to tell you that."

I finished my drink in two quick gulps then, feigning a yawn, consulted my watch and said I was going to bed. He stood and wished me goodnight with a tilt of his glass and—at long last—a sparkle in his eye.

Halfway up the stairs, a whisper in the dark called my name. Hidden in the shadows of the second floor landing stood Giuliana. She wanted to talk.

"I'm tired," I said. "I want to go to bed."

"Please, Ellie. It's important."

I drew a sigh and agreed. "Give me five minutes to wash my face and change for bed."

It was easily ten minutes before the soft knock came at my door. It wasn't Giuliana.

CHAPTER
THIRTY-FIVE

"Franco?" I said, gathering my robe tightly about my chest. Had I known it was he at the door, I would have thought to put something on beneath the robe. "I thought you'd gone to bed."

He put a finger to his lips, urging me to maintain silence, then produced a bottle of whisky from behind his back with one hand and two glasses with the other.

"No, Franco. I'm tired," I said, holding up a hand as a stop sign.

He didn't answer. And he didn't stop, either. He stepped inside and nudged the door closed with his foot. Then, placing the bottle and glasses on the dresser, he took me in his arms and planted his lips on mine. Though annoyed—and yes, disgusted—I wasn't in mortal fear for my safety or my honor. I knew that Lucio and Bernie were a door away on either side, and Tato another couple of steps farther down the corridor. Plus, Giuliana was due at any moment to tell me something important. Nevertheless, my confidence was counterbalanced by my awareness that alcohol seemed to inflate Franco's sense of his own irresistibility. It somehow gave him the daring of a smooth Latin lover when, in fact, he was more of the fumbling stablehand variety. I hadn't forgotten the night he'd tackled me on the stoop of Albergo Bardi.

"No, Franco," I said, shoving him away.

Not one to be repelled after one parry, he riposted immediately. Oh, not in any kind of violent way, but his forehead did collide with my mouth accidentally, causing my upper lip to balloon instantly and—I can only imagine—him to see stars. He staggered away, holding his head, and took a seat on my bed. In a daze, he reached out a hand to steady himself and practically tore the robe off my body.

And that was when the door opened. Giuliana peered in and was treated to the spectacle. Me, robe falling open, my lip engorged, and Franco, wearing a red welt on his forehead that called to mind the swollen rump of a female baboon in estrus.

"*Scusate*," she said, red faced, and closed the door again. I called out for her to come back. "Are you all right?" she asked once she'd returned and joined us in my tiny room.

"I bumped my head . . ." said Franco. "So clumsy of me."

I considered myself a reasonably good reader of faces, and Giuliana's wasn't buying his story. I was sure she suspected the accident had occurred as the result of some best-laid scheme gone *agley*. And that was a smear on my honor.

Things got worse. Summoned by the noise, Lucio poked his head inside just as Giuliana asked me when I'd stopped sleeping with Bernie in favor of Franco. Another in a series of when-did-you-stop-beating-your-wife questions. How to answer? And then Bernie showed up, wondering what all the ruckus was about. As the implications of the tableau dawned on him, his crest fell, and I feared I'd somehow broken his heart. The last person to witness my disgrace was Max. He'd heard the row downstairs and come to investigate. The look on his face told the tale. Perhaps he'd misjudged me. Sent Vicky away for no good reason. Not that I was pining after him, but a girl hated to witness a run on her stock.

Franco muttered an inadequate apology for disturbing everyone's rest, insisted that he'd only been checking in on me, then vanished like the little dot on a television screen when you switch it off. The one person he hadn't apologized to was me.

I shooed everyone out. This was not the time to renew the ties that bound us. I was humiliated. And, as I sat in the low light, reflecting on my blackened name and reputation, I poured myself a drink from the bottle Franco had left on the dresser. The fatigue I'd felt just moments before my public indignity had dissolved like a ghost in the night. I felt properly sorry for myself and was going to indulge in one or two more drinks until the shame faded.

And, of course, there was another knock on my door.

CHAPTER THIRTY-SIX

"*Chi è?*" I called through my swollen lips.

A soft voice came through the door. "It's Teresa."

I tucked my glass away behind the dresser's mirror and let her inside. She mumbled the perfunctory "*permesso,*" though there was clearly no one else in the small room. I invited her to sit in the one chair, offered a glass of water, which she refused, then settled onto the edge of the bed to wait for her to reveal the purpose of her visit.

"Mariangela tells me you're very kind to her," she said. "Thank you."

I brushed aside the praise. "It's no trouble. But surely you didn't come here at . . ." I consulted my watch on the bedside table, "three in the morning to tell me that."

She blushed. "No, I came to ask if you found the letter. The letter from the professor."

"It was you who left it? Then it was also you who took it at the Cavallo last Thursday?"

"I was afraid someone might steal it. It was lying on the table. Anyone could have taken it. The good professor intended it for you, and only you."

"Did he tell you that?"

"No, but I found it on his desk that day. I thought it must be important."

I retrieved the letter from my purse where I'd stashed it, opened it, and re-read the mysterious reference to our shared name.

"Do you know what he means by that?" I asked once I'd read it to her. She professed ignorance. "He never changed his name, did he? I mean, he was born Alberto Bondinelli, wasn't he?"

Teresa shrugged and declared herself baffled. I put the letter away and squared up to look her in the eye.

"I want you to tell me the truth. If you only wanted to know about the letter, you could have come to ask me any number of times during the day. You didn't need to wait until three in the morning."

She chewed her lip ever so delicately. "I don't sleep much, even less since the professor died. So I heard the noise a little while ago, and decided to come talk to you when the others left."

"What is it you want to talk to me about?"

"The professor, of course. I hear what these people say about him, and I want you to know that it's not true. Professor Bondinelli was a saint. *Un santo, digo.* The rest is all lies. *Mentiras. Bugie.*"

"Why tell me?"

"Because he wrote you the letter. He must have respected you very much. I didn't want you to leave thinking he was a bad man. He was not."

"There's so much I don't know about him. Did he share his life story with you? Do you know about his history? His marriage?"

"He never talked about his wife to me."

"What about P. Sasso? Did he ever mention a man named P. Sasso?"

She drew a blank and shook her head.

"Then there's nothing else?" I asked. "You came to my room for no other reason in the middle of the night?"

She blinked a couple of times as she considered her answer. Either she had nothing more to add or she was plucking up the courage to say it. At length, she spoke.

"I don't know where to turn, but I have to tell someone. On the day the professor died, he came home early, which was unusual. It was long after lunch. About four. He looked upset. Sad. He locked himself in his study for an hour, then he left the house in a rush."

"Did he say where he was going or where he'd come from?"

"He said he was going out."

"Those were his words? 'I'm going out'?"

She focused intently on a spot on the floor as she tried to recall. "Yes. He said, '*Esco.*'"

"Nothing else?"

"He said, '*adiós.*'"

"In Spanish? Why?"

"Sometimes he used Spanish words with me."

"Did he speak Spanish well?"

"No. In fact, very poorly. Always using Italian words. Once, when he went to Spain several years ago, he tried to board a bus through the exit."

"He didn't even know the word for exit in Spanish?" I asked.

"It's difficult for an Italian. You've seen the buses here in Florence?"

I said I had.

"Which door do you use to climb aboard?"

"The *salita*, of course."

She smiled knowingly. "In Spanish, *salida* means exit, not ascent or climb like *salita* in Italian. So the professor misunderstood and was almost trampled trying to go in through the exit. Everyone swore at him and called him . . ." she blushed . . . "*gilipollas.*"

It struck me as odd. Not that he would speak Spanish to her, but that he would have chosen that moment to do so. Was it a playful, friendly gesture on his part? I doubted that; she'd described him as upset and sad upon his return home that afternoon. Why not simply say "*a dopo*" or "*a più tardi*" in Italian?

I shook off the niggling feeling *adiós* had caused in my tired mind and turned my attention back to Teresa's story.

"What time was that? When did he leave?"

"I remember exactly because I was preparing the evening meal for later. I always start at five. Dinner is at nine. He left ten minutes after I started washing and cutting the vegetables."

"Ten past five," I said, considering the timeline.

"And that's what you wanted to tell me? That he was upset and left the house at five ten last Tuesday?"

She gave a confident bob of her head. "Yes. But also that I think someone—one of these people in this house—wished him harm."

She wasn't alone in her suspicions.

"Who?" I asked.

She made a show of not wanting to accuse, but in the end she opened up. Giuliana topped the list, but she granted Lucio might have had reasons to dislike Bondinelli as well.

"Politics," she said almost in a whisper. "They are Communists, after all. And they know the professor fought the Communists in Spain."

I took a moment to consider her assertion. From the American side of the Atlantic, especially in our household, we were used to hearing of foreigners who'd gone to Spain to fight. Those who joined the International

Brigades were revered for their courage, sacrifice, and prescience about the fascist threat in Europe. Willing to die in a foreign land to stop the rise of authoritarianism, they were labeled "premature antifascists" and "fellow travelers" after the fact for their trouble. The idea, apparently, was that there was a proper moment to become antifascist in America, and that was only after Pearl Harbor. Any opposition before that and you were branded a Communist. So, now, to hear of a man—Bondinelli—who'd made his way to Spain to fight for the other side—the Nationalists, felt perverse to me. Of course I knew there'd been Germans and Italians in Spain—they'd bombed civilians in Guernica after all—but to think a "*santo*" had taken up arms in the Nationalist cause seemed unfathomable to one, like me, who'd been raised to loathe fascists. It made me question Teresa's judgment of Bondinelli's character.

Whom could I trust to tell me about the late professor? The ones who knew him best? I'd heard both sides of that argument, and even a couple of opinions from the center. His brother-in-law painted an unemotional portrait of a flawed man. His daughter, too, offered only measured praise in describing her serious-minded father. I wanted to believe the best about him, but I was struggling in that moment. I pressed on with my questioning.

"Is that when you met him?" I asked. "During the war in Spain?"

"Yes. I am from Brihuega in Guadalajara. In March of thirty-seven, the Italians staged an attack to take Madrid from the north. There were several days of fighting. Brihuega fell to the Italians, then was retaken by the Republicans. It was chaos."

She wiped her upper lip, which was glistening as the memory returned. Gulping twice to gain control over her emotions, she struggled to find the words to continue.

"My husband was dead. Killed in battle three months before. I was with his mother and my infant son, José Maria—Chema—in Brihuega. We prayed for an end to the war. But on the eighteenth of March, 1937, our house was destroyed by a mortar. I'll never forget the date. My mother-in-law was killed. My child was trapped in the rubble of the house. I could hear his cries and nearly went mad trying to dig him out. No one was able to help. Our men were all away fighting or dead. Nobody could help me dig."

Teresa produced a handkerchief—not the one I'd given her—from a pocket of her robe and covered her mouth, hiding and stifling the silent scream trying to find release from her throat. The agony on her face—the abject terror bubbling up in her blood-red, watery eyes at the memory of the horrors she'd witnessed so long ago—struck me dumb and powerless to move.

"Chema wailed, *pobrecito*, because he had no words. Couldn't speak yet, but he called to me to come for him. I . . . he was gasping for air. I wanted to kill myself to stop his voice from reaching my ears. I lost my wits and raged and suffered a seizure. A fit. I fell to the ground and thrashed about like a madwoman until I lost consciousness."

I smeared the tears across my cheeks and snorted back the effluence threatening to run from my nose. Choking on my own breath, I strained to wheeze some air down my throat, swollen and aching from the involuntary pathos her story—her distorted, tortured face and strangled voice— had triggered in my chest. The violence of my own reaction surprised me, but there was no stemming it, consciously or rationally. The only path out was to take her hand and hold it fast until she'd finished.

"The Italians were retreating, the Republicans advancing," she whispered as if divulging a secret no one else should hear. "Night was falling when I finally regained consciousness. It was cold. There was sleet. And silence from the ruin that had been our home. I pounded on the pile of debris with my fists and wept for my lost son."

Teresa stopped. She took my chin between her right thumb and forefinger, as a mother might do to demand full attention from a distracted child. Her eyes sparkled at mine in the low light, but her voice was strong again, her weeping at an end.

"I knew I was alone now and forever in the world," she said, holding my gaze. "My husband dead, mother-in-law gone, and my Chema buried alive . . . And then four men in black uniforms appeared, looking like demons from hell. Their leader was a tall, homely man with a bandage over his left eye. Dried blood covered his entire face. Even though I was mad with sorrow over my son, I still felt fear. Fear of this evil-looking creature.

"He asked me why I was weeping. I told him about my Chema, and he insisted I show him where I'd heard my baby's cries. Then he ordered the three other soldiers to dig. Brick by brick, beam by beam, bloodying their hands on his command, they rooted through the rubble like pigs after truffles. Even as the enemy drew closer, they continued to dig. And finally, in the icy rain, the tall, ugly man with one eye and teeth too large for his mouth, emerged from the pit with my cold, motionless baby. He held him by the ankle with one hand like a strangled chicken as he climbed out of the wreckage. Once back on solid ground, he cradled my Chema properly to his chest. And he rocked and warmed my boy until he started to whimper. The man in black started to whimper, not my baby."

I cast my head down and sobbed, unwilling to hear the devastating ending. Teresa grabbed my chin again and forced me to look at her.

"The *man* was weeping. My son was giggling. My Chema was alive."

CHAPTER THIRTY-SEVEN

With my face still tingling from the emotions brought on by Teresa's story, I prescribed another short glass of whisky to calm myself. Exhausted from the long day, which had included stealing Franco's scooter and crisscrossing Florence, I needed rest. So, at length, I switched off the bedside lamp and slid between the sheets. Drawing ten deep breaths, I willed myself to embrace imminent sleep. I was drifting off, with all thoughts of murdered professors, the horrors of the Spanish Civil War, and clumsy, unwelcome late-night suitors, melting into the night. Vaguely aware of my consciousness slipping away, swirling into slumber's gentle eddy, I surrendered to the peace.

Then Ermenegildo crowed beneath my window, breaking the spell as if smashing a mirror.

TUESDAY, OCTOBER 1, 1963

I managed to sleep for three hours, but only after I'd tiptoed downstairs, armed myself with three of the *bocce* balls the others had left out earlier, and—eschewing the underarm-toss rule—flung them overhand at the source of my sleep deprivation. Impressive how fast roosters can run when given a little encouragement. Ermenegildo shot out of the garden, squawking like a dual trumpet air horn, and disappeared far into the darkness beyond. I returned to bed.

I sat alone in the *sala colazione* at nine. With each sip of coffee and bite of brioche, my tender lip provided a reminder of the ill-advised pass Franco had made a few hours before. I shuddered at what my friends must have thought had been going on. Pushing that to one side, I reflected on Teresa's story of Bondinelli and Spain.

The rescue of little José Maria was the spiritual turning point in Alberto Bondinelli's life, I was certain of it. He left the Black Shirts shortly thereafter. That cold afternoon in March 1937 was the moment he'd welcomed God back into his heart.

Teresa told me her son was now training to be an airplane mechanic in Madrid. And she gave all credit to her benefactor, Alberto Bondinelli. He'd saved the boy's life, paid for his education in a Catholic school in Guadalajara, and even sent his mother money every month for ten years. Then, when Bondinelli's wife died, he brought Teresa to Italy and gave her a job and a roof over her head.

I dipped my brioche into the bowl of coffee and conjured her face, so earnest, trusting, and sure, as she'd told me only a holy man could perform so much good. What was I to believe? Could a man change? Shed his sins, his scorn for God, and his bitterness at the loss of his sister? Could a bad man turn to good? Like Ruttonaccio in Lucio's story from our first night at Bel Soggiorno? But, I reasoned, Lucio's villain was a fraud. A scoundrel to the end, only playing at piousness. All the same, he had unwittingly achieved some good in death. The poor debtors had been released from the burden of paying back the money.

So who'd painted the true portrait of Alberto Bondinelli? Teresa, who saw a saint? Or Lucio, who saw an imposter?

"Oh, it's you," said Giuliana. She'd just entered the room. "I didn't know anyone was in here."

"Come sit," I said, eager to disabuse her of the notion that I was sleeping with Franco. Or Bernie, for that matter.

She wavered at my offer. I've seen children at the dentist's more eager to take a seat. But, in the end, she joined me. I asked her what she'd wanted to tell me the night before.

"I'm not sure I want to say now."

"Because Franco was in my room?" I asked. "I swear, Giuliana, he forced his way inside. He was drunk. After two glasses of wine, that man has no self-control."

She eyed me guardedly, still not ready to share. So I took the lead.

"I met your grandmother yesterday," I said.

That got her attention. I knew she'd visited her grandmother the very day Bondinelli died. So I wondered, was she worried? Or perhaps just curious to hear what I'd learned?

"*Mia nonna?*" she asked. "How? What about the quarantine? And the policeman at the gate?"

"Minor obstacles. Your grandmother is a lovely lady."

"Congratulations, Ellie. You wasted your time searching her out. She doesn't know anything about Bondinelli. She's not my witness."

"Maybe not. But she told me some things that surprised me. For instance, why didn't you say your father lost his job at the university when the fascists passed the racial laws?"

She hadn't been expecting that. "I don't like to share my family's tragedy with others," she said. "It's nobody's business but my own."

That hardly held water in light of my experience with her. She'd always seemed more than willing to point out that Jews and workers in general, and her own family in particular, had suffered the oppression and prejudice of Christian bourgeois society in Italy.

"I was saving that for the right moment," she volunteered when I failed to respond.

"You didn't think your turn at storytelling was the right moment?"

"I wanted to. But I decided it would be more powerful to stand up and announce it at Bondinelli's funeral."

"That would be quite a dramatic farewell. A cruel *addio*."

She seemed pleased by my observation. Then she rose to leave, but I stopped her.

"Your grandmother directed me to your uncle, Alfredo Levi. I visited him, too."

"You're still mistaken, Ellie. My uncle isn't the witness either."

"I know that," I said.

She hesitated then scrutinized me from above. "You're clever. But not clever enough."

"Will you show me the photograph you took from your uncle's house?"

"What? No. I didn't take anything."

"Giuliana, your witness is dead, isn't he?"

Feeling woolly headed after my long night and early-morning *bocce* ball match with Ermenegildo, I wanted nothing more than a quiet nap. A couple of hours before lunch, I slipped into the gazebo behind the house and treated myself to some stories from the *Decameron* I'd bought the day before, including the ones Lucio, Giuliana, and Veronica had borrowed. At length, overcome by drowsiness, I put down the book and closed my eyes. Hidden from the others, I could still hear them from time to time a short way off, chatting, laughing, whispering. I even caught bits of conversation between Bernie and Lucio as they wondered where the missing *bocce* balls had gone.

I dozed. The air was sweet and comforting. That perfect temperature created by the delicious marination of cool shade and nearby sun-fueled heat. Eyes closed, I breathed in the odors surrounding me, from earthy to spicy to pine oil. The affronts of fatigue slowly lifted their siege as an hour, then another, passed. If not for the hooded crow that fluttered into my space in pursuit of a scampering lizard, I might have slept through lunch. I started, and the crow took flight, having missed his chance at a meal. I propped myself up on an elbow and squinted at my watch. Nearly one. I became aware of wafting cigarette smoke.

"*Cucù*," came a voice to my right. Oh, God, it was Max Locanda, and he'd been watching me sleep. "Time to eat soon," he said, looking quite comfortable with legs crossed, cigarette fuming between his fingers in his usual fashion.

"How long have you been there?"

"Long enough. I was waiting to see if you talk in your sleep."

"I wouldn't need to nap in the middle of the day if you chopped off that damn rooster's head," I said in English. My mind was too bleary to work out words like nap and chop in Italian.

He chuckled, stubbed out his cigarette, and said Ermenegildo was part of the family. He couldn't bear to lose him. A long pause followed before he spoke again.

"May I ask you a question, Ellie?"

I nodded.

"Have you changed your opinion of Bel Soggiorno?"

"How do you mean?"

"You were decided to leave when the police imposed the quarantine. But now, after a few days here, have you changed your mind?"

"If you want to know if I'd like to come and go as I please, yes, I would. And if you're wondering if I've modified my views on fascism, no."

"No one is trying to sell you fascism. It's dead and gone. Part of history now. This country made a bad choice in embracing Mussolini. Especially when you consider how the war ended."

"So if the Axis had won the war, Italy would have made the correct choice?"

"*Lasciamo stare* these hypothetical discussions of politics and history. They don't matter. This is our reality, and we must live it. There's no other choice."

I sat up, smoothed my hair and skirt, and stifled a yawn that would have been unladylike had I allowed it to escape.

"Was I wrong to tell you why I sent Vicky away?" he asked.

How to answer that one? I certainly didn't want to encourage him. But at the same time, if I was being honest with myself, I'd felt dangerously flattered by his confession. It was the old contradiction: it's nice to be asked, even if you don't want to.

"I think you sent her away for reasons that have nothing to do with me," I said. "She's not right for you."

"Because of my age?"

"No. It's hard enough to find love. People should grab it where they can."

"I certainly do not love Vicky. She was a *divertissement*," he said with a Gallic flourish. "But . . ."

"No, Max, don't." It was fortunate that we were conversing in English at this point, because I was afraid I'd slip into using *tu* with him had we been speaking Italian. And I didn't want to know where that might lead. For one thing, my lip was still swollen from Franco's head butt the night before, and kissing was out of the question. For another—well—this was Massimiliano Locanda, a man of questionable character who, by his own admission, cared for nothing, followed no guiding principles except a devotion to epicurean pursuits. I didn't want to continue a relationship with him after the date I was given permission to leave Bel Soggiorno behind. Not a friendship, not a fleeting romance, not a steamy sexual encounter. Nothing. Exactly equal to the sum total of Max's values.

He respected my wishes and went no further. But I had questions for him.

"I know what happened to Alberto in Spain," I said.

He nodded in a distant, distracted manner, as if he was thinking of something else. Or perhaps weighing my exact words. "Are you referring to his eye?"

"No."

"He lost it there. He wore a glass one, you know. You couldn't really tell it was glass unless you looked closely."

"His eye meant nothing to his soul," I said.

Again the knowing nod. "Then you know about the child?"

"Yes. Why didn't you tell me before when I asked you? Why didn't you tell me just now?"

He shrugged off my accusatory tone. "Alberto wanted it that way. No one was to know. He was intensely private about his past. The way he left the Church and how he returned to it. I know of no man less prideful than he."

Had I not known better, I might have assumed Max regretted his friend's death. But he didn't. At best, he was incapable of anything beyond taking note of a sad event and experiencing a vague preference that it not be so. But true sadness? No.

"What about the war? What did Alberto do in the war?"

"He was a *mutilato di guerra*, of course. With only one eye, he couldn't serve, so he taught at the university. The army had little use for him if he couldn't fight."

"Not even to provide information?"

Max looked taken aback. "What are you suggesting? That Alberto was an informer? An agent of some kind?"

"I never met the man. I can't say. But do you think it's possible?"

"You said yourself that Alberto found his soul again in Spain. He wasn't about to turn spy."

"What about those stories that he was with the partisans? Was he recognized by the government after the war?"

"Of course not. He was too private. Too modest. He never put in for any recognition or certificates, if that's what you mean."

"Then how can you be sure he was with the partisans, not against them?"

Max said he would explain. Italy's situation had become complicated when the war started going sour in 1943.

"In September of that year," he began, "the king, Vittorio Emanuele III, signed the Armistice with the Americans and the British. Armistice is perhaps too grand a word. It was a capitulation. A surrender. The king had little choice, of course, given the direction of the war. The Allied invasion of Sicily and Southern Italy was already well under way. Two months earlier, the king had dismissed Mussolini, who remained under house arrest at Campo Imperatore.

"The armistice created confusion up and down the peninsula. Citizens and soldiers and mariners alike wondered where their loyalties lay. Were we still allied with the Germans? Should we throw down our arms and welcome the invading Allies? And what of *Il Duce*? From one day to the next, Italy's role in the war became uncertain. Many Italians were tired of the penury, the lack of food, and the humiliation the fascists had brought upon our country. Others, the Communists, socialists, and even the *liberali* and conservatives, wanted to rid the country of foreign occupiers, specifically the Germans in the central and northern regions. In the south, the Americans, British, and Canadians were greeted as liberators.

"At the same time in the north, the Germans 'rescued' Mussolini from his arrest and installed him as head of their puppet government, the RSI, *Repubblica Sociale Italiana*. A most confusing, chaotic time in our history. I, of course, was still in East Africa, a *guest* of our British friends and experienced no confusion at all."

Max seemed to relish the role of storyteller. He was in no hurry to get to the point. It left me wondering if he was nostalgic for the period he was describing or merely happy to hold forth with his considerable knowledge and wit.

"When the king signed the armistice, he gave little instruction or guidance to the military. As a result, generals and soldiers alike were unsure of what attitude to take toward our former allies, the Germans. In Rome, in fact, some troops resisted the Germans' attempts to disarm them. And our great battleship *Roma* was sunk by German bombers to prevent it from falling into Allied hands. Fifteen hundred Italian sailors perished."

He took a moment to light a new cigarette then continued.

"The Germans occupied the peninsula from the Alps in the north to the battle lines in the south. They took possession of our gold reserves, deported prisoners of war to Germany to prevent their liberation, and disarmed the Italian soldiers wherever they met them. And the resistance sprang up in the middle of the chaos. Our former allies were now the enemy. Twenty years of fascist rule and its spectacular demise lit a passion in Italians. They wanted change. Democracy, socialism, Communism . . . And they wanted revenge. Former servicemen, deserters, private citizens, even women, took up arms against the Nazis and Mussolini's puppet regime. Alberto was one of them. He became a partisan. I know it for a fact."

"How? How can you be sure he wasn't still a fascist?"

Max took a deep drag of his cigarette and eyed me for a long moment. "I know it because my father told me."

I held my tongue, sensing he was about to share something not generally known. A family secret perhaps.

"My father was an officer in the OVRA, the secret police. He knew everything Alberto was doing, or at least he suspected. And he protected him. Who do you think had him arrested in April of forty-four? My father wanted him kept safe. And Albi remained in jail until August when Florence was liberated."

"He wanted to protect him because he was spying for him?"

"Ellie, *basta*. Believe me, I have no interest either way. If Alberto was *Il Duce*'s godson or Stalin's *checca* nancy-boy, it's all the same to me. I'm only telling you he was a partisan and did not spy for the fascists. My father protected him because he loved him as a son. More than he did me, I can assure you. He wanted him to marry his daughter."

We sat in silence until Max's cigarette had burned down to his polished fingernails. Then he stubbed it out on the gazebo's railing.

"I can only imagine the horrible things your father must have done in the secret police. How do you deal with the knowledge that he arrested, tortured, and possibly murdered men and women in the name of a twisted ideology?"

"We've discussed this before, Ellie. I would never do what he did, but I do not waste my thoughts on his life, his deeds. He did things, some good, others bad. It means nothing to me."

I was almost afraid to ask, but I forced myself to do so. "Was he involved in the deportation of Jews?"

"I can't imagine how he would not have been involved. It was his job."

"And did he hate the Jews?"

"I suppose he did."

"And do you?"

He shook his head. "Not at all. I am indifferent to them."

I let the significance of his words settle in my mind. How horrible to hate so much. And how horrible not to care either way. One was worse, of course. But the other was not without blame, perhaps even responsibility. Indifference, ultimately, greases the skids for evil. I couldn't think about all that now, not while I was on the trail of Bondinelli's last movements. Drawing a deep breath, I willed myself to put Max Locanda's pathetic life and odious father to one side for the moment.

"I'm sure there's lots more you could tell me about Alberto," I said.

"Not much really."

"What about his last visit here? The day he died?"

"What would I know about that? I wasn't here. I never saw him that day."

I rose from my seat and crossed the gazebo to sit beside him. He almost flinched as I leaned to see him better in the shade.

"You don't know who P. Sasso was?"

"No, I do not."

"Your father didn't know?"

"He may have. I have no idea."

I stood to leave. "I don't believe you."

He called to me to wait, then fished a paper out of his breast pocket. "This came for you a while back."

It was a telegram. Fred Peruso had come through. I had my get-out-of-jail-free card—written in Italian, no less—to present to the inspector.

CHAPTER
THIRTY-EIGHT

Only three diners—Veronica, Bernie, and I—showed up for lunch. Berenice acted insulted and injured. Lucio had surely lost all the points he'd scored with his flirting. I didn't know where he and the others had gotten to. After dessert, Veronica loitered at the table. Bernie and I stepped outside into the sunshine of a perfect day for a smoke. But I had designs on questioning Veronica and returned to the dining room a few minutes later, just in time to catch her in flagrante as she stuffed some of Berenice's *dolci*—amaretto macaroons—into the pocket of her skirt. She blushed while I pretended not to notice. I complimented her on her clearing skin instead.

"The rash is almost gone," I said.

"The itch has stopped, too."

"Look, it's none of my business, but do you think maybe the witch hazel was to blame for the rash?"

She frowned. "I have German measles. That's what caused the rash."

"I don't think so. You never had any other symptoms, after all. I'll bet when that doctor gets here, he'll set us all free with his best wishes."

"But I love my witch hazel," she said.

"Try this. When we get out of here, test a little of it on your skin. If no rash develops, you're fine to continue using it."

She agreed that would be a prudent course of action. Then she excused herself to go to her room, no doubt to gorge herself in private on Berenice's macaroons.

"Can I ask you a question?" I said, stopping her.

"If you must."

"Do you remember the day the inspector asked everyone about Professor Bondinelli's wallet?" She nodded. "Those people—Lucio, Giuliana, and Tato—had all been seen at the university last Tuesday. Their lies were easy to disprove."

"Yes. So?"

"Who was at the professor's house that day with you? Was Teresa there?"

"Of course she was. She's always there during the day, except when she goes to Mass or to run her errands."

"And did you see the professor when he returned and shut himself in his study?"

"No. I already told the police that."

"But maybe you did see him? If only for a moment?"

She stood her ground, insisting she had not seen or spoken to him after breakfast that day.

"I'm curious about one thing," I said. "When I first met you, you didn't mention that Professor Bondinelli had returned home last Tuesday afternoon. Why didn't you tell me?"

"Didn't I? I thought I had."

"No. It was Teresa who told me. Where were you in the house that day? Helping Teresa prepare for dinner?"

"No. I was in my room studying."

"And where is your room in Bondinelli's house?"

Veronica blanched. After a brief attempt to avoid the question, she admitted that it was on the ground floor. More prodding from me dislodged the truth. Her bedroom was next to Bondinelli's study, a communicating door even connected the two rooms.

"But you didn't see him? Didn't hear him? Even though he spent an hour in his study that afternoon?"

"No. I was reading."

"He was a few steps away. Surely you heard something."

She held fast to her story, and only when I gently suggested that it was a sin to lie did she admit she'd heard him moving around in the room.

"But I swear by all the saints and martyrs that I did not see him or speak to him that afternoon."

Armed with new information from Max and Veronica, I needed to clear my head and think. I made for the hills and paths behind the house, passing Bernie in the garden along the way. He called to me, but I waved him off and headed down the long alley beneath the shady pergola toward the pines, oaks, and elms beyond. Walking briskly, determined to place the pieces together into a clear picture of what had happened the day Bondinelli died, I retraced the steps of my first foray along the back trails of Bel Soggiorno the previous Saturday. A gentle October sun shone over my shoulder, casting a lengthening shadow in the browning grass. The fresh air filled my lungs as I pushed my pace ever faster until I was almost running. The effect of the external sensations, coupled with the physical reaction to my own body's labors—deep respiration, perspiration, and accelerated heartbeat—swept all distractions and confusion from my thoughts.

Besides Teresa and, perhaps, Achille, Giuliana had been the last person to see Bondinelli alive. She hated him for good reason; at least she thought so. Could I be sure that the theory I had in mind was right? I was confident Giuliana hated her professor enough to wish him dead. Perhaps enough to help him along toward achieving that goal. Did it matter if she was correct in her suspicions? Did it matter if Alberto Bondinelli, former Black Shirt turned partisan freedom fighter, had actually betrayed his comrade Gabriele Levi? For that was now my guess. Perhaps not. Innocent or guilty of that horrible accusation, Bondinelli would have presented the same attractive target to the dogmatic Giuliana.

One niggling doubt prevented me from accepting this scenario. And that was P. Sasso. Who was that man in the photo with Bondinelli, Silvana, and her father? A name. One name was all that stood between me and the solution.

I veered left on my path, a narrow dirt track that dipped and rose and twisted obediently to the demands of the landscape. Head down, pushing up a gentle hillock, I huffed for breath, felt the burning sensation in my leaden legs, as I climbed. Like a wrestler feeling out his opponent, I circled the riddle of the name in my mind again and again with no luck. I was so engrossed in my meditation, that I didn't take notice of the noise at first. But the second snort caught my attention.

What should one do when confronted by a large adult wild boar? The beast was easily three feet tall and probably weighed a hundred and thirty pounds, which was about twenty more than I did. Bristling with coarse black and brown hair, and armed with two sharp, curling tusks, he appeared angered by my trespassing. His torso swelled as he drew a deep lungful of air, which he then proceeded to blow from his long snout with a growling threat or warning to me. With no bow and arrow to defend myself, I wasn't going to stick around to find out which it was. I had one option only. Flee.

I turned on my heels and took off at a sprint back down the hill I'd been scaling, sensing the animal on my tail. Descending the incline might have been easier than climbing it, but running at full tilt downhill presents other dangers that negate the advantage gravity has granted, namely the risk of tripping, falling, tumbling *cul par-dessus la tête*, as my polyglot father used to say. Couldn't he have said "head over heels" instead? Funny how thoughts like that one come to you when a wild boar is chasing you down a hill, his razor-sharp tusks inches from tearing to shreds your *cul*— which might just be about to tumble over your *tête* at any moment. *Zanne*, I thought as I vaulted over a large rock in my path. That was Italian for *tusks*. Another unwelcome and unhelpful thought that occurred to me as I careered down the path, certain it would be the last thing ever to cross my mind before my spectacular and bloody death.

Yet it wasn't. Huffing and snorting, the boar gave up the chase halfway down the hill. Perhaps he'd only meant to scare me off, away from the little piglets he'd been minding. Or maybe he'd tired himself out. I didn't know and didn't care. But the true reason the Italian word for *tusks* was not my last worldly thought was because another one had occurred to me seconds before the boar pulled up and granted me a reprieve. Of all things, it was the letter Alberto Bondinelli had left for me that appeared in my mind. Its clue about sharing a name. The little wink he'd sent from beyond death. And with it came the solution to the riddle of P. Sasso.

CHAPTER
THIRTY-NINE

"What happened to you?" asked Bernie as I arrived back on the *terrazza* around five. "You look like you ran a marathon."

"I stumbled upon a boar. He chased me but I managed to escape. And now, after your charming compliment, I'm going to have a bath before cocktails."

"The inspector is on his way with the doctor," said Bernie.

"Good. I can show him proof that I had German measles as a child. And I intend to speak to him about the murder."

"Murder? I thought you said that man in the paper couldn't have killed Bondinelli because he was . . . You know . . ."

"Pinching me? Yes, that's right."

"Do you still think this was murder? You really believe someone else—someone here—might have killed him?"

"I'm not sure. But I will be soon."

Dinner was served a few minutes after nine. I sat between Mariangela and Bernie, which suited me fine. After the laughter of the previous night, prompted by Veronica's story, my patience with the others had begun to flag again. From Giuliana's sharp tongue to Lucio's flirting to Franco's drunken passes, the charm had left me with bruises, both physical and spiritual. And then there was Tato's mooning over the object of his desire, Giuliana, Veronica's newfound sense of entitlement, and Max's Bela Lugosi allure. It was enough to make a girl despair. Thank goodness for Bernie and Mariangela. I found myself cherishing the moments of unspoiled innocence spent in the company of a naïf. And young Mariangela was sweet, too.

"What's that I keep kicking on the floor?" asked Bernie, and he peeked under the table to find my purse. "Why are you dragging that around?"

"There are a couple of things inside I need for later," I said. In fact, after my bath, I'd placed three important pieces of evidence inside.

We began with a traditional antipasto of various *salumi* and cheeses, followed by a first course of rigatoni *al sugo di capriolo*—tube noodles in a delicious venison sauce. Achille made busy, dispensing with great largesse a couple of bottles of Brunello di Montalcino. Apart from looking to be quite old and expensive, the wine served as the perfect complement to the antipasto and the venison macaroni.

For a Tuesday evening, it seemed Berenice was pulling out all the stops. I wondered if Max hadn't instructed her that this could well be our last night in the villa, depending on the doctor's verdict. The inspector had phoned to say he was meeting Gherardi's train and they would drop in on us after dinner. Max said he expected them sometime after ten and we were to enjoy ourselves until then.

Mariangela was the perfect young lady, a lovely dinner companion, and an engaging conversationalist. She even informed Bernie and me that the word *companion* came to English from Old French and originally meant one with whom one shares bread. I loved Bernie for indulging her and refraining from letting on that he'd already known that.

Her education had prepared her well in other ways, too. She knew which fork to use and when, and how to sit up straight and dab her lips just so with her napkin.

She engaged Bernie in a serious discussion of the tragedy at the fireworks factory in Caserta in Campania a week before. Eighteen people had died in the horrible accident. She concluded by marveling that no one had mentioned it the whole time we'd been at Bel Soggiorno. Bernie agreed that it showed a certain lack of sympathy, but said nothing more. He knew as well as I did, after all, that the explosion had occurred on the same day her father died.

The next course arrived, grilled lamb with *zolfini* beans and garlic and green radicchio, which was a kind of chicory I'd never seen back home. Achille hurriedly swapped out our glasses and poured a Chianti Classico from Badia a Coltibuono.

I stole glances at my fellow guests throughout the meal. Franco was making a big show of the discomfort provoked by the blow to his head—not to mention his pride—the night before. And maybe a bit of hangover thrown in for good measure. He was drinking water that night. I took pity on him—he looked miserable—even as I scolded myself for doing so. Shouldn't he take pity on me?

Max sat scowling between Veronica on his left and Mariangela on his right. His niece's attention was focused on Bernie and me, leaving him at the mercy of the scintillating Veronica. Served him right, the old goat, I thought. A man who looked right through plain girls as if they weren't there deserved a little comeuppance of his own.

Giuliana was flanked by Tato on one side and Lucio on the other. After the drama of the past couple of days, Lucio appeared to have lost his passion for her. She'd tossed him to the wolves, in the form of the police, by asking him to lie for her. And he'd done damage to his friendship with Tato. Never mind knocking him over with his car, stealing the woman he loved surely cut deeper. The three of them ate in silence as I watched and asked myself if she really could have pushed Bondinelli into the river.

CHAPTER FORTY

s we were enjoying Berenice's desserts, a choice between a pear torte and a *frutta cotta al vin santo*, Achille appeared behind Max and whispered something in his ear. Max nodded, wiped his mouth with his napkin, and stood.

"The inspector has arrived," he told us. "I'll have him wait in the *salone* until you've finished your *dolci* and *caffè*."

Then he motioned to me to follow him.

"Will you make sure Mariangela goes to bed once she's finished?" he asked me in the corridor. "I don't want her to hear any of what the inspector has to say."

"Of course. I'll take care of it."

A drink in his hand, Peruzzi stood near the *terrazza* door, which was open wide to let in the pleasant night air. At his side was a drooping elderly man in shirtsleeves and dark trousers. He had a kind face, but looked tired and put out to be there.

"*Signore e signori,*" said the inspector as we entered the room and seated ourselves, "this is *Dottor* Gherardi. He has examined the case notes and some cultures taken by his assistant, Pellegrini. I will leave him to give you his conclusions. *Dottore?*"

Gherardi stepped forward then coughed four or five times—mouth uncovered—just in case some of the germs he'd been incubating hadn't escaped the first three times he hacked in our direction. Then he spoke, short and sweet.

"The signorina does not have German measles. She has a rash."

Giuliana leapt from her seat and announced to all that she was leaving immediately. Peruzzi made no move to stop her this time. But I did.

"Giuliana, wait," I said. "Tonight is my turn to tell a story. Won't you stay for it?"

She refused, but Lucio, Tato, Veronica, and the inspector prevailed upon her to wait until morning before leaving. Max remained silent.

"At least do Ellie the courtesy of listening to her story," said Lucio. "After all, we endured yours."

That prompted a sneer from her, but, in the end, she agreed.

I turned to address Peruzzi. "Inspector, I'd like you to stay as well. I have some important information for your investigation that I'll share after I've finished my brief tale."

He raised his glass to me to give the go-ahead.

A word about my story. I've related the tales offered by the others, endeavoring to imitate a pleasing narrative style befitting the themes. In the case of my own effort, such a style was far beyond the reaches of my Italian skills. Nevertheless, even if I struggled and simplified the language as I told it that night, here I present it with the appropriate fluency, ingratiating tone, and suitable vocabulary that I lacked at the time.

"*Signore e signori,*" I began. "I regret to burden you with a sorrowful story of betrayal and tragedy on this, our final night together. Still and all, I trust you will sympathize with the unfortunate characters of my narrative, taking to heart the lesson it imparts. And so, gentle friends, for your consideration and amusement, I offer you the following tale.

"There once lived in Salerno a good prince named Tancredi."

Bernie eyed me from his seat on the divan, drink in one hand, a cigarette burning in the ashtray beside him. He nodded solemnly, recognizing the story I was about to tell. What he didn't know was why.

"Having reached an advanced age," I continued, "the good prince came to realize that he had for too long indulged his own selfish desires in preventing his only child, a beloved daughter named Ghismunda, from marrying. In fact, she was approaching her twenty-second birthday when Tancredi finally set his mind to arranging a suitable match for her.

"Although a rare beauty and still of a healthy young age by any natural standard, Ghismunda was, nevertheless, considered old to be a bride. For that reason, her father's search proved to be a challenging one. Still, through determination and perseverance, he succeeded in arranging an alliance with the third son of a princeling in a far-off kingdom.

"In due course of time, the wedding, celebrated amid much pomp and merriment, took place at the palace in Salerno, and Ghismunda left her elderly father to embark on a new life with her husband.

"But, after little more than two years of marriage, death intervened and spoiled the happiness of the young couple. Ghismunda's husband, whom she'd grown to love for his kindness and fairness, as well as for the carnal delights the two shared in their private congress, fell sick and succumbed to an illness that took his life. And though she'd been considered old to be a bride, Ghismunda was conversely looked upon as tragically young to be a widow."

I paused to wet my lips with a sip of whisky. My audience seemed pleased with the progress of my story. I resumed.

"After the death of her beloved husband, Ghismunda returned to Salerno to provide companionship to her elderly father. She resolved to live with him for the rest of his days. This decision forfended any eventuality of her remarrying, despite her fortune and rare beauty. Months passed and, as the period of mourning expired, the healthy young widow emerged from her grief and began to think once more of the secular pastimes she'd enjoyed before the tragic events that led to her bereavement. And among the pastimes she'd found particularly diverting was the intimate communion she'd experienced with her husband in the seclusion of the bridal bower. And so, after suitable reflection, she set her mind to identifying a discreet man of good character and pleasant countenance with whom to share her garden of earthly delights."

Lucio was grinning from ear to ear. He leaned forward in his chair as if afraid he might miss some salacious detail. Giuliana affected a bored expression, while Veronica blushed crimson.

"Now there was in Tancredi's court, a young attendant named Guiscardo who was blessed with a physical comeliness that met with the satisfaction of all the women of the court. Indeed, more than mere satisfaction, his appearance was known to provoke longing sighs and impure ruminations on the catalogue of licentious adventures that might be pursued in his company. And so Ghismunda, having had occasion to enjoy his polite conversation as well as his becoming aspect, decided to win his affections and woo him to her bedchamber."

"I thought you said this was a tragic story," said Lucio. "It sounds rather happy to me."

"*Sta' zitto*, Lucio," I said. "I am the storyteller. That means I am the queen of the evening. You will listen without interruption."

He stood and, acquiescing to my command, executed a histrionic bow. I continued once he'd retaken his seat.

"Ghismunda succeeded in passing a message to Guiscardo, proposing an assignation in her private apartment. In the note, she described a secret passage—long forgotten and in disuse—accessible through a grotto beneath the palace, leading to her bedchamber. In the course of dispatching his courtly duties, the handsome young attendant had fallen under the spell of the beautiful widowed princess and was, therefore, only too eager to do as she proposed.

"So, at the appointed hour on the assigned day, Guiscardo entered the grotto and, following Ghismunda's instructions to the letter, scaled the secret stairway and gained her bedchamber undetected. There, hidden from the scrutiny and judgment of society, sheltered from her doting father's suspicions, they embarked on a series of forbidden trysts, during which they contravened with great zeal and regularity the Church's interdictions against fornication.

"The months passed and, safe in their warm cocoon, Ghismunda and Guiscardo felt their lust bloom into tenderness, then devotion, and finally love. And, despite the frequency of their meetings, they avoided discovery and, cherishing each other, assumed the bearings of husband and wife whenever they were alone together. Their union provided both with bounties of joy and contentment and harmony they'd never thought possible between two hearts.

"Then one afternoon, Prince Tancredi purposed to visit his daughter in her apartment. Finding her absent, he thought he might tarry and await her return. Time passed with no sign of her, and, with no diversion to amuse him, the prince began to feel slumber's call. As the room was quite chilly that day—it being December—the prince covered himself in a blanket and lay down on a hassock near the bed and promptly fell asleep.

"As fate willed it, that very day the two lovers had arranged to tryst in her bedchamber. Returning to make ready for the hours of merry coupling that loomed, Ghismunda never noticed her father fast asleep beneath the blanket. At the designated hour, she opened the secret door and welcomed her lover in a most generous and industrious fashion. So pleased was Guiscardo that his thews and sinews defied fatigue and responded to her entreaties with great endurance and stamina.

"At some point during the couple's energetic communion, Tancredi awoke and found himself the reluctant witness to his own daughter's wickedness. Consumed with rage, he nearly sprang from his blind to confront the two in the midst of their rutting, but he reined in his fury and devised a plan to punish them instead. Hours later, after reviving and quenching their passion a multitude of recurrences, the lovers parted company and left the chamber to the old prince who had remained undetected beneath the blanket."

"*Brava*, Ellie," said Lucio, unable to resist interrupting me again. "But can you pause one moment while I refill my drink? This story is so exciting my mouth has gone dry."

I agreed on the condition that he also refresh my whisky. I was the one doing all the talking, after all. A short moment later, everyone, including Peruzzi and the doctor, had topped off their glasses and were ready for more. I obliged.

"Wasting little time, Prince Tancredi ordered the arrest of his attendant, Guiscardo, and locked him in the dungeon. Then he visited his daughter to confront her with his knowledge of her sin. She could not deny his account of the night before, since he'd been in the very room, not ten paces from her bed. He told her that he'd clapped the disloyal Guiscardo in irons and would decide his fate once he'd heard Ghismunda's plea.

"The princess feared nothing she might say would quell her father's ire. She was, after all, guilty of the offenses he'd witnessed, and she was too proud to beg for mercy for herself. With great sadness she resolved to accept the cruel truth that her lover was sure to die by her father's hand no matter her appeals.

"'I confess to you this and this only, Father. I love Guiscardo with an ardor you will never comprehend. If you kill him, you slay me as well, for I shall not walk this earth bereft of his company.'

"Tancredi took leave of his daughter and, furious at her obstinacy and disobedience, he ordered his men to murder Guiscardo, tear his heart from his chest, and deliver it to the princess in a golden goblet. Once the deed had been done, and the severed heart had been dispatched to Ghismunda, Tancredi repaired to her chamber once more to see if the shock might open her eyes to the sins she'd committed with the lowly born Guiscardo and lead her to repent. What he found instead was his beautiful daughter lying on her bed, clutching her lover's sundered heart to her breast.

"'Are you prepared to beg my forgiveness?' he asked her.

"'Nay, Father. Only moments before your arrival, I poured a powerful poison into this goblet, over my lover's heart, and gladly drank it down. I have but moments to live and I shall not waste them seeking your forgiveness. Instead, I pray you grant me one last mercy: leave me in death that which you denied me in life. Permit me to be with my love, the worthy man of humble birth whose heart rests here atop of mine. I beg you to bury me together with Guiscardo.'

"And having thus spoken, she drew her last breath and surrendered her soul to the Almighty. Realizing too late the error of his cruel actions, Tancredi wept bitter tears of regret. His stony heart softened and he granted his daughter her final wish. He decreed that the two lovers be entombed in the same coffin, together for all eternity in their love."

I paused. "The end."

If my audience had intended to applaud my tale, they never got the chance. At the very moment I announced *finis*, a bat flew into the room from the open *terrazza* door, sending everyone diving to the floor. He was a medium as bats go, not rat-sized but larger than a flying mouse. He frightened even the hardiest souls in the room as he circled, dipped, and wheeled just above our heads. It occurred to me as I lay flat on the stone floor, covering my curly hair with my hands, that a bat's flight does not resemble that of a bird, at least not when indoors. The bat flies more heavily, bobbing up and down as if tethered to a great rubber band from above.

Veronica screamed, *"Pipistrello! Pipistrello!"* which really wasn't helping the situation.

Achille arrived at a gallop, wielding a broom, and set about chasing the bat from one end of the room to the other. I judged by his preparedness and graceful form that he'd either herded flying mammals many times before or he'd once been a fine tennis player. Cutting off the bat's escape route via the corridor, he gradually waltzed the animal toward the door from which he—the bat—had entered the house. And then—poof—the intruder found the opening and disappeared into the night.

The crisis over, we all pushed up off the floor and glanced about the room. The only person among us retaining more than a shred of dignity was Achille, who, though winded after his chase, smiled and wiped his brow with the back of his hand. The rest of us were cowards and useless, and we knew it.

"That was an interesting story, Ellie," said Bernie for the benefit of the others. "Boccaccio, again. If I remember correctly, it's the first story of the fourth day. Tell us why you chose it."

CHAPTER
FORTY-ONE

I was ready to play my cards, inform the inspector that he'd bagged the wrong man, and I had a good idea of what had actually happened to Professor Bondinelli exactly one week earlier.

"Before I answer your question, Bernie, I'd like to invite the inspector to reconsider the arrest of Leopoldo Migliorini."

Peruzzi chuckled, dismissing my effrontery out of hand. "Why would I do that? The man murdered Bondinelli. He was carrying his wallet."

"He did not kill the professor," I said as forcefully as I dared.

"Tell us why, signorina, I pray," he said, his words dripping with sarcasm.

"Can you remind us of the time of death you established for Professor Bondinelli?"

"Between five twenty and five thirty on the evening of Tuesday, September twenty-fourth."

"Later or earlier would not be possible?"

"*Assolutamente no.*"

"Thank you, inspector. It's a universally accepted scientific opinion that a body cannot occupy two different spaces at the same time, and Signor Migliorini is subject to the laws of the universe, as are we all."

Peruzzi's sarcasm turned to impatience in a trice. "*Ma che cavolo sta dicendo?*" he barked at me, demanding to know what the heck I was trying to say.

"Migliorini couldn't have robbed, beaten, or murdered Alberto Bondinelli at that hour, because he was making a lewd proposition to me on the Ponte Vecchio. Furthermore, he pinched a part of my anatomy I'd rather not name publicly, leaving a small, tender, bluish bruise."

"What is this farce? How do you know it was at the same time or that it was Migliorini who gave you a *pizzicotto sul sedere*?"

"Inspector, I didn't say where on my person he'd pinched me. But now that you've named the spot—my *sedere*—yes, I do know for sure. I'd just arrived in Florence last Tuesday and had stepped out to snap some photos of the sun setting on the Arno. And I checked my watch after I'd run back to my hotel. It was five thirty-five."

"It could have been anyone. We have lots of perverts here in Florence."

"I took a photo of him," I said, producing the picture from my purse. "See for yourself."

He took the photo from me and, once he'd aimed his right eye at it and recognized the pervert in the dark glasses, he huffed and asked sheepishly if he could keep the print.

"Of course. Now, back to Bernie's question about my tale. I came across it this afternoon as I was reading in the gazebo behind the house. It struck me as an apt parallel to an important event in Professor Bondinelli's life. You've all shared with me various anecdotes, histories, and opinions of him and his character. Some of you loved and respected the man, while others despised and reviled him for his associations with the worst elements of the fascist regime. Some of you knew that he turned coat and fought with the partisans to expel the Germans at the end of the war. He was even arrested and held for months on suspicion of anti-German activities."

"How lucky for him that he wasn't executed like so many others," said Giuliana. "Could it be that he was a spy for the OVRA and their Nazi puppeteers?"

"Giuliana poses an interesting question. It's one I'm afraid I cannot answer with certainty. I simply don't know. But her very suggestion that Bondinelli may have been working with the secret police when he was with the partisans leads me to a piece of evidence some of you are familiar with."

I reached into my purse and retrieved the photo I'd borrowed from Mariangela, the one of the four people in the café.

"This photograph was taken during the war. April twenty-first, 1944, to be precise. You can barely see the post office in the background, which places this in Piazza della Repubblica. I doubt that detail is important, but it does help tell the story.

"Now, we know three of the people in this photograph. There's Alberto Bondinelli; his future wife, Silvana, née Locanda; her father, Rodolfo, and this fourth person, seemingly identified on the back of the photograph as P. Sasso."

I held up the picture for all to see the date and names.

"We can also see that someone has scratched out a fourth name. The handwriting, by the way, belongs to Professor Bondinelli, and this photo was taken from his office by his daughter, Mariangela, upon her return to Florence Saturday."

"May I have a closer look?" asked Lucio.

I took a few steps toward him and held out the frame. He studied it, turned it over twice, then handed it back to me.

"P. Sasso? Is that the third man's name?" he asked.

"First of all, no, the third man is not P. Sasso. His name is the one scratched out here." I indicated again the blotch on the back of the frame.

"Then who is P. Sasso?" asked Franco.

It was not lost on me that neither Giuliana nor Max had spoken up about the photograph or the missing name. They both knew, I was sure.

"Although it may be impossible to prove from this sample," I said, ignoring Franco's question for the moment, "I am, nevertheless, certain that the scratched-out name beneath the ink here is Gabriele Levi."

"Who?" asked Franco.

I looked to Giuliana, giving her the chance to answer if she wanted to. She declined.

"Gabriele Levi was a young partisan combatant," I said. "A comrade of Professor Bondinelli's. He was Silvana's . . ." I paused and turned to Max. "Was he her fiancé? Or just her lover?"

As had Giuliana, Max said nothing. But his eyes remained intently focused on me.

"Let's say the two were in love, Silvana and Gabriele. I'm sorry. Did I mention that Gabriele was Giuliana Pincherle's cousin?"

The inspector, for one, wanted to know where this was heading. Giuliana and Max, for their part, surely had a good idea.

"How does this all tie in with your story of Ghismunda and Guiscardo?" asked Franco.

One last glance at Max before he would hate me forever. Or perhaps he wouldn't care at all. I couldn't know for sure with a man like him. I forged ahead.

"As you've just heard, Ghismunda's lover, Guiscardo, was murdered by her father. Gabriele Levi suffered the same fate. In fact, the very day this photograph was taken—April twenty-first, 1944—Gabriele was picked up by the Italian secret police on the orders of Rodolfo Locanda, and summarily executed by the Germans an hour later."

Max held his tongue, even as the entire room turned to see how he'd react. I'd just accused his father of murder, after all. Yet he suffered it in silence, in his own home, as I drank his whisky and savored the memory of the delicious dinner he'd just served.

Giuliana felt no need to keep quiet now. "Gabriele was betrayed by Alberto Bondinelli. My family has always known he was given away by someone close to him."

"Maybe it was one of his other comrades," said Franco. "You can't assume it was Alberto who betrayed him."

"Look at the photo," she said. "He's sitting there with a senior official of the OVRA. And there's Bondinelli, smiling at the camera."

"Maybe the girl turned him in," said Franco.

"No," came a voice from the other side of the room. We all turned to see who had spoken. It was Max. "Silvana was in love with Gabriele. Though he used the name Marco Bianchi at that time. It was his nom de guerre."

"Who set up the meeting in the café?" I asked.

Max didn't hesitate. Didn't try to evade my question. He answered simply, "Alberto."

"I told you," said Giuliana, practically spitting at Franco. "Bondinelli betrayed my cousin and the other men in his *squadra.*"

Chaos reigned in the room, with arguments breaking out along party lines, as it were. Giuliana and, to a lesser degree—or at least with less vitriol—Lucio and Tato, went on the offensive. Franco and Veronica defended Bondinelli, Bernie and I could do no more than watch in horror as the people who had been friends and colleagues only days before, now lobbed insults and threats at each other. The inspector silenced the free-for-all with a booming voice I would not have thought in his power.

"Everyone will remain calm," he began. "Alberto Bondinelli is dead. And no one can say with certainty that he betrayed his friend or was a traitor to his partisan comrades."

"I can," said Max. "I was in a prisoner of war camp at the time the meeting took place, but my sister told me later that Alberto had organized the meeting at her request. She was in love with Gabriele and wanted to marry him. But she feared my father would disapprove and, so, she asked Alberto to intervene."

"But he was in love with her too," said Giuliana. "He married her after my cousin was murdered by the Nazis, didn't he?"

"He loved her so much that he was willing to sacrifice his own happiness for hers. And, according to Silvana, he loved your cousin, Gabriele, as well."

"Lies!"

Max drew a sigh. "As in Ellie's story, it was the father who betrayed the lovers. My father."

"How do you know this?" asked the inspector.

"How? He told me himself. He told me his daughter would never marry a Jew. A Communist Jew."

The room fell silent for a short spell, until Giuliana spoke. Subdued for the first time since I'd met her, she asked if Bondinelli had known Rodolfo Locanda was an officer in the secret police.

Max offered a shrug. "I have no idea. It was the *secret* police after all. But I knew Alberto. If he had wanted to kill your cousin—or any Communist, for that matter—he would have done it himself. As a young man, he was cruel and without pity. He would have butchered this Gabriele without a second thought. So I am certain he did not betray anyone. It was my father. He told me so and swore me to secrecy to protect my sister."

Peruzzi stepped to the center of the room and assumed control. "*Bene.* The police will open an inquiry into this matter and determine if it is indeed Gabriele Levi in the photograph. That's our job, and it's the easy part. But you, signorina," he said addressing me, "you've neglected to close the circle. What I want to know is who is P. Sasso?"

The opportunity to feed hot crow to a man who is trying to humiliate you without cause—other than the fact that you're wearing a skirt—doesn't come along every day. So when it does, you have to make the most of it. And I did.

Reaching into my purse a third time, I produced the letter Bondinelli had written to me. The one Teresa had delivered, rescued, then redelivered. I unfolded it with deliberate care and read it to the inspector.

Finally, I'd like to divulge a secret. You surely do not re-
alize that you and I have more in common than your fa-
ther's work and a passion for medieval literature. In fact,
dear Eleonora, you and I share a name. Or at least we
once shared a name for a time.

"What is this riddle?" demanded Peruzzi. "What does it mean?"

"It's a letter Professor Bondinelli wrote to me before he died. He goes on to say that he would explain everything to me once the symposium was over. Of course he never got the chance."

"Then we'll never know," said Franco.

"I know. The name we share is Stone."

CHAPTER
FORTY-TWO

Bernie and Max got it as soon as I'd said it. So obvious, yet hiding in plain sight. P. Sasso was Alberto Bondinelli. I'd assumed it was the name of the unidentified man in the photo, Gabriele Levi. But no. It was his nom de guerre. Bondinelli's. It was written right there on the back of the photograph he'd kept in his office for twenty years.

"*Non ho capito*," said Franco.

"The name Sasso. Sasso is Italian for stone. And I believe—no—I'm sure it was Bondinelli's assumed name while he was with the partisans. To protect themselves from discovery and betrayal, they used *nomi di guerra*. Bondinelli's was P. Sasso. I may be wrong, but I would bet that the P stands for Pietro. Peter. Which also means stone. Or rock."

After a few moments of chatter revolving around the discovery of Bondinelli's nom de guerre, Peruzzi invited Max and me to join him in the library. Once we were alone, the inspector bore down on me as if I were a suspect.

"If, as you say, Leopoldo Migliorini did not rob and kill Alberto Bondinelli, then who did?"

"No one robbed him," I said. "And no one killed him. He took care of that himself. It would have been a singular coincidence if he'd been robbed on his way to commit suicide."

Both the inspector and Max expressed their doubts about my theory. Peruzzi may have been willing to believe Leopoldo wasn't his man, but that didn't mean he bought the idea that Bondinelli had killed himself. And Max insisted his brother-in-law would never have taken his own life.

"I've been told that several times," I said. "And I ignored the obvious for too long."

I proceeded to outline the reasons for my conclusion. "Giuliana visited her uncle—Gabriele's father—the Sunday before Bondinelli died. There she searched through her cousin's things in search of something.

And she found it. A photograph. It was the same picture that she'd surely seen several times hanging on the wall in her professor's office."

"And she hadn't recognized her own cousin in that photograph?" asked Peruzzi.

"Not at first. It's a grainy old picture. And her cousin died when she was a small girl. Three or four years old. But when she stumbled across the very same photo among her cousin's belongings, she came to believe Bondinelli was the one responsible for Gabriele's death."

"But why?" asked the cop.

"Because, sitting in her cousin's bedroom last Sunday, she saw the date on the photograph."

"*E allora?*"

"*Allora*, directly above her cousin's bed hangs the recognition certificate of his service as a partisan. And the date of his death is listed there clearly. April twenty-first, 1944."

Peruzzi rubbed his chin. "The same day the photograph was taken."

"Right or wrong, Giuliana believes Bondinelli betrayed Gabriele. I'm convinced she confronted Bondinelli with her accusations last Tuesday afternoon. The day he died."

"And you think that caused him to kill himself?" asked Max. "*Non ci credo.* I've already told you he didn't betray that boy. It was my father."

"Bondinelli rushed up here to see you, perhaps to hear you assure him of that very fact. But you weren't in. He returned home and locked himself in his study for an hour. Veronica and the Spanish woman, Teresa, were both there. Then he left in a rush."

"That proves nothing," said the cop.

"Max, do you know if your brother-in-law spoke Spanish?" I asked.

He scoffed. "He tried. But he had no talent for languages. He used Italian words mostly. He knew a few expressions perhaps. Nothing more."

"Teresa told me the same thing. She saw him that day, as he was leaving the house less than thirty minutes before he ended up dead in the river. She recalled the last thing he said to her."

"What was that?" asked the inspector. "'I'm going to drown myself in the Arno?'"

"Almost. He told her he was going out. Then he said 'adiós.' Bondinelli was a man who didn't speak Spanish well. An Italian who used

Italian words when he meant to use Spanish ones. He wasn't simply telling her goodbye. He wished her farewell. *Addio*. Final. Permanent. Forever."

The two reflected on my linguistic argument, and I sensed I'd dented their resistance. The inspector asked me to continue.

"Let's accept for the moment the idea that Bondinelli took his own life," I said. "How does that illuminate the rest of the evidence that you have? First, it fits your time of death, Inspector. And it makes sense given the fact that Leopoldo Migliorini was far from the Ponte alle Grazie at five thirty last Tuesday evening. What's missing, of course, is a suicide note."

"I'm sure you have a theory on that as well," said Peruzzi.

"I do, Inspector. I believe he wrote it in his study just before he left the house. He locked himself in that room for an hour. I asked myself, what does one do in a study? Read books. Pay bills perhaps. Or . . . write letters. I think he wrote his suicide note. Remember, he'd been upset by his conversation with Giuliana at the university. He then rushed up here to Fiesole to see you, Max. His next stop was his house. Then the Arno, not a half hour after telling Teresa 'adiós.'"

Peruzzi began to pace the room. Max and I watched him complete three turns before he planted his feet purposefully before us and retrieved his notepad from his vest pocket. He pushed his glasses up onto his forehead and aimed his right eye at his book. Then he flipped a few pages and scribbled a note.

"I will interview Signorina Pincherle about the photograph," he said as he wrote. "I want to know how it happened to be among her cousin's belongings if it was taken the day he died. Someone must have delivered it to him. Or mailed it."

"I wondered the same thing. And I think the photographer must have sent the photo to everyone at the table."

"Or maybe Bondinelli sent it?" asked the cop.

"Maybe. But if so, it points to his innocence, doesn't it?"

"*Perché?*"

"Because he'd have had no reason to do so if he'd betrayed Gabriele and sent him to his death. Why bother? Why waste a stamp? But if he'd had nothing to do with his comrade's discovery and arrest, or if he'd betrayed him inadvertently, he might have sent the photo."

A thought occurred to me. I remembered the night Bernie and I had searched Max Locanda's study. To be perfectly accurate, I did the searching, Bernie did the sweating. And he watched the coast to make sure it stayed clear. But as I was snooping through the old documents on the secretary, I'd discovered a print of the now-infamous photograph in an old studio envelope. I reminded Max of it now.

"I knew you'd been spying," he said. "You never lost your *mutande* in here or anywhere else."

Peruzzi choked. I blushed. Max had managed a small measure of revenge for my snooping after all. Or perhaps it was for the Ghismunda and Guiscardo tale I'd told earlier.

"My point is that the photograph is just over there on top of the secretary," I said. "It might be in the original envelope. We should take a look."

With my guidance, Peruzzi located the envelope and the photograph. He pointed his good eye at it, turned it over and, finding the backside blank, turned it again.

"This is the same photo," he said. "But no names or dates on the back."

"What's the envelope say?" I asked.

"'Sig.na Silvana Locanda, Villa Bel Soggiorno,'" he read. "The postmark is April twenty-fourth, 1944."

"But Gabriele was already dead and Alberto was in jail on that date," said Max. "My father told me he had him picked up shortly after the meeting in the café."

"It must have been mailed by the photographer," I said.

"But that is Alberto's handwriting on the envelope. I'd know it anywhere."

"All of this is consistent with the theory that Alberto was either innocent or unaware of his betrayal. I would love to see if Giuliana's photo was still in its envelope. And if Bondinelli had addressed it himself."

Max and I saw Peruzzi to his car. He reluctantly agreed that my photo of Leopoldo Migliorini probably cleared him of the murder of Alberto Bondinelli, but not quite of theft. Not yet, at least.

"What will you do next, Inspector?" I asked.

"After I've spoken to Signorina Pincherle, we'll search the Levi residence for more evidence of the April twenty-first meeting. And then I'll interview this Veronica girl and the Spanish woman. If they know anything about a suicide note, I'll get them to talk."

"They'll both try to deny its existence. They're devout Catholics and loyal to Bondinelli. They'll do anything to hide evidence that points to suicide. Anything that might keep him from a Catholic burial or salvation."

Peruzzi stared at me, bemused. "You realize that God knows if Bondinelli killed himself, with or without a suicide note? Those two women can't hide that."

"I may not be a Catholic, Inspector, but I am well aware of the basic tenets of the Christian faith and the power of its God. Still, I believe their devotion is so strong—especially Teresa's—that they will do anything to protect his everlasting soul."

EPILOGUE

I arrived back at Idlewild three weeks later. My dearest friend in the world, Ron "Fadge" Fiorello, owner of the ice cream shop across the street from my apartment, was there to meet me in his beaten-up Nash Ambassador. The driver's side door was still dented shut, as it had been for nearly two years. But the heap ran well enough, and there was plenty of room in the trunk for my bag and souvenirs.

We discussed the tragic events of my first week in Italy as he motored up the Taconic Parkway. And I told him I had a special gift for him. Two gifts, actually. A pair of 45s for the jukebox at his store.

"You'll be the first in New Holland to have these songs by the Beatles," I said.

A true music fan and incorrigible collector, he seemed to recall having read something about them somewhere, but couldn't say if he'd ever heard their music.

"Your teenaged customers will love them."

"At a nickel a pop, I can retire to the racetrack," he said and drove on.

The three weeks that followed my time at Bel Soggiorno had passed without incident, if one didn't count the handsome man I'd met in Portofino after my stay in Florence. And I didn't mention him to Fadge. He was more than a little sweet on me, and I knew he wouldn't have understood.

But before I'd taken off for the balance of my tour of Italy, which included the Riviera, Milan, Venice, and Rome, I spent several days more in Florence with Bernie. After whirlwind tours of the Uffizi, the Pitti Palace, and every church in town, I met with Inspector Peruzzi. He filled me in on the developments of the investigation.

"We released Leopoldo Migliorini this morning," he told me as we sat at his desk in the *questura* on Via Zara, not far from Piazza della Libertà. "And my men did an admirable job of tracking down the old woman he claimed gave him the wallet. It turns out she's well known for begging from the tourists on the Oltrarno."

"You're not going to tell me she robbed Bondinelli, are you?"

He didn't laugh. "No. But I will tell you that she met the professor moments before he threw himself into the river. She approached him on the Lungarno near the Ponte alle Grazie to ask for money and noticed he was praying. She asked him what was wrong, and he waved her off. Then he called her back and handed her his wallet. He told her to keep it. He didn't need it."

"Did she see him go into the river?"

"No. She hurried off before he could change his mind. She told us there was five thousand lire inside. She's been thanking the saints for him ever since."

"I suppose that tells us a lot about his conversion," I said. "He truly did change."

Peruzzi nodded, perhaps not as sentimental as I was when it came to reformed fascists. Then he told me about the search of the Levi residence on Borgo Pinti. Old Alfredo Levi regaled the investigating officers with tales of his son's heroism, pointing out with glee the certificate hanging on the wall of Gabriele's bedroom to anyone who stood still for two seconds.

"Did you find any other evidence of the April twenty-first meeting?" I asked.

"There were a few love letters from Silvana Locanda. Nothing else. The photograph Signorina Pincherle took from her cousin's room was not in an envelope. It must have been lost years ago."

"That's a shame. It would have been nice to see who had addressed it."

"We know who addressed it," he said and produced a folded sheet of paper for me to examine.

The letter was dated—September 24, 1963—and written in a precise hand in blue ink. It was Alberto Bondinelli's suicide note, addressed to his daughter. "*A mia figlia* Mariangela."

I scanned the letter, reading it quickly once, then going back over it a second time. It consisted mostly of a long, rhetorical treatise on the responsibilities of a Christian, a comrade, and a traitor. With brilliant, if cold, logic, he explained to his child that a man is responsible for his actions, in the eyes of men and of God. He wrote that his love for Jesus had saved him from eternal damnation once, and he trusted that God would understand his last act on earth for the justice it represented and the sentence his crime demanded. For make no mistake, Alberto Bondinelli did not view his death as a suicide. He wrote in clear, unambiguous terms that he was merely carrying out the execution that he deserved for having betrayed his comrade and friend, Gabriele Levi, also known as Marco Bianchi.

I was stunned. So persuasive was his case, so unassailable his reasoning, that I found myself reluctantly agreeing with the equity of his judgment. What I couldn't accept, however, was the burden he'd placed on his fourteen-year-old daughter's head. He'd admitted in his farewell that he'd worshipped her mother, even when she loved another. He'd given his poor Mariangela knowledge that she'd perhaps have been better off not knowing. Through the most boneheaded oversight, her father had revealed Marco Bianchi's true name and address to a senior officer of the OVRA by filling out the photographer's envelope right there at the table in the café.

> Your mother and Gabriele had left the café moments earlier, leaving your grandfather and me alone. It was then the photographer asked if we wanted prints of the picture he'd taken. He asked for our addresses, and I wrote them out myself on the three different envelopes. One for me, one for your mother, and one for Gabriele Levi. And with that envelope, I signed his death warrant.

Bondinelli took pains to explain that his betrayal, though unintentional, was nevertheless unforgivable.

> The punishment for informers was—and should be—death. And so it will be. It was only when Signorina Pincherle came to me with her suspicions that I'd betrayed her cousin that I realized what I had done. She showed me the photograph, told me her cousin shouldn't have had it since he'd died that very same day. She said he'd been betrayed by someone close to him, and my heart sank when I came to the only conclusion possible. I was that person close to him. Through my own stupidity and carelessness, I was responsible for his death. I accept my punishment now.

Bondinelli went on to urge his daughter to honor his memory as a man who served his country and his God, even if he'd failed and paid the price for his negligence with his life.

Far better men than I have died on the gallows or tied to the potence. I go not as a coward, but as a guilty man who accepts his condemnation and asks only for the mercy of God to absolve his sins. I have tried to be a good Christian, a good husband to your mother, and a good father to you, Mariangela. If I have fallen short, the Almighty will take custody of my soul and dispose of it as He deems fit.

He finished his letter with an admonition that his daughter follow the teachings of the Church, study assiduously, and obey Teresa and her uncle, Massimiliano, to whom he conferred her care.

I have not been an affectionate father. But know that I have loved you more completely, more perfectly because of the spirit of almighty God that saved me from perdition. My faith inspires and justifies this, my final act, and I pray you use my conviction to understand the glory of God. Addio, figlia mia. Che il Signore sia con te.

"You got this from Veronica?" I asked.

He clicked his tongue. "*La spagnola.* She got it from Veronica. Together they decided to suppress the note, as you said, to hide the suicide."

"They didn't destroy it?"

His face twisted into one of those rubbery expressions as he shrugged—just as Mariangela had done—to convey his bewilderment. He said he had no idea why they hadn't simply burned the letter.

"Have you shown it to his daughter?" I asked, and he nodded.

"What else could we do? It was his will. And her right to see it."

I attended Alberto Bondinelli's funeral at the Chiesa della Madonna della Tosse, officiated by his confessor and old friend, Padre Fabrizio. All my fellow rubella survivors were there, with the exception of Giuliana. She must not have been willing to accept Bondinelli's self-execution as adequate punishment for his crimes.

It was a restrained reunion. We all did our best to be polite, exchanged addresses, and later paid our respects to Bondinelli graveside at the Cimitero di Trespiano. Then Bernie and I fled to a hotel halfway up the hill to San Miniato above the Oltrarno. We took two rooms and spent a weekend eating and drinking ourselves into a contented stupor. He flew back to New York on Monday and I carried on with the two weeks left in my Italian holiday.

I returned one last time to Bel Soggiorno the day before I was to leave for Portofino. Achille met me at the door and showed me to the *salone*, the lovely room where I'd enjoyed so many laughs and witnessed even more strife. I'd gained and lost friends there. I knew I'd never see any of them again, even if we'd promised to do so. That was probably for the best. Did I really need another fat lip, the result of an awkward pass from Franco Sannino? Or another love-song serenade, begun then abandoned, dedicated to me by Lucio Bevilacqua? No, I could live the balance of my life without Giuliana's intensity and Tato's cow eyes. And Veronica? Well, she could pile mattresses on top of each other at her own place.

But I did want to see one person. I couldn't leave without saying goodbye to Mariangela. She greeted me with a big hug, and we cried on each other's shoulders. Our reunion was more emotional than I'd expected. She'd told me once that her father was more like a teacher or a priest to her. Yet now that she'd read his execution note, she knew more about his past, his failures, and his courage. I believed her opinion had changed. No, he was never going to win father of the year. And she wasn't about to break into a tearful rendition of *O Mein Papa* at his memory, but I could sense a burgeoning awe in her eyes. Her father, who'd always appeared to her as a square, somewhat homely man who would never understand what was so great about the Beatles, had actually been a remarkable individual of great passion, intellect, and spirituality. We talked about his goodness, his selfless dedication, and his large teeth. She laughed, then wept, even as she marveled at how any teeth could be too large for such a tall man.

I had a couple of gifts for her. First, I gave her the photos I'd had developed at the *cartoleria* in Piazza dei Cimatori. The pictures weren't great on the whole, but two or three of them—the ones she'd taken with my long lens, had come out surprisingly well. Better than anything I'd managed. And so I presented her with my 135mm Elmar lens. Her eyes grew nearly as large as anything she might have magnified with the lens and she threw her arms around me in a bear hug.

"Do me one favor, Ellie," she said.

"Anything."

She handed me her BOAC bag. "Take this."

I opened it and found the two 45s inside. "Please Please Me" and "She Loves You."

"This is too much," I said. "These are your favorites."

"I can buy them again in England. What I'd like you to do is make sure America discovers the Beatles. I simply don't understand why they're not a sensation there. Please do that for me."

"I promise," I said. "I'll make the Beatles the most popular group ever in the US."

It was time to say goodbye. With great care, I retrieved one last gift from my purse and handed it to her.

"What's this?" she asked, peeling back the brown paper to reveal a red flower in a small vase.

"It's a poppy. I hoped you might place it on your father's grave."

"But why?"

I put an arm around her shoulder and squeezed her tight to my side. "I thought it would be fitting for him to rest in the shadow of the flower. The flower of the partisan ... *morto per la libertà*."

A taxi was waiting outside. And so was my favorite Tuscan cat. The brown-striped tabby was squatting on the pebbled drive near the cab. He perked up when I emerged from the house and trotted over to meet me. He'd come to say goodbye. Or *addio*. I reached down and scratched him behind the ear, and he purred.

"Goodbye, Antonio," I said.

He rubbed his neck against my fingers, savoring the caresses, until he'd had enough. Reeling around, he swiped at my hand with his sharp claws, drawing a faint trickle of blood. Then he darted away into the shrubs, never to be seen by me again.

Pressing a handkerchief to my scratches, I climbed into the car and looked up one last time at Bel Soggiorno. I decided to take with me the pleasant memories and try to forget the ugly. But that plan was thwarted before the driver had even shifted into gear. There in a window on the second floor, peering through the curtains, stood Massimiliano Locanda. His cold, blue eyes gazed down at me from his expressionless face. Then I saw the figure behind him, seemingly undulating like a ghost thanks to the gossamer curtains waving in the breeze. It was Vicky Hodges. She'd come home to roost with Max and Ermenegildo.

As the taxi pulled away, tires crunching over the gravel drive, I reflected on Bondinelli's last act in life. A gift to an old woman. Alms for the poor. To my thinking, he had disproved Lucio's cynical tale of the wretched soul who feigns piety in his last moments on earth. Alberto Bondinelli's life bore witness to a true miracle of conversion. A journey from spiritual despair to salvation. Despite his doubts and sins and crimes against humanity, he'd ended up living the life of a saint. Cruising down Via Boccaccio in the back of a taxi, I smiled to myself, scratched hand and all, happy to have shared a name with such a man.

ACKNOWLEDGMENTS

I've made a lifelong study of languages, Italian front and center, and know from experience that there is no substitute for a native speaker's eye and ear when it comes to editing words, phrases, and references that are not your mother tongue. For that reason, I relied on some wonderful friends for feedback on the Italian usage in this book.

Tante grazie to Ilaria Verdi and Francesca Romana Riggio who did most of the heavy lifting on the Italian, reviewing and analyzing every word I used. This book would have been much poorer without their expertise and generous help. The multi-talented writer/translator Gabriel Valjan also took a fine-toothed comb to the Italian textual and cultural references, weeding out inaccuracies and urging restraint when I strayed *fuori pista*. Two dear Florentine friends, Morgan Fiumi and Elettra Fiumi, shared their upbringing, experience, and intimate knowledge of their native city with me. I am deeply indebted to them, as I am to former colleague and fast friend Professor Stefano Albertini Mussini, director of New York University's Casa Italiana Zerilli-Marimò, who advised me on language, history, politics, and universities.

The first beta reader I approached for this book is a remarkable friend I've never met in person, Fred Glienna. We've maintained a correspondence for some time now, and I knew I could not write another book without knowing his objections before publication. He roots out historical errors for fun, and he challenges me on every detail.

As always, sincere thanks to my editor, Dan Mayer, who has shepherded all seven Ellie Stone books to publication, and to my agent, Bill Reiss for his support and advice.

I'm thankful to my family beta readers, Jennifer Ziskin, Bill Ziskin, Joe Ziskin, Dave Ziskin, and Mary Beth Ziskin, as well as to my medical experts, Dr. Kunda and Dr. Hilbert.

Finally, to my pillow and my crutch—my one and only—for everything.